Praise for *The King of Infinite Space*

"Lyndsay Faye plays a kind of l̶i̶ likes to riff on the standards, as she jams. . . . This above all: a fleet-footed delight and a true of its source. It is a tragicomed , a pastiche and an original yarn and achingly melancholy novel. All this, Faye can truly deliver." —*Los Angeles Times*

"In this highly anticipated must-read for the year, magical, queer, and feminist elements collide in a fresh take on *Hamlet* set in modern-day New York City. . . . Surprising, captivating, and masterfully written, this is *Hamlet* as you don't want to miss it."
—*Veranda*

"A queer take on *Hamlet* set in modern-day New York City . . . The most intriguing story line could be that of Ophelia's counterpart, Lia, whose mental illness and addictions are examined in a more enlightened, feminist mindset." —*Fortune.com*

"I think it's safe to say that we all hope Lyndsay Faye will never stop cleverly reimagining landmarks of literature. *The King of Infinite Space* is a clever pastiche of *Hamlet* taking place in New York City, uniting mystery, fantasy, and slings and arrows of outrageous fortune." —*CrimeReads*

"Sumptuous . . . Fans will delight in the many asides and references strewn throughout the text, and murder mystery buffs will be pleasantly surprised by the many different aspects of crime that turn up in this book. I am no great admirer of *Hamlet* myself, but even I was dazzled by Ms. Faye's masterful understanding of the original and by her ability to turn that understanding into something at once suspensefully fresh and relevant to our modern age." —*Criminal Element*

"Shakespeare devotees will be impressed at the variations Faye introduces to the play's plotline, and Faye's considerable descriptive gifts are on ample display. . . . Fans and newcomers alike will delight in Faye's remarkable achievement."

—*Publishers Weekly* (starred review)

"Faye's latest is not only a richly realized mash-up of mystery and fantasy, it's also a clever pastiche of *Hamlet*. . . . [Ben and Horatio's] evolving relationship is brilliantly realized, as, for that matter, is the entire book, which is, alas, ever faithful to the original, which is, remember, a tragedy. The curtain falls."

—*Booklist* (starred review)

"Lush and magical, thoughtful and provocative, *The King of Infinite Space* is a remarkable achievement, staying true to Shakespeare's tragic play in ways that will surprise and delight while reveling in neurodivergence, queer attraction and quantum physics. . . . [T]his is a novel to stick with for its rewards of a surprising plot and Faye's delightful storytelling."

—*BookPage* (starred review)

"Wildly imaginative . . . Faye perfectly juxtaposes corrosive ambition, jealousy, and madness against the ineffable strength of love over distance, time, and space. . . . [Faye's] exciting new work should be especially appealing to readers who were intrigued by the reimaginings of Anne Tyler, Margaret Atwood, or Jeanette Winterson for the Hogarth Press Shakespeare project."

—*Library Journal*

"Bardolators will enjoy the clever changes Faye rings on his story lines and characters. . . . The ending is just as bloody as Shakespeare's and nearly as poignant. Smart and suspenseful; top-notch popular fiction."　　　　　—*Kirkus Reviews*

"[A] mind-bending update on the classic tragedy that cleverly keeps its spirit intact while modernizing relationships and plot points. . . . Faye drops the Bard's best beats into a blender with thought experiments, existential dilemmas and some snicker-worthy double entendres, then sets it to delirious fun. . . . An intriguing mix of the mystical and rational, *The King of Infinite Space* wears its heart on its sleeve down to its explosive and sentimental conclusion. . . . [A] dazzling mesh of wit, philosophy, and romance."
                                                                —*Shelf Awareness*

"Lyndsay Faye is one of the most intelligent and versatile writers working today. Never before have her immense talents been on display than in the artsy, colorful and brilliant *The King of Infinite Space*."
                                                                —Bookreporter.com

Praise for *The Paragon Hotel*

"The great strength of *The Paragon Hotel* is Ms. Faye's voice—a blend of film noir and screwball comedy. . . . The jauntiness of the prose doesn't hide the fact that Ms. Faye has serious business on her mind. At bottom, *The Paragon Hotel* is about identity and about family—those we're born into and those we create."
                                                                —*The Wall Street Journal*

"Utterly winning . . . Faye writes a good puzzle . . . [and she's] a person meant to write, who thinks and jokes and understands by writing. It's a rare gift."
                                                                —*The New York Times Book Review*

"With complex, believable characters and an intricate plot, this is a sprightly, enjoyable read."
                                                                —*People*

"This books succeeds wildly on several levels. First, as a beautiful period piece, slangy and jazzy and bringing 1921 to brilliant life. Second, as a lesson about the racist history of Oregon . . . And third, as a suspense story . . . I love so much about this book."   —*Raleigh News and Observer*

"A fast-paced mystery that's also steeped in a fascinating, and unfortunately all too prescient, part of American history. If you ever dressed up as a flapper for Halloween or love to stay up all night reading mysteries, *The Paragon Hotel* is for you."
                                                    —*Refinery29*

"Lyndsay Faye continues to be the queen of smart, feminist historical crime writing."   —*CrimeReads*

"Faye once again vividly illuminates history with her fiction. . . . Remarkably fluid fiction, framed as a love letter and based in fact."   —*Booklist* (starred review)

"This historical novel, which carries strong reverberations of present-day social and cultural upheavals, contains a message from a century ago that's useful to our own time: 'We need to do better at solving things.' A riveting multilevel thriller of race, se, and mob violence that throbs with menace as it hums with wit."   —*Kirkus Reviews* (starred review)

Praise for *Jane Steele*

"Witty and exquisitely plotted, this is such a delectable treat 'tis a pity it has to end."   —*People*

"[Jane Steele's] crimes are wonderfully entertaining."
                                        —*The New York Times Book Review*

"Faye's skill at historical mystery was evident in her nineteenth-century New York trilogy, but this slyly satiric stand-alone takes her prowess to new levels. A must for Brontë devotees; wickedly entertaining for all." —*Booklist* (starred review)

"Young Jane Steele's favorite book, Charlotte Brontë's *Jane Eyre*, mirrors her life both too little and too much. . . . In an arresting tale of dark humor and sometimes gory imagination, Faye has produced a heroine worthy of the gothic literature canon but reminiscent of detective fiction."
—*Library Journal* (starred review)

"I loved this book! The language rings true, the period details are correct. Jane Steele is a joy, both plucky and rueful in her assessment of her dark deeds. The plotting is solid and the pacing sublime."
—Sue Grafton, #1 *New York Times* bestselling author

"This is a wonderfully wicked book. The deadly first chapter actually made me gasp. Jane Steele is a character you will not soon forget. Great evil fun!"
—R.L. Stine, author of the Goosebumps and Fear Street series

Praise for *The Fatal Flame*

"As always in this series, the research is impeccable and the period ambience dazzling."
—*The New York Times Book Review*

"Lyndsay Faye's New York trilogy is immersive, compelling, convincing, and yes, thrilling. Read it today for solid-gold entertainment, but don't be surprised to see it taught in college tomorrow." —Lee Child

THE
KING
OF
INFINITE
SPACE

THE
KING
OF
INFINITE
SPACE

LYNDSAY FAYE

G. P. PUTNAM'S SONS
NEW YORK

PUTNAM
— EST. 1838 —

G. P. Putnam's Sons

Publishers Since 1838

An imprint of Penguin Random House LLC

penguinrandomhouse.com

The Library of Congress has catalogued the G. P. Putnam's Sons hardcover edition as follows:

Names: Faye, Lyndsay, author.
Title: The king of infinite space / Lyndsay Faye.
Description: New York: G. P. Putnam's Sons, 2021.
Identifiers: LCCN 2021021036 (print) | LCCN 2021021037 (ebook) |
ISBN 9780525535898 (hardcover) | ISBN 9780525535904 (ebook)
Classification: LCC PS3606.A96 K56 2021 (print) |
LCC PS3606.A96 (ebook) | DDC 813/.6—dc23
LC record available at https://lccn.loc.gov/2021021036
LC ebook record available at https://lccn.loc.gov/2021021037

p.   cm.

First G. P. Putnam's Sons hardcover edition / August 2021
First G. P. Putnam's Sons trade paperback edition / August 2022
G. P. Putnam's Sons trade paperback edition ISBN: 9780525535911

Printed in the United States of America
1st Printing

Book design by Pauline Neuwirth

This one's for the Groundlings.

DRAMATIS PERSONAE

BENJAMIN DANE, son of Jackson and Trudy Dane
HORATIO PATEL, Benjamin's closest friend
LIA BRAHMS, Benjamin's former fiancée

JACKSON DANE, owner of the New World's Stage Theatre, recently deceased
TRUDY DANE, Jackson's widow, now married to his brother, Claude
CLAUDE DANE, brother of the late Jackson Dane
PAUL BRAHMS, Lia's father and administrator of the New World's Stage Theatre

RORY AND GARRETT MARLOWE, friends of Benjamin's from Columbia

ROBIN GOODFELLOW, an event coordinator

MAM'ZELLE
MOMA } three very weird sisters, owners of a floral boutique
MAW-MAW

ARIEL WASHINGTON, the doorman of the New World's Stage Theatre offices
JÓRVÍK VOLKOV, the late janitor of the original World's Stage Theatre
JESSICA ANNE KOWALSKI, a client in need of a bouquet
VINCENTIO, a tailor

DETECTIVE YING YUE NORWAY, an NYPD detective
DETECTIVE BARRY FORTUNA, her partner

No longer mourn for me when I am dead

Than you shall hear the surly sullen bell

Give warning to the world that I am fled

From this vile world with vilest worms to dwell;

Nay, if you read this line, remember not

The hand that writ it; for I love you so,

That I in your sweet thoughts would be forgot,

If thinking on me then should make you woe.

O, if (I say) you look upon this verse,

When I (perhaps) compounded am with clay,

Do not so much as my poor name rehearse,

But let your love even with my life decay,

Lest the wise world should look into your moan,

And mock you with me after I am gone.

SONNET 71
William Shakespeare

THE
KING
OF
INFINITE
SPACE

LIA

i am not police sirens
i am the crackle of a fireplace

—*Rupi Kaur,* milk and honey

L IA NEVER KNOWS WHEN she'll appear in one of Benjamin's nightmares. But since it's started happening, they tend to meet in the charred shell of the original World's Stage Theatre, the smoke hanging as solid as proscenium curtains.

Sometimes the damage is the way it really happened. Total annihilation on the lower floor and a dragon-razed mezzanine. Sometimes the destruction is rendered pretty and whimsical. The ruined velvet seats crowd against either wall, creating a proud aisle like an apocalyptic road. Or granite-sparkling ashes flit toward her pupils. Or the roof is gone, and Lia looks up to see stark, perfect constellations.

Unheard of in midtown Manhattan, what with the light pollution.

But the artist in Lia can easily imagine it anyhow.

Always, there is the terror. Even when nothing more significant happens than her boots sloughing through cinders.

This theatre burned twenty years ago.

Lia knows there isn't any logic to dreams. But it's nauseating, and she always thinks a little petulantly, *spectacular, another nightmare, being in the cremated bones of this place is automatically a nightmare, and it isn't even in* my *head.*

Because it's all in Ben's.

This time Ben sits downstage left, staring into the orchestra pit. He's ropy and pale in a red T-shirt and torn jeans—a towheaded, manic-eyed eight-year-old instead of her towheaded, manic-eyed ex-fiancé. His shiner is pulpy, and the sweet curve of his lower lip gapes like an extra mouth.

So that helps to date things. It's Ben before therapists, Ben before meds. Ben the toilet plunger, the lunch money source, the punching bag.

Looking down, she sees a pair of green corduroy pants she lived in throughout the late nineties; so she's Ben's age, too. It's before she got the hang of her coarse nut-brown corkscrews, for instance. They're cropped at her nape, much longer on top, like they were for that heinous school picture. A Halloween wig from the discount bin.

Ben has a song stuck in his head, seemingly. From all corners of the building, "Harvest Moon" by Neil Young croons its easy melody. A deeply harmless ballad. Still, Lia's blood runs thin and bluish in her wrists.

Hear what I have to say
Just like children sleeping
We could dream this night away

"Neil Young is pretty cheesy for you, isn't he?" Lia observes.

"Oh my god." Ben scrambles to his knees with a look of pure hunger.

Please not this again.

"Hi," she says.

"You're back," he blurts, standing. "I mean you're, like, you're *here*. Again."

"Don't ask me how. We went over this maybe ten times already."

"Sorry. No, I wasn't going to. Just, you know, there you are."

"Let's not make a scene of it."

"I'm literally on a stage." The premonition of Ben's adult smirk appears. "Wouldn't a scene be, dunno. Appropriate?"

"No scenes." Lia's heart thuds like a doomed heretic's. "I'm here against my will."

"Right, but. God, you can't understand how much I've missed—"

"Benjamin, change topics, or I swear I'm going to walk away and keep walking till I—I have no idea. Fall out of your ear."

"You—"

"*Do not* discuss me. Us. There's too much to . . . there's just too much. We tried it last time and I could barely function for three days after I woke up. Tell me a different story."

Longing, anger, and disappointment threaten to crumple Ben's face like a child's after a terrible fall. But Ben isn't a little boy—he only looks like one. Straightening, he nods. It was a kaleidoscope of emotions, *longing* and *loss* as a high-pitched garble.

The last flicker looked simply like *love*, though. Which is excruciating.

"So this theatre was built in nineteen-thirteen," Ben forces out. "Um. Right, sure, you know that. Please bear with me. This is offhand, and I generally prepare my lectures. World's Stage survived the Great War, the Great Depression—which I gotta add is geographically waaaaaay more impressive—World War Two, Vietnam, and the dissolution of the Brit-pop boy band Take That, which prompted dozens of emergency suicide hotlines to be set up in the UK. Horatio has firsthand *tales*. And anyway, then one spark, one instant when the temperature surpasses the flash point in the presence of both fuel and an oxidizer, and what happens?"

Lia's arms are bare and cold. The ceiling sends a drizzle of plaster to the ground.

"The fire tetrahedron begins!" Ben sounds like he's walking

a tightrope. "Wheeee! Oh shit, and don't forget gravity has to be present, that's what, like, prevents the flame from being snuffed out immediately by the waste material produced via its own combustion. But yes, so then the solids and gases create visible particles, the red-orange-yellow spectrum we associate with incandescent things, and *poof.* A historical Broadway land-mark vanishes. As permanent as a cigarette. Left behind only in records, photographs, online, and in the memories of those who experienced it. Us, for instance."

Little-boy Ben talking like present-day Ben makes Lia's neck prickle.

"And in your dreams, which I now share."

"You sound kinda pissed about that."

"I can't leave until *you* wake up."

Ben's blue eyes glimmer. "Yeah, dreams are never consensual. They're like, I don't know, having a shitty frat boy Sigmund Freud in your brain, and he's throwing a torture party. I don't do it on *purpose.*"

Lia shivers. "Who would?"

"Who would talk with the long-lost love of their life subcon-sciously?" Ben shifts gears so fast Lia hears the brakes skidding. "Half the products in this country are marketed on nostalgia. If I could bottle this crap, I'd be rich."

"You *are* rich. Your family is from oil money, your dad first bought World's Stage and then rebuilt it, and it was only dark for three years."

"Richer, then."

"You don't give a damn about wealth. Unless you're throwing it at people you think deserve it, that is."

"Well, that's because I've always had tons. Paradoxical, right?"

A silver-tinged wind brushes along crumbling pilasters. Lia remembers afternoons here after her father picked her up from first and second grade. Flipping down a burgundy velvet chair seat, dropping her patch-covered JanSport in the third row. *War is unhealthy for children and other living things* with sunflowers embroidered around it, Kermit leaning on a rainbow, a vaguely defiant UK anarchy flag pin. Then Paul Brahms would ruffle her horrible bushy head, duck his own bald dome, squawk at any stage crew present, and disappear back into the general-manager-of-theatre-operations office to make calls and crunch numbers until the lights blinked on throughout Lincoln Center.

Lia did fractions while the carpenters swore like pirates, watched rapt as dancers dropped and curlicued. Stage managers sneaked her paperbacks—*Island of the Blue Dolphins*, *The Hobbit*, *The Borrowers*, *The Great Brain*. Actors made her a combination stray cat and mascot. She learned about musical phrasing from first violin chairs, drop pleats from Tony Award–winning costumers. After befriending the ballerina playing Louise in *Carousel*, she refused to match her socks for three years straight.

Lia went to school, and slept at home, and did her art projects. But she *lived* here with Ben.

He coughs. "OK, look, I'm sorry you're here. I mean, not *sorry*, I like to see you—I love to see you actually, like, love in the exploded firecracker sense, something irreversible you couldn't possibly put back together again because we're all hurtling hell-bound toward total thermodynamic equilibrium, but. Christ."

"Yeah."

"What do you make of . . . of *any* of this?"

"When I'm awake, I never think about it. You're the one dreaming."

Lia is lying. She thinks about Ben and the old theatre constantly, in fits and spurts and sizzles and pops. After the cacophony of glitter-blessed chorus boys came the silent time. The lonesome, post-fire time. A swing set at Riverside Park creaked as the sun dragged shadows across the playground in darkening claws. She collected flowers and twigs, wove grasses into huts for mice. The apartment's lock clicked as her father arrived home exhausted from haranguing insurers, backers, corporate patrons. The radiator hissed in the ripe yellow-grey gleam that passes for the dead of night in New York, and she'd think about a set of little girls' school photos shuffled in front of her own little girl eyes.

Pick a card, any card, the thick consonants of the old man rumbled. *You love magic tricks. You want to, yes? Pick a card and I will for you make it to disappear.*

Seven times Lia was shown a selection of miniature pictures by the World's Stage head custodian, stooped and smiling in a worn denim uniform. Seven times, she picked a card.

Seven times, he made the card disappear, and she smiled up at him. Rapt.

Lia's after-school hours reverted to haunting stage doors and lighting booths upon the opening of New World's Stage. But it wasn't the same. The head custodian never returned, for one. Many of the immigrants didn't. And here were brilliant dressing room lightbulbs instead of flickering fluorescents, this stairway curved sinuously up instead of diving headfirst into the bathrooms. Still. Something in the new structure pulsed as if all the passion of the performers inhabiting the lost building were a scent persisting even after the fire. Lia wasn't always happy here. Far from it. But she was *alive.* There were so many sly jokes and not-a-bit-secret affairs, all the chaotic champagne-colored froth of adult relationships.

And Ben, of course. There was always Ben.

Eight-year-old Ben scrubs his hand down the front of his elfin face. When he draws it away, his palm is painted with the gore from his lip. It's always awful to see him like this, golden-haloed and hurting.

"Aaaaand I'm bleeding," he drawls. "When was I *not* bleeding at this age, though? Simpler question, let's use Occam's razor here."

It's only a dream, and dreams can't hurt him or you.

Lia shakes herself. "Look, Ben, I don't know why you *aren't* more creeped out by this."

Ben shrugs. "Nothing about the way our minds interact surprises me anymore."

"But why the old World's Stage?"

"Why not? All's fair in love, war, and REM sleep. Does it really bother you so much?"

"Seeing you?"

"No, not that part, please don't answer that question, just let me, like, keep my illusion you treasure our time together. I meant the wreck of the theatre."

"Of course it does. Someone *died*."

Pick a card, any card, Jórvík would say to her. And she did. *Seven times.*

Ben pulls her hand out of her pocket in one of those sudden gestures that sends blood rocketing through her veins.

"But maybe that's why we're here, huh? Maybe whoever it was who died in the fire is trying to, you know. Tell us something, settle scores."

Lia doesn't bother repressing a shudder. "I don't want whoever they found incinerated in this to tell me anything. Ever."

Lia knows who died. To everyone else, he was an unidentified husk. Barely a corpse. But she has never breathed a word of it to a living soul. Especially never to Benjamin.

"Some journalist you'd make," he teases. "Aren't artists supposed to have just a liiiiiittle smidge of investigative reporter in them? You know, really peel the skin off reality, see what lies beneath?"

But I'm not an artist anymore.

Lia has spent practically all her days expressing herself through the language of flowers, wild and weird installations, and she lost that lifeline when she needed it most.

ROSEMARY: *For remembrance, and woven into sacred garlands by the ancient Greeks to bring mental clarity.*

"Artists have to make art," she snaps, "and I haven't since the night two years ago when we stopped being us."

Ben looks chastened. Then he nods, swinging the hand he still holds. It feels like a soft slide of *home* against her palm.

"All right, sure, we quit the gumshoe stuff. How about . . . oh, I know. Here's a riddle for you: Is the reconstructed New World's Stage even World's Stage at all?"

Lia nearly smiles before it catches in her throat. Ben loves these mind games, has played them forever, and he always stares at Lia as if world peace depends on whatever answer tumbles from her lips. She glances down before replying and sees a symbol carved into the stage. It's a five-pointed star, with a smaller one nestled perfectly inside, and a third tinier pentagram within that one. She's seen it before. But can't recall in what setting.

"How do you mean, is it World's Stage?"

Ben lifts his arms and makes a dramatic circle. "I mean the Ship of Theseus."

"The what, now?"

"This is actually one of my favorites. A classic. OK, so you have a boat that's being replaced plank by plank. Once every molecule of the vessel is new, then is it still the same ship?"

"The human body discards all its cells every seven years, but you don't imagine I'm a stranger."

Ben claps, delighted. "Good one. No doctor is capable of replacing every piece of you and preserving your, like, consciousness, your *you*, your Lia, whatever."

Ben always did have a ferocious attachment to individualism and individuals, Lia remembers with a pang. It was never just his obscene wealth that drew devotees. Prove yourself a bully or a hypocrite, and he would eat you for breakfast with a dash of Cholula. Prove yourself worthy, and he would lie in the middle of the road to stop traffic as you crossed the street. People slavered over his genuine laughter as much as they hinted needing six-figure astronomy textbooks. It's why he and Lia were together so long. Christ knows nobody else would have fed her for the fifteenth time because she couldn't hold the spoon herself.

"But theoretically a boat could be a boat until the end of time. It's inanimate," he continues.

"World's Stage isn't inanimate, and I don't care which one you're talking about. This building or what replaces it."

Ben grins wolfishly. There are dry-bones scuffles here always, sounds like the spectres of flames chewing at plaster.

Gnawing at flesh.

"Then what if you never threw away any of the pieces of the original ship, and you reassembled them when the fresh one was complete? Which ship is *more* real?"

"Who came up with this?"

"Plutarch."

"He must've been a real pain in the dick."

This produces a yapping laugh with his face thrown skyward, and Lia feels the old joy flooding her body before she can plug the hole in the dam.

Fuck you, she thinks. *Fuck you, Ben, and your beautiful brain, and your even more stupidly beautiful, generous, loyal heart, and forever and for always fuck the fact I still managed to torch us to the ground.*

Ben recaptures her hand and plays with the fingers, knuckle by knuckle, which does wretched things to her blood pressure. "Wanna know my two favorite solutions?"

"Do I have a choice?"

"The first is conceptualism. There is in reality no ship. The ship is a human concept applied to a particular mass existing at a particular instant. The way love is a particular feeling during a particular period. It carries no significance whatsoever outside of human linguistics. Love doesn't exist objectively, and neither do Theseus's ships."

Lia wills her heart to slow. "And the second one?"

Ben takes a shaky breath, concentrating on her fingertips. "The second one is easier to explain with rivers. You can never step in the same river twice if you think of it in three dimensions, according to perdurantism. But if the river is four-dimensional, then it's completely logical to step into, like, *different* time-slices of the *same river*. It's always there."

"What is this about, Benjamin?" Lia whispers.

He presses his lips to her palm. "Then love would always be there, too. In another time-slice. It doesn't vanish just because the person left."

Ben releases her just as impulsively. Looks away, shoves his hands in his pockets.

"Anyway," Lia sighs, "the modern building's wall has that one section made of the blackened bricks, with the plaque. By the box office. So it isn't a hundred percent new."

Ben prods at his lower lip to explore the damage. "Maybe its personality was somehow, like, transplanted."

"I thought you said buildings were inanimate?"

"Well, that was clearly pretty dumb of me. You of all people should realize my capacity for, um, stupidity. Considering."

"Why do you bring me here?" Lia's temples pulse around her eye sockets.

"But . . . I don't. I *wouldn't*, I've never deliberately hurt you in my life."

He's right, Lia thinks. *He has hurt dozens of people, but never deliberately, not a single one of them. Even the ones who deserved it.*

Ben sounds so dismayed that a cold salt swell of guilt submerses Lia, which makes her angry, which combined with the grief finally bursts the floodgates.

"You must be bringing me here. Who or what else could be? And it's cruel to put me in your head like this. You don't even love me anymore."

Ben's tender young jaw clenches. He puts small fists on his hips in a parody of manhood, glares up at where the fiberglass safety curtain hung before the fire turned its function into a dark joke.

"Lia, I've said a lot of things to you over the years—a pretty, like, daunting array of both vocabulary words and their shades of emotional nuance, in an exponential growth of combinations. I never said I stopped loving you," he growls. "Not once. And I never will."

"Ben—"

"Radioactivity doesn't, it doesn't *stop*, that's what half-life means." Ben's eyelashes sparkle wetly. "It just, like, halves, and halves, and *halves*, forever, and I don't even have that luxury, it diminishing, you were always everything to me."

HELIOTROPE: *Endlessly devoted affection.*

COWSLIP: *You are my divinity.*

HELENIUM: *Weeping.*

Lia can't stand this. They can't be together, but she can't get out of his head or get him out of hers. The words would wound in any setting—a coffee shop, a park, some street corner where countless nameless people suffering small tragedies have scuffed their shoes against the cement. But the old World's Stage creeps along her follicles, the cobalt sheen of its walls stately and menacing.

This is the place, this is where you stood, exactly here.
Pick a card, any card.
I will make for it to disappear.

Lia races down the stairs into the theatre's house.

She's never attempted to leave before. That was asinine. She's going to bang outside and find herself on West 64th Street, or else wake up, or else fall off the edge of the known universe's ocean into a dark nothingness of rudderless ships that might or might not belong to this Theseus son of a bitch, she really doesn't give a damn anymore. So what if she's a coward?

Fine. She'll be a coward, then, belly as yellow as asphalt paint.

Nothing ever really happened to you. Not really. Just pick a card, any card.

There are no excuses for the things that you've done.
"Lia! Wait!"

Lia is already through the double doors, next to where the downstairs bar stood. It's a sullen shell. Leering at her with charred teeth, licking rotten chops.

The problem, she concludes, is that Ben doesn't understand why this place makes her throat close. If Lia were Ben, she could look at it the way he sees the world, like a lyrical theorem or a mathematical poem. She can't, though, and not just because Lia is herself and Ben is himself.

Ben doesn't know key aspects of this narrative.

Neil Young is still crooning his way under her skin. If burning down the inside of Ben's head weren't a horrifying prospect, and one very unlikely to work since nightmares aren't fucking *real*, she'd consider conjuring up a flamethrower just to stop her ex's mental soundtrack.

Lia freezes. Slowly turns.

She's reached the section of wall where the scarred bricks will someday commemorate the new building. But here, although the Sheetrock is blasted and the Manhattan street beyond flickers like a snowy TV set, three portraits in oil hang just where they will when World's Stage is resurrected: the chairman of the board of directors, the president, and the executive vice president. Ben's family.

Jackson Dane, his father. Trudy Dane, his mother. Claude Dane, his uncle.

Something rivets Lia to the floor. It isn't the spirit shining through the portraits' brushwork, far from it—she might work in three dimensions and painters in two, but Lia knows these might as well be mall posters. The faces coolly shine, eyes glazed. They're not Whistlers, not Sargents.

When her lips do part, Lia's voice has been switched off.

It's only a dream.

Plenty of people get turned to stone in nightmares.

Plenty of people can't scream.

A smear of black nothing creeps across Jackson Dane's likeness. At first it looks like virulent mold accelerated into a few seconds. A fast-motion portrait of Dorian Gray.

Lia's hand rises in mute horror when she understands it isn't decay at all.

It's combustion without any visible flames.

ICE PLANT: *Your looks freeze my soul.*

Lia watches Jackson Dane's features warp into a surrealist's mute shriek. But there's no snapping, no hissing—only the incessant melancholy breeze. By the time Ben pads up, the portrait has vanished, ashes delicate as moths' wings littering the carpet.

"I'm sorry." Ben sounds close to breaking. "I shouldn't have . . . said anything. Yep. Sometimes silence is vastly underrated. Did you know that many social animals consider silence to be an indication of imminent danger? Apparently in some vestigial part of me there's a leftover ring-tailed lemur, and I absolutely *needed* to initiate a contact call. What I mean is, I'm less of a lemur. More of a jackass."

"Stop talking," Lia orders.

"Right, yeah, I get it. The subject is upsetting you."

"It's not."

"Oh. You ran out, so I guessed it . . . was? But admittedly the obvious conclusion isn't always correct, and when the observer is at a loss, it's better to ask. Although it can feel inelegant to barge ahead like that, verbal battering ram."

A tear spills down Lia's cheek.

"Articulate wrecking ball?"

She shakes her head.

"Jesus Christ, what's upsetting you? Other than me."

"Your dad." Lia points a shaking finger where the painting ought to be.

"Huh. The portrait's gone. What did that magnificent bastard do this time?"

"He didn't *do* anything."

"Soooo, then what about him?"

"Don't ask how I know it but, Benjamin . . ." Lia forces herself to breathe. "He's dead."

HORATIO

Myth is much more important and true than history. History is just journalism, and you know how reliable that is.

—attributed to *Joseph Campbell*

HORATIO, BLEARY-EYED AND UNDER-CAFFEINATED, takes in his surroundings.

The air in the corridor is too cold and too close simultaneously. A discoloration on the industrial carpet reminds him of Australia. Barking a walrusy cough, the very old man at the front of the queue checks his mobile with a hand gloved in crepe paper skin. A baby emits weird shrieks that might possibly be laughter—otherwise it's distress or, at the outside, demonic possession.

This is a decidedly unromantic opening scene for a homecoming journey, Horatio thinks, and then mentally smacks himself.

What did you want, a moonlit moor? You aren't Jane Eyre returning to Thornfield.

Horatio's chest aches.

The bored, eager snake of passengers fidgets onto the plane. There's nowhere else to be, everyplace to get to, and all in a terrifically slow hurry. Somebody's headphones blast at ear-melting volume, Taylor Swift's "Bad Blood" battering plastic walls. Wedging himself along, Horatio pauses at precisely the wrong moment—and as he attempts to abort the maneuver, sends his elbow smashing against the latte of the woman behind him.

"*Fecking* hell!" she squeals, glaring at the coffee plume staining her blouse.

"Oh my god!" Horatio exclaims, horrified. "That—that was so very, very far from intentional, ma'am. One moment, here's—"

"Get yer snot rag out o' me face!" she shrieks.

A widening ripple of the transatlantic aircraft turns. Morbidly curious. Meanwhile, Horatio detests being the center of attention for any longer than it takes him to shave.

"Please do accept my apologies, I'd no idea—"

"That there might be somebody behind ye whilst boarding a fecking *jet plane*? Great mammoth git like you?" The woman waves the hem of her cheap rayon shirt in happy rage. "Had to run me arse off just to get a drop of coffee afore takeoff, and now look! Didn't mean to dye me blouse with it, did I?"

"Um. You'd hardly mar such a flattering top with abstract expressionism," he agrees helplessly.

"Are ye taking the piss, young man?"

"On the con—"

"Now, you just listen here!"

Family border disputes over seat-back pockets and earbuds pause their negotiations to listen. The woman hooks her index finger into Horatio's button-down and beckons him forward, a carp on a reel.

"Do forgive me," Horatio pleads with white flags in his deep brown eyes. "Any man of my size is inevitably something of a menace when it comes to air tra—"

"How much cash do ye have, then?" she demands.

Five minutes later and ten quid poorer, Horatio collapses into 37A (window). His elbows don't quite fit, which seems like Fate's cruelest blow yet. He didn't sleep a wink, wore holes in his socks until dawn hemorrhaged through his curtains. A solid pain has been lodged above his breastbone ever since the text message yesterday morning:

> so I know you're busy you always are now but
> get here please I think I'm losing my mind

Well, no, the pain has been there rather longer than that.

Allowing his inky head to droop, Horatio wonders how many things he forgot to pack, though he's not much fussed. In every nation, people sell necessaries like toothpaste and a change of pants. Double-check for your meds (paracetamol for the headache, Telfast for the hay fever), make sure there aren't any stray drugs in your briefcase (his weed is in a carved teak box budged up on the bookshelf against *Tennessee Williams: Mad Pilgrimage of the Flesh*). Taking mental inventory of his suitcase is a meditative exercise. One which is barely preventing him from worrying himself senseless.

You didn't even say goodbye the last time. You didn't, and now he needs you, and you'll have to talk about it, won't you, the whole nightmare will have to be discussed, you ghastly human being.

"Beg pardon."

A trim man with white hair slides a leather duffel under the seat of 37B (middle). He's a short fellow—though at six foot three, everyone in the British Isles seems diminutive to Horatio. The chap owns the deft movements of a card sharp or one of those sleek ferrety creatures they show on nature channels. He's strikingly magnetic, with a wry mouth and Jermyn Street clothing. A flowered pink pocket square peeks out of his light dinner jacket, which oddly has a few needles tucked in the lapel. He's either sixty and has been kept in a jar like preserves, or he's forty and has lived every instant. If Horatio were attracted to posh older men instead of brilliant fellow Columbia alumni—*well, one in particular*—he'd have a go during the seven-hour flight.

The little man thrusts out a hand. "Robin. Always best to introduce oneself to the fellow whose knees you'll be knocking up against, eh?"

"Oh, quite. Horatio Ramesh Patel. Pleased to meet you."

"Are you?" Robin winks as he seats himself. "Needn't be, we can get on perfectly well without any pleasure. Or with pleasure as a bonus, just as you wish."

Fast mover, Horatio thinks, but he isn't offended.

Just tired, so tired, and very much in need of a good long cry.

Robin produces a tiny sewing kit and a button. "Fond of this coat, shouldn't like to let it go to seed. Thankfully the spare was in the inner pocket. I won't trouble you?"

"Not at all." Horatio watches as the feline man threads the needle.

Discreet dings punctuate the low chatter of dozens of humans slotting themselves into a flying sardine tin. Horatio wonders what that horrid woman will do with his tenner—his money will likely subsidize a trip to the pub rather than to the dry cleaners. A nip or two of something would go down nicely, he reflects. He ought to have shared a pint with some mate or other before leaving for New York. Let off some steam, howl like Marley's ghost, jangle the chains.

But he's only been back in London for a year, and there isn't anyone. Not anymore. His boarding school friends are either scattered round the globe or else have married suitable acquaintances with sensible retirement investments and clear skin. And he was never minted like they were to begin with; he's shockingly poor, only frightfully bright. They've all moved to places he only knows about from train timetables, and anyway he doesn't much care for going out these days. He's fit enough, but he's thirty-three. Sleeping with starry-eyed young colts cantering from club to club is highly agreeable, and so is getting shagged by studious men wearing frameless eyeglasses he meets in bookshops, but none of it *matters*.

The work matters. It's time he made his mark on the

world at large since he didn't manage to carve it into anyone specific.

"Won't go at all well, you know."

He blinks to discover Robin tilting a brow as if he's doffing a bowler hat.

"Beg pardon?"

"Arsenal versus Chelsea match tomorrow." He tugs the needle dramatically. "Put fifty pounds on Chelsea en route to Heathrow, online you understand, but they haven't a prayer."

"Then why did you bet on them?"

"Principle of the thing. Been my club ever since I was a tyke, Chelsea. Dad used to take us to Stamford Bridge—made a day of it, carrying the flag on the Tube, face paint. Once a blue, always a blue."

"But fifty quid?"

His dancing eyes slow from a jig to a waltz. "What's fifty quid? If they're enough a part of you, you'll stand by them, come hell or high water. I'd back the underdog for love over a sure thing for money any day, even when all hope is lost."

Horatio wonders whether they've started the air circulating quite yet.

"Sudden trip?" Robin asks, his eyes back on his sewing.

It's not a very impressive deduction; Horatio rubs at his chin and finds dark stubble. His coffee-warm eyes are already hollowly set, but he knows the amiable pouches beneath are swollen. With a prominent nose curving like an hourglass and a shoulder-length spill of black waves, he knows he's embracing the suffering-academic trope a bit too literally.

"Um, yes, I suppose it is sudden."

This is the loudest person he has ever encountered on an airplane; surely the man's breaking an unwritten code. But inwardly, Horatio winces. This isn't the least bit sudden. He hadn't gone to the funeral last month, hadn't broken into a run that tore the sound barrier, hadn't leapt clear across the Atlantic. He'd waited to be called for, and that burns hot trails of shame along his neck.

"And what about you, then?" If he won't shut it, Horatio wonders whether Robin can be redirected. "Business? Dare I say sport?"

"Never know which it'll end up being."

"How extraordinary."

"Oh, I am extraordinary. A regular *pukka sahib*, you'll find me."

Horatio freezes, spellbound by mingled feelings of second-hand embarrassment and mild umbrage.

"Did it again, didn't I?" Robin exclaims, lowering his needle. "Just a turn of phrase, not the first time I've put my foot in it and no offense meant, Mr. Patel—Horatio?"

Mollification ritual complete, Horatio sighs. "Quite. Well, there's chutnification for you."

"Beg pardon?"

"Sorry, um . . . Indian diaspora. Viral linguistics."

A shake of the head.

"Salman Rushdie, the author? He coined the term in *Midnight's Children*."

"More of a talker than a reader myself."

"So I've noticed."

Horatio hopes that this reply is rude enough to rebuff the stranger entirely. When the irksome tit swings a chummy knee toward him instead, Horatio ponders the odds of a pleasanter flight if he asks to sit next to the coffee-stained woman. His neck-tie paws at his throat like a puppy, and he tugs it off with severely quashed rage when he realizes that he wore it in anticipation of who might, just might, meet him at John F. Kennedy airport.

You forwarded all the flight details.

Just didn't have the bollocks to pose the question.

"Event planner. That's what you were asking, wasn't it? Free-lance event planner, mainly weddings. But you, you're a horse of a different feather." Robin nods at Horatio's seat back, which cradles two books, a laptop, and a legal pad. "Writer, eh? Work or hobby?"

"Oh, I'm an assistant professor at the London School of Economics and Political Science. This is my doctoral dissertation. I mean, it's going to be."

"Topic of choice?"

"An in-depth biography on the Right Honorable Keith Vaz."

"The story of a politico with a taste for sex without using a jimmy? Why write anything about his life, let alone in depth?"

Because he's a high-profile British Asian in government, and the Sunday Mirror *outed him for shagging male prostitutes and bribing them with cocaine, and he was still bloody married afterward, and it's all cracking, cracking mad, and I'm drawn to flawed stories about cracking madmen.*

Horatio shrugs. "Dad's a social worker with the NHS, and Mum volunteered for Sadiq Khan's run at mayor of London. So I'm predisposed to politics, I've a knack for words, and I'm keen to teach somewhere and spend the rest of my time publishing books on . . . well, the rest of my time as a biographer. It's an old-fashioned word, but the best description."

Robin nods sagely. "Written in your DNA, eh?"

"You could say that. It's in the blood, I suppose."

"Is it?"

"Er, I've just said so."

"No hiding from what's in the blood, is there?"

Robin finishes the knot he's tying with a neat flick. He tucks the jacket beneath the seat back, triple folded. Attendants in neatly pressed polyester uniforms march up and down the cabin, patting things as if they're stroking the flanks of a mechanical steed.

"Listen, friend," the little man says more intently. He brandishes a sleep mask with cat ears and Horatio blinks in disbelief. "Hear me out for a mo' and I'll be off to dreamland like you flipped a switch. But I have a . . . let's call it a sixth sense about people. Care for some free advice?"

"Er, is there any way of declining?"

Robin chuckles, snapping the feline mask onto his forehead.

He seems an impish creature. One who might materialize before the throne and offer fathomless wealth, eternal life, the Moon, and only remember to mention later that by the by he wants oceans of blood for his trouble.

"Obviously a great whopping load of feelings tied up in this trip for you, eh? Sleepless nights, gnawing at your thumbnail . . ."

Horatio stops.

"Not pretending to know what's the matter, am I, but there's no hiding from the blood, carry it about with us, don't we, hearts pumping away, we lug it everywhere, gallons of the stuff, and if you ask me . . ."

"Um, I didn't."

"You're in danger, me duck."

"Of what?"

"Of yourself," Robin whispers conspiratorially. "Bloodsick, you are. Well on your way to being a terminal case."

When Horatio parts his lips to ask what in hell this prat is talking about, nothing emerges.

He doesn't know what *bloodsick* means. But he's monumentally sick at heart, and his mind plunges deep into a river of images of Benjamin. Benjamin stirring dolsot bibimbap at The Mill, half-smiling as the beef and egg and rice mingle, salty steam hissing upward. Benjamin listening to something Lia just said, laughing at the skies. Benjamin gripping his sandy blond hair so hard his knuckles whiten as he drops his jaw and screams, and screams, and *screams*.

Oh fuck all, not that night. Any night but that one.

Benjamin that first morning at Columbia. Horatio fluttery over studying European History, Politics, and Society, his shadow superimposed over those of Kiran Desai, Langston Hughes, Allen Ginsberg. Benjamin starting his master's as well, only in Philosophical Foundations of Physics. Brisk river-bright September breeze larking through the campus, a birdsong day, a screw-top-bottle-of-wine-and-a-blanket-in-Morningside-Park day, his future best friend motionless outside Pulitzer Hall staring down at his wristwatch as if it held every secret ever kept and saying absently to Horatio—a total stranger—an odd combination of incredible words.

I'll be late for my first class, I think, but it's gonna feel sweet to be a student again, have that structure. I was off for two months and losing my goddamn mind, you feel me? Time is only there because we notice it's passing. We create these markers to know where we are, entirely based on perspective. That's nuts, right? Trying to perceive empty time is like trying to judge a mile in the desert with just your eyesight. That's why people locked in solitary go rampantly bananas. God, I'm late for General Relativity and Black Holes and grad school is already saving my ass.

Robin snaps the ridiculous cat mask over his eyes.

"Did you mean heartsick?" Horatio asks.

Robin yawns. "Could have done, but no. Sorry, friend. Might have been able to help if we'd met earlier, but it's . . . metastasized. Heartsickness degenerates into bloodsickness, and bloodsickness is one of the leading causes."

"Of *what*, for god's sake?"

"Why, tragedy, of course."

The eerie little man inserts a set of foam earplugs and within three seconds is snoring.

But it happened last month, Horatio thinks helplessly. *Tragedy's already struck like lightning from the blue.*

He knows, however, that tragedy is nothing like lightning. Horatio made the mistake of mentioning to Benjamin long ago that lightning never struck twice, following the first time Lia landed herself in hospital, and the only two things that comforted him were Horatio's presence and intellectual tangents. Only Benjamin could ground feelings by hurtling his brain into the aether like a Frisbee, and Horatio could pinpoint the exact instant when his one true et cetera escaped the confines first delineated by Newton. The sad, soft stare of the prophet tinged with the electric crackle of the hermit. Well, after all—Isaac Newton was also a magician. Horatio loved Benjamin so much whenever he looked that way that he himself would forget every law in the book, including gravity.

No no no no, lightning discharge is made of between threeish and thirtyish separate strokes. Whenever you get hit by lightning, you've already been hit, like, a fucking dozen or so times by definition. People should say lightning never strikes once.

Horatio changes his mind. Tragedy is a very great deal like lightning.

A month ago, Benjamin Jackson Dane's father, Jackson Jefferson Dane, was found dead in the bedroom he shared with his wife of some forty years, Trudy Dane, on the third floor of their Upper West Side townhouse. Eyes wide and empty as fishes' dreams. The toxicology report concluded he died of organ failure due to ingestion of multiple painkillers, alongside the generic sertraline his wife asserted he had been taking for years to treat mood swings and anxiety, and a hefty dollop of Xanax. Jackson Dane was sixty-two; his wife, Trudy, sixty; and his only son, Benjamin Dane, thirty.

An in-depth examination of the New World's Stage books soon revealed that key donors had recently departed. And their last production, a gender-swapped version of *The Bacchae*, hadn't exactly rained pennies from the fly system. Which must have been ungodly depressing.

Horatio knows all of this from what Benjamin still calls "the Google machine." When he'd first heard, he rang Benjamin twice. Both times, his friend's high, expressive voice announced cheerily, "Hey, it's Ben! If you really want to leave a message then sure but you could just text me and save us both some time, and time, *that* is the most precious commodity in the universe. Don't just toss that shit around like you have an endless supply. You *do not*. Thanks, I'll get back to you soon. But in a text."

Ending the call each time in silence made Horatio disgusted enough with himself he wanted to peel his own skin off and toss it in the nearest skip. He was not cowardly. Cowardice was just another word for selfishness, and his family had practiced Jainism for literally centuries, *the function of souls is to serve one another*. But Horatio imagines that if you fled the love of your life following a misguided, drunken one-night stand, voicemails were not the done thing.

And if only that were all of it.

Two weeks thereafter, Horatio opened Facebook to discover via private message that Trudy Dane was already remarried: to Claude Dane, her brother-in law. The marriage was conducted in secret at City Hall, but that didn't stop theatre employee Ariel Washington from sending him a darkly worded *your friend is not in the best place*.

He'd received a text not ten minutes later:

what ho cheerio giddyup see I still
speak the Queen Mother's
English you daft left goolie you

Followed by:

asked Ariel to give you the
latest gossip from the Dane family
because typing it will make my
hand fall off

And the next day:

have you bought the happy couple
a butter dish yet?

Still Horatio said nothing. Not up until *get here please I think I'm losing my mind*. That prompted a brief heart attack and Horatio's response:

Oh god no, of course you aren't losing
your mind. I'll be there as soon as I can.

And then, a few minutes later:

I didn't know you wanted to see
me again. But I ought to have done.

And finally:

I'm so very sorry, Benjamin.

*The wounds we inflict on our own opinions of ourselves are
past solving,* Horatio decides.

Then he decides to get royally smashed.

Swallowing the last of his fourth scotch, Horatio does his
utmost to rest. His eyelids buzz and his shoulders twitch as he
tumbles toward sleep only to be yanked back, over and over
again, by his own very present waking failures.

*You weren't there for him. You said you'd be there for him
always, always isn't conditional. It doesn't matter how you
parted ways, you sack of shite, and now look at you.*

*Look at all the things you aren't that you imagined you
would be.*

WHEN HORATIO WAKES, THE plane has already landed. Light
streams in through lewdly spread shades. Overhead compart-
ments yawn open as if likewise startled from sleep. The small
fellow—Robin of the cat mask, of the portentous diagnoses—is
nowhere to be found.

The rote procedures of Immigration and Customs take place
behind a sheer plastic curtain of weariness. Reality ripples.
He's here for personal reasons, he tells the squat woman with
the steel-wool hair. No, he doesn't have any fruits, he tells the

razor-burned man with the Flatiron Building nose. Horatio's ankles are the wrong circumference, and his limbs feel like Cheestrings, which for some perverse reason Americans call string cheese.

He's half sleepwalking toward the taxi queue from baggage claim when he glimpses the man he never expected to see again except in the sort of dreams that leave him brittle and drenched. Oh-so-very-British dreams, his dick receding, abashed, *terribly sorry about all this fuss*, and his heart spreading like a net under a suicidal jumper, *here, love, I'll catch you, tear holes in me, I was made for this, can't you understand?*

Benjamin slouches back and forth. A thick, expensive-looking black leather cuff encompasses his right wrist. The Nirvana T-shirt he's wearing is rumpled but Horatio knows it's clean, Benjamin is always neurotically clean, and the dark jeans over his Converse lack much to work with in the way of structural support. This implies that Benjamin is living off Klonopin, Adderall, and sporadic forays into gourmet markets for sushi. He looks like an expensive catastrophe—which would be exactly accurate if he weren't also absurdly funny, and ungodly brilliant, and recklessly devoted.

Benjamin Dane spies him. Sharp chin, sharp nose, sharp attentiveness, sharp shards of sea-glass glittering under his friend's lashes, sharp thoughts like sunlight sparking off breakers. The softest heart in the world, underneath all of that. Benjamin purses his lips in a grateful, worried way and the entire airport comes crashing down in an operatic tidal wave.

I really do need a life vest, Horatio realizes.

Strangers glance at the very large Gujarati Londoner wordlessly enveloping the wiry flaxen American, and something hot and sweet spills into Horatio, like tea pouring into a beloved mug.

"All right," he sighs. "Yes, this is . . . Um, good."

"How was your flight?" Benjamin pulls back.

"Fine. I slept a bit. You don't care about any of that, though."

Benjamin grins. "Nope. I mean, I care about *you*. I just don't do small talk. Don't make me sound like a dick, man. But right now I'm caring about a number of other things. The number being, like, laaaaaaarge. As an integer."

"I am aware."

"Hefty."

"Yes, substantial. I'm very sorry, Benjamin."

"For what?"

"Your loss, to begin with," Horatio replies, helpless and ashamed.

The emptiness in his friend's expression echoes cavernously. "Yeah, that's old news. Funerals might be sad and stuff, but funerals are inevitable, right? Look at all these people, their cells decaying, bones drying out, arteries clogging. That was like watching a dog sniff a tree—unavoidable. Or watching a dog die, come to think of it, they do that too, I was kind of getting lost in the wrong simile there, sorry."

"Not a bother."

"Anyway, dying is easy peasy, but remarrying after you lost your first husband *this* quickly? That is the shit that truly impresses me. Are you hungry?"

"Er, not parti—"

"Good." Benjamin pivots, striding for the revolving doors. "Because my new stepdad is also my uncle, so we have a lot to talk about. My family life is entirely, royally fucked."

BENJAMIN

A knowledge of the historic and philosophical
background gives that kind of independence from
prejudices of his generation from which most
scientists are suffering. This independence created
by philosophical insight is—in my opinion—
the mark of distinction between a mere artisan or
specialist and a real seeker after truth.

—*Albert Einstein, Letter to Robert Thornton, 1944*

B EN PROPS HIS ELBOW on the lip of the cab window while
Horatio checks his email post-flight.

The bigger man pretends to work, *death in the family
couldn't be helped well I guess you'll just have to suck it won't
you the kids can teach themselves about the Anthropology of
Kinship.* But Horatio keeps glancing at Ben in little sips like Ben
is a very very nice whiskey and that's fine, Ben likes Horatio, he
loves him actually, he's never been ashamed of that, they even
slept together on one memorable if experimental occasion, and
even this strained flat-fare cab ride from JFK to Manhattan is
totally fine as long as Horatio is being good and gentle

here

right here

here

motherfucking present and accounted for

instead of doing whatever good, gentle things the good, gentle son of a bitch does in London.

It's not like Ben demands allegiance. Ben not only detests himself often, he hates the cocksure narcissism favored by red state governors and the front men for shitty bands. It's just that people sometimes like him now that he's learned at long last and after intensive study how to speak their language and when he likes them back supposing he's convincing or barring that even sincere then people feel good around him like it's a privilege or something, which it kind of is really because most people are pretty dull.

But Ben is hurt that after All The Shit That Went Down a year ago, Horatio had the *cajones* to run back home to his enchanted little isle and his *boring-normal-lovely* mom's curries and his *nerdy-glasses-sporting* dad's pipe smoke and have drinks and opinions and boyfriends and all those other things he's totally entitled to granted but not *without Ben*.

"All right," Horatio concludes. "I'm sorry, had to respond to a few of my colleagues, I sort of did a runner there. Er. Not my usual style."

"It kind of is, though," Ben notes.

Horatio winces. He looks pretty good, Ben decides. Been hitting the gym as well as the books. The pouches under his eyes make him look anxious, but Ben doesn't really mind Horatio being worried as long as it's Ben he's worried about. This is, Ben knows, outrageously selfish. He doesn't give a shit. Horatio was born to be concerned about people, he's like an empathy factory, with those Godiva chocolate eyes of his and his way of squinting at you like you're an archaeological dig.

"Sorry," Ben says. "Yeah, how's London treating you? Still wet?"

"Like living in a damp towel."

"That must be sort of uncomfortable for you, considering."

"Considering what? I'm sane?"

"Sure, that, too."

"Um. I'm brown?"

"Yep. I don't understand people from tropical climes with killer local food moving *to* London on purpose. You guys are like Scott Weiland leaving the Stone Temple Pilots. Actually, I could totally see you Patels as a family producing a record titled *Happy in Galoshes*, too. It's like you're on the verge of a Christmas album."

"Benjamin, are you really so wealthy you don't comprehend people migrating to metropolitan areas? My grandmum refuses to bin takeaway napkins in case she ever needs them for the loo."

Ben has so much money that he's unaware of the exact figure. He's a prince in denim and sneakers, he's well aware. That's why he's always, always, always trying to give it to people who actually *need it*, like Horatio. They both know this to be true and settled matters forever after one spectacular brawl over who was paying for street falafel: Ben is allowed to buy things for both of them whenever he wants, and Horatio is allowed to tell him to piss off.

"All right. I'm hopelessly out of touch, and it was a bad joke anyhow. I'm sorry."

"Benjamin," Horatio interrupts, a pleading note in his deep voice.

Peeling his eyes from the scenic graveyards of Queens, all that loamy, gut-rich soil growing its concrete-slab underbrush, Ben grants his friend his complete attention.

"*I'm* sorry. About . . . everything."

Ben enjoys Horatio fretting over him. It's a little like being wrapped up in a
   GREAT
   BIG
   LONDON-FOG-GREY
   FLANNEL BLANKET
   (WITH A FRESH PLATE OF COOKIES AND A HOT
      CHAI AT HIS FINGERTIPS).
But he doesn't enjoy Horatio in actual pain, like *pain*-pain, this nose-crinkled, eyes-tearing remorse. Ben detests seeing *any-*

body in pain, he's had enough of pain to last five fucking lifetimes, and this is *HORATIO*, so Ben instantly waves a dismissal.

"That was deeply not your fault. Or not *just* your fault. Nobody's fault."

"God, Benjamin, I—"

"Yeah, dude, you decamped, and we didn't talk for, like, a year and then you missed Dad's funeral, but you tried calling, I mean my phone only rang twice and I was making arrangements and you didn't leave any messages. But weddings are super-way more fun anyhow, you know? Not to mention the *efficiency*. This way, they can take the cold cuts from Dad's funeral and put them in those pinwheel sandwich thingies for the wedding reception. Reduce, reuse, recycle, am I right?"

"Benjamin—"

"They're already secretly hitched, but we're heading into the New World's Stage yearly benefit gala in, like, a week, so maybe they'll make some kind of massive announcement. That'd be perfect, come to think of it, since they seem so into keeping a low carbon footprint—there'll already be champagne, flowers, whatever. I have to add you as my plus-one, I wasn't sure . . . well."

When Horatio sighs, Ben hurries on. No more pain. Not for Horatio, not if he can help it.

"But here you are! You'll make this event much less ravaging to the psyche. Shut up, dude, half of Broadway will be there. We'll get you a chorus boy with no gag reflex."

"Um, lovely."

"Aw, come on, you looooove those bari-tenors, I'll be your wing—"

"No, I mean—Benjamin, what is going on? I don't . . . I'll wag off with you, whatever helps, anything, just . . . What the bloody hell? Your mum married her brother-in-law?"

Ben doesn't say anything
tries to say something anything
can't say anything.

Ben's had issues with insomnia since childhood. Ditto nightmares, anxiety, panic attacks, ADHD, borderline autism, all the mental bells and whistles *ring-a-ding-ding-ding-clang-shriek-hiss*. So he knows his own mind pretty intimately. When you're messy between the ears, you have to chart it out, identify your nicer hilltops and your crappier chasms. Currently (in this topographical depiction of his consciousness), he's been dying of thirst in this boneyard desert that is devoid of answers to the one simple question:

Why would Mom be
fucking
Uncle Claude
in the first place
let alone
in a contractually binding, china pattern way?

"It wasn't a suicide," Ben announces out of the blue. "It just . . . my dad, it wasn't a suicide."

Horatio shakes his head. "How, um . . . What exactly are you saying? The toxicology report—"

"Oh, you've been *researching*."

"Well, naturally. God, you've every reason to think me a complete wankstain, but of course I have been."

"Noooo, I do not think that you are a, as you so charmingly term it, wankstain."

"Good. I wasn't entirely certain that would be the case. Or whether I quite agree with you."

"Hey, now." Ben throws his friend a fond look. "Recall when that cup of cat piss Jules Darden called you an ambassador for impoverished exchange students? I mean, we're at Columbia, this international vanguard of higher learning, and he whips out 'exchange students.' Pretty sure I punched him in the face in that amazing Harlem dive bar, remember? So it makes me super conflicted when you talk shit about *yourself*. Do I headlock you?"

"Um. No need."

"The enemy of my friend is my enemy, even if the worst enemy of my best friend is his own worst enemy."

Horatio smiles, and the cab's atmosphere warms by a cozy five degrees.

"The toxicology report," Horatio says gently. "It seemed to have indicated that your father was depressed. Why do you suppose that—"

"Because my dad would never commit suicide."

"I don't know quite how to say—"

"Then don't say it. I know the whole speech."

People have been telling this to Ben for four long weeks now, *AND IT ALWAYS MAKES HIM WANT TO TURN INTO A VERY SMALL EXTRA-FUZZY TERRIER AND SINK SHARP LITTLE TEETH INTO THEIR SOFT SWEET NECKS.*

His father apparently took antidepressants and benzos (who doesn't). His father was sad and distant (who isn't). His father was born to conquer the world and then the solar system and he started with the New York theatre scene because that was the opposite of the family petroleum business and it turned out that mastering the arts was actually harder than vanquishing the Milky Way. Jackson Dane was grasping and critical and always networking with old East Coast wealth, but then again after all, *who fucking isn't.*

Ben's head chirps. With his father's voice, when Ben was around twelve.

Benny, what are you doing taking that shit? Pull your head out of your ass and learn to deal like a regular guy. You think people respect pill-poppers? Or you think they want to line up behind the man who actually knows what he's doing?

I only want what's best for you, son.

Horatio has gone quiet. He's just following orders, but Ben now regrets those orders.

Ben clears his throat. "Yes, Dad was depressed, but he didn't commit suicide. I was talking to him just the day before, he sounded exactly the . . . I would have known. You're going to say that the theatre was getting too much for him, that the drugs could have led to self-destructive tendencies, that it's always the sure and steady ones who end up pulling their own plugs because the world can't beat them and only they can beat themselves, but it didn't happen. Call me crazy, call me not handling the Kübler-Ross model, but I'm still going to prove it was an accident. All right?"

Horatio's shoulders under the soft blue shirt are stiff from distress and from the plane, and he should drink some serious electrolytes. But he's Horatio. He's always so very *him* that it aches, and so finally he says, "All right."

"Thank you." Ben's head falls against the seat.

"Don't mention it."

"Man, I just asked you to fly across the Atlantic at a moment's notice. Kiiiiinda seems like that could inconvenience a regular person."

"Oh, well, I've already skived off just before finals, so I needn't go back at any particular time. The teaching element was mainly finished, thankfully. My colleague owes me a good turn after I took her cat when she was shooting a research film. I'll have a spot of grading to do while we're, um, conducting inquiries. But otherwise . . . I'm quite at your disposal."

"Really?"

"Always," he says simply, and Ben feels something knotted loosen in his chest. "You know that."

"I do," Ben admits.

Once, when waiting at home for Lia to arrive back grew impossible, Ben left their apartment to prowl the streets. The August sunrise was a pretty pink-and-grey, the palette of an eighties movie where the girl remakes herself by taking her glasses off but still wears sweatshirts with the neck cut out. And for a guy fretting holes in his stomach, Ben felt strangely fine, like by leaving the house he was also leaving his fiancée's well-being in the hands of quantum mechanics.

- She either was or was not curled up in their bed.
- She either was or was not passed out in some community garden like a possum.

He stopped for coffees and two orders of egg and cheddar at the Bernardo Brothers Café by Horatio's apartment on 155th and Riverside (which had been their apartment before Lia, and would be their apartment again after Lia, and is now Ben's apartment), used his key, and found his friend sitting at the table under the window with his laptop and a steaming World's Stage Theatre mug. They had a staggering collection.

"Get dressed," Ben ordered. "They're playing *Blade Runner* in Bryant Park tonight."

Horatio stared. "Get dressed for *Blade Runner*? I've been up for all of twenty minutes."

"We could walk the High Line maybe and when we end up at Chelsea Market we could eat, like, something from each continent—including Antarctica because ice counts."

Horatio rubbed at his morning stubble, cogitating. "Wasn't Lia at that Alphabet City gallery opening last night?"

Ben pulled a stringy blob of cheese off his sandwich paper. "It was great, she said. It might be a perfect space for her to show."

Horatio, clearly choosing his words, went to the fridge and returned with a bottle of Sriracha. "Have you seen her, or was she texting you?"

Ben took a bite of fried egg and squishy bread. His heart interfered with its passage down his throat, the traitor.

"Shit, I'm being such a tosser," Horatio declared, clapping his hands. "Bernardo Brothers coffee is greatly improved with a splash of bourbon. I'll top us up, pop in the shower, and this article shall be postponed. Please don't eat my egg on a roll. No,

shut it. We've been mates for years, I can tell when you're about
to nick my food. Even when you bought it for me."

And they had a very nice day and Lia texted to say she was
home around eleven A.M. and that she was so very sorry and that
it would never happen again.

"I had a nightmare about it, before it happened," Ben admits.

Horatio's head twists. "About . . . your father?"

"Yeah. It's sorta grainy, like the satellite feed isn't quite tuned
in. But Lia was there. She *saw* it, she. Something about Dad's
portrait, the one that burned in the fire all those years ago. It
ignited or, or something. Anyway. She told me in the dream he
was dead. And then I woke up that morning, and. *Ffft*."

The quiet is now a deafening blare of words unspoken and
muted traffic noise. Ben worries at the thick black leather cuff
around his right wrist.

"I thought you hated wearing jewelry."

Horatio seems less curious about this than observational, like
he's updating

> file: Benjamin Jackson Dane//grooming:
> accessories.

"This isn't jewelry."

"Oh. Is there a ring or a lock I'm not seeing? I hadn't realized
you'd got into kinky sex."

"Everyone's into kinky sex, especially people who claim not
to be into kinky sex, but no." Ben grates his nails over the back
of his neck. "This is a chunk of Dad's commemorative belt from
the New World's Stage gala opening. I had it converted."

The only sounds are the humming of the tires and whatever
language Mr. Hamza Farooqui speaks into his Bluetooth. Ben
is rabidly jealous of people who get to have boring conversations
just now.

"Um." A line appears above Horatio's patrician nose. "So you don't wear jewelry, but you do wear a piece of your late father's belt."

"Yep."

"Do you want to . . . talk about that?"

Ben pulls in a deep breath. He can't ever seem to get a full breath these days.

"It kinda takes some adjustment, feeling it there, you know? Dunno if I should blame thermoreceptors, mechanoreceptors, or nociceptors, but they're still, like, *hello there*, you're basically wearing a manacle."

"Why not take it off?" Horatio asks softly.

"Because it's only an outward manifestation of an inner condition. I'd be feeling it anyway."

A few seconds later, there is a wide, warm hand inserting itself hesitantly into Ben's

FINGERS AND
    THE NEW FINGERS
        SLIDING INTO PLACE FEEL
           SO PERFECT BEN SWALLOWS PAST
      WHAT'S CHOKING
        HIM AND SQUEEZES THEM BACK
      FOR ALL HE'S WORTH.

"You remember how Dad's side of the family is all in Texas?" Ben asks, eyes swimming.

Horatio nods.

"When the theatre reopened, Dad kept pushing and pushing and pushing. With the construction and the big donors and whatnot, and he kept saying 'we just have to pull up our bootstraps.'"

Horatio's eyes crinkle.

"Like, whenever anyone tried to say 'yo, Jackson, we already just gave you fifty grand last month,' or Paul tried to say 'hey, Jackson, the insurance wants to know whether this was arson, *again*,' Dad would just tell them *the bootstraps*, they will not hitch themselves and it was *so Texas* it hurt."

This time Horatio does smile.

"They'd sorta shrug, like, yeah, I guess you have a point, and tooled 'bootstraps' onto a belt. The part I cut out has the quote on the back. You think it's nuts, I suppose."

"I rather think it's brilliant," Horatio corrects him.

"Yeah, I don't know that it's brilliant to cut up a two-thousand-dollar belt." Ben laughs as a fat tear slides down his cheek.

"Did Jackson wear it often?"

"To premieres, so the board could see. He thought it was ridiculous."

The sob is not planned, but it happens anyhow.

please come back I know I wasn't everything you wanted but if you'll just come back I can run a business run a marathon run for president run them all down and there you'll be at the finish line and clapping and—

Then his friend is pulling his hand away **no**, and that's to put his arm around him **oh**, and his friend smells familiar in a way nothing has for ages, **yes please**, like that black amber-based cologne he always wears and this is incredibly embarrassing.

"I'm sorry," he says.

"No," Horatio says. And then, "No, never that."

Ben feels the sounds coming from his friend's chest, waves that wash over his eardrums and pinnae and make meaning out of arbitrary frequencies. Ben finds language the single most remarkable artistic achievement of humankind. The *Mona Lisa* has nothing on Mandarin. It's safe here in Horatio's neck, and even his friend's lungs are talking. Horatio shifts, but only to pull his bracelet up for closer inspection.

"So what we have here is a memento mori. 'Let us balance life's books each day.'"

"Remind me?"

"Seneca claimed that if you lived each day to the fullest, that you would never run short of time."

"It would be beautiful," Ben replies, moved, "if that were how time worked. But it's just infinite pieces, all in a row. I wanna go back to some of them. Several of them. Better ones."

Horatio was twenty-five years old and Ben twenty-two when they dragged their meager furnishings up to the second floor of their new building. Benjamin insisted he just wanted *to be a real American who mows his own lawn and shit.* Horatio replied *I don't believe we have a lawn,* and Benjamin joked *we have Riverside Park, Morningside Park, St. Nicholas Park, and Central Park, we need to buy a lawn mower, like, immediately,* and felt a small click in his chest like a key fitting when Horatio laughed. But they aren't roommates any longer, and Horatio lives in London now.

Time isn't a crop that grows more bountifully according to how fertile you are. Time eats everything in the end, from stones to stars.

Horatio stretches stiff legs. "Whenever Roman generals prevailed in battle, there was always a slave chosen to ride behind whoever was being feted, and the slave's only task was to keep repeating throughout, *Respice post te. Hominem te esse memento. Memento mori.*"

"Look behind you and remember that you will die. Nice."

"Indeed."

"Hey, Horatio?"

"Benjamin."

"I can't help but feel like this is kinda gay."

Horatio snorts into Ben's hair before retreating to his side of the car, leaving only their fingers linked.

"It's been a spell since I held hands with anyone in the backseat of a cab," Ben admits.

"We don't countenance this sort of dodgy behavior at all back home. There are especially draconian laws."

"Christ, I've missed you so much."

It takes another half an hour to reach upper Manhattan, trying to breathe past the anchor resting on Ben's chest, trying not to think about an entirely different quote about death, made by C. S. Lewis in his memoir on loss.

No one ever told me that grief felt so like fear. I am not afraid, but the sensation is like being afraid. . . .

Ben is frightened.

Strike that, he's terrified of something he can't see yet. Something just around the bend.

They ooze unsteadily onto the pavement. Horatio tries to pay for the cab, but Ben pushes him away in genuine annoyance. His friend is a compact, competent traveler, so there's only one rolling bag to match the carry-on briefcase, and this Horatio handles himself.

So Ben turns to what used to be their shared apartment on 155th Street, a whole floor of a redbrick townhouse, and he's digging in his pocket for keys when he looks up and the world

goes dark

"Hey, Ben!" Uncle Claude pushes to his feet from where he's clearly been waiting on the stoop for them, a dented cardboard box resting beside him. "Sorry if this feels like an ambush, but you haven't been that easy to find by phone lately. Or email. Anyway, I've got some stuff of your dad's for you. Can I come in?"

LIA

Ask the woman where she going, or
    dare to ask her
where she been. You'll find bluing
    water on ya
doorstep, and ya breathin dis-eased by
    the wind.

—*Luisah Teish, "Hoodoo Moma"*

LIA SITS OUTSIDE THE flower shop, taking a nonsmoking break at eight in the morning, when the trouble starts.

It's not that she minds cigarettes—she understands the sins that make life meaningful. She's adamantly against asking smokers to cease smoking. If they want to, they will, like Ben picking up his socks when he took them off. You can't just *compel* a person to do something because it would be objectively better.

No, Lia doesn't smoke because she looked truly stupid (a friend's words) the one time she ever tried it, holding it with her knuckles to her lips like some cave dweller who'd never so much as seen a TV show before, or a movie, or even a gas station.

Lia hates looking terrible at something.

So during her nonsmoking break between the flower market and the shop opening, she sits outside the Three Sisters' Floral

Boutique on the bench that's a slice of tree, knots and bark and all, fretting. The chill in the darkness has nearly vanished, and shabby birds trill showtunes from traffic signals. An old man wearing duct tape sandals with cardboard soles shuffles past, smelling of provolone. Lia feels dull-headed and desperately anxious.

But there's nothing to be done about that last item. If Ben needs her, he'll ask.

And he doesn't need you anymore.

But he does know that he can always ask?

Lia yearns for a mindless errand. She could peek into the nearby art galleries and kick herself for not being featured in them, or head for the vintage stores to survey the latest socialite discards. She could pretend to want caffeine. Most of the trendy young people swarming the coffee shops with the AC cranked up to refrigerator temp order something either incredibly simple and single-sourced or else shockingly complicated.

But she doesn't want a crowd. And she tormented herself with the galleries not three days ago, and she's already wearing a beloved yellow-and-white striped Free People shirtdress she picked up for eight dollars. Perfect for her late mother's genes, the Sicilian Jews, the source of her perpetual tan and wiry coiffure. She's even wearing her late mother's scarf, the long one with the sweet little strawberries embroidered on the edges, making a coronet over her hair. She almost always craves it lately. Like a good luck charm or a talisman.

The Tompkins Square Library, maybe, where she can look up residencies. Maybe even apply for them.

Or grad schools, her ex's voice murmurs.

Shut it, Ben, she responds, accustomed to arguing with him in her head.

Please be all right, Benny. I'd come the instant you wanted me.

She attempts some impromptu studying in her head, hitting on flowers at random because they weren't given to her alphabetically in the first place—she'd jotted down notes gleaned from around twelve different recipe books lent by the sisters. None of which were so much as paginated.

FORGET✦ME✦NOT: *Fosters depth and wealth of friendship, even after a parting. Forgiveness (both sides) following a dispute. Loyalty in the marriage bed.*

PEONY: *Primarily for luck, health, and success. Pay attention to root vs. bloom. Guardianship and healing for those in your close circle.*

Lia fluffs her shock of curls. Only honest-to-god sleep will remedy this stupor. Not that she minds being a zombie when half of New York has barely slapped their morning alarms. This city keeps all hours, like poets and addicts and thieves. And she adores rummaging through the 28th Street wholesale florist shops—skirting sidewalk water, dodging forsythia branches straining their electric yellow fingers toward her, searching for the insane vines and blooms and boughs her employers require. All freshly decapitated, waiting to be arranged into holy oblations.

What's a bouquet if not an offering on the altar of love, or gratitude, or forgiveness? Wasn't that what every one of your own pieces meant, once upon a time?

What's a guillotined rose if not a sacrifice?

DOG ROSE: *Pleasure liberally mixed with pain and heartache.*

RED ROSE: *Unconditional, unending romantic love.*

LAVENDER ROSE: *Infatuation, mystery, the unattainable.*

Funeral wreaths and prom corsages are floral demise in the hope of human redemption, and Lia feels hallowed doing that work before the sun rises. But she's also absolutely wiped whenever the sisters send her wholesaling. She's been clocked in for four hours now because they needed hyacinth—as blue as humanly possible—and it was an "emergency."

"Oh god, please be open, please be open."

A woman has materialized, one wearing a wrap dress in a bold black-and-white DVF pattern, sporting mussed flat-ironed blond hair and a stunned expression within pools of mascara.

"What are the hours here?" she hisses. "When does it open, is it open?"

Lia rouses herself. "We open at ten."

"Ten o'clock? Oh, *fuck me*. No."

"I'm so sorry, but yeah, ten." Lia squints, pulling vintage Coach sunglasses from the pocket of her dress.

The woman shifts from stiletto to stiletto. "No, please, *please*. Don't they live above the shop? That's what she said, her name is . . . oh Christ, *how long* have you worked with this woman? She said that they're always home."

The would-be customer bangs on the heavy door with the antique cut-glass window inset. Very hard.

"Hey, whoa!" Lia leaps up.

"I *have* the money, here!" She produces a credit card and slams it against the glass pane.

"Please, will you try to stay calm?"

Lia tips her glasses down, blearily registering an Amex reading **JESSICA ANNE KOWALSKI**.

"They really don't like early customers." She glances at her phone: 8:06 A.M. "Late customers when the rum bottle is open, sure, but—"

Jessica quashes a sob. "You have to be open, I need *help*."

Lia sighs—the sisters do live above the shop. So does Lia, since they took her in. They make a batshit-insane found family of four. Sometimes one sister or another will vanish for a month or two, returning to feasts of homemade gumbo, court bouillon, and lemon pies. Sometimes they bake weed-laced sweet potato turnovers and dance to scratchy jazz records as the bodega tomcats yowl. As a creator, Lia soaks up the chaos. As an employee, she spends her life baffled. As a resident, she feels inexplicably showered with affection. But then, the sisters were open devotees of her work, cooed over hulking hills of fairy moss or hundreds of tiny tea roses suspended from the ceiling with fishing line. They loved her art, and her art is her soul.

So it isn't really so mystifying they love Lia, too.

"He's going to kill me," the stranger whispers. "I-I can't . . . oh god, what am I going to *do*?"

The hedge-fund-looking girl makes sounds like an elderly Yorkie in distress. It isn't even faked, which moves Lia to pity as well as sympathy. Jessica Anne Kowalski really cries like a purse dog.

"Take the bench." Lia shoos Jessica off her fuck-me pumps. "Be right back, OK?"

Lia tugs the cool iron of the handle and slips into the spacious, darkly wood-paneled room, lit with soft Edison bulbs and waxed amber shades. There's just the four of them living here, but the place thrums with life. At first, Lia assumed it was all the plants. Dangling from reclaimed industrial buckets, spilling out of upcycled kegs. Lately though, she suspects it isn't just the flora. There's another quality here, one that pours down through the ancient skylight, bordered in stained glass and always seeming to catch moonbeams—even when the moon isn't out. Lia knows it's just the glare from the taller office building nearby.

It sends an eerie static zinging through her chest all the same.

Before her is an antique display table offering succulents and deco glass terrariums and soaps made from goat milk and vetiver oil. To her left, beyond the built-in shelves, is what passes for an office with fiddle leaf figs for walls. And to her right, past the sleek black and gold industrial refrigerator, is the scarred oak work counter with its exit like a saloon keeper's bar top.

"Lia, is that you? No rest for the weary! We'll need peach blossom tomorrow, *chouchou*, barely blooming or no way this order for Mr. Goldsmith's ever coming out right," Mam'zelle announces in her musical way from deep in the jungle. "Oh, and a cypress branch, *s'il t'plait*. Now don't fuss, I know well and good that's two days running you ragged."

Mam'zelle pokes her head around a rubber plant. She is round and shining, like a golden pearl. She has the subtlest accent of the three New Orleans natives, but seasons her speech with the most French and slathers her croissants with the most butter. She manages the store, pays the bills, and balances the books, all while wearing variously blinding shades of pink. Her hair forms a huge kinky halo—Madonna of the fuchsia velour sweat suits. Lia adores her. Mam'zelle's gracious bulk and lilting French are not mere manifestations of her Southern hospitality; they are also knives to pry open the oyster, see what makes her customers come back begging for more. She seems to be around fifty, give or take a few years—but who could say?

"Mercy yes, I need some peach and palm what ain't hardly figured out it's dying yet. How I'm gonna satisfy Mr. Rivera else? Lia!" Moma calls from behind the counter, wrapping a red ribbon around a curious mixture of sweet peas, chamomile, and peppermint. "Supposing you can get there by five in the morning and hustle on back, then there's beignets in it for you, baby."

"You keep giving our *petite chou* so much lagniappe, you'll bankrupt us. She's no customer—she's our own," Mam'zelle teases, sipping café au lait as she slinks into full, fabulous view. It's a hot-pink blouse today over a swishing petal-blush skirt. Lia used to try in vain to identify any of Mam'zelle's designers and concluded that every last piece was bespoke.

"What you said, my sister?" Moma asks.

"I said we *pay* her, no call to cook for her every time she has to set her alarm clock."

"Y'all spoil little Lia here rottener than I do." Stretching her back, catlike, Moma ties the bouquet's silk. "What you give her outta the till this very morning for fetching them bluer than blue hyacinths, twenty? Sixty? Don't you think I don't see it. I see everything, me."

"You surely do, *chère*." Mam'zelle offers a Cheshire smile.

Moma looks nothing whatsoever like her sister. She is skinny and muscled and cinnamon-colored and wears her hair in tiny little braids woven with golden threads, ending at her waist in those soundless bells you find edging fabrics in incense shops. She sports cropped tees that flaunt the abs of a woman who could stand on her head at any moment (and often does). The master craftswoman when it comes to floral artistry, Moma handles all the most difficult orders. She's always offering Lia lucky bundles made from scrap blooms. Lia adores her too, and knows that they both have a horror of flowers being discarded at all, which explains her generosity with cuttings. She seems to be around forty, give or take a few years—but who could say?

"Beignets are worth more to me than money," Lia admits. "Who needs money for beignets when you can just eat the beignets?"

"F'true," Maw-maw grunts from the corner, where she wields a spray bottle at a shelf of spidery air plants. She looks less like she's giving them a drink than like she's holding them hostage at gunpoint.

Maw-maw too fails to resemble her siblings. She is very square and squat and old and burnished. She maintains the shop's houseplants, curating and arranging the displays. Shuffling about in sandals and pale linen sack dresses of the sort women pay hundreds of dollars for on vacation in Boulder, muttering to herself. Whenever she does expound audibly, it's in sweeping decrees that make no sense. Lia would adore Maw-maw too, but it's tough to adore anyone who speaks magic eight ball. She seems to be around a hundred and eighty, give or take a few years—but who could say?

Mam'zelle makes a note on her iPad. "Hurry yourself up with that bouquet, Moma, and leave off the mint or you'll hex the whole block. *Vite.*"

MINT: *Guards against unsummoned spirits, repels those who threaten your well-being, when mixed with other ingredients can break very strong curses.*

"There's a customer outside," Lia reports.

Clicking buttons with immaculate acrylic nails, Mam'zelle hums. Moma's scissors slice a sharper angle on her ribbon. Maw-maw ping-pongs off, monologue too low to hear.

"She's very upset and wants your help. Now, not at ten. The poor thing's all dolled up in last night's club shoes. She's a mess."

"*Pauvre petite,*" Mam'zelle intones.

"Too many lonesome girls in this big dirty city," Moma clucks. "How I'm gonna make enough bouquets for all? Not enough love to go around, baby, and ain't it a crying shame. Tell this child to come back at ten. Maw-maw! You done took your pills, my sister?"

An indecipherable grunt emanates from the bromeliads.

No. There's too much love in the world, just like there's too much food in America. The problem is getting your hands on it.

"It's a real emergency. And she just waved her credit card in my face and she's good for it. Her name is Jessica Anne Kowalski. Also, she knows you're in here, FYI."

Mam'zelle snorts prettily, fingers clicking.

Moma flips shining braids over her shoulder as she plucks an unsatisfactory mint leaf.

Maw-maw could be anywhere by now. Lost in the topiary section. Playing tarot. Violently spritzing the ferns.

Lia angles a shoulder. "If you wanted to give me some pointers, maybe I could handle Jessica myself? She's too sad to be wandering the streets, seriously. It'll bum out all the pigeons."

The crinkle of tissue and the tapping of scratch-resistant glass are the only replies.

"OK. Well, I'll just tell her to come back, but she said something about how he'll kill her."

The small noises cease.

"What exactly she said to you, baby girl?" Moma wants to know as she tapes the golden crepe paper—a signature touch at the Three Sisters'—around her latest creation.

Lia leans her elbows on the rough countertop. "She said *oh god, what will I do,* and *he'll kill me.*"

"Oh, I can hear your heart, *chouchou*." Mam'zelle slides a motherly arm around Lia's shoulders. She smells like the signature sea salt and melon eau de parfum they carry in cobalt bottles, the one called La Sirene. "She reached right in and touched the strings. Moma! We'd better let her in, hadn't we, my sister? We can't let Lia's new friend pace the banquette for two hours!"

There's just too much pain in the world. Lia's throat aches. *There's so much that's already past mending. We should do everything we can, when we can.*

"And you sure what she say was he gonna *kill* her?" Moma repeats, a midnight gleam in her eye.

"Completely," Lia assures her.

"And this Jessica called on God, *help me*, what I gonna do?"

"Yeah, I was standing right there."

"What good'll God be to that poor sweet girl?" Moma laments with growing glee.

"Not one little bit," Mam'zelle trills.

"She sound like she need help in this *here and now*, not hereafter, you feel me, my sister?"

"*Ma chère* sister preaches truth, sure enough."

"Oh, this man of hers sounds mean." Moma smiles without using her mouth, wrinkling her nose like a rabbit.

"I think he sounds sick," Mam'zelle agrees with visible delight.

"Up to no good no how."

"A snake in the grass, *chère*, as I live and breathe."

"Reap the harvest," Maw-maw proposes, wielding her spray bottle on high. She's back.

"All right, *chouchou, allons-y*!" Mam'zelle claps her pretty hands together. "Maw-maw, you throw wide that door!"

Maw-maw budges the door open, grunting. Lia beckons to Jessica, who now weeps in little hitching coughs on the hewn bench.

Jessica startles to her feet. Then she wobbles indoors, hazel eyes wide. She isn't pretty, but she's expensive-looking, and that sometimes counts for more.

"Welcome to the Three Sisters'." Lia smiles.

"Thanks for letting me in. Jesus," she breathes, clutching a wet Kleenex to her breast. "It's a fucking rain forest. Are there toucans?"

"No, but I wouldn't put it past them to install a koi pond."

They walk to the gilt-adorned leather desk nestled in the corn palms, where Mam'zelle beams at the arctic light of her computer screen.

"*Bonjour et bienvenue!*" The proprietress offers a queenly hand palm down, as if Jessica is meant to kiss it. "I hear tell that you're in need of our services. *Bien!* You sit right here, and my sister Moma will bring us some coffee with good thick cream, and you tell me every trouble you been suffering."

At the opposite end of the long countertop, Lia watches Moma and Maw-maw's mouths stretch into carnivorous grins.

"I don't even do dairy." Jessica seems mesmerized.

Lia strides alongside Moma for the coffeepot and the mini fridge, straining to hear all that Jessica has to say. This is the perfect distraction to prevent her from letting loose a floodgate of anxious text messages and possibly even voicemails.

Anyway, Ben loathes voicemails.

Sometimes, the Three Sisters' Floral Boutique sells wedding packages. Sometimes, they sell by the stem. Sometimes, they send out deliveries to restaurants and hotels and private clients. But every so often—for a price, a very *high* price Lia suspects— the bouquets get just plain weird. And the people who order these always do so with a shocking level of urgency.

"Thank you for this," Lia says to Moma, pouring Ronny-brook cream into porcelain covered in cabbage roses.

"How I'm gonna say no to this face?" Moma runs fingers over Lia's chin. "Anyhow, two years you done been here and it's high time you helped me. Every step with this one, let's get those artist's hands of yours dirty again."

"You're kidding." Excitement flits down Lia's spine.

"Cross my heart, baby girl." Moma lifts the steaming cups

onto their mirrored tray. "Now we go and listen with all our might."

Back at the client desk, Jessica is in full swing. It turns out that she's a hand talker, so Moma delivers refreshments with care. It also turns out that Jessica was absolutely right to demand entrance. Lia wouldn't have faulted her for employing a battering ram.

Jessica has an ex-boyfriend named Jeremy, whom she met through their work at the Wall Street hedge fund Two Sigma. They dated for three months before deciding in a whirlwind of romance to move in together. She delivered her things to Jeremy's place on Central Park South, where the sunsets trailed fire across the horizon and the trees rustled Americana ballads. Her father was overjoyed she wasn't "out in some warehouse wasteland" any longer (Williamsburg was in fact a mecca of double-digit sandwich prices). Her mother was thrilled she was "finding herself" (she'd actually found a boyfriend). Jessica was delighted that she was no longer living solely with Mr. Marbles (her cat). A storybook ending seemed on the horizon after she got promoted to sector head, and eventually portfolio manager.

There was only one problem.

"Whenever I wanted to go out with my girls, he went insane," Jessica says. "Don't you care about us, don't you love me? At first I thought he was just being romantic—and that he would mellow out. But then months went by, and it didn't get any better."

"Seems really lonely," Lia offers.

Jessica gnaws her lip. "I missed my crew from when I was an associate. We used to have these sprees, we'd wear Prada and get bottle service and just dance till our feet were bleeding. We all came up at the same time, you know? So finally I thought, what the hell, I'll plan a ladies' night. They were shocked I even texted. We were all so excited."

"That sounds wonderful," Lia observes.

"It should have been wonderful. It all went wrong, though."

Jessica shreds the tissue into sad confetti. A few minutes after having finished her makeup, two minutes before the Uber would arrive, Jeremy smashed her iPhone on their "cute" exposed brick wall. Then he said she looked sexy as hell and she was such a dirty girl and she didn't have to play hard to get and he pushed her into the bedroom, where they had sex. Very rough sex.

"I didn't even know whether—if I wanted to." Jessica's eyes are soft and glittering. "I was really scared after the phone thing, you know? He must have thought it was hot, I guess, the drama. Maybe I figured it would get sexy if I played along. Or I thought if I didn't fight, then . . . then nothing that bad could be happening to me."

Mam'zelle stirs sugar and cream into her coffee, smiling like a saint about to give a benediction. "Eh, la la. I know the feeling, *à la lettre*."

Lia does not. Not precisely. As always, she finds herself reflecting, and the reflections splinter into cutting edges.

Nothing ever really happened to you. Not really. Only pictures.

Nothing like this.

Pick a card, any card . . .

There are still no excuses for the things that you've done.

Lia snaps herself out of it, annoyed. "What did you do?"

Jessica left Jeremy after he started reading her texts and hacking into her email. The same group of girlfriends from her first hedge fund showed up one morning when Jessica was pretending to work from home. The five dumped all her belongings in boxes, revved up the U-Haul, and escaped. Jeremy required a restraining order, Jessica became a new roommate with her girl gang back in Brooklyn, and the skies seemed to clear.

"Then last night I was out on a date, and . . . and Jeremy was at the club," Jessica wails. "When he saw me, he punched Arthur—that was my date, Arthur, he's in environmental law. Poor Arthur! And Jeremy said he was going to kill me, and I'm too scared to go back to my place with my friends. A coworker of mine said that her fiancé used to hit her sometimes, and she sent me here. She said you fix things. What am I going to *do*?"

"Oh, we have *just* the tonic, pretty pet," Mam'zelle coos. "Moma, *chère*?"

"What you said, my sister?" Moma appears at her side.

"I'm thinking that Miss Jessica here owes Mr. Jeremy an apology."

"I . . . excuse me?" Jessica says.

"Oh, you couldn't be more right," Moma agrees.

"A bouquet would go a long way toward mending what's broken," Mam'zelle muses.

"Surely would settle that poor man's troubled spirits, and a man with troubled spirits is a plague on all the land. I'm thinking something nice in white clover, me."

WHITE CLOVER: *Ends hexed conditions, guards against hostile forces, brings about closure.*

Jessica frowns, confused.

"Now, this bouquet would come with a Three Sisters' Floral Boutique binding money-back *guarantee* that your relations with your ex *petit ami* will be nothing but amicable henceforth." Mam'zelle produces a single-sheet contract and a stiff card edged in gold leaf. "You, Miss Jessica, need only pay us our fee, sign this document, and personally inscribe your signature on the note that'll accompany the delivery. The aforementioned delivery will be made by us to you, but *you* must deliver it into Mr. Jeremy's hands yourself. We'll take care of the actual message, *ne t'inquiète pas*. Only the freshest, choicest flowers, herbs, and our signature pure aromatic oils will be used for your gift to Mr. Jeremy. We ask in addition to our usual rate only that you recommend us to others."

"And how much is the usual rate?"

Mam'zelle taps a Montblanc pen against a line in the contract. Lia's jaw drops.

Jessica slaps her credit card down with a *clack*.

"Oh, baby, we gonna have *such* fun with this order, I can't hardly wait!" Moma pecks the top of Lia's brow.

The sudden touch warms her scalp. Lia can't help but feel that this transaction marks a significant shift. *She* coaxed the sisters into allowing Jessica inside, and now she's been invited to assist with their peculiar art form. It's a stepping stone of some kind, or a marker, and those always ring Lia as if she's a bell in a church tower.

"Reap the harvest," Maw-maw repeats in an approving rasp.

"What does that mean, Maw-maw?" Lia wants to know.

But Maw-maw doesn't answer. She has a broom now, wide-headed and scraggly, and she smiles with her teeth but not her eyes as she pushes it past Lia, dragging a dustpan tunelessly behind her.

Mam'zelle gifts Jessica a small purple crystal in a velvet bag for lagniappe and tells their new client to keep it close as she departs. The sisters make murmured comments, consulting. Lia is about to ask Moma when they plan to start work on the bouquet when the door flies open without a knock and a man darts inside—perfectly coiffed, designer suit, white-haired, and wearing an expression as if he's either about to emcee a six-year-old's birthday extravaganza or murder a puppy. The showroom lights flicker, frizzle, then glow once more.

"Why good lord above us, if it isn't Robin!" Moma exclaims darkly.

"*Merde*, look what's washed ashore at high tide," Mam'zelle says in a low growl. "How are you faring, *cher*? Step into the light, let your old friend have a look at you."

"Well met indeed, my dulcet darling duckies!" the man cries. He's extremely short, with the burning yellow eyes of a jungle lizard, and a similarly posh accent to her dear old friend Horatio's. The thought makes her heart twinge. "How come our crops for this season? Berries plump? Fruits groaning? Lambs well-suckled?"

Lia stares. The sisters hoot, raising praise hands. Thank god Jessica is gone, or she'd have been thunderstruck. Yes, that's exactly the word, this is a thunderous entrance, because the air hops and thrums with static.

"Harvest *full* to *busting*," Maw-maw announces.

She lifts the dustpan reverently, like a ceremonial urn. Tipping it, she pours it over her head, bits of dust and ribbon and leaves and hair and other dead things fluttering as they anoint her brow.

HORATIO

My words have become fractures as of
    late;
splintered bones, dark skeletons of lost
    poems and journeys home
from places where love sinks beneath
    the floorboards.

—*Shinji Moon, "Fragmented"*

HORATIO APPRECIATES THE ALARMING distraction of Benjamin's uncle Claude, he of the perennial golf attire; otherwise Horatio would be drowning in nostalgia just seeing their flat again. They haven't talked about *it* yet, not really. Referenced it yes, but discussed, far from it. *We might never talk about it. Would that in fact be better?* As matters stand, he's quietly observing, ready to leap in if Benjamin should need him.

It's incredible you made it so long in London without practicing your life's vocation.

"Hey, I just figured you'd prefer I drop these off in person." Claude spreads his hands. "I had to wait because I don't know what kind of schedule you're keeping, you get me?"

"The dig about being presently underemployed? Yep, I get you, it wasn't subtle." Benjamin makes a tiny circuit, two or three steps toward the leather sofa they bought at Housing

Works and arrowing back at the chipped granite countertop dividing the kitchen from the sitting and dining area.

"Hey, hey, kiddo, offense is not my goal here. We're family, OK?"

"I might be your family twice over, but I'm not your fucking kiddo. That's offensive in and of itself. Goal failed."

"Wow, what's with the walls?" Claude juts his chin at the cheap wooden panels screwed into the drywall, the scrawled quotations from grad school days crammed into every corner in various penmanships.

"They're anecdotes." Horatio bites his lip at the reams of multicolored Sharpie devoted to their grad school witticisms.

"They're snapshots from parties you weren't invited to," Benjamin hisses.

Benjamin has been this toxic for over ten minutes now, but Horatio doesn't wonder why Claude lingers. He's always had the patience and placidity of a friendly cow. The man appears to find insults genuinely clever. Absolutely everyone on earth likes him with the exception of his nephew.

What might be still more relevant to avuncular lingering: Claude Dane is now wed to Trudy Dane, and Trudy is positively obsessed with Benjamin. Horatio shouldn't be surprised if her new husband had been given his marching orders and instructed to report on Benjamin's status in full, juicy detail.

Claude is strikingly unlike Benjamin's late father. Jackson Dane was decidedly Texan—large personality, large head with a large mane of leonine hair, large goals. Claude is quite small, a half-brother from another marriage who grew up in Florida and listens with the incredible attentiveness of a successful businessman. As if he's both memorizing your wife's taste in wine and studying your tax return. He sports khaki pleated shorts in the heat, khaki pleated trousers in the cold, and when he's undecided about temperature, he actually ties a pastel cashmere sweater around his shoulders. Claude sells lavish New Jersey properties in places like Alpine or New Vernon, Horatio can't recall. He is very handsome in the way all real estate agents tend to be and has blue eyes like Benjamin and his lost father. But where the elder's were coldly keen and the younger's like a clever stretch of sky, the brother's are flat and self-satisfied and caring. Horatio suspects that Benjamin detests Claude because he isn't even the slightest bit introspective. He likes action films. He likes specific sports teams.

Not everyone needs to conduct inquiries into their own mortality six or seven times a day, mate, Horatio thinks with a rare flash of pique.

"I get why you feel so hostile toward me right now." Claude's exaggerated patience sounds like a person bragging about charitable donations, but Horatio expects it's entirely sincere. "Everyone loses their parents eventually, but none of that matters if it's *your* loss we're talking about, Benny."

"Sooooooo, one of all, you will never ever again call me Benny, because we've had that conversation, like, half a dozen times. Two of all, yes. It is *completely* understandable that the sight of you gives me hives."

"Under other circumstances I'd have mailed this old stuff." Claude crosses his arms over his polo shirt, aqua today. "But I wanted to check in. Your mom—well, of course I mean your mom and *I*—miss seeing you, especially during this difficult period."

Aha, Horatio thinks. *You are merely the emissary. Got it in one.*

Benjamin drags his hand through his hair. "Somebody had to actually make mortuary arrangements other than Paul Brahms. He's already loco over the benefit gala."

"And we deeply appreciate it. All the care you took. You really stepped up to the plate there, Ben. Trudy was just . . . beside herself."

"No, she was beside you," Benjamin corrects sweetly.

"But my brother can never be replaced, and his family has to move on. He's buried—buried the way such a great man

deserved, with the utmost respect, thanks to you. He's at peace.
We're past that now."

This, Horatio thinks. *This is the sort of unromantic pragmatism that will set Benjamin whizzing like an arcade game.*

"Yes, and I am *so happy* for you!" Benjamin rubs at the heavy
leather bracelet. "Sorry I missed City Hall, but I wasn't invited.
Did you pick out, like, a pattern for fucking salad tongs?"

Claude's neck reddens. "Listen, you are in a very hard place
right now, but remember that Jackson and I lost our father, too.
And our dad lost his dad."

"Are you aware that the number of mammalian heartbeats—
no matter the size of the animal, it makes no difference because
shrew hearts beat suuuper quickly and elephant hearts really
slowly—in a lifetime is always approximately one point five billion in number? Isn't that cool? I hope my dad cracked a billion,
the thought makes me feel better. Anyway though, there were
not enough."

"I'd never argue with you there, son. Tragedy is a fact of existence."

"How many salad tongs will you be needing exactly? I'm
good for at least five."

Wincing, Horatio does what any steady-nerved friend would
do under the circumstances; squeezes Benjamin's ropey biceps
and goes to make them all a cuppa. The beloved red kettle waits
on the stovetop. He unearths a stack of half-crushed tea boxes,
black and green and chamomile that all smell like dust, and
clicks on the gas. It splutters, shocked out of a deep hibernation.
Horatio resolves with a fresh jolt of guilt to buy groceries. By the
time he turns around, the Danes are scrapping over living arrangements.

Not this again, he thinks, now hearing Trudy in every argument Claude is making.

"There's the whole third floor of the townhouse, yours for the
asking again," Claude points out.

"I'm not asking, though," Benjamin returns icily. "You could get five or six grand a month easy subletting it. Hell, *I* should sublet it—that's my new job, all figured out. Forward me the rent checks."

While Jackson applauded Benjamin's bid for independence, Trudy never comprehended why her precious son, newly arrived back from a year of post-undergrad studying moral philosophy in Wittenberg, Germany, wouldn't want to return to the family manse. Horatio recalls the contrast well—his own mum in London fiddling with Skype and never looking directly into the camera, his dad grinning at him from across the ocean. *So awfully proud of what you've achieved,* they said, all aglow. It wasn't very English of them to big him up like that over Columbia. But then again, they are activists. Socialists. His mum wove her own macramé in the seventies, and his dad supplied the hashish. Meanwhile, Trudy Dane questioned why Benjamin didn't have dinner with them and did he need his ski equipment?

"Trudy needs you to consider being a present part of the family again. You haven't even stayed the night since you started grad school," Claude persists. "What, five years ago?"

What a trusty messenger you're being.

"Eight," Horatio puts in, because Claude really is being horrible without meaning to.

"Time flies when you're having fun," Benjamin growls. "Literally. Perception shifts according to sensory stimulus, emotion, and attention. For instance, when I'm *not* around you, time just *whizzes.*"

"Sure, eight years," Claude agrees reasonably. "Listen, what do you say about you coming home for a bit? It would mean a lot to your mother. I could even pick up the payments for this place."

"Yeah, quick thing, did you not notice that I too have this family's money?"

"Not that I really get the appeal, all the way up here in the Heights, no elevator, no mail room . . ."

"What's worse than hives? Leprosy," Benjamin says through his teeth. "The sight of you gives me fucking leprosy."

Hiding a smile, Horatio glances through smudgy glass at the opposite brick buildings and at the fenced-in trees fluttering dappled shades of silver and green. Benjamin when sad and stricken is excruciating. Benjamin when riled like a hyperactive puppy though is rather brilliant.

Claude rests his palms on his hips. "Don't you think it would be better for everyone if we all pulled together?"

"I sorta think you guys are pulling together enough for everyone."

"Benny, we're all on the same team here."

"If teamwork involves banging my mother, then consider me benched."

"All right, that's enough, isn't it?" Horatio chimes in, dismayed. Claude may be acting as Trudy's drone, and he may shrug at matters of life and death, but he isn't a monster. The kettle shrieks as Horatio shuts off the gas.

Claude holds his hands up. "I came with a peace offering and you're not in a place right now to receive it. But I do want to remind you that I'm family, and—"

"As if I can ever forget you're my uncle for as much as a *single second*!" Benjamin explodes. "Were you having an affair all this time? Is that it? Were you—"

"Right, ta very much for the box of sundries, but you ought to clear out, Mr. Dane," Horatio suggests, abandoning the tea mugs.

"Do you see this guy right here?" his friend snarls, pointing. "He's extremely loyal, to a fault actually, anyway my point being that I am about to request that Horatio beat you to a quivering pulp."

"Um, that is not in line with compassionate *daya*, or with nonviolence, or really anything in my belief system," Horatio objects.

"That's cool. You're a good enough person that you're probably going to achieve nirvana this time around anyway."

"Well, I don't care to risk it, if it's all the same to you?"

"You hear that, Uncle Claude? The only reason Horatio isn't

punching you is because it's against his *religion*. That is how shitty you are."

Claude looks genuinely downcast. "Just . . . I hope you find some good things in the box, all right, kiddo? It's stuff from Jackson's New World's Stage office, and your mom was too upset to look."

"Maybe she was actually just too distracted, looking at your tiny misshapen—"

"OK, I'm going." Claude shoots a meaningful look at Horatio. "I'm real glad you're back, Horatio. Keep an eye on this one, will you?"

"Always," Horatio answers, newly irritated.

"Please do let the door hit you in the ass on the way out," Benjamin adds.

When Claude has vacated, Horatio makes the slide of the dead bolt audible. Turning, he watches as Benjamin fishes a pill bottle out of a lidded linen storage box on the bookshelf. The fact that his friend's brain operates as part philosopher, part scientist, and part torture device is obvious to most everyone. But outsiders have no idea the lengths the Dane heir goes to in order to make sense of the world around him.

"Don't look like that, it's just Xanax," Benjamin snaps.

"Good."

"Goooooooooo on," the smaller man drawls, crossing his legs and sinking to the arrow-patterned rug.

"Nothing."

"You are not-saying something, chummy chummy matey. It's super annoying."

Still, Horatio hesitates. "But it was, er, worse than Xanax just afterward, I take it? Because Ariel wrote me, and he said you were not . . . well."

His friend looks somehow both impish and tragic. "I don't remember, I was on too much weed and alcohol and Klonopin and occasionally coke other than the usual Adderall and antidepressants."

"Benjamin," Horatio says helplessly. As if invoking his name will heal it somehow.

The smile vanishes. "You could think of it as, like, removing a threat to myself. And the danger was, you know. Between my ears."

Fetching a pair of scissors to deal with the box and gathering up the mugs, Horatio joins his friend on the floor. The familiar hot pinprick of mingled guilt and anxiety sizzles in his chest.

It isn't your fault that he's obsessed with death. Death is objectively fascinating, after all.

And Benjamin's father just passed, so morbidity surrounds him.

No, morbidity surrounds Benjamin when he's ordering trash pizza, or waiting for the subway, or breathing air.

Death will end everything Benjamin's ever loved, and he flirts with this like a drunk left alone at a bar. *Why does death seem so particularly spellbinding to you?* Horatio asked once, sharing whiskey straight from the bottle as the midnight traffic painted neon graffiti on their walls. Benjamin cackled and said, *It doesn't seem particular, it* is *particular, because we can only do it once. It's not like I can say, hey Horatio, remember how it went that time I died?*

Horatio wants to take his friend's heart and wrap it in sunlight and goose down so that Benjamin is never battered again by all the shocks that humanity is so naturally subjected to.

"Maybe I'm being stupid." Benjamin tosses the pill bottle from hand to hand. "I mean, I know I said Dad would *never*, but. Take me for example."

Horatio passes his friend the tea. Tea ought to solve more than it does, he reflects. Tea made by someone who loves you, specifically.

"Last year, I was teaching at Fordham talking Socrates, I had that side gig at the Henry Street Settlement, and I *still* thought about dying, like, nonstop because there were these kids, Horatio, and they wanted to know *why*."

"Why?"

"Why they'd been raped, why their mom was a crackhead, why their dad never came home from Iraq. And philosophy has a metric fuckton of questions, sure, but answers are pretty lean on the ground. There was like, nothing I could say, and I felt like a complete waste of oxygen. I just put one foot in front of the other, but. It's not supposed to be this hard."

"No," Horatio agrees, raw and ragged. "It isn't."

Benjamin warms to his subject. "It's commonly thought that if your life is *difficult*, if you're in *pain*, that's when you want to pull the trigger. A person living under a bridge might get sick of it, right? Meanwhile a joint study found that the American states with the most life satisfaction were also the ones with the highest suicide rates."

Horatio sips his Earl Grey.

"Suicide is about saving everyone from the burden of fucking carrying you," Benjamin concludes, shrugging.

"I rather thought it was a chemical disorder?"

"Yep, yeah, that, too. But it's also removing yourself from the equation because you are a comprehensive drain."

"You make a difference."

"Well. Thanks, but that's not accurate."

"You make all the difference in the world to *me*," Horatio volleys.

Benjamin's assessing face appears, the one where he realizes he accidentally mucked with someone's head. And this is where his innate kindness factors in, and it's heartbreaking to watch. Benjamin sometimes looks terrified of *infecting* people with his own pathologies. When in fact he'd give ten years off his own life just to know that his loved ones would carry on happily until they were a hundred and three.

"I don't know why you're telling me all of this," Horatio says with a sigh.

"It's interesting."

"It's hurtful."

"Good god, why?" Benjamin genuinely wants to know, the wanker.

"Because it's not fucking theoretical for me, it's a genuine nightmare," Horatio snaps.

"Oh!" Benjamin lifts his tea, a peace offering, blowing on its surface. "That was not meant to distress you. I'm sorry."

Horatio remembers Benjamin in his dorm, cross-legged on the floor exactly the way he is now, sorting through black plastic milk crates of vinyl albums. He kept lobbing musical opinions at Horatio without expecting replies, and Horatio was happy to provide none. Music is everything Benjamin loves wrapped into one; it's mathematics and harmony and philosophy and feeling, and here he was, unaccountably trimming his record collection.

Oooooh snap—every Brit loves The Clash, yeah? Good. Man, Daptone killed it when they recorded Back to Black, *and if I weren't already with a stupidly hot crazy artist type, I would have so massively crushed on Amy Winehouse. Ugh, Parliament,* Mothership Connection, *how hard do I love thee? So, sooooo hard. These go in your pile, man.*

Horatio wanted to know why, supposing these were Benjamin's favorites, he was now gifting them.

I dunno, I like you—you've got soul, or something. Depths. And anyway, I won't be needing these for that much longer. My internal clock is very . . . loud.

Horatio promptly made plans with Benjamin, this brighter-than-daylight creature who wanted so perversely to die, every single evening for the following week. They moved in together shortly thereafter. Horatio fantasized about heroic rescues, emergency services calls, even mouth-to-mouth that led to more carnal activities (in his guiltiest, most deeply shameful moments). And then he learned that fiercely burning beings naturally exist in the darkest depths of space.

That is the habitat of stars going supernova.

"I sorta, um, did just say I'm sorry. Should I say it again?" Benjamin offers without a hint of sarcasm.

"It's fine, it only . . ." Horatio stumbles over the right words. "Um, I'm not attempting to censor you."

"You just don't enjoy me waxing on about the harrowing nature of pushing a rock uphill." Benjamin smiles in encouragement. "One must imagine Sisyphus happy after all, even though nothing he does matters."

"No, I . . ." Horatio feels woefully wrong-footed. "Some things *do* matter."

"Which ones?"

"Loving someone matters." Horatio shouldn't be subjected to this conversation. "Not, er, not being loved, a person can be loved all day and up and down and sideways and that can still not make a difference. I mean that loving someone else, when they're more important to you than you are, that ought to matter."

Benjamin's brow furrows.

Horatio hastens to cover the silence. "But I know it sometimes matters in the wrong way. If you feel like the people you love are better off without you. Then it matters . . . backward. Christ, I'll shut it. I've always believed love makes a difference."

"Are you paraphrasing Corinthians or the Beatles?"

Horatio laughs. And then Benjamin does too, because that is how this works. They just need to brush the dust off, get back in the hang of this. His friend scrubs his hand through blond hair again, on the brink of something. He reaches for the black leather cuff, unbuckling, and everything is still fine till Horatio sees a scar. A vertical one, on his friend's wrist.

"Oh god," Horatio exhales.

Benjamin only squints in commiseration. The bastard.

Horatio considers in due course storming out of the flat, succumbing to jet lag and curling up on the rug, thanking his friend for being honest, or possibly throttling the love of his life himself because he's beautiful, *can't he see that he's beautiful*, and this is all a fucking bad dream.

"When?" Horatio reaches out, unthinking. Benjamin doesn't move. The scar is raised but smooth, like a little strip of bone jutting through pale skin, and this touch feels more intimate than any of the far more sordid ones they've exchanged.

"Almost six months ago." Benjamin to most would sound clinical, but Horatio hears the strain. "Uncle Claude might be a fly on a warm smear of dog shit, but he was right about my, like, altered schedule earlier. Before that I was productive, two entire jobs for the philosophy of physics degree holder, whoopee and *felicidades* and praise baby Jesus, and then, well. Ha."

"I should have been here," Horatio states miserably. "In every conceivable way."

"Hey, I did . . . very selfish things before you left. We should maybe even talk about those, yeah? Drunk. We'd want to be drunker than this. But anyway, you could have completely ghosted me, but I needed you, and you essentially said *where and when would you like to have me*? That was you being amazing."

"I'm not at all amazing."

"You don't get to decide whether or not you amaze me. You don't deserve any of this drama, you deserve a nice cottage where you, I dunno, keep bees and have fresh wildflower honey with your tea. Can we just get back to the part where you don't need to be angry at you, and I don't need to be quite as angry at me, either?"

"But you aren't—it's not like that for you anymore, is it?" Horatio pleads. "You aren't still—"

"No." Even if it isn't a promise, Horatio will interpret it that way, because otherwise he'll bloody well fall apart. "I'm back in the saddle, my friend, there are ranges to ride once more and I'm riding the shit out of them. Now hand me those scissors. I'll use them exclusively for approved purposes. Sorry, sorry, kidding! Let's see what Uncle Claude just dragged over here."

Horatio hands them over. His friend puts the cuff back on, burying the evidence, hiding the clues. Only Benjamin could have a conversation about attempted suicide and then breeze straight into sorting through his late father's junk drawer. Horatio's head pounds and they haven't even discussed why Horatio fled back to London in the first place. Apparently they're skipping that part save for Benjamin admitting *I did very selfish things before you left.*

The contents of the box are, at first, predictable.

There's a picture of Benjamin and Trudy, Benjamin in black cap and gown, graduating summa cum laude from NYU, his mother with platinum shoulder-length hair and the lazy smile she wears for the camera. She has the same clean features as Benjamin, an artful creature of Botox and powder and Chanel. Then a Lee Child novel with a bookmark midway through that makes his friend flinch, because life shouldn't stop in the middle of an unfinished story. A nearly empty bottle of cologne Benjamin sniffs morosely, a lint brush, a shoehorn, and then his friend pulls out a sleek digital camera.

At first, he numbly scrolls through photos. But then he opens the video files and a voice that neither of them expected ever to hear again fills the room.

"This is probably the last of these I'll get to make," Jackson Dane says to the camera.

Horatio swings himself around to Benjamin's perspective, bumping his shoulder. Benjamin's hand shakes. He rests the camera on his knee.

"I did what I could," Jackson says lowly, "but I still must have failed, if anybody is watching. I hope it's not my son, Ben, and then again I hope that it is, because I don't know that anyone else would believe me. Claude says I need to see a professional, Trudy says I need a vacation, and Paul says I need to sleep more. Whoever finds this, give it to Ben, please?"

Jackson stops, struggling for words, then looks straight into the lens. "I think that someone is trying to murder me. And the only person who has the kind of access I'm talking about is my own brother. Claude Dane."

BENJAMIN

If there really is a complete unified theory that governs everything, it presumably also determines your actions. But it does so in a way that is impossible to calculate for an organism that is as complicated as a human being. The reason we say that humans have free will is because we can't predict what they will do.

—*Stephen Hawking,* A Brief History of Time

T'S CRAZY SOUNDING, I know," Jackson says near the end of the first chronologically recorded track (thus the last viewed). "And so far it's only this *feeling* I have, of corruption. Like a tar pit guzzling down everything that touches it."

Ben is incapable of meeting his father's pixelated eyes any longer. His hands are palsied.

CAN HORATIO TELL, IS HE WATCHING?

HE'S ALWAYS WATCHING.

REMEMBER?

Ben tucks the traitor appendages under his legs. *Corruption.* He knows the feeling intimately. He once read an article about Armageddon and how it wouldn't be by drowning in polar ice, or a super-germ, or even the Sun dying, it would be by insect extinction, all the

MANY
ANTSGRASSHOPPERSFLEASMOSQUITOES
BUTTERFLIESFLUTTERBYES
DWINDLING DISEASED
DYING
AND THEN THE SEAS WOULD ROT AND
THE ANIMALS WOULD STARVE
AND CARCASSES WOULD LITTER THE FORESTS THE STREETS
NOT FOOD FOR GENTLE SOFT FLIES MAGGOTS WORMS
SIMPLY
LEFT
ALONE

Pull it the loving fuck together, your dad is still talking.

" . . . sensation of being the center of a conspiracy." Jackson doesn't look threadbare yet, and Ben battles the illusion he's watching time flow in reverse. "But what is it they say—you're only being paranoid if they *aren't* out to get you?"

Jackson's hair is more silver than blond, why didn't Ben notice that *before*? He wears a grey cashmere V-neck (on his goddamn body, not wrapped around his stupid shoulders like Uncle Claude, that limp lizard dick), and Ben recognizes the sweater as a Christmas gift he bought years ago at Saks.

"I hope I'm wrong." Jackson sips his drink. "And I probably won't need to make any more of these . . . confessions. It just feels like someone is always watching. I can't shake it. It's driving me up the wall."

A brief black flash, dark matter massing, then the screen flicks back to life the way his father never can. It's just a preview image now, the stubborn ridges of Jackson's forehead furrowed with doubt. The man who taught Ben how to ride a bike in Central Park, who yanked him away from that speeding cab so hard when he was six that his arm hairline-fractured, who spit hardened plastic platitudes about *tough love* and *pull yourself together* and *be a man about it* when he first—

Never mind about wanting to die, not now.

He outlived his old man, after all.

"'More is unknown than known,'" Ben quotes, dizzy with grief.

"Beg pardon?"

Ben grinds his palms into his eye sockets. "Dark energy comprises sixty-eight percent of the universe, dark matter twenty-seven percent."

"I don't understand."

"Under five percent of the universe is normal, physical matter, so it isn't really *normal*." Ben's voice shakes as badly as his hands. "This, you, me, Manhattan, civilization—this is barely possible, statistically speaking. Almost everything in our reality is invisible, untraceable. We're surrounded by Plato's fifth element. Aether. *Quintessence.* We ourselves are the most unlikely beings we've ever discovered."

"Um, yes. But what does dark matter have to do with your father?"

"It has to do with the insane percentage of the universe that's utterly unfathomable and yet here's my own dad telling me he was murdered, and I don't know *what to do*."

"Benjamin." His friend's voice rings steady but frightened. "I'm afraid you aren't making any sense."

Horatio is comfortingly solid and Earl Grey–smelling, leaning with his shoulder against Ben's quaking one, and Ben knew, he fucking *knew* it wasn't suicide, but it should have been an *accident*. This is a game of Clue on a bad LSD trip.

Uncle Claude? With the pill bottle? In the bedroom?

"It's like he was here," Ben whispers. "Asking us to, I don't know. Avenge him, maybe."

Horatio slips his thumbnail between his teeth. "This is completely barking, Benjamin. Why did your father record a series of messages implicating your uncle in his own murder, then leave it in his office, only to be delivered by the killer? None of it's sensible."

"Truer words," Ben says and laughs.

"Not to shift topics, but when did you last eat actual calories?"

Ben springs to his feet, charmed by Horatio's concerns, but his dad

> wouldn't have died on purpose
> couldn't have died on purpose
> so here is the perfect explanation
> although one that has them both
> staring in unseeing bafflement
> at the walls.

Their walls were once hideously white. As if they lived in one of the sleek gallery spaces where Lia exhibited. Ben has always detested white walls, that tabula rasa, the impersonal starkness. No worse fate was possible than being locked in a white room with himself. So when Ben found three huge slabs of plywood in the trash area, he screwed them into the wall. *That's . . . quite industrial, I didn't know your aesthetic ran to warehouse chic* said Horatio, and Ben laughed and whipped out one of the Sharpies he'd just purchased and wrote on the rough veneer:

"I DIDN'T KNOW YOUR AESTHETIC RAN TO WAREHOUSE CHIC."
—Horatio

Half the time when we're being hilarious, we're drunk, Ben explained. *Now I'll never forget anything you say.*

The bigger man had suddenly become fascinated by the meager contents of their fridge. Over the years, the plywood background filled with letters into words into clauses into sentences that were never placed in that order previously, even considering the approximately 1.5 billion global English speakers and the myriad English speakers marching down the vast time line before them. Ben found it wildly beautiful, setting down moments that would otherwise be lost to tequila.

"It wasn't the fact of the boa constrictor, it was coming to terms with the guy using it as a scarf."—Ben

I just want to collect all the tourist photos where we happened to be in the background and use those for our family album."—Lia

"BUT I DON'T UNDERSTAND. WHEN JESUS COMES BACK, IS THAT MEANT TO BE AS A BABY, OR AN ADULT MAN?"—Horatio

"Do you remember saying that?" Ben nods up at the wall. "Telling Lia, 'You are on track to be the Captain Ahab of the idealized al pastor taco'?"

"It was an awfully long time ago."

"Yeah, but that's *permanent* marker. Like, unchanging. Eternal. Sorta."

Present-day Horatio looks wrecked. He folds himself into a better lotus position, flinching at a twinge.

"You should rest," Ben advises. "This is not really, like, technically your circus. It's my primates, bought and paid for."

"After *that*? Don't wind me up, I haven't the patience. We should call the police."

"Um, I talked to the police during their initial investigation."

"Well, you might have said so!"

Ben's skull is a bell and his mind is a clapper. Throwing aside the curtains, he shoves open scraping windows.

Let there be light.

"The light from our sun is obviously from an active star, but it's only morbid romantics who claim the stars you see at night are so distant they're already dead," Benjamin notes. "The vast majority of the visible ones are alive and kicking. What's sadder is that stars are born all the time that we'll never see. We'll die long before their light reaches us. If a star shines in the sky and nobody sees it, does it still combust? How's *that* for poetic melancholy?"

"Benjamin," Horatio groans. "Please, just. What did the police tell you?"

Ben strains to remember. Four weeks ago, four minutes ago. What was it he just took, Xanax over seeing Uncle Claude, that cystic ass pimple? Adderall, he needs Adderall. He flips open his storage box again and ignores the distress blurring his friend's features like static over a radio tune as one drives farther into the wilderness.

"The guy's name was Detective Fortuna, old school type, red sauce Italian," Ben reports after he dry swallows. "Girthy. Earthy. Underarm sweat stains as his main accessory. Guest starred on *The Sopranos*, that kinda cop."

"And what did he *think*?"

"I kept screaming at him to, like, prove it wasn't suicide. He thought I was out of my mind."

To be fair, this was *immediately* after his dad's passing, and there were a lot of drugs involved, prescriptions squandered so freely that Ben marched to the Columbia campus and the ass-numbing plastic chairs of Brownie's Café and his favorite drug dealer, a white kid from the Hamptons who'd been catering to vacationers since he was, like, wearing light-up sneakers. Brownie's was a staple of Ben's twenties. You descended a spiral staircase inside Avery Hall, traversed the architecture gallery, and dove down into a white-walled bunker smelling of falafel. The ideal place to buy illicit benzos. And to kiss Lia on one of her last visits to campus before Ben graduated, his fingers tangling in her fairy forest of curls, her laughing and *cut it out* and *god, you're just bones, I'm buying you a sandwich* and *I have an installation to get back to.*

Something brushes Ben's shoulder and he jerks.

"Sorry, I'm so sorry!" Horatio steps back. "You, um—may I use your mobile?"

Ben hands it over.

"Indian or Thai?"

"You're the vegetarian, is either one any easier?"

"They are equally vegetable-focused, which you are generally well aware of, when your brain isn't actively on fire. You were saying, about the cop?"

Ben recalls the comprehensive runny cow tit who was Barry Fortuna as the new pill metabolizes *too slowly far too slowly.* "He thought I was certifiable, and, like—oh yeah, he took special objection to the fact I employ 'like' as an interjection. He said he'd broken his kids of the habit, and I replied that the use of pause words is simply an indicator that your brain is going faster than your mouth, so that wouldn't have been a problem for any of his offspring."

Horatio settles on the sofa as he taps in their delivery order. "And this fellow didn't take a shine to you? How extraordinary."

"Not *everyone* appreciates me, and I very often agree with them."

> There were all those people at school, for instance.
> And then at school again.
> And again.
> Everyone except for Lia really, not until Horatio, and Lia isn't here.

Ben takes his cell phone back when Horatio extends it, not remotely curious about food. Wanting to see something else, though. Clicking open his messages—*don't——don't——don't*—he finds Lia's most recent communications. They aren't very long.

But he reads. And he reads. And he reads.

"Benjamin?"

Horatio sounds like he's directly above him. Ben rips his attention from the screen. The Adderall is kicking in, so screens are now

d e l i c i o u s c a t n i p f o r t h e e y e.

"Do you often, um . . ." Horatio's pupils glitter, wet-pavement-on-Fifth-Avenue black. "It's none of my business, of course. Well. Look, do you . . . often read messages from her?"

Ben jabs the screen blank.

"Because you weren't reading them, before," Horatio continues helplessly. "I know you never deleted messages from her, but—"

"Lia? We're not doing names now?"

"Yes, Lia. But you didn't, I mean to say, look at them very often?"

"Define *often*?"

"For god's sake, Benjamin."

"No!" Ben growls. "I don't often read text messages from my beautiful and brilliant ex-fiancée, I save them for when my dead dad just returned from the grave like a zombie—no sorry, that's impossible, he was cremated and his remains interred at Trinity, I was there—but my point is, that, like, just happened, so I genuinely wish she could figure this bullshit out with us but I'm putting my cell phone away now. Are you happy?"

"Of course not," Horatio snaps.

He goes to refill the kettle, his back looking freshly defeated. Ben detests ruining Horatio's endless good nature. Horatio once asked what he was thinking about and Ben said *whether it would be subversive or masturbatory to write my own funeral dirge for solo guitar* and his friend barely spoke to him for two days.

"I'm sorry. Again." Ben winces. "You're talking to someone fraying apart. I'm that sweater from the Weezer track. Pull the wrong thread, and I'm a pile of yarn."

Horatio rubs the base of his skull.

"There are shittier things to be." The silence is worse than the fighting. "Yarn can even, you know, become a sweater again. It wouldn't be like forcing every atom of carbonation *back* into a Coke bottle, or turning all the magma from a volcano into its original rock, things that go against the arrow of time itself. Somebody dedicated, a totally epic knitter, could repair you. If they were very patient, and forgiv—"

"All *right*, Benjamin."

"But I'm saying—"

"I hear exactly what you're saying, you mad twat."

Ben sags in relief. The apartment grows quiet, which sounds much better than silence. That was a near escape with the phone screen and the Adderall, but with the drug fully kicking in, Ben feels the familiar euphoric sensation like being sprinkled with gentle petals all along the back of his neck and he begins to calm and to

F
O
C
U S

We can re-knit the yarn.
We can still be fine.

"All right. Tell me more about the World's Stage woes, I only read a few tattler articles online," Horatio suggests. "The gossip rags claimed it as a major cause of his depression. Jackson was the chairman of the board, Trudy was president, and your uncle Claude executive VP, correct?"

"Yep, and I have a big chunk of votes, too. Essentially Mom wanted more commercially viable productions and Dad wasn't having it. He hated what Times Square turned into, like Disney vomited all over it and nothing is risky anymore except for touching somebody in a giant Elmo costume because *that* shit can get you instant syphilis."

"If not something even more arcane. Apoplexy."

"Right? Lockjaw. As you are well aware, the Danes have oodles and scads and kajillions of dollars. But Dad always resolutely refused to support the theatre with oil money after it was founded. Total point of pride with him. Donors, sure. Patrons, bring it. Box office success, hallelujah with praise hands. But to him, following its initial creation, using, like, family moolah to keep the theatre afloat would have meant it was a jerk-off vanity project when all he ever wanted was a world-renowned production company."

"Yes, I recall. Someone even once suggested it in my presence during some fundraiser or other and he answered, 'Raising money is one thing. But I don't take handouts, not even from myself.'"

"Nailed it. Anyway, Dad wanted to do a new adaptation of Goethe's *Faust*, for example, a super-dark one with freaky marionette puppetry that sounded outstanding, and Mom had a whole cadre of people who wanted to do *Annie Get Your Gun* but with, like, not *just* white people."

"My goodness."

It wasn't that Jackson Dane was a visionary—he was simply a ruthless businessman trying to build a creative legacy without compromise, a man who blended the timeliness of The Public Theater with the renown of the Lyceum Theatre, and he could rake in millions on a musical version of Kerouac's *On the Road* supposing he cast Adam Driver as Dean Moriarty.

Ben folds all his fingers together. "Just so you know, I can think now."

Horatio produces more tea. The man is a loaves-and-fishes miracle when it comes to stewed herbal beverages. "So, what thought is most pressing?"

Ben bounces on his toes. "You were so so so right, Horatio."

"Er, which bit?"

"These videos fail to achieve, as you would definitely not put it, the full shilling. Because Dad would have rooted out the culprit and destroyed him, and since we know he considered that puckered pig anus Uncle Claude the likeliest suspect, if he'd had any evidence whatsoever, he'd have cut him into so many pieces that the roaches wouldn't even get a light nibble."

Horatio blows on his tea. Ben attempts to emulate him, cogitating.

Action.

Do something.

Anythingdosomethinganythingdosomething

The time has come

The walrus said

To chop the cabbages

And avenge the kings.

"How hungry are you, like *exactly*?"

His friend actually face-palms, which Ben loves—Horatio claims to have picked it up in America, but it suits him. "You're having me on."

"Cut it out, man, you paid for whatever-it-is on *my* account, which means it's technically my food. Looky here, I'm writing this note and I'll have the delivery guy buzz my neighbor and I'll text Eduardo that it's for us and then eventually we eat something, OK?"

"Why do I get the feeling that you've been putting off your next meal for several weeks?"

"Because you're a clever clever boots. Do they say that over there? We don't say it over here, so they have to, I guess."

"But where, and why must we go *right now*?" Horatio begs.

"To the offices of the New World's Stage Theatre. To interrogate the man who knows everything, the guy behind the guy behind the curtain behind the guy, Paul Brahms, my almost father-in-law."

Ben's blood shines cold and mercurial in his veins. Horatio helps a great deal, so does Adderall, and this is a puzzle—and what is Ben better at than investigating the most profound mysteries of the universe?

"Vengeance is a dish best served cold, but rice noodles are not," Horatio mutters.

"Vengeance? Huh, I've never heard of a philosopher bent on revenge, but there's a first time for everything. And Paul Brahms is going to help me send my uncle to the deepest hell I can find."

Ben already has tape affixed to his scrawled message for the delivery man. He leaves the door open but forgets to look behind him. He is on the cusp of shouting back over his shoulder when he hears a light curse and the rattling of keys, and Ben's grin when he steps outside is brighter than the sun-soaked summer clouds.

THE NEW WORLD'S STAGE Organization offices—management department, human resources, ticketing, and the priceless historical archive—are south of the physical theatre, in Times Square. They soar like a melody through the orchestra of street traffic, the yells and sirens and chatter of cabbie radio that Ben grew up with. There are days when he hears almost everything in music. These times aren't unpleasant, just loose and languid. A homeless man on 56th wearing a placard reading **NO ONE IS COMING FOR YOU** shrieks at passing cars while far above them on countless sills, pigeons coo filthy lullabies to one another.

Ben is clarity personified now, every fiber *willing* their cab forward. It doesn't even need an engine. Inertia doesn't stand a chance against the power of his resolve. He can hear his dad, in a rare show of genuine praise, the day Ben graduated from the Philosophical Foundations of Physics program at Columbia.

> **I knew you had it in you, Benny. We might not always see eye to eye, but you're just about as sharp as they come, and accomplishing something like this is goddamn bullheaded.**
>
> **You've done us proud.**

"What do you intend to ask Paul Brahms?" Horatio's dark head slumps against the cab window.

"What *don't* I intend to ask him, after he's seen these?" Ben waves the digital camera in a grim circle.

At West 44th Street, he shoves cash through the driver's partition and they land on the pavement between a dirty-water-dog cart and a caricaturist who is accidentally making all of his subjects appear Asian. That the man himself is decidedly *not* Asian but rather sports enormous Rasta locks is puzzling but then *swishwhish* they are through the revolving doors and *clipclop* ladies in corporate heels glide across the marble and *thrumwahwaaaaaaoh* croons the instrumental version of that hit song from their world premiere stage production of *Labyrinth*.

"Hey, Benny, how's that music career coming?" calls Ariel from behind the security desk.

Ariel Washington has worked here for thirty years and thus gets a pass on calling him Benny. As Ben stops to shake hands, Ariel's face folds into about a hundred chestnut wrinkles. When he was twelve years old and obsessed with playing guitar, Ben had the misguided notion of asking Ariel, whose family was Nashville royalty, how to crack into the jazz business. It turned out that being a session player required more than a good ear, a phenomenal brain, a few hours of practice a week, and a thrift store hat treated with Febreze.

"I'm, like, hitting the big time any second now."

"Don't let me die before seeing my Benny live at B.B. King's!" Ariel winks.

"You remember my friend Horatio? I asked you to shoot him that message?"

"Sure, sure. Missed your face around here, man."

Horatio smiles. "Um, likewise. And thank you for writing, truly."

"Not a problem, I could always see how tight the two of you was. You musta been in my Benny's band, that it? Trombone? Trumpet?"

Ben replies, "He's an eighteen-karat hide hitter."

"Beg pardon?" Horatio starts to laugh.

"You play the drums, dude. So, Ariel! Do you know where Paul—"

"Ariel! What a relief, I tell you, I was catching the elevator and you're off your shift at four and here it is, only ten minutes left for me to find out did you make sure that the donations from the Lauder family for the gala auction are in the *front* of the mail room?"

The new voice is high-pitched, Brooklyn-born, and airy, as if the speaker just crested a peak.

"Never mind, Ariel." Ben pastes on a smile. "Hi, Paul. I need to talk to you, OK?"

"Oh!" Paul Brahms looks up from a clipboard, on which rests a cell phone he's tapping. The same hand also cradles a pen. Both hands hold pens, oddly. "Hello, Ben. And oh my god! Horatio Patel, really so nice to see you, I never dreamed—Ariel, those boxes are in the *front* of the mail room, so anyone authorized can pick them up without a problem, do you remember taking care of that?"

"Sure do, Mr. Brahms."

"Because the auction coordinator a couple days back said that she was looking for, let me see, I have it here or I did a second ago, for Pete's sake—yeah, it was the Englander package, and she needed the glass pieces for the photo promo?"

Ariel's face scrunches tolerantly.

"And she looked and looked, and thank god finally found it, but there just isn't any time left, we have *five days*, and I always say this kind of thing is ninety-five percent preparation and five percent perspiration—"

Ben mouths the saying in chorus to Horatio.

"And the Lauder packages are crucial, so we are sure they are in the *front* of the mail room?"

"Anyway, Paul." Ben coughs.

He's experiencing the awful feeling he always gets around Lia's father, that *nagging biting itching bitching* suspicion that maybe-just-maybe Ben is a horrible person at heart. Because there isn't really anything wrong with Paul.

Ben wants to strangle him anyhow. And literally always has, since the day Jackson hired him. Ben has so much practice battling the urge to choke Paul Brahms to death that he could have any neck in the world spread out before him—Kid Rock's, whoever wrote the Kars4Kids commercial—and be able to walk away without so much as an itch on his pinkie finger. Something in the neutral stare that might be calculating anything or everything behind it, something in his pathological insistence on going his own pace, something in his appearing almost *willfully* ridiculous, makes Ben homicidal.

"Like I mentioned, we need to see you immediately. Ideally that would be now. It's kinda what the word classically means."

Paul's brows wriggle above his horn-rims. He's bald as a cue ball and ricochets off things nearly as much. Not unhandsome, not rude, not visibly remarkable except for his capacity to flit around like a moth that doesn't care whether or not the light is even switched on. Somehow, every detail ends up perfect anyway. It makes Ben insane. Neatly dressed in slacks and a striped button-up, Paul purses his lips in a way Ben hates much more than he should, a way that means:

My concern for this dear deranged boy should be expressed in private,

uselessly and also at tremendous length.

"OK, sure, Ben, what do you say I maybe just knock a few minutes off before I meet with the *Playbill* people and, Ariel, those Lauder packages are—"

"So far in the front of the mail room, you could mistake them for outside," Ariel answers.

"Oh lord, but that's not going to work at all, they're not actually *in* the hallway, surely?"

"Nope." Ariel serenely taps his pen against the sign-in sheet.

"Because it would be—"

"They're not in the hallway, Mr. Brahms."

"Oh, thank goodness. All right, so, Ben and Horatio, could you both just please sign in to the buil—"

Ben takes Paul by the arm, frog-marching him. He tolerates the old bastard, and he even enjoys his care and company sometimes, but he would give his eyeteeth for just one go at bashing Paul's head in like the egg it resembles.

"What's this about?" Paul squeaks.

"About the fact my dad didn't commit suicide."

"Again?"

"I don't think that's technically possible. Or rather, temporally possible. So, *still*. Still didn't commit suicide."

"No, I mean, when we met those several times just after Jackson passed, you were . . ."

Paul pauses, embarrassed, and hides it by pretending to get a text message from a still and silent phone.

Yes, I realize I was off my fucking rocker but when you trail off that obviously, you might as well have written a poignant short story, published it in The New Yorker, *and handed it to Horatio for review.*

"Now I have videos, Paul," Ben soothes. "Videos from Dad. Turns out that actually he was murdered. Is that pretty crazy or what? Anyway, I have these, these clips he took. About who he thought was responsible, and we're going to make the son of a bitch suffer like no one has ever suffered in human history."

Paul polishes his glasses, gazing owlishly at them. "Is this evidence you're talking about recorded on a small Sony digital camera?"

Several impossibly slow instants pass before the lead bullet of this question nails Ben in the chest.

"You . . . you *knew* about this?"

"Well, all things considered, sure thing, Ben, I had to have known about them." Paul replaces his glasses. "Your old man, may his memory never be forgotten, didn't know much about technology. It was surprising, coming from a guy with his grasp of—"

"Your. *Point*. Please," Ben grates.

"Look, I'm terribly sorry, but this isn't news to me." Paul spreads a speckled hand over his heart. "I *took* the videos."

LIA

The wait is just about over, the breath
of intervention ragged.

—*Kamilah Aisha Moon, "Coup in Progress"*

Lia ventures into the realm where the wolves roam free. *Neon-lit bodegas with sleek, evil refrigerators. Bars where pretty people offer conversation, escape, have another? Plastic people who can have two, six, eight drinks and then walk away without ordering a ninth and a twelfth.*

She traverses the savage backwoods most people think of as 90th and Broadway.

This is the stupidest place you could possibly go.

BITTERSWEET: *A fruit-bearing vine. Cut three of its climbing branches and twine them to repel enemies, or use them to cross a foe's path after dark.*

Lia worries at the braid of twigs in her dress pocket.

When Lia was still an artist—not in the sense that she saw the world around her in color and form, in squalor and splendor, but in the sense that people paid her for art—she wanted new things. New friends to debate, new techniques with glue and needle. New ways of interpreting the feelings she kept locked in the smooth spherical marble in her chest.

Lia doesn't want new things anymore.

She wants comfort, thick socks with a hole starting in the big toe. She used to spend entire days walking the streets with Benjamin. They'd debate over how to cut across Central Park under a vermillion May sunset (*forest or duck pond*), which Village to wander through (*East or West*). By most standards, an idyllic existence.

And if Ben ranted for an hour about how jumping off their fire escape would be a hilarious answer to the Kantian argument that people's innate value lies in their capacity to choose, well.

Nobody's perfect.

And if six spare mini bottles of Tanqueray were hidden in various purse niches for an Emergencies Only scenario that somehow ended up *always* happening, well.

Life isn't perfect, either.

CAMELLIA: *Our destinies are forever inextricably linked.*

In these lonelier times, the yearning for the rote is strong. So this evening, instead of reading or sketching while the three sisters flutter like a silken breeze, Lia wanders around the Upper West Side wearing her mother Laura's scarf.

Just stick your head in the lion's mouth, sure. Check if he's been flossing.

FIVE✦FINGER GRASS: *Lucky for the gambling tables, drawing money, and can be used to help travel safely and prevent the loss of self.*

The commonplace is a thousand thousand times more precious than the rare. These slender trees witnessed five-year-old Lia forking overcooked spaghetti into her mouth. Watched through their window as Dad wept silently onto his plate. This coffee shop casting a golden coin of light onto this bench was where Ben met her between classes. She'd bitch about the price of art, how everyone should have access, everyone should scrape the feelings from their rib cage with a paint knife, and he'd listen as if Lia were Frida Kahlo.

The old Lia is reemerging. She's known it since the dreams with Ben started. The Lia who felt everything, fenceless, no traffic lights, attacked open-ended projects with passion and clarity and rolled-up sleeves. The one Ben used to love. Still might love, even.

Ben used to say that everything possible is so, in one corner of the multiverse or another.

Just someplace we can't ever get to.

She reaches the City Diner on 95th Street, where the tall old man with the hairnet works. Lia and Ben would laugh hysterically over eggs and hash and spinach pie, guessing his country of origin. Nothing worked—the waiter was as nationless as the air. They tried to draw him out with loud talk of soccer, or observing whether he ate any pork products. Lia eventually created Bulvmania and the game changed—hours expended crafting their imaginary country.

That's what we were, Ben and me.

An imaginary country. No army, no navy, no ramparts.

Population: 2.

Ben might not even be in New York. He could have flown to Chiang Mai for a curry or taken a Metro-North train to inspect the Hudson River.

But it's the most likely out of anywhere on earth that he's here.

She feels the pure transgression of this foray lodged in her chest, nestled between her legs. Ben used to belong to her and then he didn't anymore and she shouldn't be within any of his space at all, but she could hardly leave the planet, could she? She could hardly leave *New York*, could she? She'd dissolve into stardust, which was what Ben always insisted she was sculpted from.

And here's the side street, yes. She floats through the honey-thick night air into a pretty Episcopal church on 101st. Next comes a much less pretty flight of stairs with its green paint flaking, into a concrete-floored basement, and onto a rusting metal folding chair.

A swift progression into what she deserves.

The room, as ever, smells like a janitorial war zone. Windex vs. subterranean windows. Lysol spray vs. Goodwill sofa. No side is winning, nobody is ever winning. A huge sign reads **SO-BRIETY IS NOT AN ANCHOR IT'S A PAIR OF WINGS.** Someone drew what Lia considered a very stylishly rendered cock and balls on it once and instead of replacing the poster, they just tore that corner off.

She crouches, willing herself invisible. Which won't work, of course, not when she came to an AA meeting run by a man she and Ben have known for nearly two decades. Not when she likes Ariel Washington enough to *want* to be brutally honest.

"OK, everybody." The deacon smiles like he's laying his hands on their foreheads, his dark skin crinkling kindly. "Congratulations to each and every one of you for being here. Now. My name is Ariel and I'm an alcoholic."

Hi Ariel, everyone choruses.

The meeting progresses. One man's addiction is sentient and appears as a chameleon with wily rainbow camouflages. A lady weeps about her grandfather biting her infant son after the toothless baby chomped on the bastard during bath time. Another woman's mother used to punish her by making her kneel on a cheese grater. A rawboned auntie type in her sixties pulled a knife on her ex, but apparently because she's Puerto Rican, not because she's an alcoholic—she's that too, but claims credit for *not* having swung a blade before, because of the whole Puerto Rican thing. The stories shouldn't blend together, not when they're about things like walking twenty blocks with a glass shard spearing the sole of a flip-flop. But they do.

It doesn't spare her the usual mantra.

Nothing ever really happened to you.

Once upon a time, an elderly immigrant from Eastern Europe named Jórvík worked for the first World's Stage Theatre. The one that burned like hellfire. He wielded a janitorial broom with soft grace, wore a simple, clownish smile, and liked to perform small magic acts he brought from the old country. Ben and Lia were his devoted natural audience. For Ben, it was flashy showers of coins, disappearing wristwatches. For Lia, it was subtler— card tricks, her favorite. But the old man never used a deck. Instead, he spread in his gnarled hands the miniature mass-printed school portraits of other little girls her own age. Ones with braids, ones with freckles, snub noses, cornrows, missing teeth.

Pick a card, any card . . . and I will make for it to disappear.

There are no excuses for the things that you've done, Lia thinks.

"So then this guy he calls me, right, and I know not to pick up, I *know it,*" a youngish woman laments. Pixie haircut, sparkly pixie nails, liquid eyeliner swooping like pixie wings.

Ariel nods, understanding. He understands everything at the World's Stage corporate offices too, and Lia can't count how many times she and Benjamin have separately broken down with him in the mail room over some new transgression of hers or dark thought of his.

Of course, the mail room isn't an AA Room. The point of these Rooms is to say out loud, in solidarity, *I too fucked a raccoon for heroin.*

"And this guy's 'hey, just want to hear your voice,' and this guy, he *hit* me, you know?"

They know. This person has been coming to the identical AA meeting for four years.

"And see, *that's* when I got it." The girl nods, pushing cat's-eye frames up her thin nose. "The clicker."

Lia fights a smile. *What's her name, Franny? Frances?* Whatever her name, she doesn't know the term *kicker.* And she has told the Tale of the Clicker so many times she might as well be a ballpoint pen.

"That's when I realized that this guy, and the opiates I was getting from him, you know, they were *the same*. The pills, and the booze, and the relationship." Her eyes well with tears. "I'd be feeling amazing and then it was *hurting* me. They *both* were gonna kill me, you know?"

Ariel shifts in his seat. "That's powerful, Frankie. Anybody here relate to that feeling? Like what's around you and inside you gonna get you killed?"

"It killed my aunt," a man says. "It killed my best friend, too."

"It killed who I used to be, anyway," Lia states. "My life was over."

Ariel nods. His eyes where they feather contain a past too, darknesses, acts that can't be taken back or forgotten. "All lives end, but we sure can want to change the how and the when of it, can't we?"

She'd had a plane ticket, was meeting Ben at JFK for a romantic Christmas jaunt to London that she figured was probably mostly about avoiding his parents. But it would involve Christmas trees, and whiskey-spiked apple cider, and her fiancé, and so she was happy. It was snowing hard, and she left the apartment with bag in hand to get to the airport. Decided to stop by her East Village studio space first, have a nip of something and check her email.

She never arrived at the airport. The sisters found her the next morning.

"I died on the hospital table but they got my heart going again," a reedy guy notes with pride.

"Oh, I'd have died." Frankie nods. "But . . . it's hard not to still think about it. That familiarity. That *feeling*."

Lia studies an ancient ceiling leak. She once created an illegal installation in an abandoned New Jersey shopping mall that was just ivy growing violently, voraciously, over a defunct escalator.

It got her featured in *Time Out* and reminds her of what's-her-name: entangled, very pretty, and not going anywhere. Frankie is sad tonight, which saddens Lia in turn—the Tale of the Clicker generally perks her up.

"It was this roller-coaster, right? There's the wind in your face and you've got this shit-eating grin. Then come the bruises and *that's* even kind of OK, you know? Romantic from the right angle."

"You can still see the stars from the gutter," Lia agrees.

"It's pretty somehow, or else you *make* it pretty so you can stand it. Anyway, they both were this thrill ride. Afterward, without either . . ."

One man has his cap pulled low over his eyes as he nods off.

"Afterward, you might as well have flatlined," Lia supplies. "Since it feels exactly the same."

CATNİP: *Useful in drawing a particular man to you. Either sprinkle it in a man's food or in the four corners of your bath.*

After an hour, everyone scatters like so many nestless ants. At least tonight the meeting calmed her. Occasionally Lia wanted to take the entire box of cheap black-and-white cookies plus the stale coffee and dump it all over her own head. Just to shake up the narrative. But the interlude spent during the meeting helped, if not the meeting itself.

It was stupid to come to this meeting. One with Ariel.

One from the old days.

Lia thinks about the word *trigger*, and how trite she used to find it, and how much it now feels like a gun to the head.

She reaches 104th Street and a plain glass door in a plain complex from the 1920s. They've been capable of moving for twenty years or more. They never have. Maybe because her mother, Laura, lived and breathed and very slowly died here. To the right of their door hangs their mezuzah scroll, now covered in a dozen layers of landlord-approved industrial white paint.

Lia touches it, because she always does.

ANGELICA: *To sanctify your home, keep stray men from your home, bless a baby in your home, protect your home, create a border for enemies and crossings into your home.*

Inside the Brahmses' two-bedroom, the TV shouts merry partisan vitriol. One politician wants a nature preserve, and the other feels indifferent to rare water bugs. Lia used to paint picket signs about this kind of thing. Now she leaves the sound on because Paul likes it that way and goes to join her sleeping dad on the couch, nudging him affectionately.

"I wanted to catch up. Jesus, it's only ten at night," Lia teases.

His open mouth twitches into a fatherly half-smile. Paul Brahms was always small, Lia thinks as her own lips curve down. A small man with big burdens. She sometimes wonders whether he sheltered inside them. He's a curious figure, her father. Dithering and efficient, clearly innocuous but ferociously determined. Paul isn't hiding anything definite that she can pin down, but he always did seem like *more* of a person to her than the person he showed to the world at large. What an odd thing—for a man to loom larger in a two-bedroom rental than he did running a massive production company. But it might have been easier for her dad to be a melancholy man in public, a worried man, an almost ridiculous man, and not be anything more noticeable. Maybe the cloud of woe took solid form, hardened into a crab's shell. After all, it requires a special kind of ego to take on the world.

"No, don't hang the lights from those cords," Paul mutters. "Two to a ladder. Always."

"What's that, Dad?"

"I said two to a ladder."

"I love you, and you're absurd."

She covers him with the crocheted quilt he insists does *not* smell like a stale microwave. Lia glances down at the coffee table and her lips part again. This time in shock.

Paul was working. He never stops worrying about other people's jobs—so maybe that's why he seems to encompass more than himself alone. That's where Lia learned to pick up strangers' burdens, she supposes. Then again, maybe it was her dad's personal grief that trained her to thrum along with pain like a tuning fork. As if suffering had to be shared, like a concert or an art exhibit. Paul used to thumb through family albums prominently featuring Laura Caruso Brahms, leaving them on the countertop for his young daughter to put away. Again.

And again. And again.

But this isn't a documentary of family loss. They aren't even the benefit gala spreadsheets. These are grainy, sordid, CSI-looking pictures. Of Ben's mother and his new stepfather.

But taken two decades ago. At least.

"What the hell, Dad," Lia breathes.

Her hand hovers before them in a grotesquely long depth of field. Something Hitchcockian, featuring bell towers and lethal falls.

With a creeping sensation, she carries the prints to the kitchen where the overhead light still coolly hums. Out of love and habit, she investigates the fridge. He's living off cottage cheese again. Sniffing a container of lunch meat, she gags.

It's as bad as just after Mom died.

You need to take better care of him, since you can't take care of Ben anymore.

Lia refuses to slide to the floor in a lake of tears. This feels like supernatural bravery.

Are you really so brave though if you're supernatural—isn't the point of bravery that you're, like, shitting your pants but you do it anyway?

Shut up, Ben, she pleads.

Sitting at the counter, Lia flips through the photos.

"What the fuck," she whispers.

Her dad didn't take them, first off. These were paid for. Photographer Paul Brahms directs everyone closer together, *we all like each other here, aw, sure we do,* until Benjamin would stick his elbow straight into Lia's ear, and her dad would take several blurred shots of his own finger. No, a detective or a cop must have been involved. Second, there's nothing but pictures here—no notes, no reports.

Lia's stomach roils. She needs to know what this means. Because she's read the articles about Jackson Dane's dubious death, she saw the painting shrivel into ashes with her mind's eye, or maybe with Ben's mind's eye. And afterward, when the death turned all too real, they ruled it a suicide.

Would discovering a decades-long affair drive a grown Texan over the edge?

The first is a shot of Trudy Dane framed in the sort of outdoor hotel corridor you find in LA. Looking like a circa 1960s bombshell who just fucked someone's brains out on a beach. Trudy's always been stunning, stunning and calculated. Lia has lost track of how many times Trudy's been featured on the *BroadwayWorld* website or photographed for Page Six.

Lia glances at where Paul Brahms is now fully snuggled into the old-soup-can-smelling caftan. Her dad knows everything about New World's Stage, from whether the restrooms are being properly serviced to what brand of coffee the concessions stand sells. His fingerprints are on every inch of the building. And he doesn't share that information, not even with Lia—he hoards it like a dragon crouched over its gold.

But why this, Dad?

Why the hell should you know this?

Next come the money shots. Claude Dane exiting the same hotel room, kissing Trudy on the cheek. She smiles with her eyes closed. Ben got all that manic drive from his late dad, but Trudy has always been languid. This identical expression is the closest her son ever gets to looking like he just lapped up the cream, and it was always from lapping at other things entirely.

Lia shifts on the chair, her eyes watering even as she flushes.

In the next shot, a breeze whips Trudy's hair into a wide

blond smudge as Claude rests lips against her ear. It's the second floor, because Lia can see the parking lot filled with sleek, powerful machines, dancing palm trees. The Danes aren't hiding in some roach motel. Even though they're the wrong Danes.

Lia returns the pictures to the coffee table. Lots of people have affairs, even within families. But these photos frighten her.

In light of the death.

In light of the dreams.

She desperately wants to pepper Paul with questions. But Paul protects all the Danes like some medieval knight. Worse, this inevitably has to do with Benjamin. And her dad would rather sew his own mouth shut than broach *that* subject with Lia. She watches the shallow, almost concave movement of Paul's chest.

In-out. In-out.

They were desperate when the Danes changed their lives. Only a little girl, still hugging her late mother's pillow to her chest, she doesn't remember it well. But the story has become the stuff of legend. And like all legends, it leaves room for its various narrators to be unreliable.

Paul and Lia were living off tinned tuna when Lia wasn't gratefully eating her school lunches, and they'd missed the rent twice. Drowning in her mother's brain cancer debt, her father with a leaky rowboat, a pair of hip waders, and a thimble. Trying like hell to save them, choking on the salt spray. Then one night, young Lia alone with the flickering television glare as Paul begged the bank for another loan in midtown, he came to an alleyway. An extraordinarily well-dressed and imposing man was being held at gunpoint.

What was I gonna do, just keep walking? was how Paul Brahms put it.

What everyone agreed on was that Paul—weak, nebbishy Paul—walked straight into the corridor yelling and waving his arms, lying that the cops were on their way. The thug (sentenced to fifteen years at Rikers Island thanks to multiple violent priors) howled with laughter.

Which was the only opening Jackson Dane needed. He'd smashed the attacker's gun hand against the brick, and seconds afterward that little shit's skull.

Guy wanted my blood. Saw it in his eyes. I owe Paul my life, my family's happiness, everything—and we Danes repay our debts was the way Jackson Dane told the tall tale.

The Danes employed her father, refinanced their crippling hospice bills. Paul and Jackson worked like partners. Lia and Benjamin fell in love. Their lives were a nest of forgotten jewelry chains, and people either sit picking eighteen separate necklace strands apart with a needle, or else accept the entire lump.

And Lia is discovering that their lives were even more entwined than she'd imagined.

"Why do you have these, Dad?" Lia touches the streetlight reflecting off her dad's head and he snuffles gently.

She's taking one last queasy glance at them when Paul's phone flashes briefly. But it's enough. A millisecond would be enough. It's from Ben.

> hey thanks for earlier today I know
> I was asking a lot of you but it is
> pretty urgent so can we this time
> not underestimate said urgency and do
> ten thousand other things instead
> please?

What could possibly be going on?

And Trudy and Claude, they're . . . Christ, they're married now.

Lia traps her hands against her sides to keep from flinging herself at her father, begging for information. It won't do any good.

As a last recourse, if only to assure herself this isn't another nightmare, Lia selects a picture of Claude looking at a wind-warmed Trudy from inches away. His eyes are so full of her. As if that doorway led to the wide world entire.

Lia trudges down the hall with the glossy print, taking refuge in her old room. Childhood idols study her. Freddie Mercury scowls at her distress, but David Bowie offers asylum in a wonderland of astronauts with eyeliner. Reflexively, Lia slides a hand into the depths of her pillowcase. But there aren't any bottles there.

Lia is so far gone, she doesn't know if she's relieved or furious.

Her late mother smiles at her from a portrait on her dresser. Bigger briar patch of curls, sharper hook to the nose, fuller lips, cat's-eye glasses. Laura Caruso Brahms was more beautiful than Lia can ever imagine becoming. She gently touches the scarf.

Crawling onto the mattress, Lia surveys her memorabilia. Certificate from the Congressional Art Competition, when her work was first displayed freshman year of high school—at the United States Capitol.

You peaked too soon, Ben teased.

Scholastic Art & Writing Awards, when she was petrified of what to wear to Carnegie Hall.

Do body paint—I'll help, and it's totally legal in New York, Ben suggested, all sly smiles, and they hadn't even slept together yet. The first time for that was in a locked dressing room at the theatre when she was seventeen, sizzling makeup lights illuminating fevered skin.

The crystal paperweight of the Milky Way galaxy. *It reminds me of you,* Ben said about what ought to have been a knick-knack and instead felt like his heart, heavy and pulsing in her hand.

"Fuck this noise," Lia whispers, casting around for her phone.

No matter what I did, I love him, I just fucking love him, and you help people you love no matter how many times you may have stabbed them in the heart.

Lia's teeth grind as her screen lights up and she begins to type.

When the phone falls from limp fingertips, she's too exhausted to even know whether or not she pressed *send*. Lia snuggles under sheets that still smell like her. She has to be up at four in the morning again, anyhow.

As Lia lets the mental cacophony smother her, a strange image plucked from earlier today keeps reoccurring. One of the man named Robin, the little guy the sisters might adore or despise. And how, catching sight of a fraying seam on Moma's cropped tee, he pulled out a miniature sewing kit. Leaning over, licking his lips like a gourmand, he threaded a needle. Lia's muscles twitch and start until she falls into a fitful near-slumber, dreaming of monsters captured in photographs.

HORATIO

Books and drafts mean something quite different for
different thinkers. One collects in a book the lights
that he has been able to steal and carry home swiftly
out of the rays of some insight that suddenly dawned
on him, while another thinker offers us nothing but
shadows—images in black and grey of what had built
up in his soul the day before.

—*Friedrich Nietzsche*, The Gay Science

SPARROWS ARE FAFFING ABOUT outside, and they sound
absolutely *appalling*. The walls, extraordinarily thin for a
pre-war building, thump with salsa music. Horatio's teeth
feel sandy and he's facedown with legs tethered in knotted sheets
and he imagines that a witch turned him to stone.

"Bollocks." Horatio rolls onto his back. "Bollocks, bollocks,
bollocks."

He scratches his hairline, disentangling. Marveling that he is
here of all places—he nearly thinks *home*, but no, *here* in his old
bedroom across from his old . . .

"Benjamin?" Horatio croaks.

The door is wide. No answer. Surely if there is a God in
heaven, the nutter is still passed out with his hair standing up
like a punk porcupine.

Well, there you are, then. Jains don't believe in a God in heaven.

You're buggered, sir.

Horatio cracks a stupid smile, blinks at his brass statue of a *Tirthankara*. Still here after all this time. He must've been too distracted to pack the poor soul. Horatio doesn't pray as often as he should do, and certainly not when he was at Columbia. The figure appeared here after a foray with Benjamin into St. Mark's Place and a very great deal of weed and ramen. Rishabhanatha's eyes are closed. Lucky, considering what Horatio—new to American appetites and American boldness too—got up to in this bedroom.

He presses his palm against the heartache that never dissipates. In a sense, it's unsurprising Benjamin acted glibly after their unspeakable (apparently) error. Horatio'd had a different red-blooded, red-pricked Yankee in here every week. Teaching assistants, pre-med students, coffee baristas. Alcohol, marijuana, meat, sex—they're contaminants, like sun leading to skin cancer. Bodily pleasures. Horatio enjoyed being shagged senseless by that ginger-headed lab tech about as much as he relished a good whiskey.

Purify yourself afterward. Gift deli flowers to your idols, return that full-price shirt to Brooks Brothers. Spare the life of a mosquito. He's a modern man and he was in grad school abroad, for heaven's sake. Sex was worth about ten Hail Marys in Catholic terms and giving up his seat on the 1 train in Horatio's.

Sex with Benjamin, though.

"God, what a cock-up," he whispers. "Benjamin! You awake, mate?"

Sex with Benjamin derailed Horatio's entire belief system—he'd give up dharma, abstain from non-attachment if it meant he could hear Benjamin's breath catch that way every night. It has tainted every casual encounter since. As generous and as ecstatic as losing himself in flesh proves, by the finish line, he's just a mindless pulse of pleasure. A car engine, a mallet, a thing of cock and pistons and no soul. Every song suggesting that he could imagine his way out of this, picture Benjamin while with another man, was laughable.

He knows Benjamin tastes like bitter lemon. He knows he smells like a freshly snapped spring twig. He knows how the ceiling arches its spine whenever he walks into the room. He could glut himself on all of it.

"Were you as pure as they say?" Horatio asks his statue softly. "Or did you ever want something so badly it was killing you, too?"

Rishabhanatha doesn't answer. The teaching god's contentment lends Horatio peace. Benjamin may think time is a flat circle, but that doesn't mean Horatio wants his life to be spent orbiting the drain of infatuation.

"Benjamin!"

Linking his fingers, he pulls them over his head in a stretch. Just as well Benjamin should still be sleeping, after yesterday. Yesterday was . . . well, it was not fruitful. Horatio remembers Paul Brahms as a fast, fretful turtle with a shell-like skull. He has darting eyes, clear and deep and brown, like his daughter's—though Lia seemed drawn to those in distress, while Paul spends so much time actively avoiding hurt that he's ridiculous enough to attract it anyhow. Mourning bursts into his gaze occasionally, and something else Horatio has never put his finger on. Paul is a good egg, the glue holding together New World's Stage, and the absolute bane of Benjamin Dane's existence.

Benjamin reacts to Paul the same way he reacts to cheap perfumed detergents.

Paul ushered Benjamin into a small conference room yesterday afternoon and explained that whereas once Jackson Dane saw obstacles and razed them, he now had started firing cannonades into empty space. Where once he shrewdly avoided his enemies, he suspected his own board of directors.

"It was, I tell you, Ben, not pretty," Paul's nasal voice informed them. "Your father, rest his soul, he always had that edgy streak under all the bounce and bluster. So at first when he said that there were these forces acting against him—"

"Which forces, specifically?" Benjamin interrupted.

"But that's the issue, Ben. There weren't specific forces."

"He's dead." Benjamin flashed an axe-bright smile. "Ergo there were specific forces. Unless this was, like, *Murder on the Orient Express* and everyone my dad ever met was trying to ice him."

Paul placed fatherly hands on Benjamin's arms. Horatio thought Benjamin's shoulders might lodge in his ears.

"Ben, the last time you visited, when we spoke—"

"The last time we spoke I was lit up like a twenty-four-hour pharmacy!" Benjamin shook him off. "Are you really saying that you watched my dad record himself figuring out he was going to get murdered, then he *got* murdered, and the two things have, like, nothing in common?"

"That level of anxiety, Ben, it wore on him."

"Yeah, imminent death is stressful. Like having a long commute, or a roommate who won't take out the trash."

"Ben, your dad? These problems were longstanding and he was taking so many medications. I'm sure you can empathize with that situation, right?"

Matters went rather downhill afterward.

Horatio sits up blearily. Sheets pool in his lap. His friend then asked Paul whether he had any other useful comments about substance abuse, which was remarkably cruel even for Benjamin. Of course he apologized instantly, which was the most infuriating part; his amends were so sincere that you felt culpable supposing you didn't forgive him. But Paul was useless by then, repeating *I have the benefit gala to think of* and *I just truly don't know how to help you with this*, until Benjamin literally threw his hands up.

"You're going to compile every detail you can pertaining to the relationship between my dad and my uncle," he said flatly. "Whether Dad once wore mismatched socks or Uncle Claude ordered the wrong bagels. Report back. And if you make this about my meds again, I *will* be bringing you to the board. Which is, at least fractionally, me."

They walked back to the flat, lazy July lightning flickering. They'd hardly begun to discuss what to do next before Benjamin curled up on the couch like a cat, and Horatio dragged his jet-lagged bones into his old room. After throwing a blanket over the man who caused the slick, half-thrilled, half-frightened feeling in his stomach. Naturally.

Because I am an incalculable, incurable idiot.

But that was yesterday, and this is now.

"Benjamin, we've plans to hatch." Horatio shuffles into the living room, pulling a heather-grey T-shirt over his head. "Though cheers for conceding that the human body requires basic maintenance."

His friend is not on the couch.

Rapping on Benjamin's door, Horatio promptly throws it wide. Every wall is obscured by the bookshelves that were his friend's one admission he owned what could be termed a "library." Horatio finds nothing save books, a sleek triangular turntable, the 1960s Silvertone Teisco shark guitar with the teal patina Benjamin treats like his own child (the 1954 Sunburst Gibson is in its case in the closet, and whenever it makes an appearance they are all in very deep trouble), a small amp, a thrift store desk with the latest MacBook, an antique clock from his mum, Trudy, and the cactus named Thelonius that Lia gave him.

Horatio's belly flips, a fish on a dry shore.

He is out of the flat after throwing on yesterday's trousers.

The air shoves back, a hot damp against his shoulders. It should have rained last night. Construction workers clatter on the corner. Horatio wonders how many secrets lie fallow here. Champagne bottles swigged by mobsters, a Dutch girl's tortoise-shell comb. He doesn't know where he's going. There's the park nearby, any number of them, really, and the Columbia campus, and *what if Benjamin isn't in any of them*, what if Horatio held his friend's hand in the back of a cab and love doesn't matter, after all?

When Horatio narrowly dodges a bus outside Bernardo Brothers Café, his neck crawls with fear. But there Benjamin slouches under the ballooning green ash tree, on their favorite bench. Naturally—because he's a free New Yorker without any obligation to keep Horatio apprised of his whereabouts.

And I'm a bloodsick muppet.

Horatio nevertheless reads Benjamin's mobile screen from over his shoulder.

"Please tell me you know what you're doing reading texts from Lia, you complete tosser," he begs, sinking down beside him.

Benjamin doesn't look up. "Uh, I know what I'm doing?"

"Perhaps state it in the form of, um, a statement?"

A French bulldog approaches, resplendent in a kinky spiked collar. Horatio watches as it moves along. It looks so easy, the moving along, but truly traveling is the hardest thing in the world. Horatio could take tiny step after tiny step, and still. He would carry Benjamin and Benjamin would drag Lia, and Lia weighed as much as Australia, the beautiful creature.

"Have you already breakfasted?"

Benjamin waggles his coffee cup.

"How lovely."

Horatio opens the bag Benjamin proffers to find another coffee and a poppy seed bagel with cream cheese. Resigned, he crosses his legs. It's astonishing, in a way, how a man who is clearly running on fumes, drugged to the tits, obsessed with his ex, and investigating his father's alleged murder still has the generosity to foresee that Horatio would be not merely addled with worry, but hungry as well. And to deposit himself exactly where Horatio could walk (or run) in a straight line to find him.

It's actually very easy to love the man. Even if he's never believed that.

"I had *such* shitty dreams last night." Benjamin's eyes are still bloodshot, but his skin looks less like wax paper.

"Regarding?"

"Lia. Stop that, I'm fine. Lia, yeah, and also the guy who used to do custodial work at the old theatre before it burned. I'm sure I told you about him before."

"The immigrant janitor who kindled your interest in riddles?"

"Whoa. Dude, if you ever run dry of, like, every genuinely interesting person, you can write a biography of *me*. Sleeping has been . . . intense lately."

"Er, yes, you told me you dreamt about your father's portrait burning."

"Yeah. It was just sooooooooo visceral. Brains are crazy complex mechanisms for being lumps of water and fat. Anyway. These dreams feel like I'm actually with, you know. People."

"Like this head custodian?"

Benjamin nods, eyes distant. "Ancient guy from someplace where the bus stops have bullet holes. Jórvík Volkov. He did the most amazing magic tricks. Cards, coins, numbers, knots. He was, like, maybe a leftover from some Siberian circus, can you imagine—wooden carts with blue and red and gold paint, trailing horse shit through empty frozen tundra."

"Sounds ghastly, to be honest."

"But legit, right? Jórvík said all he wanted after 'these long, cold times' was to make kids smile. Lia tried to learn card sharping, but you know her, too many tells. Meanwhile I picked up a book of shell games, which led to math puzzles, which led to Lewis Carroll's unfinished *Curiosa Mathematica*, which led to an affinity for mortality, humanity, philosophy, and the absurd, which led to the unequivocal success story before you. Cheers, Jórvík."

"You've not spoken of him to this extent."

"Yep, Jórvík never came back after the first theatre burned, but the questionably documented ones needed new gigs. He's probably mopping something somewhere."

"What was so shite about this dream, then?"

Benjamin shakes his head. "I don't know, just. It was terrifying. It's always nice to see Lia again, but. Yeah."

Crumpling the foil wrapper, Horatio sinks a neat shot into the rubbish bin.

This track calls for immediate shifting.

"Right, here's what's cocked up most thoroughly regarding the case, from what I can tell. You think it out of character for your dad to have . . . aided his own demise. Very good. Paul Brahms thinks he was managing his paranoia and met with a sad accident. We have evidence left behind electronically by your father—let's call him a material witness—suggesting actual foul play. Meanwhile, neither of us are sleuths."

His friend scowls. "A biographer and a philosopher? You unearth the secrets of the human soul and I lay bare the mysteries of the cosmos. We're, like, the best dynamic detective duo ever to be formed."

"Benjamin, you are aware that you're ridiculous, I hope?"

"You always pronounce 'brilliant' wrong here in the States."

"Oh Christ, not this early in the morning."

"We should have iconic looks. I've got this mourning cuff, that's kinda edgy. Or emo, I can't tell. Maybe add a jaunty scarf for me, a hat for you. What kind of hat do you want?"

"Um, no hat."

"You don't have your hang of our dialect back yet, I said what *kind* of hat?"

"Benjamin, we don't know what we're doing!" Horatio exclaims.

"Sooooo untrue." Benjamin beams. "We found my dad's ghost tapes and we weren't even *looking* for them."

Horatio closes his eyes. "I can't win. Arguing with you is like arguing with gravity."

"Pretty damn easy, then. One bro jumping in the air just whupped the ass of an entire mid-sized planet's gravitational force, literally a child can do it. What you mean is that gravity always comes back, and *then* it always wins. Like me."

Horatio contemplates planting a kiss on Benjamin's mouth, or a punch. Either would prove satisfying.

"Fine, fine!" Benjamin chuckles. "Killer summary, very police procedural. I think it *wasn't* suicide, Paul thinks it *was* an accident, Dad said it *would be* a murder."

"Yes, exactly, but we're both too close to this problem to actually *see* it."

His friend freezes like a startled rabbit. "The coastline paradox."

"The what, yes?"

"Hoooo boy, I couldn't see it before, but you're totally right!"

"Please speak English, or American, just not . . . not Benjamin, I can't cope. What are you on about?"

"The coastline paradox!" Benjamin rubs his hands in glee. "You're so brilliant, dude, I *owe* you. It's impossible to get the same results twice regarding a coastline's length if you use multiple units. Let's say, hypothetically, I measured Manhattan's coastline in inches, and then I measured it in centimeters, I'd end up with two completely different figures. And the closer zoomed in you get, the *longer* it gets. I'd end up with a solid length using miles but a batshit insane length using molecules. The math involves geometry and fractals, which none other than Benoit Mandelbrot described as beautiful and damn hard."

And there's the title of your biography. Ta very much for writing it for me.

"So the closer we look, the more complexity this will inevitably develop." Benjamin frowns. "Examination on a microscopic level will produce results increasing in convolution while they narrow in scale. What *unit* do we need to use to measure this coastline, Horatio? It's OK, that was rhetorical, I'll tell you, because you're brilliant brilliant *brilliant*. We need a much blunter tool."

"Meaning?"

Benjamin's eyes gleam emergency-siren blue. "Meaning he

who rights the wrongs and orderlies the disorderlies, Detective Barry Fortuna. C'mon, we can walk to his precinct from here. I'll even give you time to comb your hair, since you apparently ran out of the house. Don't say I never did anything for you, OK?"

I grant forgiveness to all living beings. May all living beings please forgive me. I have friendship with all living beings. I am hostile to nothing and no one.

Horatio matches Benjamin's jaunty stroll. He'll change at the flat. He'll have another coffee. Benjamin will calm down. Surely?

He trudges onward, the day barely begun and already exhausting. The endless jagged teeth of fractals and the countless sharp waves of coastlines nipping at the edges of his mind.

DETECTIVE BARRY FORTUNA IS not impressed by the digital camera.

Horatio palms the hair he forgot to comb earlier. He can't help fidgeting. Horatio always feels like a terrorist when he walks into American police stations. The cops look at him perfectly blandly, but he still looms enormous and embarrassed.

"So about these videos." Benjamin's smile turns serpentine.

"Yeah, about these." Fortuna adjusts a creaky swivel chair.

"What do you think of them?"

"See, that's one approach. But you're the one brought 'em in. What I gotta ask is, what do *you* think of them?"

Benjamin stares, disbelieving. Detective Fortuna shrugs. The gesture owns a certain bullish eloquence.

It's just past eleven and a footlong sub sandwich rests on Fortuna's desk. The meal resembles its owner: saggy but solid, dense with occasional bright bits, leaking at the corners. Fortuna's watery brown eyes are so sunken that there are mere folds where eyelids should be, and his shoe-polish-toned hair is thinning.

"Any time I get fresh evidence, I gotta consider the source.

Now, your old man was losing his edge, on plenty of dope for it, too. Sure, sure, the legal kind."

This dynamic, Horatio thinks, is all wrong for *protect and serve*, not to mention *courtesy, professionalism, respect* but it is entirely understandable for an NYPD officer and Benjamin Dane. His friend reeks of privilege, was illegally high throughout the beginning of the investigation. Fortuna studies Benjamin with the sluggish cunning of an iguana.

"I get you barging in here ready to call this a murder, but that there's how *you* see it. And if somebody else brought that camera to me, I'd be wondering, huh, how are *they* seeing it?"

"Your investigative methods are truly groundbreaking."

"How do *you* see the recordings, Detective?" Horatio intervenes politely.

The sleuth aims hooded eyes at him. "These here remind me of my aunt Giuliana."

An exquisite spasm of annoyance warps Benjamin's face as the air conditioner drones to life, rustling the papers tacked to a corkboard. A map of the Upper West Side, takeaway menus, a couple of suspect sketches that only resemble the same human being in that all the requisite features are present.

"My aunt Giuliana was always hassling us about mice, God rest her. Mice in the kitchen, mice in the basement. She made the best baked ziti in history, no bullshit. This woman, though? Mice on the brain. Me, here I am a uniformed cop, Zia Giuliana, I would say, don't send me on another search for mice what ain't real."

"OK excellent, and there were no mice," Benjamin prompts. "Can we please—"

"Oh, there was mice all right." Detective Fortuna allows his impenetrable eyes to descend. "In the carport what they renovated in nineteen-eighty-eight."

Horatio pauses. "So . . . you give this new evidence some credence, then?"

"I ain't saying that, either. There was equal chances of there being mice or no mice, on account of there weren't no *evidence* of them other than her say-so."

A slender Asian woman in a neat grey suit enters, heading for the filing cabinet.

"Did you for real just apply the paradox of Schrödinger's cat to mice in the garage?" Benjamin's face lights up. "These mice were in a quantum mechanical superposition, and by committing the action of looking for them, you forced the universe into there either being or not-being a pest issue at your zia Giuliana's?"

"Nice one, Barry," comments the woman shuffling through papers.

Barry Fortuna pulls his sandwich closer. "You know what, I should introduce you to my partner, Detective Norway. You might get on better. Norway took some interviews right after the body was found."

"When can that happen?"

The woman—perhaps Chinese American, but Horatio never likes to guess—turns around with a folder in her hand. She's sharply attractive, with severely defined red lips and a cutting chin-length bob.

"Detective Ying Yue Norway," she says. "What did I tell you about lunch before noon, Barry? Next it'll be breakfast cigars."

"Oh." Benjamin has the presence to look contrite as he shakes hands. Clearly he didn't foresee anyone of Asian descent being called by the name of a Scandinavian country. "Sorry, Detective Norway."

"Don't worry about it. I'm not Norwegian."

The detective pushes her partner's sandwich aside with obvious censure to lean on the desk. Everywhere Fortuna spills over, Norway is trim. Her hair is as dark as her partner's, but naturally, rather than from what Horatio assumes to be a can of spray paint. If a new drama titled *CSI: Flushing* or *CSI: Elmhurst* were proposed, they would hire Ying Yue Norway.

"What kind of grief are you giving these two, Barry? He just got a prescription for his blood pressure," Norway adds apolo-

getically. "He says it's genetic, I say it's his daily dose of morta-
della. Makes him irritable. What can we do for these gentlemen?"

"It's the Dane kid, come again about the suicide. They have
tapes now, of Dane senior saying his life was threatened."

"Tapes? Do you see a cassette deck on this camera?" Benjamin sniffs.

"We never met during the initial investigation, Mr. Dane. I
think you dealt solely with my partner here. But in the course of
my questioning, I found your father to be highly respected. I'm
sorry for your loss."

Since Benjamin is mute, Horatio says, "We deeply appreciate it."

"Are you his partner?"

"Yeah. Kinda. Not as such," Benjamin answers as Horatio
spiritually sinks into the floor.

"So." Norway frowns. "I spoke with at least half a dozen
parties. The fact that the substances found in Jackson Dane's
system were prescribed to him, and that he had a history of
anxiety—"

"Well-founded anxiety," Benjamin adds dryly.

Norway nods. "But under the circumstances, although his
death was certainly unexpected, there was no reason to look
into it further."

"Mice." Fortuna unwraps a corner of his sandwich. "The old
man pegged his brother in the tapes, Ying."

"Believe me, if I had seen anything, I would have said something. Kind of our slogan, you know," Norway adds with gentle
irony. "But there was nothing to say this wasn't self-inflicted,
and the bereaved were against our digging any further. I was
ordered off your lawn."

Benjamin gestures, the cuff looking impossibly weighty.
"What do you mean, the *bereaved*? You were asked to stop
looking into this? By whom?"

Detective Ying Yue Norway angles her shoulders back. "I

would have thought this was a decision the entire family was privy to."

"Yeah, I am the *least* privy person. Who told you to stop investigating Dad's murder?"

"Your mother." Norway rubs her chin. "And since there was no evidence of its being a murder, we complied. Who else do you imagine would have the authority? Your mother, Trudy Dane."

BENJAMIN

What a Chimera is man! What a novelty, a monster,
a chaos, a contradiction, a prodigy! Judge of all
things, an imbecile worm; depository of truth, and
sewer of error and doubt; the glory and refuse of the
universe.

—*Blaise Pascal*, Pensées

"N O NO *NO*, THIS is not me fixating, this is not mania or any
of the things your eyebrows are broadcasting, because goddamn it, Horatio, you have magnificent eyebrows and they
are *mocking me*."

Horatio's jaw spasms. "Um, just. Explain to me why it's such
a great notion to descend on your mum immediately instead of
giving this a think first."

Ben yanks in a lungful of tar. A measurable amount of chaos
is tamed by inhaling sizzling particles of poison.

Granted, he's adding to the world's *overall* disorder and
speeding the eventual cold death of the universe. You can't
unsmoke a cigarette. But it's a small, achievable goal, and it's
something to do with the hands that both want to rub his
mom's smooth perfumed arms pleading *what are you doing*,
but also *a bit just a bit* want to wrap around her swanlike neck
and

T
   W   I
       S
         T

Ben eyes the ghost of his last breath. "Why put off till tomorrow what can send you into an emotional abyss today? If I go now, I don't have to go tomorrow . . . if I don't want to do it tomorrow, it has to be now . . . but if it isn't now, I still have to do it tomorrow."

Anyway, Ben is so glad to be drinking afternoon beers with Horatio that the thankfulness joins the smoke, searing in his chest. When they initially discovered the rooftop was unlocked, they promptly improved on its Overflowing Ashtray Utopia aesthetic. Kiddie pools happened for five summers running, but their favorite features were year-round: a moldering patio umbrella branded **CAMPARI** and a trio of lawn chairs. The oasis smells of baked blacktop and the trash cans Lia filled with lavender and ivy. Her chair currently hosts a cooler and a container of mixed fruit Ben supposes Horatio bought out of witless optimism.

It looks less empty that way.

They used to come here, just Ben and Lia, to sip cocktails out of red Solo cups. Watch their planet's personal star exploding above the horizon like some gorgeous galactic disaster. Once in the dead of night he locked the door and convinced her to spread her thighs open and was on his knees for an hour. Benjamin can't even look at *water tower, housing project, fire escape, rooftop garden* without seeing Lia's regal nose silhouetted, laughing at some crack he just made about the cult of Pythagoreans agreeing it was only healthful to screw women in the wintertime.

Benjamin listens to the chemicals upping the tempo of his lungs *a poco a poco.* Like siphoning stimulants into a metronome.

"Yeah yeah, there's a reason I no longer live with Mamma Dane, yet she's the obvious next person of interest. *You* could always do those work things—I don't need a chaperone to talk to my own mom."

"Anyhow," Horatio segues coolly, "not two hours ago you said you were too close to this problem to measure it, something about coastlines, and now you want to give Trudy the third degree. Your *mum*."

"I know who she is to me biologically."

"And emotionally?"

"She runs me in circles like a show pony."

Lighting a new cigarette with the butt of his spent one, Ben endures the sour flicker on Horatio's face. *Two entire cigarettes, Jesus, just look at you knocking all these tasks off the to-do list this afternoon.* Somehow he managed to forget how much his friend's care

~ ~ ~ ~ R A D I A T E S ~ ~ ~ ~

like a retro neon diner sign.

"OK, we're no longer talking coastline paradox. This is now Brunelleschi's vanishing point, and the zero mark—the dimensionless speck, the impossibly smooshed compressed coordinate that allowed for three-dimensional illusion on a two-dimensional canvas after all those ghastly pictures of flat baby adult Jesus during the medieval period, the black hole of the art world drawing everything into its infinite gravitational pull—is Mom. So I need to talk to her."

Ben shoots a cheerful[*manic] smile at Horatio. He's aiming for confident[*jaunty] but it lands somewhere between forced[*deranged] and sickly[*pinheaded]. It's distressing, because either he's getting a nicotine rush or causing Horatio distress is making him nauseated.

"You know that if you just go tearing in there, she'll have you by your bollocks." Horatio pulls two more bottles from the cooler. "The NYPD isn't going to call off a murder investigation just on the widow's say-so, though in the case of what looked like an overdose, I can see why they might be prevailed on to keep quiet. But what *good* reason could she have had to do such a thing?"

"She had a square football field of reasons. But she only needed two."

OK sure Ben was not at peak operating capacity after his father died and *yes granted* sometimes processing grief is a bullet train going in a circle to no place and *yeah possibly* that meant he wasn't really there for his mom but he remembers the

«F»

«L»

«A»

«S»

«H»

«I»

«N»

«G»

of paparazzi cameras outside New World's Stage as his mom left an emergency board meeting dressed in jet-black Chanel like a Kennedy, and the yells of the Page Six maggots, and the way Trudy looked sitting on the couch with that lingering urine aroma Uncle Claude as she said, white-faced but weirdly happy,

courthouse ceremony // I know it's sudden but it feels so natural // didn't want the tabloids making something filthy out of true human affection // agree not to say anything just yet // will always and forever love your // wanted so much to tell you—

"Which two reasons were paramount, then?" Horatio queries.

Ben shakes his head, fighting the static. "Sorry. First, if she let the police investigation drag on, fallout from an official inquiry could potentially have negatively impacted New World's Stage's investors. Second, fallout from the whole marrying-my-uncle thing. Which is disgusting. She must have paid half the city's bloggers not to out them. No, not even *we* have enough money for that—they can't have found out yet."

Horatio nods, a piece of hair escaping the knot at his neck. "You told Ariel to tell me. I imagine several lawyers must be well aware. Who else does that leave?"

"I don't know, but Mom keeps texting me hints that the benefit gala is, like, capital-*I* important, imploring me to speechify. Asking whether my black-tie options fit, which lets her take a dig at my eating habits simultaneously. Speaking of which, can I pay for your tux to be airmailed?"

"Airmailed? My god. I don't even own a tuxedo, remember?"

The look Horatio gives him is so *concerned* and about his *memory* of all things. Ben is an idiot, he realizes. It's been going on practically since they met, but he doesn't know anymore how to be the center of devotion so loud that it tolls from bell towers. *May I remind you that I'm breakable, but do break me if need be . . . I've never owned a tuxedo.* Lia didn't care for Ben like this. She loved passionately in her concentrated, cerebral way—immersed in her art, preoccupied with dissecting her own psyche on a petri dish. To Horatio, Ben is the sun. Ben acclimated so quickly after meeting the man that he stopped registering it, this deluge of love, the way the smell of a simmering pot vanishes after half an hour or so. He'd always told himself

It's OK
This isn't cruel
                              Because I love him back
                                        I love him too

And if we both know that
Really know it
                              Then it'll be fine somehow
                                        Despite the fact

He might not have
All the rest of it

                              I'll love him so much
                                        I'll *make it* fine

But now Horatio has been gone for a year and Benjamin has lived without him. It's like sharing a space with a neutron star—threeish solar masses squeezed into a radius of approximately twelve and a half miles, its gravity crushing protons and electrons into unfathomably minute particles.

We are really really really going to need to talk about What Happened.

"Yes, I know you don't have a penguin suit." Ben coughs, abashed. "Since it's my dumpster fire, may I pay for a killer tuxedo? Please?"

"Ta very much, but no." A wrinkle forms above his hourglass nose. "I could probably—"

"Nope. I'll call Vincentio."

"Right, then, we'll fight about whoever the hell Vincentio is later."

"Vincentio is my tailor and the most authentic human I've ever met other than you."

"Um, lovely. What function does your mother want you to perform at the gala, exactly?"

"We can find out when I see Mom."

"When *we* see her."

Horatio's smile feels like John Coltrane's "I'm Old Fashioned," and the stray lock of hair keeps bashing him in the eye, and Ben thinks that he doesn't belong in the same world as this man, and best to face that and decide for about six seconds to make somebody else happy even if that can't be sustained indefinitely. Sustaining something indefinitely is impossible—it violates the law of conservation of energy, which would matter less if you completely eliminated dissipative forces like friction and were left with only smooth surfaces to create power for mechanical work from nothing. It was a pipe dream of scientists for centuries. But unfortunately, there is always friction. And thus making Horatio happy forever isn't in the cards.

"OK," Benjamin says, as a gift. "Come have a tea party with Mom and me."

"OK," Horatio agrees, relieved.

Ben puts out the second cigarette barely smoked, a second gift. "My family is a disaster of, like, Chernobyl proportions. I'm going to sprout a third eye. Can we pretend that your friend isn't a massive tool and that I asked you all about the Patel clan maybe yesterday?"

The snuffed cigarette pleases Horatio more than the question. So does Ben taking his usual lawn chair, their feet almost touching. Horatio talks—the funding for his dad's social work program for elderly veterans is shaky, his mum is saving to have the kitchen improved. Ben nods in all the right places and snorts when Horatio describes his gran leaving her purse in the fridge and the eggplant on the countertop.

They sit for an hour, make a run to Bernardo Brothers for another sixer. Shadows lengthen and Lia's shade slips among the ghosts of telephone wires and satellite dishes, the imprint of her footsteps stamped on the concrete. They share their rooftop

yellow lorry slow
nowhere to go
but oh that magic feeling
nowhere to go

until there actually is somewhere to go and Ben pointedly reminds Horatio that he never showered and by the time the water flows, Ben is already texting:

please don't kill me but
mom will talk way more if I
go alone

Plus after a moment's thought:

tell me a country of origin
and I'll bring back cuisine
within a couple hours promise

The door closes soundlessly. Ben didn't live with a consummate alcoholic for five years without learning a trick or two about escaping detection. Lia was an artist (read: brilliant) and a perfectionist (read: meticulous) and a star pupil (read: wily). She could buy a mini bottle or five in the ten minutes it took Ben to wash his crevices.

Horatio doesn't deserve to get ditched like that, but some of the things between Benjamin Dane and his mother can exist in the fragile space between Benjamin Dane and his mother alone.

CRUDE CHATTER OF MIDDLE schoolers clustered around an ice cream truck. Smells from the bagel shop, the churned detritus of the 86th Street subway grate, the window boxes of seasonal flowers Lia knew all the names of. Standing outside their door, Ben can see Jackson Dane six years ago, striding down the curved stone steps between the lions' heads, hailing a cab on his way to the New World's Stage offices.

The Dane townhouse is too familiar—nothing whatsoever is different. Everything has changed.

If you weren't well aware that ice, water, and steam were all identical, if they weren't all such everyday sights, it would look like astonishing black magic as they shifted. But that doesn't mean they aren't all

~ H2O ~

Ben's hands shake, but this thought always grounds him. He shoves them in the pockets of the jacket he threw on over his Kill Ugly Radio T-shirt. Mostly to reassure himself he has both Adderall and Klonopin at the ready.

One never really knows with Trudy Dane.

He lets himself into the foyer of grey marble with its grand staircase and fiddle leaf fig trees. From deeper in the townhouse, Joni Mitchell softly sings "Coyote" with Jaco Pastorius flitting around her guitar chords like an insect flirting with a porchlight. To Ben's right is the formal dining room with its huge bay windows. To his left is the living room no one ever really lived in, unless Ben was doing what his dad called "tormenting" the grand piano.

Or sitting on it, staring out the window to see if the kids from school had run out of eggs yet. Or hiding under it. Or bleeding under it. Or . . .

" . . . and I'd hate to leave it where it was, so I need to go to the offices," comes Uncle Claude's voice from down the echoing hallway toward the kitchen.

Ben isn't thinking as he

D
   I
     V
    E
     S

under the massive musical instrument that once protected him from eighty-pound bullies. Ben listens from his lair wedged between the piano's seat and its housing, on the carpeting replaced every three years with a fresh fall of fairy-tale white.

"But do you know *what* specifically Paul's upset about?" Trudy's voice follows Uncle Claude's toward the front door.

"Just what we're all upset about, pumpkin. Jackson's death, our getting married so suddenly. Ben's attitude, his mental health. Your son's not familiar with the policy of sparing the messenger, I guess. Even after I told him the box was from you."

Pumpkin. Ben longs to spit up a catlike amount on the snowy carpet. Claude sounds affectionate toward his mom, genuinely. He's reporting back to her, accurately. Ben loathes him, nevertheless.

"We all knew what poor Jackson was suffering through," Claude continues. "Still. Those tapes though, what a nightmare. Suspecting things like that about me of all people. Paul's been so upset about the gala, of course he didn't look through a box of junk from Jackson's desk, but to think I delivered these crazy conspiracy theories straight to Benny . . . what a complete mess.

Paul called me not five minutes after Ben's visit, of course. Now we're just looking at damage control."

Ben bites his lip, tasting pennies. This tracks with what he knows so far—why would Uncle Claude, that rancid gallbladder, deliver videos implicating himself in a murder? And if Paul never believed Jackson was in danger, why wouldn't he immediately warn the new happy couple about the mistake? What Ben still can't get at is the meat of the matter. Claude doesn't seem remotely concerned about this new evidence other than for Trudy's feelings. Which means either Jackson Dane was out of his mind, or that Claude Dane is a criminal genius.

"Poor Ben." Trudy sighs. "He's always been so *far* in his own sad, sweet head. He was two years old before he spoke—I thought dear god, what is wrong with him, what is wrong with *me*—and then he announced, 'I don't like banana, please.'"

"It's awful to think about you so unsure of yourself as a mom."

Get the fuck out of my house, you caked-on oven scum. And thank you for being kind to my mother.

"It wasn't Ben's fault he was so difficult, Claude. Brilliant people are always difficult. Not to flatter myself, but you wouldn't believe the trouble I had at school in rural Texas before I learned how to bleach my hair. I have no idea what to do about my own son, and it breaks my heart."

"Which is why I'm going back for another talk with Paul. Anyway, I need to see him about our gala plans."

"The poor thing. He's impossible when it comes to delegating, he oversees everything from swag bags to ice sculptures. Sometimes I wonder what that man *doesn't* know."

Having never thought of this, Ben presses his teeth into his lower lip. Paul does know almost everything there is to know about his family. Ben's pill problem, his mom's alcoholism, his dad's depression. They're all tangled up like sailors' knots technically a knot is only a circle embedded in a three-dimensional Euclidean geometric space with Paul as secret keeper a knot invariant is a descriptor for knots that look topically different but are mathematically identical and the possible values of crossings and bridges for the knots Ben is faced with at present don't even get into the Alexander polynomial of the knot please please god please make Ben suspect that if Paul weren't also an idiot, he could solve this whole mystery over a Dunkin's coffee.

So why the hell won't he?

"Are you sure we're doing the right thing, Claude? I feel off-kilter, like a thunderstorm's coming."

His mom is correct. There's been something in the air since Ben's father died, something toxic and stifling. He's shocked the flowers in all the sidewalk planters are still alive. It's tangible, the rotting taste.

"I'm serious," Trudy murmurs. "I wake up sick with worry every morning."

"But you love the gala! Come on, we have to put a brave face on this. What are you wearing?"

"I don't even care."

"Hey, hey there, pumpkin. It's going to pan out fine, I promise. How old were you exactly when you started bleaching your hair?" Claude's voice lowers suggestively.

Ben blocks out the next fifteen seconds through sheer force of will. Goodbyes are exchanged. *Saliva, too*. The front door closes.

He breathes, resetting the rhythm of his lungs. Listening. Trudy kicks her ballet flats off in the hallway, leaving them there. The fridge door opens. Wine *glugglugglugglugs* into a fancy stemless wineglass because Trudy likes both the opulence of Riedel and the youth of drinking from an expensive fishbowl.

Crawling out from under a grand piano is never dignified, Ben reflects.

He heads for the kitchen, pours himself an equally hefty glass of Sancerre but in a coffee mug, and follows his mother into her sanctum sanctorum.

"Hey, Mom."

Trudy whirls around, clutching figurative pearls. Ben almost smiles. She's highly theatrical—but she actually does that without thinking when she's startled, touches her slim neck in an antediluvian Southerner's gesture.

"Where's Uncle Papa?"

"Benny," she breathes. "Honey, you startled me!"

"You asked me over."

"That was *weeks* ago!"

"But the texts were vague about any exact time."

"I've been worried half to death."

"Whew! At least you didn't get all the way there, in that case."

Ben samples his drink. The sitting room at the back of the brownstone's first floor, speaking of *time*, is an ode to the fourth dimension. Steel clocks, bejeweled clocks, wooden clocks. Portico clocks suspended in arches, ships' clocks with nautical grips for elfin helmsmen, dial clocks from four separate centuries. Oddly, they bother him today. He generally finds them soothing, like taking an Ambien or thinking about being cremated. Look one way and there's a painted grandfather clock, look another and a porcelain timepiece representing an entire English garden.

Found that gorgeous little gal stuck behind a counter at a junk store in Johnson City, Texas, while the car shop was fixing my flat, his dad used to boast. **Surrounded by army surplus and Mickey Mouse mugs. But she'd taken this set of clocks and shone 'em up so pretty, anyone could see they were her pride and joy. Boy did I get her number quicker than an eye can blink.**

Of course, that was before the sweeping off of feet, the successful modeling career, the business degree, the transition to powerhouse socialite. Currently she's head to toe lululemon in dusty pink, with her buttery hair swept up and her blue eyes wide. Ben's mother burns so richly, she turns everyone in the room into an insect. When she slides her arms around him, he can't help relaxing into a haze of tuberose.

"My poor sweet boy, I heard that Claude delivered some of

your father's office things. I didn't know how to deal with them, and you weren't answering. I had no idea how you were feeling about . . . the situation between Claude and me. I *had* to get your attention."

Ben steps back. "My attention was gotten."

Trudy takes him by the elbow, puzzled. "What is this you're wearing?"

"Oh. It's a chunk of Dad's signature belt. Wedding rings seem to have lost their significance, so I sorta thought I'd do what I could to make up the deficit."

His mother's face goes carefully blank.

"What a, what a surgical choice of words, Benjamin. Here I've been devastated, taking comfort where I can find it—god knows not from my son—and then when I do finally get a visit, it's for you to refer to me as a deficit. Would you speak this cruelly to anyone who *wasn't* your mother?"

Ben downs half his wine, reflecting on his complete pigheadedness in approaching the familial stronghold without a wingman.

Sometimes instant surrender saves hours. "Sorry. I'm kind of not through the Kübler-Ross stages, you know?"

"Of course I know, honey. I'm your mother, I've called, I've barely thought of anything else."

"Except Uncle Claude."

Her back straightens. "Yes, I know I ought to exist for your grief alone, but what about when you won't *allow* me to be close to you? Hmm? Don't blame me for turning to my closest friend after my son has already shut me out."

Closing his eyes, Ben allows himself five seconds of the dozens of time machines (aren't they that, in a way, machines about time?) going relentlessly

clickclick tick click click clock ticktock click clock clickclick
      click clock ticktick
tock clickclickclick clock click click click click-

click   click   clickclick   click   tockclick
click click click click   clock   clickclick   tock   click click   click   tick
click tock tick   tock   click

and tracking seconds that feel horrifically out of whack before trying again. His mother once estimated owning seventy clocks. If it were even seventy-one just now, a single addition to the museum, he'd choke to death on his own throat.

"How's your collection?"

"Benjamin, if you're just going to deflect when I bring up real feelings, then I don't know how we're going to get anywhere. My collection is fine. I found the sweetest little baby Plato calendar clock last week, a nineteen-oh-two model. I almost texted you a picture."

Trudy points to a squat timepiece on the coffee table, drawing her bare feet up under her on the couch like a vintage bathing beauty. The cube of glass in its brass case displays two numbers, a month and a date, that flip if you wind them with a key. They used to love hunting for these temporal treasures together at flea markets. The shapely chronometer on Ben's desk was a graduation present from her, a Victorian striking lantern clock. Trudy inscribed it with a quote from Saint Augustine:

"THERE ARE THREE TENSES OR TIMES:
THE PRESENT OF PAST THINGS,
THE PRESENT OF PRESENT THINGS,
AND THE PRESENT OF FUTURE THINGS."

"I love it," Ben admits. "That is a seriously useless clock. You can know exactly what day and month it is, like, *all day long.*"

When his mom smiles, the old understanding sparking, Ben can almost forget she betrayed his dad's memory by marrying his uncle.

(ALMOST)

Facts. No more feelings. Feelings are like chum to his mother, and he loves her endlessly, but her teeth are very sharp.

"You stopped the police investigation into Dad's death."

"Of course I did." Trudy stares into her wine. "Your father loved that theatre company almost as much as he loved us. Do you think he'd have wanted it to be torn apart by petty rumors just when we needed support?"

"Your marrying his brother would accomplish that waaaay faster."

Her cheeks flush. "I thought this was about the police, and my allowing them to cease investigating."

"Yep. Without consulting me."

"Benjamin, honey," she sings, "do you *know* how worried I was? About how any little thing could send you back to . . . well, we won't talk about that catastrophe. I know it's not good for you."

Do not bite. Disengage.

"Dad made videos about people being out to get him. Before they got him. They were in his box of office crap."

"Oh, my sweet precious son, I didn't know how to tell you this. Paul showed them to me *ages* ago."

Ben wishes he could do something other than gape.

She knew. She didn't believe him, either. She knew this whole fucking time.

"God, Benjamin," she groans. "You were so *angry*, and I couldn't convince you that your poor father was sinking into delusions, and I thought if Claude brought them and you found them yourself . . . I couldn't tell you, not when you've made it so *clear* you need distance. You had your memory of your father in perfect health, but I began to lose him years ago."

Tears spill down stark cheekbones. Ben wonders whether, if he dismantled a clock and stabbed himself in the neck with the minute hand, Trudy's tears would increase to hysteria or vanish in the wake of supernatural mothering skills. It strikes him as fifty-fifty. She's good at split-second decision making.

His head pounds like a blown speaker. The fuzzy dread ampli-
fies. It's the clocks. But he loves the clocks, it *can't be the clocks.*

clicktickticktickclicktocktocktockclicktickticktockclickclickclicktockticktickticktock-
clicktockclicktickticktockclicktocktocktocktickclickclicktick

Ben pops a pill from the Klonopin bottle as Trudy watches,
unsure whether it's more strategic for her to be hurt by this action or angry over it. He quickly tires of watching her run the
odds in her head.

"So, Dad was going senile and you skipped telling me. Neat."

"You're being so critical. Is it a coping mechanism?" Trudy
presses silver nails against her temple. "This is the most difficult
time that I have *ever* gone through, honey, but I'm the mother,
I'm not allowed to have feelings."

"You're having them, like, right now."

"But I'm not allowed to *express* them, am I? How are we
supposed to talk if I'm continually in the wrong?"

"I—"

"Look at you—your weight, your pills, that morbid *shackle*
on your wrist, it's all screaming that you aren't up for learning
what my life's been like since you and your father both essentially left me. Now you're going to be punishing me for months
for even mentioning your father's decline, when you're the one
who *cannot* handle it."

BREATHE blink BREATHE blink BREATHE

"OK!" Ben cheerily claps his hands. "Let's discuss Dad's decline."

"Absolutely not. *Later*, maybe, when our heads are clearer."
Trudy shakes her head. "I'm too hurt, Ben. I love you more than
anyone will ever love you, I'm your mother, but everything we
argue about lately regards who I am as a *person*. It's exhausting,
honey."

"Actually, by definition, everything everyone ever argues about is regarding who they are as a person. As in, how they're acting. If we stopped having arguments about who people are, there would be no arguments. Just, I dunno, debates about systems of economics and which one is the hottest Jonas brother."

Trudy leans over, lifting a pocket watch resting with several others in a dish. She's opening her mouth to answer with something emotionally castrating when the

$$S$$
$$\qquad W$$
$$\qquad\quad J$$
$$\qquad N$$
$$\qquad\qquad G$$
$$J$$
$$\quad N$$
$$\qquad G$$

of the little timepiece sends Benjamin's heart rolling away like a marble.

"That's it." He lurches forward, chest tight. "That's what I saw, *that's* what's been eating at me, Christ, it's like a fucking maggot in my brain."

"Benny? What's the matter?"

He'd reply, but Ben absolutely cannot stop seeing:

THE DREAM HE HAD LAST NIGHT THAT HE ALMOST
TOLD HORATIO ABOUT BUT NOT REALLY
BECAUSE HE JUST REMEMBERED IT FULLY:
A DRAMA IN ONE ACT

In the deepest darkness, Ben fell through a crack in his sleep. He scuffed in gently bruised twilight through twigs and decay, surrounded by a forest festooned in spiderwebs. The sun was setting faster than usual. Either the Earth's rotation had hastened, or else something fouled the atmosphere.

He wanted to turn back.

But he didn't know where he had traveled from.

And he wanted to speed up and arrive.

But he didn't know where he was going to.

He was as free from directional orientation as Einstein's equations (true weightlessness is indistinguishable from free fall). All Ben knew was that he was headed somewhere *as the scratches and chitterings of the woods grew louder.*

The land fell off into a bayou with a promontory. He stood high above this finger of solid ground. Near the edge of the miniature peninsula was a monstrous tree, millennia of rings curled up in its trunk, crowned with enormous garlands of glowing spidersilk. When he saw Lia step out of the woods, he understood.

This wasn't his dream. This time, he was in Lia's.

She was a young Lia, perhaps ten or eleven. Her face was round and constellation-freckled, her eyes huge. Ben's tongue tasted Lia's name until he remembered how little she liked sharing dreams with him.

So he stopped.

Jórvík Volkov's grey head emerged from the lake. Then his long, drawn, hangdog face, then his wiry neck, then his slumped shoulders. He was dry and unhurried as he walked up the shore. When his hand became visible, Ben saw a plain metal pocket watch swinging, a prelude to a trick he'd seen the man do a thousand times.

Lia's mouth opened wide enough to split her face from ear to ear.

"Hallo, pretty little thing." Jórvík stood on the green shore, lips moving as pendulously as the hypnotist's prop. "Are you ready for the magic show?"

Lia scrambled away, spine hitting the mammoth trunk. Ben had seen Lia terrified before. But he'd never realized how frightened she was of their theatre's head custodian.

Why are you horrified by a janitor?

"For you I have made many times things to disappear. Yes?"

Jórvík held in his other hand, as if he were playing poker, a series of wallet-sized school photos. They were all little girls, chubby cheeks and skinny chins, all smiling.

"You choose a card, and I make her disappear. If you do not choose a card, more will vanish. So choose."

Ben did not know what kind of sick game he was watching. But he did remember headlines from those years. The sort of headlines that could happen anywhere, in any small town, in any huge metropolis, always terrifying.

CHILD REPORTED MISSING FROM
MORNINGSIDE PARK
SEARCH CONTINUES FOR EIGHT-YEAR-OLD GIRL
PRETEEN VANISHES FROM UPPER WEST SIDE

It was Jórvík.

Ben didn't know this because he understood it. He only knew it because somehow, in her mind, Lia did understand.

Ben leapt forward. He clawed up thick, dripping hunks of earth to get to her. Lia was shrieking without making a sound. Fixated on Jórvík's watch moving closer . . .

And closer . . .

And when Jórvík dipped the watch into her open mouth, she swallowed it down to the very end of the chain.

FIN

"Oh god," Benjamin gasps.

He's on his mother's couch and her hand is on his face. So small and so soft, like worn linen.

"Honey, what is happening?" She's frightened. *He didn't mean to frighten her.*

"A dream. No. The memory of a dream that wasn't mine."

"What the hell did you just take?"

"Brain candy."

"Do I need to call an ambulance?"

"No, they don't come for dreams." He sits up. "Especially if they aren't yours."

"My sweet boy—"

"Don't you understand, I *can't* control this? Dreams are a *short film*, and you can't even close your eyes because the dream is fucking *behind them*. They were bad enough when they were mine."

"Benjamin, honey, dreams can't hurt you," Trudy pleads.

Ben steps over spilled wine and ceramic mug shards. Probably of his making. "Apparently they absolutely can. But this is also a panic attack. Which . . . well, does feel exactly like dying."

"And you would know, after all."

Ben rubs his hand over his wrist cuff. "I . . . Jesus Christ, Mom."

Trudy instantly looks on the verge of tears. "God of course, of course I go and blurt out the wrong thing. We were so close once. Will it ever come back? First you try to leave me on *purpose* with a knife to your own wrist and then your father sinks into a paranoid depression. You both just . . . departed. You all at once and Jackson by degrees. If it weren't for your uncle, I don't know what I would have done. At least Claude is *sane*."

Shaking his head, Ben runs, he *runs*.

He pelts away from the clocks, throwing the front door wide and leaving it gaping like a wound.

LIA

Love is a funny thing shaped like a
   lizard,
Run down your heart strings and
   tickle your gizzard.

—*traditional New Orleans blues song,*
   Gumbo Ya-Ya: Folk Tales of Louisiana

O
H, HOW I WISH you'd been there!" Robin, at his ease in an
overstuffed armchair, shows milk-white teeth. "Here's the
groom confessing his love for the divorced ex-stepmother
of the bride—and to think if I hadn't been so tragically careless,
she'd never have discovered her picture in his wallet at all—the
bride being sedated, groom weeping into his flask. Already
pocketed my fee in advance, naturally, can never tell with weddings, what?"

"Not when *you're* running them, *mais non*. And here you
turn up at our doorstep, nursing your wounds?" Mam'zelle
reigns from the ornate parlor sofa, her curves draped in mauve
velvet.

"Comical notion! Didn't breathe a word about personal in-
jury. To correct all misapprehensions: I am here to *celebrate*, old
friends."

"Ain't so very old, us," Moma notes from the ballet barre

installed against the wall. Sweat glints from the deep scoop in her racerback shirt.

"Aren't you?"

"Nor so young, neither."

"Timeless as the winds, that's my sisters!" Robin pushes his tissue-thin sweater up his forearms, squinting at the dress sock he's darning. He always seems to have a needle in his fingers. "Only meant to say that I bodged together an annulment, a whopping lavish destination elopement, and a perfectly swish reception for the *new* happy couple! Quite the coup, eh?"

Mam'zelle rolls her eyes while Moma's nose crinkles.

"Bitter fruit," Maw-maw rumbles from the kitchen. She fans the neckline of her linen dress, hovering over a vat of oyster stew. It's another garment inspired by a trash bag that costs four figures at Bloomingdale's. Ever since Robin turned up, she's been cooking and making weirder than usual pronouncements. Deviled eggs and rice-stuffed baked tomatoes rest on the dining room table. Onions, celery, and bell pepper have been sizzling like hellfire.

"Every fruit turns bitter in the end," Robin teases.

Lia can't figure out whether the sisters are friends with the newcomer, enemies, ex-lovers, business associates. So she sketches, listening. The flower market this morning was a blur of violently yellow ranunculus and delphinium of a blue she could drown in. Now she sits at her artist's nook, pothos vines surrounding her, sketching a new installation.

It's the first she's attempted since she came here. It terrifies her in the way she imagines pregnancies are terrifying. Exhaustive and excruciating. But for the first time in a long, weary while, she feels compelled to *make*. As if a long-dormant virus woke up. Normally her sketches here own all the purposefulness of a cat stretching—she does them because she always has.

But this. This is a plan.

Lia adds leaves to the braided vine-monster she's drawn. She hears his progress in her dream last night, squelching through the mud, and she moves to touch her mother's strawberry-stitched scarf. She's been wearing it for days. Months, maybe? Is it years now? But she remembers with a pang that she couldn't find it in her attic room after her post-market nap. It's wedged under a pillow or lurking in the folds of the bed. It's not here to defend her.

"How did the four of you meet?" Lia calls.

Moma answers upside down, one leg on the barre. "We lot met back in N'awlins. Professionally speaking. He put around he's a 'wedding coordinator,' is how come we get to know him, working the same circles."

"Working from different ends of the same circle." Mam'zelle smiles. "If you follow me."

"Amen to that, my sister," Moma snorts.

"Circles within circles," comes Maw-maw's rasp.

"Indeed," Robin purrs. "I am a wedding coordinator in *precisely* the same way you ladies are florists."

Putting her pencil between her teeth, Lia squints. She's never been very observant, physically speaking. Whether the light switch was on the right or the left in the hotel bathroom, what color the waiter's eyes were. She'd be crap at a murder investigation. Earrings wander off, MetroCards vanish, Ben huffed in frustration when the electric bill went unpaid and unseen.

Spiritually though, Lia has been through enough to be a goddamn water witch, and her divining rod is twitching.

The sisters' floral arrangements are careful, intricate, meant to influence. They nudge people in a desired direction; sometimes they downright shove. Every time, they tend toward resolution—a person really does get well soon, a contrite philanderer is forgiven, a happy birthday is indeed enjoyed. Robin seems remarkably akin somehow to Lia's friends. But he's shared several anecdotes, and they all involve havoc. A wedding day ends in disaster. A sweet sixteen party catches fire. An anniversary dinner hurtles into divorce.

If you're at opposite ends, but the shapes are circles, how are you meant to know which side you're on at all?

DEVİL POD: *Used to reverse jinxes and to repel evil intentions back upon the sender.*

"So you had new business last night." Mam'zelle's liquid brown eyes slit. *"Félicitations et bonne chance."*

"Yes, matters are certainly . . . percolating. In fact, I met a chap on the flight here from London who may have something to do with it."

"Why you say so?" Moma inquires.

"Was bloody well sat next to him, wasn't I! Never a coincidence. Great brawny Anglo-Indian fellow, eyes dark as temples. Handsome chappie, could've sworn I was sat next to a young Naveen Andrews. Poor lad was bloodsick as anything to boot. Could smell it from the boarding gate, my darling duckies."

Mam'zelle clucks. "Bloodsickness . . . you ought to have said, *cher.* That could end up in tragedy if *someone* doesn't mind their manners."

"Leads to no end of trouble," Moma agrees.

"No *end* of trouble." Robin looks up from his sewing, winks. "If we might only be so lucky! And would I could soak in your spiffing company all the lazy day long. But I've appointments with the client who imported me here and simply must see whether I happen to bump into my transatlantic acquaintance en route somehow."

"Stirring the pot, you," Moma states.

"Not at all. Beginning to gather the threads, what?" He snaps his needle free with sharp canine teeth, and a shiver drips down Lia's spine.

"Have you anything else to share, you sly critter?" Mam'zelle prods.

"Safer to let the pages of the love letter unfold, as it were. Chummy of you lot to let me kip here, though. Always game to take in a stray, it seems."

Lia feels Robin's eyes scorch like a sunbeam across her face.

"Eh, la la, don't be ridiculous." Mam'zelle pats the nimbus of her hair. "We don't allow *gens du commun* above the Three Sisters' Floral Boutique."

"Apologies for any unintentional insult, then. I've not put you out, have I?"

"If space is what's needed, we ain't got no end of it, us." Moma saunters over to the sitting area, sipping from a rainbow-patterned water bottle. "There's room after room after room at the Three Sisters'."

Lia knows this is true. When she couldn't be with Ben anymore, the last spectacular disaster already played out, the sisters installed her in a tiny third-floor bedroom. It's like a princess's mullioned tower, and like a dragon's glittering cave.

"Limitless occupancy, eh?" Robin spears a fresh glint of emerald through the needle's eye.

"The bedrooms might be full, but this settee's surely welcoming," Mam'zelle agrees.

"Settee might be occupied, but ain't that couch in the flower shop plush." Moma adjusts the towel around her neck.

"Room in the oven, nice and toasty," Maw-maw calls.

"Maw-maw! For shame! *Comment peux-tu dire ça!*"

"Maw-maw, when you took your pills this morning? Lands sake, what I'm gonna do with you?"

Robin grins, fingers moving like silverfish. Lia has no idea where he slept, having gone straight from her childhood bedroom to the flower market before pale lines of dawn had even scarred the sky, but the sisters have a seemingly endless supply of space. Their rooms swell to suit them. The two floors above the flower shop are walled with recessed shelves groaning with exotica, esoterica, erotica, idols, cookbooks, crystals, antique perfume atomizers, and one statue of the Virgin Mary decked in Mardi Gras beads. Lia was exploring once and came upon a baby grand piano. She never found it again.

Moma has sidled up behind Lia, pressing thumbs into her stiff neck. Happy sparks shoot down her spine. "What you scheming and dreaming, baby girl?"

Lia frowns at her sketch. She woke up to her dad's bedroom door open, a curled lump under the quilt, and the sweet rhythm of his snores. The awful pictures of Ben's mom and his uncle were gone. But her rising panic had surprisingly little to do with her hapless father, or even the Dane family.

Moma used the right word, because she was dreaming again. Dreaming of *him*. The urge to get this vision out of her system and into artwork is like the desire to vomit up poison. Art scrapes off toxic sludge. Telling stories to save her soul—her mom's slow cancer arranged into floating flower biers, her own clawing guilt rendered in thistles and thorns.

"Our *petite chère* has been like this ever since she lugged all those juniper branches home," Mam'zelle notes.

JUNiPER: *Symbol of the fertility goddess Astarte in Canaanite lore, an aid to sexual health and virility; burned for its aromatic smoke in rituals of sanctification and purifying.*

"Wouldn't even take a buttered biscuit, just grabbed her colored pencils and set *to*," Moma agrees as she studies the rendering.

After her mother died, Lia fashioned miniature funeral pyres from iris leaves and seed pods, gave them twigs for masts, and sailed them to their watery doom. Which led to the middle school display of the 3-D floral arrangements with their frames rendered in metallic Sharpie against the gym wall. Next came the rotting sofa she transformed into a planter, and the anatomically immaculate little girl's skeleton (freeze-drying enough white rosebuds to wire together proving the hardest challenge).

Artistic purging of emotion vanished after the final calamity. Why recite tales of failure when you've already lived them a hundred times over? When they were all your fault? She buys product for the sisters, tries to help Moma with the serious gris-gris and gets shooed affectionately away.

This is art, though.

I forgot how fucking painful art is.

"You saw this, my *chouchou*, in your mind's eye?" Mam'zelle is hovering now, too.

"No, I had a dream, and it felt like this."

The sketch shows Lia lying under a huge tree draped in sickly green tinsel. A hideous golem composed of swamp detritus looms at her feet. Spanish moss slithers from the ground like roots, binding her arms and legs to the earth. A huge clump restrains her neck.

"*Love* it," breathes Robin from behind the pair of sisters. "She ought to plan events with me—there's an entire tale here just for the looking."

"Mademoiselle Lia's our own perfect angel, so just you scram," Mam'zelle coos.

"Our baby ain't no lousy event planner, her," Moma brags, sliding coconut-scented arms around Lia's neck. "She's a *visionary.*"

"But with such an eye for *narrative*!" Robin insists. "Why, the events she could orchestrate from behind an executive desk in an all-chrome office. Nation building, regime toppling—"

"*Tu es villain parfois,* you sick thing," Mam'zelle hisses.

"Even weddings," Robin chuckles. "Which are, as we well know, the hardest of all. Have you ever been engaged, me duck?"

"Have I *what* now?" Lia returns.

Moma snips a creeper of ivy off a hanging basket and starts weaving it into Lia's thicket of hair like a crown.

"Oh, topping!" Robin rubs his hands together. "The heart-shattered always plan the very best events."

"She is never heartshattered," Mam'zelle snaps, crossing her arms. "It's broke, it is not in shards. *Tu comprends?*"

"Her man, he loved her so." Moma releases the ivy. The leafy diadem is as secure as it would be knotted into lambswool. "We saw for ourselves, us."

"My sister, we surely did," Mam'zelle agrees.

"Can this topic maybe be tabled indefinitely?" Lia wonders, her throat contracting.

"This scar what she carries gonna be *powerful*," Moma continues as if she hadn't heard. "Because *such* a love that was! Mmmm, I shiver just to think on first seeing them."

Lia hides her burning face in her sketch. Because she remembers it too, her debut gallery opening in Alphabet City. A white birch tree suspended by its roots from a ceiling with real grass affixed to it, hundreds of crystal-speckled filaments strung from branches to sod, the rain falling endlessly upward. She wore a tattered ivory maxi dress like a Grecian ruin, Ben passing her glasses of champagne while she soaked up the accolades.

He whispered in her ear, *It's too magnificent to exist.*

It's normally necessary to have connections, to rub elbows and kiss ass, to get a gallery show. But for Lia, somehow everything fell into place. This always struck her as vaguely bizarre. And yet . . . The three sisters were always present. Among the art lovers, minor critics, and people who liked free prosecco and cheese cubes. Lia remembers the women who would save her vividly, though she didn't know why at the time. It was like recalling someone from the future. Mam'zelle wore a coral-pink blouse and massive hoops, looking like a sculptor or printmaker. Moma was in a black velour Sugarhigh jumpsuit with a scandalous neckline, obviously a local yoga instructor or psychic. Mawmaw was dressed in a raw silk sack, clearly an eccentric art-hoarding millionaire. They fit right in. And yet they didn't, somehow. They carried their own space with them.

They were all looking at Lia when Ben whispered, *You're also too magnificent to exist.* But they were gone when he said, *I'd*

*have married you under that tree, I shoulda called, what do you
need, a priest these days or just a notary or something?* Later,
after they'd laughed and made love and two of his fingers were
still inside her, he said, *You know I love you everywhere, but I
think it's everywhen, too. Every universe. In all of them at
once, I love you the same.*

"That boy loved her as hard and as long as he could," Moma
continues. "Till it was once too much too many and he couldn't
no more. And every time she kissed him, he found *I love you too*
behind her teeth."

"So when our *petite chère* came to hard times, we nursed her
like our own," Mam'zelle concurs.

"Please, I can't talk about this," Lia begs.

"It took a long while to get the devil out of her, spooning her
broth and sugared tea." Mam'zelle sighs, unhearing.

"Some might've called us crazy, but we knew her *spirit*, and
what I'm gonna do when I sees a busted work of art on the cement? I'm gonna glue it up, me," Moma affirms.

"OK, actually, I'm not a work of art, I'm a fire in a trash can,
so you really shouldn't have," Lia chokes, feeling sick. "I never
fully understood why the hell you did."

"*Why* did we? How you say that at us?" Moma cries.

"Why, we loved you from sight, precious girl." Mam'zelle
grips Lia's shaking hands in her soft ones. "*Un coeur comme un
artichaud.*"

"Heart *just* like an artichoke, lord bless me. A leaf for everyone," Moma explains. "Your man, did he ever adore you for it.
He'd have torn down the stars just to spell out your name with
them."

Lia rips herself loose. Rises, blind and clumsy.

"Quite right! Perfectly reasonable to be cross with them,"
Robin crows, white hair gleaming as he cocks his head. "You
ought to come over to my side. Shall we commence your career
as an event planner this evening, or would morning suit better?"

"Fuck you very much." Lia shoves her drawings under her arm.

"Don't get your knickers in a twist." Robin rocks on his heels, golden eyes twinkling. "Fortunes are grown from the mulch of broken hearts. Well. *Misfortunes*, rather. Made several myself."

"Misfortunes or broken hearts?"

His teeth when he smiles are predatory. "Only offering you a piece of the pie, what?"

Lia flees. She nearly collides with Maw-maw in the kitchen, the older woman holding a tea tray with a mad gleam in her eyes.

"Sausage puff?" Maw-maw offers.

The hall is only three yards off. The distance passes like the Sahara. *A drink, I need a drink.* She could have swallowed every drop of Ben for the rest of her life and still found space in her belly for a pint of whiskey. She remembers biting skinny hip bones, choking him eagerly down, everything in her brain quiet for the blessed seconds that were only about breath and love. Ben in awe, always in awe, that she *wanted to.* And she did. Ben might have been a sarcastic bastard at times, and a morose lump at others.

But he was also the single most generous person Lia had ever encountered. And for Lia or for their friend Horatio, he'd have walked into the middle of the Long Island Expressway.

When she reaches the stairwell leading down to the shop, standing there bereft with a sketchbook under her elbow, she realizes that she desperately needs a specific task.

Tasks are very important.

Enough tasks in a row, and Lia will stop feeling this way.

Jessica Anne Kowalski.

Her rapey ex-boyfriend is not going to eliminate himself.

She charges down the stairs, past where the sign is flipped to **COME AGAIN PLEASE**, and down the claustrophobic, dim metal flight to the flower storage and deliveries basement. The wedding vases live here, the chicken wire and floral tape, the candleholders, the water buckets for armfuls of larkspur and cherry blossom and iris and much stranger plants.

LARKSPUR: *Flower to lift the heavy spirit, raise hope, loosen the tongue for laughter.*

CHERRY BLOSSOM: *Impermanence in Japanese culture, useful for changing streak of bad luck or unwanted situations.*

IRIS: *Named for the Greek goddess who linked the heavens and the earth by means of the rainbow; planted over women's graves as a beacon to guide them to the afterlife. Nothing more powerful for ensuring that your message reaches its addressee.*

Oh, and the altar. The altar lives here, too.

From a few yards away, it just looks like someone with a very strange aesthetic styled a table. A glass vase contains no flowers, but instead anisette liqueur—licorice floods the air whenever one of the sisters tops up the heart of the shrine. But when you come closer, things get pretty weird. Eight cups of plain water surround the central chalice. That would still look like décor, maybe, without the shallow abalone shell, a dish of birdseed with satiny feathers sticking out, the husk of a cockroach, the skeleton of a mouse.

There's the symbol too, hanging above. It's a pentagram. Inside the pentagram is a five-pointed star. Inside that star is another five-pointed star, and so on. Lia once tried to count them and afterward vowed never to let her eyes linger on the goddamn thing again. Sometimes Lia suspects there are infinitely smaller and smaller stars in the symbol. It reminds her of Ben trying to explain how since a black hole forces its tens of solar masses into technically zero space, it has literally torn a gash in the fabric of space-time.

Ben.

Ben, what are you doing right now?

Lia wishes she could cry. The way she started to upstairs. She loses the ability at the oddest times, when she needs a snot-drenched sob fest. Then a week later, she'll watch a life insurance commercial and have a graphic meltdown.

The sisters can't possibly know how it feels to be so craving alcohol that you start eyeing the antiseptic in the bathroom cabinet, calculating. Or to drop a wine bottle, break the neck, and still drink straight from it, just *very carefully*. And they don't know how it feels to lose someone by accident, like a cell phone or a credit card.

The mantra returns, as certain as sunset.

Pick a card, any card, what's the harm?

You killed them, you as good as killed all of them.

There are no excuses for the things that you've done.

Lia goes to the computer to look up Jessica Anne. They haven't had an order this detailed in months now. Those who sense something mystic about the shop tend to drop coded words like *sympathy* or *romance* or *get well*, and the sisters always send them off contented. But this is going to get *highly* specific. Herbs, prayers, the smallest words etched along the thickest stems in the obscurest tongues. Moma has about two dozen oil blends stashed down here, and on days when she mixes them, the place is heady with myrrh, vetiver, almond, and lily of the valley.

Soft footsteps behind her. Fearing it's Robin, Lia turns.

"We done pushed our lamb too hard, my sister," Moma says sadly.

"*Je suis désolée*, sweet girl, truly so," Mam'zelle apologizes with hand on heart.

Maw-maw stands with her arms crossed, nods.

And this, *this* is what sets Lia crying.

"There's nothing to be said about my broken engagement." Her face burns with searing tears. "I don't remember anything, you *know* I don't, I was supposed to be on a plane, bags packed, and then I almost fucking froze to death and then you dragged my useless carcass inside and nursed me and then four days had gone by without talking to Benjamin. Not even a text. I can't talk about the worst thing I ever did when I can't *remember* it."

"Anything you have feelings about surely can be discussed," Mam'zelle replies.

"This not-talking ain't doing you no good, child, and you been doing it for two years." Moma moves her braids behind her shoulder.

"Yes, well, I was catatonic when I arrived, so," Lia whispers. "Maybe I still am. In a way."

Occasionally she wonders why the sisters didn't take her to an emergency room or call an ambulance. But nothing they do is normal, and Lia feels safer here than she ever has shaking till her bones clack on a hospital bed.

"That sketch you just finished, *chère*?" Mam'zelle points an elegant finger. "That is about your *history*. These two years you've kept your head down and fetched and carried from the market, and this is what we *waited* for."

"That weren't for no client." Moma shakes her head. "That weren't a dozen red roses with a splash of voodoo nights oil. That there who you really are. Gotta be shown, Lia, for you to be any use to you, use to *us*. Gotta be *aired*."

"For Christ's sake, why? I already *lost* everything. I can never go back to Ben, to my old life."

"We got stakes in this our own damn selves. Trust in that. You ain't got no fairy godmothers, Lia, believe me when I *say*."

"But what is the point?"

"You gotta understand where you come from, baby girl, or how you can know where you aiming to get to?"

Lia laughs. "Where did I come from? I barely had a mother, my dad's grief was like a straitjacket, we owe everything we have and are to another family, and I . . . I had secrets. Cruel ones. I had alcohol. It helped me to drown them. I had Ben, and my art, and now nothing."

"That's a whole lotta nothing to have to carry around on your back," Moma observes. "Heavy load. Plenty enough nothing for a lifetime of talking over."

"Fine," Lia snaps. "You three couldn't be any more mysterious, not if you walked around in Mardi Gras masks. Where do *you* come from?"

"I'm descended from French royalty and Negress slaves,"

Mam'zelle answers, "the *crème de la crème* and the dirt under their feet. My ancestors were plantation men in tall silk hats and barefoot quadroons so beautiful they could stop your heart dead in your chest. That's a lot of nothing on my plate too, *chère*. But all Creole stock were *sorti de la cuisse de Jupiter*, and Jupiter's thigh lives in me still."

"I grew up with poor white Cajuns in the deep woods, me," Moma replies. "Where I come from ain't nobody recall, but they done taught me to fish for shrimps and oysters, cure sunstroke with willow tree branch and kidney stone with a swamp lily. Little black child belonged to everybody and nobody and some folk fed her and some folk whupped her and that's a whole bag of nothing to carry around. But I can tell your future from which way the steam in your tea rises."

"Devil shaped me from clay and fucked me to life with his red-hot tail," Maw-maw rasps.

Her sisters' hair stands on end.

"There ain't no *way* you been taking them pills right!" Moma shouts.

"Maw-maw, *quelle honte*, have you been smoking the Moroccan again?" Mam'zelle cries.

"You talk sensible now, or you *get* on back upstairs!"

"*Dieu me donne la force!*"

"I come from nothing and going back to nothing," Maw-maw sulks.

A collective sigh of relief sounds.

"That's better—lord above."

"Beg pardon for my sister, Lia, *jamais* have I seen her this bad."

Lia laughs helplessly, the tears no longer burning her. She can breathe. She is sad, very sad, but she is also safe. She's wearing an ivy coronet and this is all ridiculous. These sisters who aren't really sisters, who talk like no one she's ever heard. In fact, they talk like Lia imagines N'awlins residents spoke a hundred, two hundred years ago.

"All right," she coughs. "I'll keep sketching. But I had a shitty night, OK? No more chitchat about Ben."

The sisters, comically contrite, nod as one.

"I, uh, came down here to study up on Jessica Anne Kowalski. We're making her bouquet day after tomorrow, yes?"

"*Mais oui*, and we must do all we can for her, my sister," Mam'zelle clucks.

"Oh, have I looked forward to *this*, sister mine," Moma chuckles.

"I really can help you this time, then?" Lia hopes.

"You just try *not* helping me and see where it gets you." Grinning ferally, Moma plants a kiss square in the middle of Lia's brow.

Something knotted loosens inside her. It hurts, but a pain like moving a stiff muscle. Shaking a sleeping limb. Jessica Anne Kowalski deserves their help. Tasks are what's needed, tasks are her friend, and these women saved her. And certainly these voodoo-infused bouquets are harmless objects, it's impossible for them to have any real power, but the *belief* Jessica and others feel simply after laying that much cash on the table . . . it gives them confidence.

Nothing works better than an outrageously expensive product, so long as you trust that you got what you paid for.

Anyway, they're works of art. And works of art genuinely can accomplish miracles.

Lia doesn't feel happy. But she's so much more settled by the time they've been consulting for half an hour about scents and charms that she nearly stops seeing Ben's final handwritten letter to her. The sisters handed it over almost as soon as she woke up, retching. They didn't say a word, just shook their heads. It's been floating before her eyes like the afterimage of a photograph stared at too long and too longingly.

I loved you then. I love you now. I love you everywhere, and everywhen, and after what you did this time, I can never be with you again.

How am I ever going to recover from something like this?

HORATIO

There is enough
human suffering in you
to collapse a building . . .

—*Robert M. Drake, "Enough Is Never Enough"*

HORATIO POKES A CYLINDER of eggplant rollatini he suspects was prepped last week. Italian food does well with a spot of refrigeration. But these ingredients are less infused and more . . . coagulated.

"Please stop being mad at me." A miserable Benjamin sits opposite at a booth at the City Diner, an old haunt of his and Lia's and sometimes Horatio's, too. After-hours hash brown aromas and the clanking of pots fill the air. "I know I'm a complete piece of shit, but it's soooooo painfully loud."

A tall man wearing all black save for a ludicrously long white apron shuffles up, refilling acrid coffee. Ben keeps glancing at him, the way one might look at a curious zoo animal. The hoary old fellow has stark, tanned features. He puts Horatio in mind of those enormous scraggly seabirds that dive for fish.

"What's the story about that one, then?" Horatio wonders when the server ambles off. "You persist in staring."

"Lia and I used to come here, like, a lot," Ben answers.

I know that, Horatio doesn't say.

"We obsessed over where this guy was from. He's not Muslim or Jewish, we once saw him eating an unedited Cobb salad. He always mumbles, but it's no language we'd ever heard. Lia decided he was from a place called Bulvmania and made a whole map with French fry landmasses, ketchup war zones, parsley forests, torn-up Equal packet lakes, and salt and pepper beaches."

Horatio smiles. A gush of sad fondness suffuses him. He always protected Lia like an older brother might, even when he wanted to borrow her skin for a disguise.

If there were a hell instead of accumulated goodnesses and evils, you would be heading there this very minute for that thought.

"Oh my god, that's the first time your eyebrows have parted ways with your cheekbones in, like, an hour, thank you." Benjamin pushes away half a club sandwich. "I never *mean* to hurt you."

The fury returns, hot and humiliating, and Horatio clanks their plates together mid-table.

"Sorry, come again? You didn't mean to ditch me while I was starkers, or fail to come back till ten at night, or be off your bloody gourd when you did?"

His friend collapses tragically. "It was an accident."

"It doesn't matter."

"I'm kiiiind of sure it does, because people do not schedule panic attacks for right when they're chatting with their moms about their dead dads and their taint stain uncles."

"Sorry, carry on then with the vanishing and the general larking about, and I just won't ever get angry about it. Would that suit?"

"None of this suits!"

"Yes, and I recall wanting to assist you, not wanting to come out of the loo with a towel over my knob only to find a wisp of air curling upward like a vanished cartoon character."

"Oh yes, I *asked* for this to happen. I can even see the future and know impulsive decisions will work out badly."

Horatio waves his hands like a referee stopping a football bloodbath. "When you're like this, you're . . . you're awful. You're dismissive and self-pitying and truly difficult, do you know that?"

"Everyone has been telling me I'm terrible company since I was four, so yes," Benjamin snaps.

Horatio very nearly rolls his eyes. He knows his friend's history the way he knows *Leaves of Grass*, but at some juncture in every person's life, he believes, they must stop blaming spilt milk and traffic jams and yes, their own dodgy behavior, on what happened before they had reached double digits.

"Um. Listen please, every human in history is difficult at times, but you're turning your version into something extraordinary. You aren't a martyr or a devil or a saint, so if you can, stop sodding acting like any of them. Just own the mistake, apologize, and exist in the middle for as much as ten seconds."

"As I mentioned to Mom earlier, I physically cannot always conform to societally acceptable parameters, so—"

"You might not always enjoy life, but absolutely everyone else feels the same way," Horatio growls. "Sometimes it's harder to be utterly brilliant and a bit mad, yes, but in other situations, it's harder to be dense as a brick, so buck up."

"Sure, pull up the bootstraps, as it were. Spoken like a very neurotypical . . ." Ben pauses coldly to consider. "'Pillock,' I think is the word you would use. Derived from 'pillicock,' meaning dumb as a rooster? Yep."

Horatio takes a calming breath, nodding in apology. "Forgive me, that was . . . quite horridly unfair. I *am* absurdly neurotypical. But, Benjamin, please. You *can* listen when I'm stroppy with you, say you're sorry, *not* climb up and strap yourself to the rack, and bloody well carry on."

"That's the drill, then? You explode, I'm contrite, game over?"

"It isn't a sodding game, and I've every right to be angry," Horatio hisses. "And not just about this."

Benjamin's eyes widen almost comically. "You want to talk about *that*? In, like, a diner? Wow."

"No, I want you to understand I'm this furious because I was worried sick. You want me to stop whinging? Fine, lovely. I don't *give a toss* about you anymore."

He drops his napkin over his plate while Benjamin gnaws a fry. Horatio feels his muscles uncoil. He's broadening as he always does in America, wide shoulders winging outward. A Greek family a few booths away chatter among themselves. They remind him of his own kin, with an ache like sugar hitting a bad tooth. An elderly couple sit opposite, bowls of soup between them. To the right, a burly bearded man frowns ferociously at a newspaper. Horatio thinks he knows why his friends liked coming here. You could be anyone and not look out of place because City Diner wasn't anyplace in the first place.

Where's a better spot to feel perfectly at ease than nowhere?

"Do you see that, by the bar?" Horatio juts his chin.

Benjamin's reddened eyes flick sideways. "Damn."

The waiter sips a light beer as he sorts through his receipts.

"So, no restrictions on alcohol in Bulvmania. Could be a solid clue. Thank you."

"Not a bother."

"Horatio?"

"Hmm?"

"I could totally do that."

"Sorry?"

"I'm gonna apologize to you without either nailing myself to a cross or hiding in a nuclear bunker. And I'm sorry for sneaking away to visit my awful, wonderful mother."

"Cheers. All's well." Horatio is genuinely touched.

"Won't happen again, swear to god." Benjamin pushes thumb and forefinger against his nose. "It was a three-ring shit show."

"Considering your views, God is an odd one to swear to," Horatio teases, aiming for the fondness to return.

"What are my views?" Benjamin asks dryly, recovering himself.

"Oh, um . . . that God is dead and we murdered Him, some-thing along Nietzsche lines?"

His friend blows on his burnt coffee. "Well, not exactly. God is our explanation for entropy."

"You've mentioned this, I think. And that means?"

Benjamin squares his lecturing shoulders, sits up straight.

Good, thank you, that's better. Horatio wills himself not to see Benjamin as he was a few hours ago. Unconscious whim-pers, unconscious twitches as he rocked on the sofa. Horatio begging to know what the matter was. Benjamin begging him back *I can't I can't, you'll drag me to the sixth floor and lock me in, it could only have been a dream, or the drugs, please let it have been only a nightmare.*

I will be your straitjacket, Horatio thought frantically. *Put your limbs in me and anchor yourself. I can do this for both our sakes.*

"OK. Presenting my 'God Is Entropy' lecture, one-oh-one. Carefully place a distinct layer of oil over a layer of water and you're looking at a very simple system," Benjamin declaims. "Black sand on white sand in two segments, an ice sheet floating on water. All of these configurations are pretty uniform."

Horatio manfully battles the urge to sigh. "Benjamin—"

"Wait, look, exactly like cream and coffee—you can layer cream on top of coffee if you're careful enough." Holding an open plastic creamer over his mug, Ben struggles to look dis-tantly ironic. "But after this very careful layering process I'm not attempting, if you stirred it, you'd get a completely brown liquid. That's another fairly featureless substance. Everything mixed evenly, also quite basic. Like, pumpkin-lattes-and-pottery-with-cheerful-words-on-it basic."

"Is this leading anywhere? Because—"

"*This,*" Ben persists, "the creamer *outside* of the coffee, is before the Big Bang, if you can even say there was a before the Big Bang, which we can't, because did time itself exist? Probably not. *This,*" he continues, adding the creamer and stirring it with still-trembling hands, "is the cold eventual death of the universe when everything is motionless freezing nothingness."

"I thought we were talking about God."

"We are. I started with the idea of two distinct layers and I ended with a homogenous liquid. Both are nail-gun-to-the-head boring. But suppose we'd just done that creamer pour in a clear glass, with a slo-mo camera."

He rests his chin on his palm. Horatio might be impatient tonight, but he is also helpless to resist when Benjamin paints these surrealist dreamscapes that somehow seem more tangible than everyday life.

"Picture the plunge of white into brown, the initial swirling, the impossible labor required to accurately track, like, every atom as it shifts and eddies and fucks and permeates and penetrates this frankly maaaaaaybe eight-hours-old substance they call coffee. Vector after vector, unimaginable complexity. Sublime chaos along the way to being featureless. That's God, my friend."

Horatio nods, beginning to understand. And as ever, the way Benjamin sees the universe isn't quite scientific, and it isn't quite spiritual. It's an unholy marriage of the two that must reverberate through his head like a cathedral organ.

"The universe began and will inevitably end," Ben says, staring at his mug. "Cream outside of coffee becoming cream stirred into coffee. But for a flash, right at the outset? Unfathomable intricacy. Michelangelo. Isaac Newton. The Beatles. We're in the swirl, Horatio, and it's so complex that we invented God to explain its *purpose*. It doesn't have one. God is chaos before it reaches uniformity. God is Beyoncé and Richard Pryor. And we get to see it."

"I think I'm looking at it right now," Horatio says before he can stop himself.

The words float in the air between them. If Horatio could breathe, which he can't at present, he would breathe them back in. His pulse starts hammering. He's usually more careful, and he can't un-say it, Benjamin would remind him that time doesn't work that way.

You utter shite, now you've gone and done for us both, haven't you?

Benjamin stares very hard at the tabletop. There's a brush-stroke of warm blood over his cheekbones. When his lips move, the smile is sweet and sad and *something else*, and Horatio's feelings are everywhere at once, in his brain, in his fingertips, his groin, the left side of his chest.

"People think it's defeatist or lazy to say *que será, será*," Benjamin tells him softly. "But it's a scientific fact. These lives we lead, we were always going to lead them that way. It's just how the cream was poured."

If there weren't a table covered in cold diner food between them, Horatio would be kissing his friend with one fist in the back of his shirt and one cradling his head already, propriety be damned.

"You're saying that no matter how hard we try, divinity shapes our ends, and that divinity is random chance?"

It's terrifying, and beautiful in the way most terrifying things are.

"Entropy," Benjamin corrects with a smile that could raze city blocks. His lifts his coffee. "This particular entropy tastes like ass, by the way."

"What the . . . no way. Oh, Christ guys, it is *so* crazy to see you both here!" comes a new voice.

"Benny, what is *up*, it has been too long!" another chimes in.

Horatio's and Benjamin's eyes raise as their mouths drop.

"Er, hullo," Horatio manages. "What on earth are the pair of you doing here?"

"Rory!" Benjamin exclaims. "Garrett, what the hell?"

"Right, dude, it's *so* random!" Rory Marlowe exclaims.

"What are the odds?" his twin brother, Garrett Marlowe, crows.

Or perhaps it's the other way round?

"Seriously. A divinely instigated accident." Benjamin grins, edging over in the seat. "Well shit, sit down, you bastards! How are you?"

Horatio mirrors his friend as the new pair slide into place, both leaning and clapping Benjamin's back. He isn't upset by seeing the Marlowe twins, exactly. He's had copious laughs in their company, and copious alcohol to boot. But they were finally fucking getting somewhere, he and Benjamin, *finally*, so Rory and Garrett's appearance is as enraging as it is mystifying.

Where Benjamin is chiseled and blond, the twins are slab-jawed and what Horatio imagines when he pictures the descriptor "raven-haired." And where Benjamin is astronomically rich, Rory and Garrett are merely flamboyantly rich. They are already finishing each other's sentences and egging Benjamin on. The Dane heir has always liked them because they're genuinely funny and clever. But Horatio has always been ambivalent about them because he and his parents are in debt to Columbia and Eton for a stupefying figure, and he doesn't wear three-hundred-quid shoes, so they ignore him.

As they're doing now.

Horatio feels his hands curling into what resemble fists. He relaxes them, shocked at himself.

"And then that time in Professor Bob Cordell's class, oh my god—"

"When we had to present the theoretical physics proof we'd been trying to write based on a philosophical text—"

"Such a bullshit assignment. 'Search for a core of provable mathematical truth in the wildly romantic or speculative.'"

"Professor Cordell was so far up his own ass, he could check for strep throat."

"And here you are in front of the class," one of them says to his brother, "talking about quantum physics and their curled-up minuscule dimensions—"

"One dimension in particular, right, and finding a way of accessing it—"

Horatio doesn't know which twin sits next to him, Rory or Garrett. He supposes it doesn't matter, as there won't be a quiz, and he yearns to throttle them both equally. To his extreme alarm.

I shall have humility and amity for all.

Recalling that one of them uses *right* as a verbal tic, he decides that's Rory from now on.

"Then you get to the part about using an as-yet undiscovered particle to access this quantum dimension." Garrett hunches forward in glee.

"Right, with plenty of Einstein shit about light speed and bending space thrown in." Rory giggles helplessly.

"And preserving the mass and energy profile of an object, and Benny here raises his hand and says . . ." Garrett concludes with an invitational flourish.

Benjamin is smirking when he supplies, "'Even supposing you could build a hyperdrive, how are you going to navigate hyperspace without a map? It ain't like dusting crops, boy.'"

The twins are the definition of mirth, faces contorted and arms flung. Horatio smiles faintly, reflecting that while he never would have survived switching his master's over to philosophy of physics, he really ought to have given it a go.

Think of all you missed whilst fretting over the triangular slave trade.

"'Without precise calculations you could fly right through a star or bounce too close to a supernova,'" Benjamin continues quoting as the Marlowe twins howl, "'and that'd end your trip real quick, wouldn't it?'"

"He did it just like that too, totally deadpan." Garrett's face flushes, which resembles a distressingly handsome sunburn.

"Right, no Harrison Ford impression, just straight called us out on trying to build the *Millennium Falcon*." Rory wipes wet lashes with a napkin. "Professor Cordell was too confused to even be pissed, never having seen *Star Wars*. I swear to God that man was born in a bunker."

Twisting, Benjamin calls out, "Hey, man, not to interrupt your break, but could we get two bottles of wine for the table? Like, the very finest of your red flavor? Thank you. You're in for a treat, guys. This will be the best wine within eight to ten yards of us. So." Benjamin straightens as the rail-thin waiter drops four wineglasses on the table with one hand. "I thought you both took tech gigs at Google's main Silicon Valley campus?"

The twins are going a mile a minute again. Horatio wonders whether they remember his name. When he and Benjamin used to throw parties, they'd never interact much. Horatio would be chatting up less stunning but less straight men, or skiving off with Lia to sip from a bottle of gin on the fire escape, talking of art history, or each other, or Benjamin.

Lia. It's coming back in a great pounding rush, the way they all used to be together. Because he loved Lia, before, deeply loved her. It was impossible not to love her, with her pale freckles and regal profile and that hair like fireworks on New Year's Eve. She was funny and kind and utterly brilliant at the oddest things, and she never laughed when she didn't mean it. Ever. That alone was worth loving. He can see why Benjamin did, he always could do.

A stone forms in Horatio's stomach.

"A toast," Benjamin proposes, raising his glass. "To old friends in unexpected places."

"Hear, hear," Rory proclaims as the four of them clink.

Garrett flips through menu pages. "Their coffee is listed as 'our legendary coffee.'"

"That's totally accurate, and they should be congratulated for managing to brew coffee in a vat of dead fry oil," Benjamin comments. "Guys, though, seriously—what are you doing here?"

A strange neutrality infuses Benjamin's tone.

Garrett goes back to the menu while Rory examines the wine bottle's label. "We're spending a week in the city, man. Old stomping grounds! We were going to look you up but running into you like this is more fun."

"Way more fun," Benjamin concurs, blue eyes squinting. "I mean, I didn't see you at Dad's funeral, that would not have been the slightest bit fun, but I assume you're maybe coming to the gala, so at least you won't miss Mom's wedding reception, which will be suuuuuper fun."

"We didn't really know how to bring that up." Garrett rubs the back of his head, abashed.

"Oh, so you're not *surprised*, then." Ben's lips are closed as he smirks, but Horatio can sense the sharpness of his teeth. "Interesting. Seeing as the marriage is not, like, public knowledge. Not that I'm gobsmacked the Marlowe family knows about the blessed event, since Mom always considered you folks primo inner circle. Kinda shocks me she didn't ask you to be Dad's pallbearers. Oh, wait, *I* planned the entire memorial. That's right. Slipped my mind."

"It sucks, Benny," Rory offers quietly. "It all sucks. But yeah, our whole family is still on her invite list as donors to the theatre, and she does still keep in touch, and our folks are stuck out in Cali, so here we are."

"We weren't sure if you wanted to discuss it—"

"But we're so sorry."

"It's cool, at least I won't have to, like, struggle to remember my new stepdad's name," Benjamin purrs. "OK, so. I am a ready worshipper of the gods of chance, I was just talking with Horatio here about that, but this is really all an accident?"

"Of course." Garrett frowns.

"Right, why wouldn't it be?" Rory adds, topping up their glasses unnecessarily.

Benjamin links his hands on the tabletop, shrugging. "I dunno, you remember that time toward the end of grad school when Mom wanted to make sure I wasn't popping too many pills for finals and she bribed you to go through all of my shit?"

"Jesus Christ," Horatio marvels aloud.

He knew that Trudy was invasive, and occasionally obsessive, but this is beyond what he'd pictured. The twins exchange moderately mortified glances. As if they had been caught copying each other's exam answers, or pissing in a pool.

"Man, that was beyond unfortunate." Rory spreads his fingers on the table.

"Absolutely ridiculously invading your space," Garrett agrees.

"But Trudy was *worried* about you. Finals at Columbia are no joke."

"It sort of felt more like an intervention than it did an invasion?"

"But we're sorry. We didn't realize that you'd caught us."

"Noooooo." Benjamin bats his eyelashes. "You didn't. I made sure Mom did, though, and she was out of my fucking hair for a solid three months, which were among the sanest of my life."

The Danes are beyond dysfunctional; Benjamin loves his mother. Horatio can hold two thoughts in his head at the same time. But there's a sharply plucked bass note of rage here, and it sends ripples through the grotty house wine. Benjamin himself looks surprised.

"Hey, Benny, we apologize," Rory offers. "As much as we might have intended well—"

"And been too out of our own minds with finals to really think it through—" Garrett continues.

"And walked away with season box seats to the Yankees," Benjamin notes.

"Right, we regret it now." Rory nods.

"Not cool, bro. Not at all," Garrett agrees.

Horatio watches Benjamin deliberately calm himself, softening. Lia always said she loved Benjamin Dane because he wanted to plunder the world's secrets to the last molecule and abandon it entirely, all at once. In more intimate moods, she'd talk about his giving nature too, about how far he'd go for either of them, which was probably somewhere in the Andromeda Galaxy. But it's *this* for Horatio, the devastating sincerity, that ends him. No matter how many times Benjamin's been spit on, nearly drowned in a school loo, taken to hospital for fractured ribs, he can still be shocked that anyone would betray him. And then he can forgive them. Benjamin fundamentally doesn't understand greed or disloyalty, even when he's being mildly vicious himself.

"Yeah, I get it," Benjamin sighs. "I worry me, too. Anyway. Enough of this shit, so you're going to the benefit gala?"

"Wouldn't miss it, man."

"Those swag bags alone."

"What was in there last time? Bottle of Pappy Van Winkle, limited edition Swatch, a spa weekend?"

"Yep, those three items in particular do sound like my mother," Benjamin agrees, but his tone is calmer.

"She kills it every year, right? It'll be an amazing event. Horatio, my man, you're down too, right? It's like the gang is back together."

Rory swings his eyes lazily. Now that Benjamin has relented, Rory's arm is thrown back over the booth, and Garrett has melted forward over his wineglass, a matched set of Roman princes poised to be fed grapes.

"Um," Horatio replies. He doesn't know whether he's more shocked that Rory wants him to be there, or that Rory addressed him.

"Yep, he's absolutely coming." Benjamin finishes his wine, studying the dregs. "Just working out the, like, salient details."

"Outstanding," Garrett crows.

"Epic," Rory concurs.

"Agreed," trills Benjamin, and he leans over to grip his friend by the wrist.

Horatio flinches inwardly. Benjamin's hand on his frozen limb is delicate and guitar-calloused and encased in a leather cuff. An inner storm is brewing, and he doesn't know whether the maelstrom will turn out to be a blizzard, a monsoon, or a tornado. Horatio only knows that if one more bloody butterfly flaps its wings in Taipei, a category five event will erupt in his aorta.

Benjamin lets go. The moment lasted how long, a second? Two seconds?

Ten or twelve lifetimes, give or take a few millennia.

The twins are making plans with Benjamin for a proper mutton lunch at Keens the next day. It's intended for the four of them, but far from feeling glad of gaining the twins' attention, instead Horatio feels as if he's fast losing something. Benjamin isn't going to blink at him in that gentle way with the Marlowes around or smile like he means to say something. Horatio wants to lash out at them like an angry animal battling for a mate, with teeth honed and claws curling.

I bow down to those who have reached omniscience in the flesh and teach the road to everlasting life in a liberated state.

I bow down to those who have attained perfect knowledge and liberated their souls of all karma.

I bow down to those who have experienced self-realization of their souls through self-control and self-sacrifice.

The rest of the conversation rolls over him like a thundercloud. And then as abruptly as they came, the wine is gone, and the twins are taking their leave.

"Yeah so, again—totally amazing seeing you." Garrett slaps Horatio's back and grips Benjamin by the hand.

"I'm fucking floored. Tomorrow is going to be *awesome*." Rory repeats the gestures.

I hate the Marlowe twins, Horatio decides with clean satisfaction. *They get on my wick like absolutely no one in the continental United States.*

The Greek family departs likewise, and for several seconds, a bleary bustle occurs. *Goodbye, goodbye, thank you, come again, thank you.* Benjamin is waving and Horatio copies him, just to be polite.

"Um," Horatio attempts, turning back round, "what were we—"

"Something's rotten, and it's not tonight's fish special," Benjamin announces, scowling in thought.

Horatio closes his mouth, raises an eyebrow. His friend taps an odd syncopated rhythm with his fingertips. Nearly a minute drifts into the aether, lost for good.

"Yeah, nope, this doesn't add up," he declares. "For them to want the cannabis seed moisturizer or the weekend in Barbados or whatever Gwyneth Paltrow–approved horse puckey Mom put in the gala bags this year, sure, I buy it. For us to run into them in the city? Sure. For us to run into them *here*? You, me, Lia, we all used to wind up at City Diner. Rory and Garrett used to end up at Rose Bar convincing Victoria's Secret models to blow them in bathrooms. No way in hell were they like hey, you know what I'm really feeling? *A Denver omelette.*"

Benjamin is right. He might firmly believe in coincidence, might even be said to deify disorder, but there's such a thing as probability.

"You think they want something?"

"Nah, I didn't say that."

"What, then?"

"I think my mom always wants something," Benjamin says slowly.

Horatio is beginning to think Trudy Dane might be the craftiest soul he's ever encountered. It's the mirror opposite of his own experience. Once upon a time in mid-April, Horatio's mum found a copy of *Gay Times* magazine tucked in a padded coat (in the pocket further from the wardrobe door, no less). She'd been trying to determine whether Horatio needed new winter wear because she could get it more cheaply off-season. Horatio had completely forgotten the magazine existed and still recalls the helpless quake in his limbs before his mum threw her arms around him and started crying first.

"You can't meet up with us for lunch tomorrow," Benjamin declares.

For an instant, Horatio is hurt. But his friend has a calculating air, the one he gets when he's mastering a lick on his guitar. Benjamin reaches for the empty wineglasses and begins arranging them like a general who's moving pieces on a war map.

With entirely too much enthusiasm.

"I," he decrees, shuffling his forces, "will rendezvous with the Marlowe twins for lunch. Kiiiinda want to feel those guys out. You," he continues, sliding one glass away from the other three, "are going to the theatre offices and surprising Paul Brahms, because he'll say different shit to you than he will to me. And then you're going to my tailor in the Garment District, Vincentio—I'll find the address, I have an account there—and getting fitted for a tux. You'll love him."

Finished, Benjamin surveys his plan of attack. He looks quite chuffed with himself. He fiddles with the cuff on his wrist as Horatio's hackles rise.

"So, er. You just . . . decided that, then?"

"Yep."

"Without, you know. My input."

"We did skip that part, yeah."

"Since when do you order me about?"

"Since we're investigating my dad's murder."

"Well, yes, not to downplay that at all, but who the hell do you think you are?"

"Here's what good actually came of my little matronly escapade." Benjamin leans forward, pale brows darting like sparrows. "I so happened to be under the piano when that sploot of gastric juice Uncle Claude was taking his leave."

"You . . . sorry, you *happened* to be under the piano?"

"Exactly. And as he left, he said he was going to see Paul about me, because Paul told them that we'd watched the tapes. But Paul likes you—everyone likes you. And he trusts you— everyone trusts you. And Paul knows seriously everything. So you're gonna go ask him questions and then get fitted for a penguin suit while I have a shamefully expensive lunch with the Marlowe twins."

"And what if I've no bloody intention of allowing you to dress me up like a Ken doll?" Horatio demands.

"C'mon! You'll be, like, a *spy*. And get outfitted for a tux by *the* Vincentio, dunno his last name. You'll be the Gujarati James Bond."

"Kindly shut it, there's a good lad."

"Please do this for me." Benjamin is using his *I've whole oceans in my eyes and you haven't any life preserver* routine, and none of it is remotely fair.

"No. There are limits, Benjamin."

"Pleeeeeease?"

"Sod off."

"It would be so *good* of you to do this for me." Benjamin angles his head. "You would make Jina for sure, my man."

"Oh, bloody hell."

"Dude, you would so escape the life and death cycle it's not even funny. This would clinch it completely."

"Do you know, I rue nothing more than I rue the occasion that I *ever* made you acquainted with the religious beliefs of my ancestors."

Benjamin does his classic head toss and barks a laugh. "Does suffering help with the total consciousness thing too, or is it just about being awesome?"

"Suffering can't hurt. So to speak."

"See, so this is also perfect in that way, then. Well, not like I want you to suffer *unduly*. I promised you a hottie chorus boy, an entire Whole Foods produce department of carefully selected male—"

"Benjamin."

The tone is far too urgent, and his friend scrubs his face with his palm once, twice.

"What?"

"Er, that's not . . . Hang it, that isn't why I'm here." Deliberately, Horatio relaxes. The smile he offers must look molded from plastic. "Let's . . . whatever else we may do, or not do, I'm frankly a bit preoccupied by the task at hand."

"The murder investigation?"

"No, not precisely."

Benjamin chews his lip before fully comprehending.

"That task being, to put it bluntly, me."

Horatio can't trust himself to speak. So he doesn't.

Blue irises gentle. "Which don't for a single instant think I fail to value beyond . . . like, half my inheritance. Whatever that is. Hell, the entire thing. So. That means you will do it, then? Or you won't?"

Horatio sighs. The waiter of mysterious origins drops the check, and Benjamin has his card slapped down before he can even fish his wallet out of his trousers.

This bloodsickness condition you suffer from? It's fixated on an absolutely irresistible total prick.

"Fine," Horatio concedes.

"Excellent!" Benjamin leaps up, all focus and angles again, lost puppy demeanor entirely forgotten. "Let's get some shut-eye. I'll find Vincentio's address in the morning. It'll be a super rush job, but this dude is used to handling people like Jared Leto, I win Customer of the Year awards by comparison. He'll get it done. He's amazing."

"I've not the slightest doubt."

"Horatio?"

He pauses as he slides out of the booth. "Yes?"

Benjamin's eyes are icicle points. "Then *we'll* get it done. We've got this, you and me. Just watch."

"One question."

"Yep?"

"Supposing that we *do* find out that your uncle Claude was in fact, well . . . Hang it. Your father's killer? What are we to do about it if he is? Your mother . . . I mean to say, this is all very complex."

"Tell me about it."

"But what's the *plan* of action if it's true?"

"I dunno. Good question. I murder him, save all those legal expenses?"

Benjamin slouches his way toward the door before Horatio can begin to process whether he was joking.

The air is too clear to be anywhere else but aboveground, on the gum-scarred streets. So they walk home. A beggar with a cat on a leash whimpers and Benjamin hands him a fiver. A rat scurries by, sleek and beautiful and muscular, while an emaciated woman in a sequined mini-dress sobs on a bus stop bench.

They reach their building and trudge up the stairs. But they don't go to bed at all. When they've flicked on the lights, Benjamin decides George Harrison is in order and pours whiskey and pulls out his guitar. Horatio doesn't object, can't object. It's practically all he ever wanted, watching Benjamin cradle the Silvertone Teisco shark and coax rasping purrs from its body, if only Horatio didn't also want so very, very much more. Flashes from the street flicker white, then red and blue, back to white again. Emergencies surging and fading like the sudden leaps of his pulse.

"You're well knackered," he observes, swirling the ice in his glass. "God knows you ought to be. You don't have to entertain me, you realize."

"Sure, I do." Benjamin's mouth tilts up. "Just. Our dinghy on the stream of time is sailing faster than I'd like it to."

Two o'clock drifts into the past, and then three, and then god only knows when, until it occurs to Horatio that his friend's guitar isn't the only one gently weeping. Even though none of the tears are visible.

BENJAMIN

An intellect which at a certain moment would know
all forces that set nature in motion, and all positions
of all items of which nature is composed, if this
intellect were also vast enough to submit these data
to analysis, it would embrace in a single formula the
movements of the greatest bodies of the universe and
those of the tiniest atom; for such an intellect nothing
would be uncertain and the future just like the past
would be present before its eyes.

—*Pierre-Simon Laplace,*
A Philosophical Essay on Probabilities

THE NEXT DAY STARTS off—as is now to be expected—
unbelievably shitty.

Ben had stupidly forgotten how often he nibbled
smoke-tender meats in the identical corner booth at Keens with
his own dad across the table. Sitting still and small and awkward. Like a frozen rodent. Judgment radiating down from the
dead-eyed portraits and equally dead deer littering the dark
wood walls.

Just walking through the door was a full backhand to the face
with grief. Ben reels with it. Not to mention shame and a sen-

sory download dump that could fill a hard drive the size of a car. Humans have no one particular organ devoted to the passage of time, which he finds odd—just a brain to record a jumbled amalgamation of the other five senses, smeared with watercolor emotions and stained by subsequent data. But here he is, at Keens again, and the movie reel won't stop playing.

You all right over there, son?

Yeah. M'good.

Well. How's the situation at school, then? You standing up to people, letting 'em know they can't push you around?

"There's no way in hell." Rory scoffs, glaring at his twin.

"A law degree is a natural career path for philosophy students," Garrett argues, flicking a napkin onto his lap. "God, I missed this place."

"So is getting some cush think-tank gig."

"You really think we can land jobs sitting on a rock growing our beards out?"

"Not a rock. An ergonomically sweet office chair."

"What about you, Ben?"

"For work? I was teaching," Ben answers.

"You always were a bleeding-heart liberal," Rory teases as the waiter pours champagne.

"Yeah, I was trying to staunch the bleeding, actually. Cauterize it with meaning."

"How'd that go?"

"Poorly."

Are you trying to figure out their angle right now, or are you showing them your updated Useless Douchenozzle CV? Make them feel comfortable, idiot.

Ben ignites a smile like a bonfire doused in lighter fluid.

"Enough about my craptastic attitude, guys. Weave me tales of sunny California and garlic festivals."

The twins oblige. Ben feels his shoulders sink in relief. There are

                                        too many past forks scraping
        too many past napkins refolding
            forcing their way into the present like
                                        sociopaths in a schoolyard
                        too many of
        these dropped spoons   these yes another, thank yous   these no,
        just the checks   these a few more cubes, pleases

Eight-year-old Ben clumsily forking mashed potatoes into his mouth. Jackson Dane checking his Rolex, reading *The Wall Street Journal*. Rubbing fingers still strong and splayed from his stint as a Longhorns quarterback against his Texas slab of a jaw.

Thing about bullies, Ben, is they're the world's biggest cowards. One push and the whole act crumbles. But you gotta push first, right?

Benny? You push anybody yet, like I told you to?

And push 'em real hard?

The problem with these attempts at happy healthy hale fatherly family fun time was that Jackson Dane was godlike. He was a fossil fuels millionaire on the cover of *Forbes* and of *American Theatre*. He'd done guest spots on CNBC's *Squawk Box* and on NPR's *Fresh Air*. Power, wealth, fame, a crooked cowboy's smile while his eyes glinted like a senator's.

Jackson had everything. Except for a common language with his only son.

Jackson tried to talk sports, and it was laughable. Jackson tried to talk theatre, and it was nearly as ridiculous. Ben tried to talk music, and math puzzles, and space exploration. This was before Ben had any knack for talking at all; his selective mutism as a child was anxiety-based. All mangled up in the ADHD and the general terror of BEING ALIVE and thus MAKING MISTAKES and thus LOSING EVERYTHING. But his silences, those revolting *gaps* in his speech, still made him look stupid and feel harrowingly alone.

And it is

F
 U
  C
   K
    E
     D

      U
       P

to be sitting at Keens like some blue-shirt stockbroker enjoying the legendary mutton chop. Ben never gave a damn about food in his life.

You fucking moron, you're supposed to be investigating. Concentrate.

"So then he says no, *I* put the sock in the microwave," Garrett concludes, grinning.

"It was the only thing left from the laundry that wasn't dry!" Rory protests.

"Dumbest shit I've ever seen."

"Hey, I wanted that sock dry, dude, and time is money."

Ben huffs. "Time's nothing whatsoever like money. When have you ever been refunded time, or saved it to spend later?"

Rory and Garrett flicker like ghosts as they blab doggedly on about cars and parties until Ben interrupts an anecdote about Megan Fox to blurt, "So when did you guys land?"

A glance is exchanged. Meaningful, for sure, but not decipherable to anyone who isn't a Marlowe twin.

"Night before last," Garrett answers.

"Right, made it in half an hour early," Rory choruses. "Good thing too, we had Google meetings in Chelsea."

Ben feigns a pout, aware it's unconvincing. After all, he only pouts for Horatio. "And you weren't gonna text me? What with everything that's been going on? Harsh, man."

"New phones," Rory explains apologetically. "We were going to shoot you a Facebook message."

"Cool," Ben returns, freshly suspicious.

"Hey, don't be like that," Garrett says. "We're really so sorry about your dad, Benny. We're not good at this shit—"

"At all," Rory adds.

"But we're here for you now, no question."

The twins start talking memories of Jackson Dane, and now Ben's about ready to slice himself open and ask if the chef would like to serve a rare variety of tartar this evening. Jackson might as well be the fourth man at the table. Six foot two inches, sandy-haired, sharply grey-eyed, leonine brow. Taking up half the air and all the atmosphere.

"He was legend, you know? You want that last piece of bacon?" Garrett asks.

"Knock yourself out," Ben hears himself saying. "Do not allow that poor delicious animal to have perished in vain."

Benny, hey there, kid. Miss you.

We never did see eye to eye on much, did we?

Shutupshutupshutupshutup, Ben thinks desperately.

But I swear to God, son.

Here I told you that my brother killed me in cold blood, and you're playing your fucking grab-ass games with your grad school buddies?

"Right, she might have been the hottest thing going," Rory admits, "but she was also obsessed with my feelings. Sometimes I'm not having any, you get me?"

"Heh," Garrett agrees.

"You're both single right now I take it?" Ben prods.

"As the lone pine," Garrett replies.

"Get any last night? Gimme the full monty. You two were always a menace at the clubs, don't tell me you haven't tapped anything yet, it's been, like, almost forty hours."

The twins broadcast identical leers across the white porcelain side dishes Ben hasn't even pretended to touch.

Why the hell did I hang out with these pricks—oh yeah, be-cause they were better at mathematical physics than anyone else in the program. It was the philosophy bit where they sucked goat balls.

"Nothing major, dude." Garrett takes a slug of champagne.

"But we were at the Electric Room, right?"

"And these French girls, I kid you not, they were absolute *tens . . .*"

Ben's lips quirk as the Marlowes describe getting hand jobs in the same coat closet. Not because Ben is enjoying this story, and not because he's a prude, either. Horatio could crown himself Slut of the Year and Ben would be there with pom-poms, cheering.

Horatio.

He smushes that thought like a bug.

No, Ben's lips sit crookedly now because he's *got them.*

"Isn't the Electric Room on Sixteenth?" he interrupts.

"Uh, yeah, I think—why?" asks Rory.

"Then how'd you end up at City Diner? Please don't tell me it was for the coffee. You dudes are freaks, but I don't think you're into scat."

It only takes a fraction of a second for both men to pause.

**BUT BEN
HAS THEM
HE TRULY MOTHERFUCKING
HAS THEM
BY THE CAJONES**

"We were meeting these other girls at Ginny's Supper Club," Garrett replies too late.

"Hotter than hot chicks we actually hooked up with in Cali-fornia, and—"

"Guys, it was so good to catch up with you." Ben throws down his napkin.

"What?" says Garrett, paling.

"Let's say we, like, order some expensive crap we don't finish again soon? Those, what was it, frog craw-stuffed burgers you told me about aren't going to eat themselves, am I right?"

"Foie gras," corrects Rory nervously.

"What the hell, Benny?" Garrett attempts.

Ben is already in motion. He doesn't care—he can walk to the offices from here, clear his head, and catch Horatio as he finishes up with Paul Brahms. The door swishes shut behind him, sending atoms and air molecules and dust and photons crashing around like Molly addicts at a rave.

Entropy, Ben reflects as he enters the sunshine, sliding on Ray-Bans. *Regrettable, but necessary for my purposes.*

Too goddamn much pussyfooting around in there, kid.

But you made it in the end.

I totally did, didn't I?

What I don't get is why you didn't confront those assholes, show a little authority for once.

Because I don't want them reporting back that I'm onto them till I know more. Especially not if it's Mom. Let them think I'm bananas, a whole banana boat, as long as they keep playing their cards.

You never did learn how to confront your peers, did you?

And after all my advice. You are one sorry excuse for a son.

Ben glances back at the steakhouse, eyes swimming. His entire being pulses with the memory of his irretrievable, unreachable father.

"Bye, Dad," he whispers aloud.

HOPE BUDS IN BEN'S chest, straining through the soil. *Everything is solvable.* He doesn't need infinite intelligence to know the wind is blowing north-northwest or to tell a pigeon from a power tool. Ben genuinely doesn't remember the journey across midtown when the doors go *swoooosssh* and he's in a building composed of sterile white light, sterile white marble, and enough filthy secrets to stuff a Chinese landfill, he's convinced.

"Benny!" Ariel is overseeing a pallet of deliveries, but his face rumples in a fond smile. "Been nice to see you around so much the past few days."

"Oh my god, I'm such a shithead!" Ben exclaims, making the older man frown in confusion.

Ariel Washington. *Why* didn't Ben think of consulting Ariel Washington? The best thing about Ariel Washington (other than Ariel being a fantastic guy and a sobriety counselor and a stellar guitar player in the style of Charlie Christian) is that Ariel is the second person—other than Paul Brahms—who has his fingers on every pulse point of New World's Stage. Doormen are like that. They deal with everyone and everything that comes in and out of the door, after all. So they own a

CERTAIN

OMNISCIENCE

ENTIRELY BY DEFAULT.

"Sorry, long night. You'd be OK talking with me for a few minutes, wouldn't you, Ariel?"

"Sure thing. Walk with me—if I don't get this mail room organized, Mr. Brahms gonna lose his shit."

"That happened, like, eons ago."

They stroll through the lobby, with its aggressive air-conditioning and its immaculate potted palms. Ben remembers his first tour of this place. His dad's chin-jutted enthusiasm, **we're building a legacy here, son,** and how somehow it made him feel smaller to be part of a legacy instead of larger. Like he wouldn't measure up. The expansive mail room is just around the back of the front desk, and when they arrive, Ben grins in delight.

"Leave it like this, oh please leave it like this."

It's clearly crunch time for the benefit. Two days out, and the place looks like the 34th Street USPS on Christmas Eve, clogged with the staggering accumulation of shit that goes into hosting a charity gala with a silent auction element and legendary swag bags. It smells overwhelmingly of cardboard and chaos. Ariel taps his pen against his lip.

"This some kinda side visit? You got business with Paul, I take it?"

"Oh, well." Ben shifts, realizing how sheepish this is going to sound. "I actually sent Horatio to do that."

"No kidding? That's an eighteen-karat friend you got there. But why send him to see Paul?"

"Paul has, shall we say, a very distinct take on my mental stability."

Ariel's eyes nearly vanish when he chuckles. "Mr. Brahms got a very distinct take on everything, way I see it. So then what're you up to? Coming from a late-night set or something?"

"Ariel, you know I'm not really a musician, right?"

"'Course you are." Ariel makes a *hah* of discovery, moving two boxes to the opposite side of the room. "You got heart and brains. S'all it takes."

"Well, some would argue talent is also key," Ben objects, though the compliment warms him.

"Practice is worth fifty times what talent is. And practice requires stubbornness, and you as pigheaded as they come."

Suddenly enervated, Ben sinks down on a biggish box. Yes, he is stubborn.

But.

This is all so exhausting.

He was hardly the mascot for good cheer before, but those struggles had to do with not mattering. Suddenly he matters a great deal due to his dad's untimely end, and Ben feels like settling down in a warm laundry basket and sleeping till all of this is over.

Is that how Lia felt with me? Like it was too much and not enough all at once?

Ben shivers. Thank Christ after that disgusting panic attack at the townhouse, once the drugs and the hormones wore off, the nightmare itself flickered and fizzled. Ben couldn't believe he thought for a few minutes that Lia was the unwilling assistant to their serial killer janitor. Absolutely ideal material for a bad dream. Absolutely absurd notion after waking up and smelling the coffee grounds. He doesn't even know why he was so sure, only remembers that he *was* sure, against all rational sense, and that his mind can be a liar and a thief, and he hates it, and he should have brought Horatio.

Horatio.

OK, knock it off, that can happen later. Soon.

"What's eating at you, Benny?" Ariel doesn't turn from his inventory, but he's all attention.

"Uh, I don't really know what to say. Maybe you heard from Paul or someone that my dad thought he was being . . . stalked, threatened?"

"Mighta heard a rumor."

"Obviously I have to do something about it. And I have a pretty solid plan in place to learn more. It involves the gala and the part I'm to play in the, um, talent portion." Ben drops his elbows to his knees. "You know as well as I do that thoughts aren't to be trusted."

"Amen to that."

"So I need to find more proof, but. Everything is just so fucking weird since Dad died. Like there's this horrible patina on the world now. Grime coating everything."

Ariel peers at a label. "You feeling paranoid, you mean?"

"Well." Ben lifts a shoulder. "Like they say, if you look around the whole bus and can't find the crazy person . . ."

"The crazy person is you."

"There's something *wrong*," Ben says miserably. "And I don't know how to *fix it*."

Ariel lowers himself onto a box across from Ben. He has remarkable eyes, a mahogany brown, and suddenly the old friends aren't in a cramped mail room stuffed to the ceiling with objects that will eventually crumble into dust. They're in the back of a

warm jazz club
and the set is over and
it smells like phantom cigarettes and white-hot notes
the carpet is filthy the lighting is dim
and everything
is going to be just fine.

"Like a smell you can't find the cause for," Ariel prompts.

"Exactly, yes! Somebody put a *dead trout* in the trunk of the world's car, Ariel, and it's driving me insane."

Ariel straightens his nametag before speaking in his usual low, even tones.

"Grief plays funny tricks, Benny. Make a man feel locked in a cage when he's free as a cloud, make him feel alone with his loved ones. Grief is as inevitable as dying. It's natural. But you've seen your share of it."

Ben passes a hand over his stinging eyes. "Listen, Ariel, you can—you can help. I think. There are these videos my dad made, claiming he thought Uncle Claude wanted to off him."

Ariel's eyebrows swoop together, creating a picket fence of disbelief. "You gotta be shitting me."

"That would be, like, so incredibly amazing if this were one of my darkest jokes, but no. Paul Brahms claims to have recorded them himself. OK, so . . . here's my dad waving these *look out for fratricide* flags. But then Mom tells me that Dad was neck-deep in prescription meds and paranoia, so I need some sort of evidence before I go and ruin what's left of my batshit family."

Ariel's mouth brackets. "So you got a plan, and the plan involves the benefit. You wanna fill me in?"

Ben's temples throb. "This plan involves the element of surprise."

"Better to ask forgiveness than permission, that it?"

"Sure. Sounds about right."

"Then what questions can I help you out with?"

Ben chews on his words before asking, "Was my dad mentally disturbed, in your opinion?"

Ariel puffs out his cheeks. "Your dad, he sure wasn't . . . settled in his mind. Mrs. Dane worried him. Business worried him. *You* worried him."

"I—do you mind saying that again?" Ben stammers.

"Not being even a little bit stupid, you'd do best to quit acting the part," Ariel advises gently. "Let's say Mr. Brahms thinks that you're crazier than a dog in a hubcap factory, and that I think you're musically inclined. Mr. Dane? He thought you were his son, and his son had too many troubles. And it worried him something fierce."

Something in Ben's chest judders like a tectonic plate.

"I, um. What . . ." Ben clears his throat. "So he worried about me. Everyone does, I even do, so. And he worried about . . . what else?"

"This theatre. Something terrible."

Ben sits forward, ready to lap up information.

New World's Stage wasn't in trouble just before Jackson Dane died . . . yet. But Ariel Washington knew most of the things Paul Brahms knew, and Paul Brahms was fretting more than the usual. About major donors, about production costs. About box office. About the theatre's investment portfolios. Meanwhile, Jackson snarled whenever it was so much as hinted that the family money would be of assistance. *This is a goddamn production company, not a tin cup getting rattled on a street corner,* he'd snap. *How in hell do you ever expect us to be taken seriously, acting like weaklings whenever we need to make tough calls?* And that was that. Paul paced from office to theatre to mail room to accounting department to publicity department and round and round again like a mouse in a maze. Muttering dire portents regarding the now-legendary *Spider-Man* budget and how all it took was one Beach Boys jukebox musical for Dodger Stage Holding to bite the dust.

"New World's Stage been too comfortable too long, is what Paul thinks," Ariel concludes.

"What do you think? Like, fall of the Roman Empire comfortable?"

"Nah, not yet. American empire comfortable. And I think you miss Lia Brahms something awful. And I think that her not being here while you go through this—that it's almost too much."

"It's," Ben rasps. "Yeah, it's a lot. I'm—Jesus Christ, I'm so sorry."

"Don't be ridiculous. I known you since you was a kid. Lia Brahms too, back before she learned not to comb that hair of hers."

The last time Ben saw Lia, she was wildly, happily drunk. Passing shots to her art world friends at an East Village house party. Exposed brick, air festooned with weed, some junkie fixated on the ripple of television lights. Ben was drunk too, *really* drunk, but the difference was that he'd have a hangover the next morning, while Lia would have the shakes till she retrieved a shot of something from her sock drawer. The snow fell softly that December night, fell like fairy dust or like forgiveness, and as it happened Ben and Lia would no longer be a couple thereafter, and he wrote her a letter a few days later.

Lia,

When we first met, you were exploring the theatre where your dad just got a job, and I was hiding from a vicious kid named Jason.

You found me in the upper balcony eating a turkey cheese sandwich. You looked like you were casing the joint, or like you might order new carpeting. You were eight, same as me. Jason was ten, ten and massive, and our theatre was the only place I could get into and he couldn't. I never told you, but my ribs were black and blue, and my hip looked like it met a meat grinder, and I couldn't breathe very well yet.

Or express myself.

But I wanted to. So I gave you half my sandwich and you said thank you, I've already eaten, but you ate it anyway. Because you knew I'd be hurt if you didn't. Because that's the sort of person you were.

I loved you then. I love you now. I love you everywhere, and everywhen, and after what you did this time, I can never be with you again.

How am I ever going to recover from something like that?

If I could shatter time and go back, I would. Smash the whole clock's face and wrench the hands in reverse.

Enough poetry, nobody remembers poetry.

You want to know what I'll remember? I'll remember that you smell like melons in the summertime. I'll remember how much you hate that you can't sing. I'll remember what a truly shitty singer you were. I'll tell myself that everything that ever has happened still exists if you look at Time from outside of Time. And so that day you wanted to watch the sun set from the fire escape, and after we undressed each other we left rusty handprints everyplace, that slice of time is always happening. Just somewhere we could only visit the once.

The rust never did come out, not from either of our shirts. You left marks on me. I'm going to imagine, because it won't hurt anyone, that I left marks on you, too.

I'm sorry that I wasn't enough to keep you. I tried to be. It was all I ever wanted, other than for you to be happy.

Ben

Ben smears away the tears from his cheeks.

"Benny, you gotta feel how you feel."

"Not like this, though," he snaps.

"Why the hell not?" Ariel's growl is fiercely protective.

"Because I'm a suicidal-optimist and philosopher-detective and that's already ridiculous enough."

Anxiety ripples across Ariel's cheeks. "Lia was in a bad way. You gotta stop making yourself sick over it. Just because you can't do for her anymore don't mean you have to forget her, nor chew yourself up and spit yourself out, neither."

Ariel is an AA counselor, and Ben knows Lia used to attend his meetings. Ariel is sworn to complete privacy regarding them.

> He still wants to rip
> every particle of information from him
> with his bare hands.

"You can't tell me, can you," Ben whispers. "About . . . about when you last saw her, I dunno when that was. What she was like."

Ariel shakes his head, lips a sealed envelope.

Ben straightens. "I would always have wanted more time with her, I know I would, no matter how long it was. That's the worst part."

"What is?"

"Time. Time will fuck with you endlessly until you're compost. You can't hide from it. There's no hiding from anything, and especially not endings."

Ariel nods, but they are interrupted. A shift in the light scuffs against Ben's awareness, and he looks up to see Horatio practically filling the entrance to the mail room. His best friend looks like he just tripped over Ben's hopelessly mutilated body in the middle of a ten-car pileup.

"Benjamin. What's wrong?" Horatio's dark eyes are wide. "I was signing out just now, and I heard you."

The silence is as lengthy as it is awkward. Ariel waits for Ben to speak. When Ben opens his mouth, he finds there aren't any words in it, empty as the day he was born. And too many days after that. Realization flushes Horatio's face that he's interrupted something intimate.

"Oh bollocks, please excuse me . . . I'll just—"

"Come in, you perfect and I do mean perfect idiot." Ben beckons to him. "Pull up a box of branded napkins, we're having a hen fest."

"A what?"

"A chin-wag. Just sit down."

Horatio casts about for a seat. He slips off his hair band, unconsciously redoing it, deeply uncomfortable. When he does settle onto a half-emptied pallet, he looks like a giant asked to get comfortable on a folding chair, and Ben laughs helplessly.

"What?" Horatio demands, embarrassment making him irritable.

"Nothing. You make everything better." Ben pulls a Klonopin out of his pocket, says, "To mental health, cheers," and swallows fabricated tranquility.

Horatio now looks annoyed rather than ashamed, and Ben counts it as a win.

"Hey there, Horatio. Good to see you. Gotta get back to these boxes." Ariel levers to his feet.

"Tell me it's all going to be OK, Ariel." Ben sighs, retrieving his phone to check the time.

"'S the one thing I can't do. Because it won't be, in the end. But you can sure fight like hell to live the best you can till you get there."

Ben is about to compliment Ariel on just how dark that bit of optimism is when he registers that his cell reads 1:27, and Horatio's tailoring appointment is at two.

"Vincentio! Shit." He jumps up, hands already steadying. "Thank you, Ariel. Seriously, I owe you. For the information and for the . . . the other stuff. Thanks."

"Don't think I ever did let you down yet, Benny, and I don't plan to start." The world's finest doorman taps his pen against his furrowed brow in a salute while Horatio, looking adrift, rises almost as soon as he sat down.

"Let me know if you think of anything else?"

"Ear to the ground, as always."

"Constant vigilance." Ben breaks a brief, back-clapping hug with Ariel and then moves to hustle his colossally broad-shouldered friend toward the door. "Good lord, man, you're like some kind of Indian lumberjack without the flannel. Bye, Ariel! Give Paul Brahms hell for me, please."

They aren't even around the reception desk yet when Horatio plants his feet. Which stops Ben because the laws governing mass versus momentum are not to be mucked with.

"Do you mind informing me what on earth that was?" Horatio sounds angry, but Ben feels vibrating currents of worry.

"Er, a smallish meltdown. Eeeeensy teensy."

"Caused by?"

"I was questioning Ariel after questioning Rory and Garrett while you questioned Paul. How is every little thing with Paul?"

Horatio rubs at his neck. "He's fine. But I've something to tell you—an idea, of sorts."

"Fantastic!" Ben exclaims. "Inform me en route to your fitting, we haven't completed the double-oh-seven aspect of this outing."

"Horatio Ramesh Patel!"

Ben and Horatio turn, startled.

"Ben!" Trudy Dane tugs off huge Versace sunglasses. "Oh, honey, I was so . . . thank god, just thank god. Hello there, Horatio! It's wonderful to see you so unexpectedly."

"Precisely what I was thinking," the man who called out to Horatio says with visible glee.

This newcomer is about the same size as Ben's mom, and his amber cat's eyes glow with intelligence. His hair is pure white, his three-piece navy suit patterned with a tiny chalk pinstripe, and several threaded needles stick through his lapel like a corsage. Why he's beaming at Horatio Ben can't imagine, but Horatio's shocked expression and Trudy Dane's sudden appearance send spiders down his forearms.

"I—er—Robin?" Horatio stammers.

"Aren't you certain?" the little man questions happily.

"Yes, of course I am. Robin. What a surprise. Hullo, Trudy."

Ben's mother embraces his friend in a miasma of designer perfume. She next angles toward her son, pretends to see hesitation when there's mainly surprise, decides to be hurt, then pretends not to be hurt, all in about 1.4 seconds.

"Hi, Mom," Ben says, fighting the urge to clap.

Robin is pumping his hand next. "The reason my mate Horatio came to New York! For you can be no other. Chuffed to meet you, chuffed absolutely to bits."

"This is a friend of yours from London?" Ben asks Horatio.

"No! Um, not in so many words. We met on the plane, actually."

Ben swings quizzical eyes to his mother, who is affecting an unaffected martyr expression. She wears a grey sheath dress with an angled neckline. It probably cost the same amount as a used car, and it's her Mom means business look.

"Robin is an event coordinator, Benny," she says with exquisite softness. "He's here to help with the gala, in a broad sense."

"Neato. And in a narrow sense?"

"Robin also works as a wedding coordinator." Trudy blushes, and it looks very nearly genuine. "He's here to help me, too. Your . . . my new husband and I, that is."

"Oh. My uncle daddy Claude, you mean. Epic."

"Wait, wait, wait!" Agitation radiates off Horatio, and Ben wants to tap Morse code into his palm, find out what's wrong. "What on earth are you doing consulting with Trudy Dane? Is that why you spoke to me so freely?"

"Wasn't aware of your association up until now, was I, my darling duckie?" Robin coos. "Anyway, life? Just a series of coincidences, innit? Can't put 'em in a novel, nobody'd believe it, but reality? Improbable events, all day every day."

There's something distinctly off about him—not malevolent exactly, but chaotic. In a weird way, this guy feels like entropy, and Ben fights an irrational shiver.

"But pleased to inform you that my business in New York is

all growing clearer by the *instant*." Robin weaves his fingers together, smiling from ear to ear. "Well, sorry to say that I really must dash. Positively marvelous luncheon, Ms. Dane, and I'll get you my notes posthaste."

He leans forward to shake Horatio's hand. He shifts to Ben's. Ben stops breathing.

Robin sports a cravat, immaculately tied. Its pattern is deftly hand-stitched, an ivory length of cloth with tiny pointed wild strawberries. It resembles an elongated scarf. The one that Ben remembers so clearly *didn't* have green vines, these tendrils of leaves and serrated foliage, did it?

No.

It didn't.

But the one Ben remembers with a pang like a lightning strike absolutely—beyond any possible shade of a shadow of doubt—belonged to Lia Brahms.

LIA

The only single women widows now
   or brides
Half married to the breeze. We lie to
   stay together.
We lie to make do. . . .

—*Terrance Hayes, "American Sonnet
   for My Past and Future Assassin"*

L IA FEELS SLUGGISH, DUSTY. So out of practice that she's
dirtying her own paper. Leaving finger smudges in thick
grey smears.

This new piece (she pictures a performative installation, her
real body tangled up in the tree with the demon looming over
her) is stuck in the sketch phase. How did she progress beyond
that before she was this corroded hull of an artist? How were
her dreams assembled into floral wire and fabric and fresh cuttings?

She needs to explore her own darkest artistic period. Excavate
the tomb.

The previous afternoon bloomed beautifully. She learned
about the powers of waters from various sources (ocean, rain,
river). Maw-maw showed her how to infuse homemade candles
to attract creativity (patchouli, yarrow, lemon verbena). But her

true assignment was sketching Jessica Kowalski's bouquet after determining with Moma its exact composition. While serving everyone vanilla-scented coffee, Mam'zelle announced that they'd deliver their product to a particularly swank Financial District event space at a fete Jessica and her dick ex were both attending. It was crucial that Jessica give the "apology" bouquet to Jeremy herself, in public, she reiterated.

That sounded melodramatic to Lia, but she coaxed blooms and grasses from the page with colored pencil anyhow. Pretending that she believed magical floral arrangements were perfectly normal—not to mention *real*. She wasn't sure anymore. She didn't even know whether or not she cared, it all suited her so perfectly, like finding a lamp-lit candy cottage in the midst of a devouring forest.

When she presented her finished rendering, all three sisters applauded, and Lia felt her face light up like a hearth fire.

Today, Lia sits in her snug chamber on the third floor of the flower shop sifting through her files. Her room is ghostly ivory under the thick chair rail, sporting wallpaper with golden trellises above. Straight out of Oscar Wilde's interior design magazines. The air conditioner rattles encouragement. There's barely room to sleep—just a bed and a glass table and one skinny dresser, with space to scooch between the bed and the wall. It ought to feel claustrophobic. But it's like a nest or maybe even a womb.

An overstuffed black portfolio rests on the coverlet. Lia settles against the wall and unzips.

"What the fuck?" she exclaims.

She hasn't opened this in the two years she's been here, but Lia knows the exact chronology of her installations and stores them accordingly.

They are severely disordered, not to say completely gone to shit. She meant to study her *Elegy for a Life Lost* project, which coincided weirdly with her engagement, because something about the new piece reminds her of that show. The one that was held in the biggest gallery yet, when she was twenty-six. But the

Elegy pictures are scattered among photos of wisteria waterfalls and an airplane made of lilies. It's like some kind of morbid infection.

You did not go through my art portfolio, Lia thinks grimly at the sisters downstairs.

Did you?

BUTTERFLY BUSH: *Effective in protection charms, hiding, privacy, or barring entrance to a sacred space.*

She separates *Elegy* from the rest. Twelve caskets, ordered at a steep discount online but still costing five figures. From a Kickstarter and from Ben, who blew raspberries on her belly till she agreed and then made her call him "Benicio DeMedici" for a week.

Lia discovered that coffins come in *golden champagne* and *ice pink*, like nail polish. *Twenty-gauge steel, cherrywood, Rocky Mountain pine.* Lia displayed one a week over twelve weeks within seasonal bowers, her nude body reposing inside, a crown of blooms tangled in her briar-patch hair. She provided items to toss on her as guests passed through. **SWEETS TO THE SWEET: FAREWELL** the sign read. Petals, herbs, good clean dirt, like at a funeral—also empty mini-bottles, gum wrappers, chicken bones from her lunch that afternoon.

Trash. Which is what people become when they're no longer people.

She began with January, half-dozed in a walnut casket bedecked with bare tree branches, gardenias, and holly while people chucked debris at her. The next week was for February, so the vessel was eighteen-gauge steel dressed in greying grasses, hyacinth, waxflowers. Full circle to December reposing in a riot of blood-red poinsettias. New Yorkers attended for three months, showering her with rosemary sprigs and fast-food wrappers. Every time, it was beautiful for the first participants and revolting for the last.

A few critics found it lovely, still fewer brilliant, some achingly sad. "A Pre-Raphaelite's adolescent wet dream, devoid of any irony or taste," that one was memorable.

You're a line of music, Ben answered when she asked on week six what he thought of her corpse disappearing under wadded paper napkins. *I could transpose your melody into any key, hum it at any tempo, and still know you.*

After the ninth showing, he said, *Since you're striking this display tomorrow anyhow, may I fuck you right into these whaddaya call them, lilacs? Destroy them? Thematically appropriate, am I right?* And a week later, *I kept a handful of those petals we mashed into the casket lining. I'm, like, trying to dry them out, keep them. But they're completely soaked. In both of us.*

An aura of mingled mischief and terror haunted her boyfriend, and it didn't take Lia long to infer there was a cunning plan afoot. She wouldn't have put it past Ben to propose to her while *in* the coffin. He was that ridiculous. But no, after the show closed, he bribed his way into the Hayden Planetarium, spread out a lavish midnight picnic under the model solar system, and affixed the engagement ring to a bookmark in *The Language of Flowers* by Henrietta Dumont (first edition, 1851).

Fucking enough of this. Back to work.

When Lia forks her fingers against her hairline in frustration, she wants her mom's scarf again and sends her arms burrowing into bedclothes looking for it. Sensitive fingertips scrabble through the goose down.

No kerchief. She needs it, really *needs* it.

It tethers her. Lia dives under the bedskirt like a gopher.

"Shit!" she shrieks when her hand touches liquid.

She scrambles backward. No scarf, what the fuck, what the *fuck?*

"OK." She holds glistening fingers up. "OK."

Odors slither into her nostrils. Rosemary, clove, a thrum of the savagely ancient. It takes a few sniffs to place this backwoods-ritual aroma, but it's always been in the room, she realizes.

"Camphor," she decides. "OK. It's cool. Everything is cool."

Lia investigates with her phone light. She doesn't find a strawberry scarf, but she excavates a camphor bowl marked with tinier and tinier pentagrams within a larger pentagram on the lip. *Neat.* The water inside—fresh, no dust—covers three coffee beans, a star anise pod, a bag of Lipton, and a sodden cigarette. Separate from this hoodoo soup are seven black hen feathers bound with twine, a rabbit's foot, and a dried bouquet of yarrow, eucalyptus, and sage.

Lia sighs.

YARROW: *For bravery in the face of adversity; also powerful in the Chinese I Ching or Book of Changes divination method, and in the regional American South, to haunt your dreams with the one you will marry.*

EUCALYPTUS: *Protects from jinxes and repels enemies to such an extent that it will work mojo on both external threats and on yourself, if you are your own enemy.*

SAGE: *Women's strength, wisdom, and the courage to follow through on that wisdom when confronted with danger; protection against the Evil Eye.*

A rap at the door disturbs her investigation.

"Yeah, come in."

Moma enters, snakelike torso on display between ripped blue jeans and a black halter crop top. When she sees the bedside table, her brows arch, thumbs tucking into empty belt loops.

"Well, what you got there, baby girl," she remarks. It isn't a question.

"There's magical shit under my bed."

Moma smiles with eyes and nose only. "I'll be damned."

"Maybe. That's the general line people take on witchcraft, you know."

The bowl, the herbs, the shared dreams—when did it all begin? Should she be amused or terrified? Lia reflects on a fire-gutted theatre cold enough to burn her skin in Ben's nightmares, on a slant-smiling boy who technically had everything and really had no one but her. At least, until Horatio came along. Sweet, perfect Horatio, whom she adored, with his kind eyes and his gluttony for punishment.

Because Horatio loved Ben too, and Lia in another way altogether, and he preferred to have both of them gracefully than nothing at all.

Her and Ben, though. It was always peculiar. She's read about people having psychic connections, *I heard his voice the very instant he died* type of stuff, *I knew she was in trouble*, Rochester screaming for his Jane. Lia has talked Ben down from crippling panic attacks simply via text message. He once found her passed out in a Chelsea hotel lobby she'd never visited before.

Maybe—just maybe—it's all real. According to her ex, quantum theory states conclusively that observation of one particle enacts an instantaneous effect on a distant joined particle, beyond light speed, beyond what's possible. But conversely, Isaac Newton himself (alchemist, magician, Ben always used jazz hands when evoking him) juggled biblical texts into proving beyond any doubt Christ would return in 1948.

Science isn't everything. Neither is magic, clearly.

Lia's heart flutters, winglike, in the cage of her ribs.

Moma laughs, tossing her head. "Where you get that kinda fool idea? I'm no witch, me. Nor none of my sisters."

"But you did stick a bunch of herbs and a camphor bowl and a bunny foot and a bundle of black chicken feathers in here."

"Not *me*."

"Fine. The three of you together?"

Eyes twinkling like holiday beads, Moma lifts her shoulder.

"Putting dead twigs under my pillow can't change my subconscious, not really," Lia protests.

Moma agrees, "True enough."

"The people who pay you so much believe what they're getting is powerful. That *makes* it powerful, the placebo effect."

"Can't cure nobody saving their faith in us burns strong."

"Right, so you can't be witches."

"Ain't that what I been telling you?"

Lia can't help but smile. "Yes, but people who do sneaky incantation shit *are* at a higher risk for drowning, burning-at-the-stake type of obituaries."

"Nobody alive can kill the three sisters saving the three sisters they own selves, and that's gospel." Twisting a few braids around her wrist, Moma adds, "Same'll go for you too, I think, your fate in no hands but your own."

"My own? You're kidding. I just found a bunch of shifty talismans, and I'm pretty sure they're meant to have an influence."

"'Course they are, baby." Moma comes a few steps closer. "You done been taught what all this, that, and t'other signify now. There ain't no malice in these herbs, so what's so sinister? Same as putting a bag of lavender in your underpants."

"Moma, there are *chicken feathers* where I *sleep*."

"Nothing gonna protect you from jinxes, hag-riding, and witchcraft quite like frizzly black hen feathers, believe you me."

"This *is* witchcraft." Lia battles not to laugh. "What protects me from *this*?"

Moma's eyes sparkle obsidian-black. "There maybe you have a problem, for sure."

"And the rabbit's foot?"

"You ain't stupid, baby girl. Everybody and their sainted mamma know those is for luck. You can get them at the Seven-Eleven."

"So you're fixing me with herbs," Lia surmises.

"Nobody fixes you. We give you the ingredients. You're the one does the root work."

"OK, now this is just sounding like therapy."

"*Allons-y!*" trills a musical voice. "Lateness does not become us at these prices, sisters of mine."

Mam'zelle arrives, resplendent in an Ulla Johnson–resembling dress in fuchsia, bare shoulders gleaming golden and lace bouffant sleeves brushing the doorframe. When she sees the table, her ripe mouth forms an O.

"Well, *je suis scié!*" she exclaims.

"That's what I said, my sister," Moma informs her.

"*Chère petite*, what's happening here?"

"Somebody left a pantry of occult dry goods under my bed," Lia reports.

Mam'zelle's hand flutters. "I can assure you, I would never—"

"She knows, her," Moma interjects with a crooked grin. "*You* might not. But *we* would."

"The hour ripens. Rots on the vine." Maw-maw's grizzled head pokes over her taller sister's shoulder. "Oh. Damnation."

"*Exactement,*" Mam'zelle tuts, frowning.

"Pretty much," Moma concurs.

"Oh, for Christ's sake, it's not like you're trying to turn me into a newt." Lia slides the objects back under her bed. "Here! Look, I'm not thwarting your, your skillfully wrought charms or whatever."

"That's the spirit, *petite chou*!" Mam'zelle laughs.

"Damn straight it is!" Moma chimes.

"Leave what will be to be," Maw-maw approves.

Meanwhile, Lia's head spins.

Can this Louisiana craziness actually make me dream my ex-fiancé's dreams? Or invite him into mine?

She doesn't ask. Asking would get her silken smiles and gentle portents. Anyway, there's something both starkly intimate and ephemeral about those visions. When she's there with Benjamin, it's for them alone. And when she isn't, it plays back like silhouettes across sheer curtains.

"*Sacre coeur*, I haven't seen your early work in too long, *chérie*!" Mam'zelle exclaims.

When Lia recalls that the bed is covered in glossy prints, her frustration returns.

"Yeah, on to the more important issue. Someone has been in my room."

Three sets of eyebrows tilt as if to say . . . *and?*

Lia throws her arms wide. "I'm fully aware you are giving me space rent-free in exchange for services. Playing weird-ass tooth fairies is cool. Really! Going through my portfolio isn't. That's private, it's . . . it's mine. It's *me*."

Frowning, the trio edge inside. There is barely space, so Moma slumps catlike against the wall, Mam'zelle perches on the bed, and Maw-maw plants herself on the threshold.

"Now, that ain't right."

"Nous n'aurions jamais."

"Not by these two hands."

"Wait, none of you messed around in my art files?" Lia demands.

The sisters glare, an emphatic denial.

"Let's be very clear here, *all* of you didn't rummage through my art files?"

"Would you borrow my lingerie?" Mam'zelle huffs.

"Would you plunder my potions?" Moma sniffs.

"Switch my sugar and salt?" Maw-maw growls.

And no, Lia wouldn't. There's a difference between tucking a rabbit's foot under a friend's care-furrowed brow and outright snooping. The sisters may make inscrutable pronouncements, believe that sprinkling graveyard dirt in your shoe will ward off trouble. But they don't lie.

At least not as such. They give you questions back, not answers.

Anyway, it's been two years—who's to say she didn't do this herself during a tear-sodden fugue?

"They're all out of order, especially the coffins." Lia sighs. "Remember those?"

Moma's serpentine body tenses. Mam'zelle darts a suspicious look at Maw-maw, who glowers. All three sisters saw *Elegy*, every single day of it. Twelve times, Lia found their signatures in the guest book, and twelve times, she discovered three antique New Orleans subway tokens in the garbage.

"Her signature work, that is," Moma notes.

"We're late," Mam'zelle announces, rising.

"But—" Lia attempts.

"*On y va, chère petite,* come! We will get to the bottom of this, mark my words. Maw-maw, you leave your pipe alone, *comprends-tu*? And behave yourself, or I swear on Mother Mary, I will curse your sourdough starter."

With wide-eyed horror, Maw-maw backs away. They can hear her dire auspices as she clomps downstairs.

"Wait, you know what's going on, don't you?" Lia accuses.

The silence is pregnant. Moma ties handfuls of braids behind her head in half a square knot. Mam'zelle picks at the lace bow cinching her hourglass figure.

"It's not clear yet, but soon enough will be," Moma replies. "Where's your mamma's scarf at? You wear it like religion."

"It's gone missing. Maybe at my dad's place, I'll look again. I feel . . . different without it. Less like me."

The sisters exchange glances in a language Lia doesn't know. Mam'zelle sighs; Moma sets her teeth in a tiny snarl.

"Wait, did you take it for some reason? Why can't I find it?"

"No, we certainly did not, and we'll find out, us. Move you along now, baby girl," Moma orders. "Bring your things."

"Where the hell are we going?" Leaning, Lia swings her bag over her shoulder. "You haven't even told me that much."

"Over Gramercy Park way, to meet with Miss Jessica. She gotta approve that sketch of yours, otherwise how I'm gonna charm it?"

"Plus there's the final payment to collect," Mam'zelle adds as they make for the stairs and the honey-yellow wall sconces. Carpeting runs through the middle of the dark wood steps, a plush stream trickling downhill in blues and corals.

"Ain't no contract saving the final payment delivered," Moma concurs.

"She's paying you even *more*?" Lia marvels.

"Oh, no more in currency, *chère*, it's just a matter of the blood," Mam'zelle muses.

"Just a little blood," Moma adds by way of reassurance.

"Une trace de sang."

"The *blood*?" Lia squeaks.

When they reach the stairwell, sunshine pours from the skylight to feed the leaves of philodendrons and Boston ferns. Mam'zelle picks up a little bundle of flowering quince. "You remembered your sketchbook, my *chouchou*, with the plan for her bouquet?"

QUİNCE: *Symbol of life, fertility, and happiness in love in the Balkan states, where a tree is planted in commemoration of newborns; posies can protect one from harm.*

"It's right here."

"I need to study it over in the cab, *s'il t'plait*."

Wordlessly, Lia passes her art pad over. She and Moma created this, but Mam'zelle is the star saleswoman.

"Just rest your mind and keep your ears open," Moma advises. "I'm a true apothecary, me. Have we ever steered you wrong yet?"

And they haven't, Lia admits as they walk out the front door. Not yet.

But again, this isn't a promise.

It is only another question, not unlike the way Robin peppers everyone with questions, and Lia puzzles again over how, if you're on opposing sides of the same circle, you could ever possibly know where you really are?

JESSICA ANNE KOWALSKI'S LACQUERED nails dig into her palms. "It's not *exactly* second thoughts. It's just . . . maybe I overreacted to a bad breakup, is all?"

She sounds miserable and looks pricey. Frosted hair flipped under, aqua cap-sleeve Badgley Mischka dress pristine. It's way too much outfit for her. It should be the first female president's. Her lips are bitten raw under the petal-pink gloss.

"Overreacted?" Lia repeats, incredulous.

"Oh, I don't think so, me," Moma dismisses.

Mam'zelle shifts, crossing strappy gold sandals. "Why, if we'd imagined this were merely a frivolous *crime passionnel* on Mr. Jeremy's part, we'd never have taken on the assignment. It is much *plus sérieuse*, you understand. Oh! Here's a bit of lagniappe for you, courtesy of the shop."

Mam'zelle beams as she passes Jessica the nosegay of quince.

"Yeesh," Jessica hisses. "Sorry, didn't know there were thorns. This is really pretty, though. Thank you."

"Je suis désolée," Mam'zelle apologizes.

She produces a tiny antiseptic packet, delicately captures Jessica's hand, and cleans her finger, collecting a single drop of blood.

"Et voilà!" she coos, putting the square in her purse. "Good as new."

"Thanks." Jessica takes another healthy swallow of wine.

What the actual fuck? Lia thinks.

They meet at the National Arts Club, a favorite of the sisters, who are all members in VIP standing (they must be for Moma to get away with a crop top and denim by adding a Smythe mini-blazer). The Arts Club looks like them, in a less-enchanted, less-feminine sort of way. Mullioned everything, walls mummified in portraits, a freshly cut arrangement or a leafy palm in every corner. The sun glows cooler over Gramercy Park, softened by the age of the window panes, the darkness of the carved walls.

"Miss Jessica, how I'm gonna unveil our bouquet while you're this wound up?" Moma says gently. "How can we help?"

"We worked so hard on it," Lia adds, encouraging. "But I can understand why you wouldn't want to, to deliver something to him face-to-face."

Pick a card pick a card any card pick a card.

Jessica emphatically does *not* want to see Jeremy at the lavish party they're attending on behalf of the hedge fund, especially not now that he's sleeping with that trashy Brittany bitch from client solutions.

"Brittany's from Newark," Jessica moans. "She wears Gap Factory."

"*Mon Dieu*, the disgrace of it," Mam'zelle breathes. "All the more reason to settle this, *mais non*?"

The hunch of Jessica's shoulders is too sharp to be about anything so petty. She's just afraid. Simple, and yet so impossible to admit.

"More important, he hurt you," Lia supplies. "You don't owe anyone anything—not him, not us. It's your choice. But what do you think of helping to stop him from doing it again?"

Jessica's Rolex ticks and the world turns. She stares through pooling eyes at her empty wineglass. "He hurt me, and he could . . . he could hurt her, too. Yes. I want to settle this."

Mam'zelle's mouth curves in approval. Moma leans forward with fingertips tented. Jessica will be perfectly safe. The sisters will be nearby, ready if needed to assist instantaneously. Jessica must look Jeremy in the face and say the phrase written on the card for a bouquet this powerful to take effect.

"But I can't *speak* to him!" Jessica pleads, freshly agitated.

"You can, sure as anything I ever did know," Moma vows.

"I don't even want to be in the same building with Jeremy, let alone *talk* to him. This is not what I'm paying you for!"

"Oh, but it is, *chère*," Mam'zelle assures her. "And it always was, from the first day. You're paying us to find out what you can do, not what you can't."

Lia shifts, unsettled. This feeling of Jessica's rings far too familiar.

Jórvík Volkov, apart from being an excellent custodian, card sharp, and prestidigitator, also dabbled in tricks to do with fire. Flames leaping from his palm, spitting orange flares, setting ice cubes alight, immolating hundred-dollar bills. He didn't perform them often, but he wriggled in childish delight when he did, saggy chops fixed in a grin as he waved smoking fingers before Lia's and Ben's rapt eyes. As much as Lia cannot stop thinking about his card tricks, the school photos that carved this hole in her, she doesn't think about his fire magic. Ever.

Trying not to think about something, she has discovered over many many years, can be the most exhausting work imaginable.

The change in perception of time as you age makes perfect sense if you think in fractions, Ben used to say. *Like, what fraction of a life is a year to a five-year-old kid? It's a fifth. To a fifty-year-old man, it's a fiftieth. No wonder middle-aged people feel like the brakes have been cut.*

"What if Jeremy causes a scene?" Jessica sniffles. "What if he freaks out and ruins me professionally, since he already . . . since personally . . . since we aren't together anymore?"

Since he probably raped you, Lia supplies, jaw tight.

"And here you are, then! Corking, and Miss Lia as well. Absolutely brilliant!"

Robin sweeps into their private circle, edging between the gold-patterned couch and the coffee table. The lamps all give a sizzle and then gleam dully again. He's as dashingly coiffed as ever, his dove-colored shirt unbuttoned beneath his pin-striped suit and vest, though Lia has only ever seen him in a cravat previously. A few needles pierce his lapel where a boutonniere ought to be.

"How you making, Robin?" Moma inquires through her teeth. "Speak of the devil."

"Were you? Anything complimentary?" The gold-dust shine in his eye brightens.

"Why, you're absurdly early, Robin!" Mam'zelle exclaims. *"Ça alors!"*

"Just wrapped up with my client in midtown, thought I'd pop over." He pivots to Jessica. "Charmed, absolutely charmed. This is the client, you said?"

"We didn't," Lia snaps.

"Hello," says Jessica. "Who are you?"

"We ain't even shown her the rendering yet, and here you come traipsing in like a carpetbagger," Moma volleys at Robin.

"Robin Goodfellow, event planner." Brandishing a business card, Robin sits too close to Lia. He smells of sandalwood and snipped threads. "Apologies for dropping in like this, Miss Kowalski—the sisters and I are business associates."

The sisters regard Robin in silence. They could be sitting in a cabin putting a puzzle together or deliberating over a verdict of murder. It's tough to tell sometimes.

Robin clasps his knees. "The grand reveal! Fair to assume that Miss Lia executed the drawing, isn't it, you lot always were rotten artists—"

"Hey!" Lia shouts, almost wrestling Robin to the ground in front of Jessica Anne Kowalski.

Quick as a white-furred fox, he has unzipped Lia's bag and spilled the contents onto the ornate coffee table. Wallet, keys with her Bowie "Rebel Rebel" fob, a colored pencil case, all tumbling out. Hot fury gushes into Lia's throat.

"You can't—"

A photograph printed in stark black and white and muddy grey. A man and a woman. Unmistakably infatuated with each other. Robin gives another shake and the compromising picture of Trudy and Claude Dane hemorrhages from her satchel like guts from a kill.

Lia's mind stutters. She stares.

What the ever-loving fuck have I done?

It's been quite some time since she had to ask this question. She does not miss doing it.

What's this bruise about? Who's this stranger emailing me? Where is my credit card/MetroCard/house key/cell phone/ mind?

She remembers taking this picture from the pile on her dad's coffee table though, all too clearly.

Robin whistles. "What the devil do we have here?"

"Them's the Danes," Moma says, glancing swiftly at Lia. They've met at numerous gallery openings. Well, *all* of the openings. "Years and years back, from the looks of it."

"But the wrong ones," breathes Mam'zelle.

"You got more dog in you than the Humane Society," Moma growls at Robin.

"Flattery will get you everywhere, darling duck," Robin chuckles. "Now! Ah, here."

Lia watches, aghast, as he flips through her sketchbook. It feels like he's lifting her blouse, like he's upskirting her. Finding the bouquet at the end, he brandishes it in front of Jessica. Their overdressed client looks more confused than ever, which Lia hadn't thought possible.

"What style, what flair, eh? Your bouquet, presented for your explicit approval," Robin trills.

"Wait a sec," says Jessica.

"What are you doing, you bastard?" Lia snaps at last.

"Why do you have a picture of Trudy Dane?" Jessica questions. "The fundraiser for her theatre, the Empire Stage or something, that's the event where I'll see Jeremy again. And, well, deliver this bouquet. Have you been researching me? That's pretty thorough work. But what's this photo about?"

"Well, what a world," Robin reflects, allowing the sketchbook to drop. "As it happens, the Danes are clients of mine as well! I'm to organize the, shall we say, more *official* portion of the grand event. And now we've all seen this . . . rather remarkable snapshot. Possibly it was meant to be kept private. Apologies! Well, back to the business at hand, what say you?"

He whisks the incriminating photo away, beaming at the women assembled as if he's a man who's performed sleight of hand. Which he has, Lia understands. Because she knows exactly what it looks like when tricks morph into terrors.

"Cracking great embarrassment, what?" Robin shakes his head. "*Sincerest* apologies, ladies all. On my way! No rush, may as well conduct my own affairs with the sisters when I've not just put my foot in it. Toodle-oo and congratulations on what's sure to be an *unforgettable* bouquet!"

Mam'zelle soon has Jessica at her ease again, and no one fakes unflappable serenity like Moma. But for Lia, the meeting passes in palette-knife blurs. She injects meaningless approvals into the conversation, nods and frowns, and seethes over Robin Goodfellow.

What the ever-loving hell does he think he's doing to the Danes?

She shivers at the knowledge Jessica's bouquet will be delivered at the gala. It ought to be shocking but seems right somehow—like chords in a great orchestra, crescendoing to an inevitable conclusion.

Somehow, Lia knows, she will be there, too.

HORATIO

Make up something to believe in your
heart of hearts
So you have something to wear on
your sleeve of sleeves

—*The National, "Mistaken for Strangers"*

I N THE GARMENT DISTRICT, a cracked Formica countertop
faces 37th Street next to a glass door strung with bells. Inside,
a halal joint called Royal Smile Taxi Terrace features redolent
Arabian spices, a cone of shining meat, and a smiling bearded
purveyor (but no terrace). At the back of the eatery lies a white
door marked **EMPLOYEES ONLY** in Sharpie.

Horatio has learned that behind this door and up a flight of
stairs flecked with white sprinkles of primer lies a wholly undiscovered country.

"What am I going to *do*, Benny, you calling me out of the no-
place like this, only two days to fit him? *Deja esa vaina!*" the
tailor snaps, swatting Horatio's hand away from the waist of the
tuxedo slacks.

Vincentio hails from Santo Domingo. He is nearly as tall as
Horatio and as thin as Benjamin, an incredibly posh gazelle. His
hair is close-shaved, green eyes lined in charcoal and flicking
over Horatio's body like an absinthe-addled fairy godmother.

Horatio feels naked, standing there in a white ribbed undershirt, arms tingling in the air-conditioning.

I am free from the four Kashäyas. *Anger, ego, deceit, and greed have no place in me.*

"Vinny, dude, I told you it was an emergency," Benjamin groans.

"It is every-time an emergency with you!"

Benjamin winks wearily at Horatio. "Is this, like, your favorite speech pattern or what? Vinny never ever met a pair of English words he couldn't smoosh into a portmanteau."

Vincentio mutters something, yanking Horatio's inseam.

"Um. Must you?" Horatio wonders helplessly.

"You see your friend over there?" Vincentio indicates where Benjamin is smeared over a leather armchair, a champagne flute in quivering fingers. "Never has he ever-once come in, said 'Vinny, take your time, make me look like the *prince* I am,' this tiny sonofabitch looks like Kurt Cobain but with good hygiene. Now he brings you, you are magnificent, and 'day after tomorrow,' he says. *Toy adelante*, but Jesus Christ."

Vincentio's warehouse is the entire floor, its ancient parquet the color of silt. Between the iron posts, oases of overlapping carpets host sofas, clothing racks, designer chairs. Light from the former sweatshop's huge windows ricochets off the brass bar cart. Horatio downs the remainder of his Perrier-Jouët. Maybe it will stop him feeling so immensely narked off.

"Please tell me what had you in such a froth about Robin Goodfellow?" Horatio requests again. "Other than the fact he, you know. Is helping with your mum's wedding soiree."

"I could ask you the, like, *identical* question. But interrogating people seems to be your job this afternoon."

Horatio links his fingers behind his neck, willing himself to be calm. Granted, Robin's appearance thoroughly put his wind up. But Benjamin had seemed shattered with Ariel, then perfectly normal with Robin, then completely crackers again as they took their leave. He hasn't even grilled Horatio yet about Paul

Brahms. He's all edgy elbows, and Horatio has had just about enough of it.

"More champagne? Yep, that's the ticket, more champagne." Benjamin lurches to his feet like a cougar, and the fresh bottle emits a satisfying *thop*. From the set of Benjamin's shoulders with his back turned, he's popping another pill.

"Which is it this time? Klonopin or Adderall?" Horatio calls.

"Heh. Wow."

"Might as well top me up too, there's a love."

"My pleasure, here."

"Ace, ta very much."

When Benjamin pours the Perrier over Vincentio's hunched back, a petit roar emerges.

"Vete pal carajo que te sorte en banda!"

"Sorry, no, that did not land with me. One more time?" Benjamin stalks back to his chair.

"I am never-more dealing with your cock-shit ways." Standing, Vincentio levels a finger at Benjamin. "I'm going to explore dinner jackets because I am no-way fitting a full tuxedo on this stunning man shaped like a pyramid you bring to me. Bullshitting me, that is what you are doing right now, *Dios dame fuerzas.*"

Benjamin sighs. He pours a third flute for the tailor who stands pointing like a Dominican Ghost of Christmas Yet to Come.

"I'm sorry, Vinny," Benjamin says. "Sip this while you look at dinner jackets, yeah?"

Vincentio slinks off like a miffed tomcat. Horatio could swear that he hears *mother-shitting cock-fuckers*.

They are left alone, and Horatio opens his mouth.

"I'm sorry to you too, even though you're probably sick to death of it, the sorry-ing." Benjamin taps their glasses, producing an icy *clink*. "This Robin guy's cravat thingy reeeeally resembled that scarf Lia always used to wear as a belt or tie her hair back with. It wasn't the same, obviously. And it had leaves on it and hers didn't."

Horatio's chest compresses. Lia has been coming up in their conversations far, far too often. Two years ought to be enough.

Would it be enough for you, losing him? You would petrify. You'd be nothing but a stump, the whorls of the years that you had him.

"And before that? With Ariel?" Horatio urges recklessly.

"That epic train collision was mostly, um, about my dad. I am super adept at going off the rails, let's see what junction I'll crash through next today. Maybe it could be about the Grateful Dead being the most overrated band of all time. Keith Richards once said that what Jerry Garcia did was *poodle about* for hours, and that is the most fantastic verb ever to verb."

Horatio pinches his nose. Benjamin's opinions about music are multifarious, strident, and subjective. So he simply allows them to drift past.

"Why were *you* so weirded out by Robin, though?" Benjamin questions.

"Um. We met on the flight, as I told you. He said the oddest things, presumptuous even. There's no reason for me to make it sound so ominous, and I didn't mean to be a berk about it."

"So he just sort of . . . rubbed you wrong?"

He told me I was bloodsick, and I think he was right.

"Rubbed me wrong expresses it."

Benjamin waves his glass in a zigzag. "Yeah, me, too. We'll keep an eye on the dude. He's in cahoots with my mom after all, so we're adding him to our list. *The* list. Persons of interest."

Benjamin, when not skittering over one's skin like static electricity, is uncannily energizing. He's a battery, either zapping you or powering you, and Horatio decides to be grateful they've moved into the latter category.

"Anything else to get off your mind?" Benjamin sings.

"Well, I, um, don't much fancy being here."

"But you're going to the prince's ball and Vincentio is your fairy godmother." Benjamin peers up through flaxen eyelashes, completely unashamed of making this horrid remark. The absolute wanker.

"I'm not meant to be wearing swish togs at all!" Horatio is being a bear with a sore head right now, but he doesn't care. "Humility in all things."

"You're not meant to add disharmony to the world either and you're enabling *me*."

"God help me."

Benjamin grins, sudden and hard. The warehouse may be empty, and maybe it's the intoxicant, but the atmosphere sparkles like gunpowder. Horatio is acutely aware of the defensive cock to his own hip. There could be a hundred phantom seamstresses in here, all stitching and stitching and slowly going blind, and it wouldn't feel as crowded as it does now.

"So, anyway, what did Paul tell you?" Benjamin asks.

Horatio reties his hair, leaving the ends tucked in. "Nothing whatsoever. But by inference, something rather odd?"

Paul had been in his cramped office—the same office he took when they first moved in, as unassuming as the man himself. Slick light from the fluorescents painted his bald head in an arc like a sickle moon, and Horatio had a barmy urge to pat it. To his left were a mass of ledgers and spreadsheets, as hodgepodge as a stew. To his right were a telephone and a photograph of Lia, fourteen or thereabouts, laughing at something off-camera, corkscrews cradling the curve of her cheek.

"I tried to approach everything delicately." Horatio and Benjamin settle into the armchairs, leather squeaking. "I implied that I needed to reassure myself of your well-being."

"Gee," Benjamin drawls. "That sounds really hard for you to pull off."

"Will you shut it?"

"Sorry, sorry, you're a superspy. We're getting you a signet ring with a poison stabby bit."

"If we're kitting me out like a superhero, then I want a sword cane."

"Oh my god, *done*. I'll have one for you by the gala. You probably think I'm kidding. So what was Paul like?"

Horatio lifts his shoulder. "He was himself, spinning like a top. He said that he had to go see to the parking garages."

Benjamin's lip quivers with mirth. "Please tell me you just said 'parking garages.'"

"Yes, yes, I did. He's been measuring the parking spaces and asking the manufacturers of luxury vehicles how wide the, well, the wingspans of the doors are, to see whether the stalls are too narrow."

"Too narrow."

"He needed to see how long it would take to repaint all the lines."

Benjamin laughs with neck-lolling abandon. Horatio doesn't savor mocking Paul Brahms the way his friend does. It's like pointing at someone who slipped on an icy patch of sidewalk.

"He did talk to me, though," Horatio continues. "He said a great deal actually, just nothing very much to the purpose."

Paul appreciated that Horatio was concerned about Benjamin. Then he mentioned statement vases, fretted whether the guests might be allergic to particular flowers. Which shifted into discussing whether the attendees should sign epilepsy waivers, since flashbulbs would be used. After which he got preoccupied by the possibility of service animals.

"He's always like that," Benjamin moans. "Like a guillotined chicken. The Marie Antoinette of chickens."

"Yes, but how can that possibly be?" Horatio objects. "How does he occupy such a central role in the theatre without being, well . . . competent? Everyone says your dad trusted him with everything. For heaven's sake, he took those videos."

"Are you saying Dad's trust was misplaced?"

"Actually, quite the opposite. I'm saying that if your dad's trust *wasn't* misplaced, then how can Paul Brahms spare the time for flashbulb waivers and parking lot demarcations? Even someone who used twenty-four hours in the day wouldn't have the wherewithal."

Benjamin's brow scrunches as Horatio recalls more of Paul's fits over the years: the meltdown about commercial floor cleaner causing cancer, the brouhaha over serving veal to the board of directors. Through all of this randomly dispersed energy ran a strong undercurrent of both dedication and of aching sorrow. Laura Brahms, née Laura Caruso, passed away long before Horatio's time. But he had seen a few of Lia's photos with Laura, as a baby, and he knew Lia herself intimately, so he could easily picture her mother—a Hasidic profile, mad hair, olive skin, a full-lipped smile. She would have been creative and affectionate, pointed and beautiful, just like Lia.

It took a mad multimillionaire obsessed with the secrets of the cosmos to net Lia. How the hell could the likes of Paul attract such a remarkable spouse if he weren't alarmingly intelligent?

Horatio itches to ask Benjamin which particular qualities Lia inherited from her respective parents. But bringing up Lia is as good as whacking Benjamin in the dial with a two-by-four. Anyway, he can see some of the lineage himself. Paul isn't artistic, so that's maternal; Paul *must* be brilliant, so that's paternal or likelier both. But Lia was also manipulative—well-intended but scheming, the way he's come to understand all addicts operate without necessarily meaning any deliberate harm.

Horatio wonders with a thrill of disquiet whether Paul might be that way, too.

"How'd this little tête-à-tête end?" Benjamin questions, pensive.

"Paul said he was thankful I was kipping with you."

"Heh, that makes two of us."

Sensing his face about to heat, Horatio deflects. "Apparently I should encourage you to play the guitar. Something along the lines of soothing the savage beast?"

Ben yaps a laugh. "That's kinda cute, actually. I'll whip out some Cat Stevens later if you ask pretty."

"He did have a point," Horatio realizes. "Your sensibilities do rather bleed into your playing, obviously. If there's a more emotional art form, I've yet to encounter it."

"Actually, musicianship is a conscious act of math," Ben answers with enthusiasm. "Pythagoras, ultimate boho cult guru, figured that one out by mucking around with monochord strings, although a waaaaay cooler legend states that he passed a blacksmith's shop and realized that the sizes of anvils that were compatible divisibly also gave off the sweetest *clangs* when struck together. There is no more purely scientific art form than music. Which is fine if you're talking about Radiohead's *In Rainbows* record and slightly less awesome if you've got Smash Mouth stuck in your head, but either way music is fractions and—"

"Here's Vincentio coming back," Horatio observes softly.

"Copy."

"You know, I always rather wondered why you weren't studying music rather than philosophy of physics?"

"You're hilarious. If I were about twice as intelligent, I miiiiight scrape by with an undergrad degree in music theory. Not graduate level and never at Columbia, it would break my brain."

Dinner jackets hang over Vincentio's willowy arm, silks and velvets and one alarming metallic paisley. "You are finished now with arguing, please tell me, because I have never-ever seen a more useless lovers' quarrel, hand to god."

This time Horatio does blush. His friend tilts his champagne a fraction too abruptly and a drop spills out the side of his mouth. Horatio does *not* think about licking it off. Vincentio lobs a tiny wink in Horatio's direction, and the Londoner longs to seep down, down, down through the floorboards.

"Yep, we'll behave now," Benjamin replies brightly. "Whatcha got there?"

"Lanvin, the Row, Ralph Lauren, Tom Ford, and Kingsman for luck."

"Sweet titties."

Horatio barely suppresses a groan over the concept of a stranger and the love of his life running commentary about his physique. He's rather proud of his physique (it's spiritually cleansing to improve it daily). And Benjamin is rather meticulous (aesthetically speaking). His friend might look like a man wearing ragged jeans and a band shirt—today's reads **SEAWOLF** over paint splatter that looks like an undiscovered constellation—but the jeans will not have cost less than two hundred quid, and the body underneath resembles a whippet's.

Stop, stop, stop, stop.

"Why don't you lot just . . . choose for me?" Horatio suggests as Vinny muscles him into a sapphire velvet coat with a black satin collar.

"Ha ha," Vincentio does not laugh.

"I wasn't ribbing you, I don't see the need for *me* anywhere in this process."

One kohl-lined eye arcs over to his friend. *"Oye ni por un de million hago yo esta vaina."*

"No habla, dude," Benjamin notes again.

"Never-way are you paying me nearly enough for this shit."

"Oh, cut it out, yes I am, you adore me. If you want more, just say so. I'll make it rain. How many private islands do you want, exactly? Hey, I like that one. What do you think, Horatio?"

"How much is it, please?" Horatio begs.

Benjamin rolls his eyes. "What do you think, Vinny?"

"Nítido, but no-how do we choose this. The undertone of the blue is wrong, never-kind of way I am making this bronze god look sallow. Right, we are trying the Tom Ford black-on-black satin camo print."

Benjamin whistles as Vincentio produces a gorgeously detailed silk tux jacket. This coat could doubtless pay for a few months' worth of Horatio's student loans. He tries it on. The fabric feels solid but airy, like wearing a mantle of black wings.

"Ay Dios mio," Vincentio says approvingly.

"Jesus, Vinny, you've been holding out on me! You've never showed me anything like *that*. Christ almighty."

Benjamin's eyes are alight with mischief and *absolutely nothing else*, Horatio vows to himself. His friend approaches, his eyes shards of sky through a window. The midsummer light has shifted as the afternoon progressed, faded and worn like antique porcelain. He's not going to reach out and start fiddling, is he?

Please do not brush those guitar-cracked fingerprints over any fabric, I'll be unraveled entirely.

Please.

Benjamin is opening his mouth when his mobile buzzes repeatedly. His expression freezes over the screen.

"Who is it?" Horatio questions.

"Yeah, Ben Dane here. No, it's totally fine."

Vincentio does something abstruse with a tape measure diagonally across Horatio's back.

"Oh, did you?" Benjamin's chin jerks toward the ceiling. "That's fantastic. Or I hope it might be."

Who is it? Horatio mouths again, batting Vincentio away as the tailor swoops to encircle his neck for a collar measurement.

Benjamin ignores him. "And this is your cell number? Can you please just tell me what sort of . . ." Benjamin's lips purse in frustration. "Fine. Right, six o'clock, One-thirtieth Street. I'll wear a silver backless catsuit with a gardenia pinned to the top of my ass crack. Fly a red kite if you need to abort the mission."

Another pause.

"The code phrase is 'shake it like a Polaroid picture.'"

The line goes dead. Horatio, unsurprised, waits.

Ben smiles with a face drained of all humor. "How does a rendezvous with Detectives Norway and Fortuna sound? They've discovered something."

"Oh my god. Six, you said? That's only a couple of hours."

"Yep, and they don't seem like they want it known they're meeting us. So down at the riverbank by all those park benches and barbecue grills on the Upper Upper Upper West Side." Benjamin winks absently. "We used to spend ages walking that bike path. Remember?"

Horatio does remember.

He stops breathing. Because he recalls the *last* evening they visited the Hudson particularly well. There was a salmon-pink skyline like an arsonist's bedtime story and the faint drone of weather helicopters, both screaming *danger, danger.*

Nobody listened.

Horatio wonders when his heart is going to snap irreparably. It is not made of kindling, and the organ always springs back, recovers. However, if he has learned one thing from Benjamin, it's that nothing is indestructible.

Entropy will win out. Time, and time again.

THE HUDSON SHORELINE DOESN'T smell like timber, seldom smells like fish, never smells like strips of venison drying in the sun anymore. The new economy has no aroma. It's steel and glass cathedrals erected to worship numbers. But Horatio loves history, chronicling individual lives. He loves the fact that salt brine still drifts along the riverbank the way it did when Canarsie tribes slipped through the glimmering trees. Sitting on this bench, he can picture them, like the afterimage of a too-bright lamp.

Benjamin rails at the police officers nearby on the grass, and Horatio ought to help but Horatio cannot be useful anymore. Partly because he's as pissed as a newt. And partly because this is Benjamin at his bloody worst, ranting rapid-fire vituperation, and Horatio can do *nothing* to put the brakes on.

Benjamin gets to do this by himself, again.

You ruined it.

But it was already ruined. A long time ago.

Horatio pushes his thumbnail against the picnic table hard enough to make it bleed. It's better than the knife that's been stuck between his ribs since they arrived. He listens to Norway and Fortuna report several outlandish discoveries, but nothing is filtering, really.

There's just the familiar caressing wind of a summer's night on a riverbank, and Horatio is absolutely fucking finished.

Detective Barry Fortuna lifts his palms like stop signals. "Hey, kid, you gotta cool off here. I ain't saying that this cold case shit necessarily had anything to do with what happened to your old man. It just . . . we had questions, yeah? There been more investigations buzzing around your theatre than we'd like, speaking geographically. Weren't never a police matter, but plenty of insurers asking questions when the old building went up in smoke. Never-identified body in the rubble, which *was* a police matter, bet your ass, but never amounted to nothing and nobody came looking for anybody. Jack squat to go on. Now we connect a few dots and see that these missing kids all those years back was from the same neighborhood. Finally, your dad's suicide—"

"Call it that again and I'll have you turned into a traffic control agent. In a *Walmart parking lot*," Benjamin seethes.

"You see what I'm up against here?" Fortuna grumbles to Detective Ying Yue Norway.

"This is insane," the Dane heir spits out. "It's not *possible*."

He doesn't sound one iota like Benjamin dismissing stupidity, oddly. He sounds like Benjamin rejecting something painful, something he doesn't want to face.

He'd sound that way if you said, "I love you and always have," for instance.

"I understand that our line of questioning itself is automatically distressing," Norway soothes. "But it'd be remiss not to contact you. See if you can recall any information for us that we'd not have asked you as a child regarding these cold cases."

"So, what, my dad . . . he was tied to decades-old missing persons cases? He was a psycho? He torched his own theatre with some mortal enemy inside and then years later lost his marbles?" Benjamin hisses. "What the fuck are you trying to tell me?"

"Nothing at all. You're leaping to conclusions." Detective Norway lifts a birdlike shoulder. "We only wanted to know what *you* might have heard. Twenty years ago."

The voices dissolve. There were seven missing children. Three of them linked for certain, all girls. They went to schools near the World's Stage Theatre, the old one. Horatio tries to concentrate, but why should he? Benjamin is right—this can have nothing to do with the Danes. And Horatio all but attacked the champagne after Benjamin informed him where they were off to and is now incapable of thought other than *I can't be here.*

"*Horatio.* What the hell, man?"

Horatio looks up. Why is there so much salt on the breeze? It isn't 1670, the New World isn't lush and wild, Haarlem isn't a bloody Dutch fishing village. His eyes sting.

It must be the salt.

Benjamin pulls his marionette strings tighter. "Right," he says to the cops. "Right, I will be in touch."

"Is everything, uh, good with your pal?" Detective Fortuna questions.

"Does it *look* good? I am dealing."

"If you think of anything," Norway says, nodding, "you know where to find us."

"Jeez, whaddaya figure is up with this guy?" Fortuna gestures at Horatio with a meaty hand.

"Say one more word about him and I swear to god I will end you, and it will not be quickly," Benjamin says in the poison-sweet tone.

"C'mon, Barry," Ying Yue Norway sighs. "We passed a halal cart. I'll teach you tact over a gyro."

The detectives shake hands with Benjamin. The detectives depart. Turn toward the towering green iron staircases. Horatio's eyes drift over the waves where the great steamers used to flock with shipments of sugar and silks and people and—

"Hey. You."

Horatio's eyes still burn, but they're dry now. He isn't built for openness. Nor for this sweet pinkening of the skyline, just like before, just like a year ago. Maybe time really is a flat circle. He's on a merry-go-round in a hell he doesn't even believe in.

He laughs, shoving his brow into his fists.

A hand drops to his shoulder. "OK, we are just—what's happening? This is scary. Scary is generally *my* job."

Horatio shakes his head.

"Horatio, *goddammit*. Look at me."

Instead he looks over the water as the sunset ripens, cherries and peaches and nectarines and plums. He can't be here. He flew halfway across the world last time.

Horatio takes a slow breath. "Um, we were here last summer. This month. Right around this hour, as I recall. We always did like twilight."

Benjamin deflates against the park bench, realization flooding his sharp features.

Horatio folds his hands together very very hard. "Did you not care, or did it not occur to you?"

"I . . . Jesus Christ. The latter. Of *course* the latter."

Horatio swallows. "So you actually want to talk about this?"

"Now that I understand . . . yes, god yes. Yeah."

"You don't want to talk about the cold cases instead?"

"Absolutely not," Benjamin rasps. He still sounds like he's hiding key information. "That . . . that can wait, I have to make sense of that first, and I've put this off long enough. I might be a moron, but I'm not cruel."

"Actually, you don't know how to avoid being cruel," Horatio notes.

The ensuing silence is small. The way tragedies are often scaled in miniature, as simple as a last breath or a first kiss. Benjamin is cruel because he doesn't understand cruelty in the first place—he thinks intentions count for everything. He can only be cruel the way an animal would be cruel, or a deity. All impulse and no regard until afterward.

Horatio places both palms on the pine table. The dirty river wind in their hair, the dirty street exhaust on their skin, the dirt under their shoes. Eventually they'll find a way out of this.

Or they won't. Every story ends, but they don't always end happily.

"Benjamin, I—I cannot sit here and not have it mean anything."

"I know that."

"Then why are you so confused?"

"Because I *do know*, before you came back I might have just guessed, but I've known for a few days, and it crushes me."

"How could this possibly crush *you*?" Horatio shouts.

His favorite human stands up to pace. "OK, OK, let's start at the beginning. That night we . . . when it finally happened, like this thing the stars spelled out and courteously wrote in English, 'Ben and Horatio love each other and will ultimately do the sexing,' we . . . you remember?"

Horatio closes his eyes.

Yes, you consummate cock, I remember where I was when all my dreams and nightmares came true.

One year ago. They were pissed, to begin with. A little. Not nearly as much as Horatio is now. Only a shared Viognier bottle over fresh pasta, then a pair of whiskeys so they wouldn't have to leave the restaurant, abandon the silk ribbons of wind. All the sharp corners sanded off their inhibitions. It was the sort of perfect-weather night that saddens New Yorkers because there are only ten or twelve per year. The city becomes an hourglass, precious grains lost every instant.

So they visited the waterfront greenway along the Hudson. Benjamin monologued about how David Gilmour's guitar effects sound like listening to music inside an endless cave, comparing it to Yayoi Kusama tricking the eye with infinity mirrors.

And Horatio loved him. He just loved him, and the night was still young and so were they, and the lights on the river were shining and so was Benjamin, and an orchestral breeze struck up, and then they were holding hands.

Aaaaaand that, Benjamin concluded, *is why recording engineers should be the rock gods, not the dudes who can shred the hardest or even the ones with the tightest pants.*

Glancing down at their fingers, he smiled and began swinging them.

You are ridiculous, he announced.

It sounded like *I love you* to Horatio, and every time he replays that night, it still does.

So when they had thoroughly exhausted the topic of illusory sound engineering, from Pink Floyd to Pat Metheny, and the wafts of cut grass and Dominican barbecues had mingled into one savory scent, they climbed the next set of stairs. Benjamin hailed a cab and *their fingers were still laced,* so when they arrived home, Horatio took his Fate by the shirt collar and kissed Benjamin in the stairwell and learned he tasted like lemon peel, and like wine, and like the sharp golden edges of the leaves shuddering under the streetlights.

Horatio's heart was in his throat, but Benjamin didn't pull away. Once inside the flat, Horatio pressed his smaller friend's back into the wall, gripping the ropes of hip muscle and just *inhaling* him, and it was Benjamin who touched the bulge at the front of his trousers, which made Horatio gasp, which made Benjamin laugh, and if all that was natural, wasn't it also natural for Horatio to slide to his knees and press his face against soft denim and for Benjamin to say *I take it you're not seeing anyone right now* and *you would look so fucking amazing with my cock in your mouth* and then for Benjamin to have his knuckles carding thickly through Horatio's hair and finally *fisting, clutching.*

Just when his friend had slumped half a foot and Horatio thought he might disintegrate, Benjamin whispered, *Hey hey, no—shh, you're OK, come over here.* They collapsed on Benjamin's bed. He kissed Horatio's throat and said, *Albert Bandura first demonstrated the cognitive process of purely observational learning in nineteen sixty-one—I'm gonna give it a whirl, yeah? Just. I'll do what you were doing.*

"I recall, yes." It comes out colder than Horatio means it to.

"So . . ." Benjamin screws his eyes shut. "And, and I know we didn't talk about it afterward, that I just. I let everything go back to normal because I thought it could. Or no, because I wasn't thinking at all. I was, I don't know. I wanted the dust to settle . . . But if I'd *known*, I wouldn't have done what—Horatio. I love you, I do."

Horatio's hands form fists. "Mutual, I'm sure."

Gritting his teeth, Horatio pictures the aftermath of the best and cruelest orgasm of his life. Because it was from sodding *Benjamin Dane*, and Benjamin was sloppy and sweet and choked twice and said, *Jesus, sorry, I guess learning according to modeling alone isn't ideal.* And as Horatio already knew from party nights when their flat was carpeted in aluminum and glass, Benjamin was a cuddler. Which had happened several times with Lia in the pile too, the trio as happy as they could imagine being, but never in this context, oh, *never like this.*

And then the next morning. An empty bed and a note from Benjamin on the kitchen counter.

Ha ha, whoa man, hell of a night. I guess you can put an-other notch in your bedpost, but I want mine to be extra big, OK? Even if I was complete crap. We can find you a bassist at that concert later, I have it on good authority bassists always know what they're doing. If you see Lance, tell him that our kitchen faucet is just a dribble again and to pull his head out of his ass.—B

"I lasted a month with everything back to the way it was," Horatio whispers. "Then I couldn't anymore. I'm sorry I didn't say goodbye, Benjamin. You were owed that much."

"Please don't talk about debt, I owe you—"

"You owe me *nothing*!" Horatio all but screams. "Or else how could you treat me this way?"

The silence echoes along the park. If Benjamin is right, and time is really a dimension, then people can hear this silence in Egypt, in Rome, in the Renaissance, a thousand years from now.

"I never meant to hurt you of all people," Benjamin says, horrified.

"Well, then maybe you shouldn't have fucked me of all people."

His friend has no answer to that.

"Goodbye, Benjamin," Horatio tells him. Standing, he heads down the riverfront.

"Horatio, please come back here!"

He doesn't. This trail is as ancient as the first native tribes. He isn't the first to follow it, and he won't be the last, this tracing the flow of running water, this choosing to walk away.

BENJAMIN

What does it mean to be a *self-conscious* animal?
The idea is ludicrous, if it is not monstrous. It
means to know that one is food for worms. This
is the terror: to have emerged from nothing, to have
a name, consciousness of self, deep inner feelings,
and excruciating inner learning for life and self-
expression—and with all this yet to die.

—*Søren Kierkegaard*

I T IS THE MORNING before the annual New World's Stage Benefit Gala, and Benjamin Dane is not drunk.

He *was* drunk though, spectacularly, which made the tone
of his texts pretty widely varied. They started at midnight, when
Ben was so wracked over Horatio that he hadn't thought about
death (his own, anyway) in a record-shattering four hours.

> Horatio I know I deserve to be
> used as a ball in one of your
> soccer footie matches and kicked
> all over the pitch (field? court?)
> but please say something

Nothing. No response.

No concept in the Western world is more terrifying than zero, Ben thought, opening a bottle of Lagavulin at 12:16 A.M.

Mathematicians took centuries to accept the void; it was detested by all save occult scholars. Add zero to any number and the number remains unchanged. Add zero to itself ad infinitum and it never grows. Multiply something by zero and shitnuggets, you've erased the whole board. Divide a number by zero and watch your own brain leak out of your nostrils as you conceptualize infinity. Zero skull-fucked the axiom of Archimedes and flipped double birds to the Aristotelian universe.

Radio silence from Horatio was incomparably shittier.

There was zero scotch in this World's Stage mug, but now there is SOME scotch, Ben thought. *Blessed, blessed coffee mug.*

Naturally, an hour later, he texted again while twitching their curtains aside to scan for a large man with his shoulders slumped:

> OK so I ordered cold noodles, mu shu, red curry tofu, sushi
> without the fishies, samosas, veggie
> enchiladas, falafel, a mezze platter,
> and two pizzas I need your help

And then:

> bad joke I know I don't need your help
> and you might be through with that gig
> anyway but seriously I've never been this
> ashamed of myself

Followed swiftly by:

> yes that was about me being ashamed
> but see I noticed right away ha ha
> whoops and now this will all be about
> you, I promise, I'm begging here

Benjamin tried to pace himself on the Lagavulin—with literal pacing, cleaning the apartment, arranging a gluttonous vegetarian takeaway feast. He finalized his PowerPoint for the gala and shot the file off to Paul Brahms. That should have felt like the final stretch of a marathon but felt like . . . nothing.

Next, Benjamin got a text from Rory Marlowe. That wasn't unexpected. But it did provoke a certain **HULK SMASH** urge.

> hey man! wanted to check in
> on you after that lunch went down,
> make sure everythings cool

Garrett Marlowe texted him too, because the Marlowe twins are total asshats.

> sup Benny can't wait to see you
> at the gala! maybe we could swing
> by your place beforehand, get our
> pre-game on

There was so much *nothing* in these texts compared to the texts Ben yearned for that the nothing sucked all the oxygen out of the room.

Nothing comes from nothing, nothing ventured nothing gained, we can only know that we know nothing. Zero was particularly repulsive to medieval scholars.

If God is all-powerful, he can do anything;
if he's all-good, God can do no evil.
Therefore, since there's *nothing* God can't do,
evil is *nothing*.

Needlepoint that on a fucking doily and hang it on your wall.
Ben took his first searing gulp straight from the bottle. This
led to Ben curled underneath the coffee table as if it were a fallout shelter typing:

you don't undrstand you and me
together were a supernova doyou
get it both one half the supernova
and I want tofix it but you keep LEAVING

And lastly:

I'm sorry I'll stop only please
come home

Now he sits on his bed as the dawn floods his room like water
on the *Titanic*, cradling his 1954 Sunburst Gibson. He doesn't
play it often. An unholy combination of lucidity and despair is
required for him to grind out chords on a guitar with this level
of acoustic resonance in a seventeen-inch body. A blade of daylight slits across his bed as a riff off "19th Nervous Breakdown"
oozes from his fingertips.

It seems to me that you have seen too much in
**   too few years**
And though you've tried you just can't hide your
**   eyes are filled with tears**

The roof of Ben's mouth is lint-dry. But he needs to concentrate now that all the leftovers have been put away (he ate a

stuffed mu shu pancake and two pieces of avocado sushi, he was good, he was responsible) so he just takes

> one-quarter racemic amphetamine aspartate monohydrate,
>> one-quarter dextroamphetamine saccharate,
> one-quarter dextroamphetamine sulfate,
>> one-quarter racemic amphetamine sulfate,

which most people called Adderall.

The trouble is, he doesn't know *what* to concentrate on. These Rolling Stones chords that keep leaking out? That weird troll Robin Goodfellow? What Norway and Fortuna told him? How very little he knows, especially about how to get Horatio back?

Stop it stop it stopitstopit.

This is not about him—it's for Horatio, to *fix it* for *Horatio*, because while Ben gleefully cuts down the ignorant and hypocritical, the notion of hurting his friend this badly sends machetes through his belly.

If you broke his heart, you shouldn't be trying to get him back.

Fiddling with the original Kluson Deluxe tuners, Ben finds that the Adderall isn't latching him on to anything useful. He can name every song in the Stones' catalogue alphabetically, but he can't remember how many days it's been since his dad died, or the names of the seven little girls he saw in the police photos. Curling up on his black duvet with his guitar, Ben closes eyelids that tremble like the starlight seen through Earth's corrupting atmosphere.

ZZZZZZEEEEEEEEEEEEEEEEEP

Ben flies out of bed so quickly at the downstairs buzzer that he lands with a faceful of carpet. He scrambles up. A peat bog has rented out his mouth. *Horatio is back.* Ben will offer him a selection of international cuisine. *But why wouldn't he use his key?* Horatio was drunk, he lost the key in a cab, at least he's all right, at least he came—

RAP RAPRAPRAP RAP

Vincentio stands on the other side of the door holding a garment bag. No makeup this early, but he's painted on designer skinny jeans and wears a batik scarf over his low V-neck.

"*Que lo que,* Benny. Wow. I'm thinking right-now is maybe a bad time?"

Ben sighs, turning around. "It's not like it can get any worse."

"Oh, well, please and thank you."

"Shut up, Vinny. Coffee?"

"Certainly."

"It's down the street, Bernardo Brothers, theirs tastes the least like it's brewed in a vacuum cleaner. Scotch?"

Ben pours two shots and clinks the ceramic. Vincentio's dainty eyebrows twist, but he downs the liquor.

"Breakfast of champions. How the hell did you finish Horatio's tailoring so fast?"

Vincentio says something in Dominican.

"Dude, *please* buy me a Rosetta Stone for Christmas."

"This is *your* tuxedo, shit-dip. Final fitting, it is on your calendar you said yesterday, you swore on the Holy Cross. Strip."

Ben shuffles to the bathroom to brush his teeth. When he returns in his briefs, just to make a point, the tailor throws a button-down and a pair of trousers at his head.

"This mountainous *amigo* of yours, he is asleeping?" Vincentio surmises with pins between his lips.

"Wherever he is, I hope so."

Air puffs out of the tailor's nose. "*Te gusta estar bien con Dios y con el diablo.*"

"Vinny, I truly will punch you. Not fire you, but. The punching."

"You like to please both God and the devil, which is impossible. That one? He is good. I'm thinking you pick him, I do wedding tuxedoes."

"You are waaaaay ahead of the game. He hates me."

"Bullshitting me again."

"And I'm not even gay, I think, just Kinsey-ish with a sprinkling of demisexual."

"And I am seeing how you look at this man. Think very-much harder."

Benjamin walks abruptly to the linen drug box. Yes, he loves Horatio and has for many years. Yes, Horatio fell flat for him about six days into grad school and Ben's been ignoring it because he was ass over tits for his childhood sweetheart. He cannot be expected to untangle this, not in this slice of time, not *now*. Ben shakes

Chemical Name:

       5-(2-chlorophenyl)-7-nitro-1,3-dihydro-1,4-

       benzodiazepin-2-one

       Molecular Formula: $C_{15}H_{10}ClN_3O_3$

       Molecular Weight: 315.7

into his hand, returns to the scotch bottle, and invites Klonopin to shut Vincentio up since there's no shutting Vincentio up by natural means.

The tailor marches Ben to the full-length mirror in his bedroom (they've danced this house-call tango before). Ben squints morosely. Vincentio insisted on velvet, saying it was *much the thing*. Trousers and jacket are a plush steel color. Ben's too thin, but it fits him perfectly, and his eyes shine electric blue.

"Perfection. Giorgio Armani, please to be the father of my children," Vincentio says, looking smug.

"I don't think it anatomically works like that."

"But never-can you stop me from trying."

Ben sheds the tuxedo and dons Columbia sweats as if to say *I give up*. The tailor is likewise quiet as he zips the garments into their bag.

"What's on the agenda today?" Ben asks when he can no longer stand himself for how dickish he's being.

"Fittings. Meetings. Your uncle is at two o'clock with their piece-of-shit event planner."

Ben discovered Vincentio many years ago, but the entire male wing of the Dane family followed suit after the premiere of their Tony Award–winning adaptation of *The Handmaid's Tale* starring Lupita Nyong'o, at which Ben looked stunning. So Uncle Claude's appointment isn't a surprise. The title *event planner*, however, wedges like a dull knife through Ben's brain.

"Robin Goodfellow, you mean?"

Vincentio's face scrunches. "You've met, then. Wash your hands and pray to Belie Belcan, who I think Americans are calling Saint Michael."

"Why?"

"Everyplace Robin goes, the ground opens up. Be careful. I'll have both suits to you tomorrow. Your friend, his will not have time for a final fitting, but *gracias a Dios* I am a genius."

"Wait, wait a sec." Ben pursues Vincentio to the door. "Why do you say Robin's bad news?"

Vincentio adjusts his scarf. "Last time I worked a wedding with this Robin, five days later the bride, she jumps off a balcony. He did a private bat mitzvah once, six figures, and the daughter turned out to be pregnant. People hire him because his events are beautiful, but among professionals he has a cocked-up reputation. We have an expression in Santo Domingo, *curarse en salud*."

Ben gestures in exasperation.

"Cure yourself when you are still healthy, not when you are already fucked. Until tomorrow, Benny."

Ben lets the Earth's mass pull him back onto his bed. It's still ridiculous o'clock in the morning and everything feels filthy. The light yellows like a sweat stain. He knew Robin Goodfellow was ominous even apart from the strawberry scarf (which must surely have been a coincidence). Anyone who rubs Horatio Patel wrong can't possibly be right.

Horatio, there is no geodetic North without you. There's only grid north and magnetic north, and I'm equally shit at navigating those.

KRR

KK   **ZZZZ**

AAAAA   CKKKKK

The front door opens.
With a key, with a key, with a key.
Before Ben can even push himself upright, Horatio is in the bedroom frowning.

"Benjamin, are you spooning a guitar?"

*Oh Thank Baby Christmas Manger Jesus
I Love You
Glory To God In The Highest
I Thought I'd Never See You Again*

Messy waves fall to Horatio's shoulders, and the hollows under his eyes have formed ripples like a pond struck by a pebble. Meanwhile, Ben feels the stone blocking the tomb entrance rolling away. He's tearing off yards of funeral shrouds. He's tossing shreds on the cave floor like so much confetti.

"Well . . . yeah?" he answers. "It . . . does appear that I'm spooning a guitar?"

"The Sunburst? Really?"

"It was pretty bad. Worse for you! But bad."

Nodding, Horatio directs his eyes at the wall.

Please don't look like that. If you break it, you buy it, I'll buy it, just tell me how.

"I'm not staying long."

"Oh," Ben says. It's all he can come up with.

"Though I'm taking a shower first and eating something."

"OK."

"But I may be back, um, depending."

Ben's pulse hares off into the underbrush. "Yeah, cool, totally, whatever you say. Depending on what?"

"Tell me what you meant," Horatio requests hoarsely.

"Yeah . . . sure, which bit? What did I say?"

"Supernovas."

"You're in your inner citadel," Ben notes.

"Beg pardon?"

"The Stoics. Then later Boethius, who had this rad life and fortune and family and everything and then, like, got screwed by the king and tossed in prison to rot. SparkNotes version is retreat to your principles when going through the sausage grinder, because even destiny can't take away your honor."

"Cracking good observation."

"Sorry, I'm sorry! What was the question?"

"You texted me, while clearly out of your tree, that we were each half of a supernova. What does that mean, Benjamin?"

Ben makes a supreme effort to, by some miracle, become sober and lucid.

Do. Not. Fuck. This. Up.

"A particular type of supernova." Ben sits, crossing his legs. "They're called type one-A. And we're not exactly a supernova yet, I was reeeeally drunk, we're actually two stars caught in a mutual gravitational pull, in a configuration called single degenerate progenitors. One of them is a white dwarf, and that one's this ridiculously intense wee bastard of a star—obviously that's me—and very often, the other one is a red giant. Shit. OK, this is not meant to sound as racist as it does when actually coming out of my mouth, this is pure cosmology, so ignore the, like, accidentally racist aspects?"

Horatio crosses his arms, waiting.

"Right yep, so the white dwarf sucks gas out of the red giant, *slurp slurp slurp* stealing all this energy. But at a specific threshold, the white dwarf gets too dense and hot, and then it goes supernova, *boom*, very big boom, and that is one kind of type one-A supernova, and I think we've, uh. Crossed the tipping point."

Horatio meets Ben's eyes. The pain is buried, but Ben can feel it, pulsating like the heat from a dying sun. "I need to know whether you actually give a piss about me."

"Nope. It's super more intense than that, the pissing. I'm not expressing myself well. What I mean is, you're geodetic North."

"And *that* means?"

"I'd be lost without you."

Horatio rakes his hands through his hair and exits. Seconds later, Ben can hear the shower running.

Better than it could have been.

Water pounds angrily into the tub. Ben stumbles into the kitchen. Even if he guesses wrong, the act of heating the food will count. When the microwave beeps he retrieves a plate of falafel and pizza, adding a few avocado sushi pieces and forkfuls of cold noodles for luck.

Horatio returns fully dressed, his hair in a damp knot and his eyes hooded. When he spies the plate, they widen in surprise. He spears a sushi roll with the fork.

Ben squashes a fond smile that will be very much misinterpreted.

"So," Horatio says after consuming most of the plate. "True north, that's . . . considerably more important than I've felt of late."

Ben's lungs ache. "You're all that matters."

"Now you've lost the more important bits? Terribly complimentary, cheers."

"No, you're everything, you're the kindest, smartest, most—"

"Don't big me up like that, it's unfair," Horatio snaps.

"Uh, excuse me?"

"Flattery is cheap."

Benjamin blinks, genuinely stumped; he never flatters anyone, let alone his closest friend. "Why the *hell* should I flatter you?"

"Because—"

"No, think this through," Ben insists, anger percolating. "What could I possibly have to flatter you about?"

Horatio's eyes flash. "Right, daft of me, apologies."

"Shut up, Horatio. You don't have any money, so I don't want any. In fact, how much are you still in the hole? Because I could make that go—"

"Stop it," Horatio hisses.

"OK, sure. You don't want my money. If money is power then I'm, like, waaaaay more powerful than you. I don't need you to cheat on tests for me, or introduce me socially, or get me a job. I'm rich and brilliant. Flattery is currency for getting something, and you have nothing whatsoever I need."

"Then I'll be looking at flights back to—"

"No no no no, sorry, *wrong*, you have nothing of *material* value I need."

"What the fuck do you need, then?"

"You. That's a hell of a reason to compliment you. I need *you*."

Ben can't look at his friend, so he looks at the kitchen floor. Its pattern repeats in interlocking stars and diamonds, the black and white tessellation unbroken save for where the decades-old tile is cracked. Three-dimensional space fades in and out, the foreground shifting to the background. He's as exhausted as he would be racing up and down M. C. Escher's impossible staircases.

"What's next?" Horatio asks quietly.

"You mean with the investigation or with us? Anything could happen. I could get kidnapped by pirates and it wouldn't even, like, surprise me."

Horatio's mouth wants to smile. "Is there anything you're actually certain of that I should know about?"

Ben walks a few paces closer.

"I don't know whether you'll forgive me tomorrow, or next week, or twenty years from now. But I know that I'll work as hard as I can, spend as long as it takes, to make that happen. If it's even, you know. Possible."

Horatio's eyes search his face. Then he closes the gap, takes Ben by the shoulders, and kisses him. Softly, just below his hairline. Lingering for several seconds before pulling away.

"It's possible," he says as he walks out the door.

Ben sways momentarily and then

```
  d
    e
      f
        l
          a
            t
              e
         ssssssssss
```

like a punctured balloon.

Oh, Christ on a Ritz cracker, that was excruciating.

Shivering, Ben forces himself upright. He touches his brow.

It might be glowing, is it glowing?

He can't tell. There are too many loose ends swirling through his addled mind—now that Horatio has been addressed, and nothing more can ameliorate that problem save time, he needs to dive back into Whac-A-Mole.

Lia was tied up in some sadistic nightmare with Jórvík. And never told me. And drank herself senseless.

You can't swing a dead cat around here without hitting a cold case in the vicinity of New World's Stage, according to Norway and Fortuna.

Rory and Garrett are spies. Really bad spies.

Robin Goodfellow is a walking curse.

Dreams come true.

As do nightmares, apparently.

KNOCK KNOCK KNOCK

He's back, Horatio must have forgotten his keys, and now that he's returned Ben can give him a preview of his speech at the gala tomorrow but firstly throw himself over the event horizon beyond which even light can't escape and kiss him until they're both—

Paul Brahms waits in the hall.

"You are, like, so deeply not who I was expecting that the disappointment can't be computed," Ben reports. "It is an impossible quantity, it is not Lebesgue measurable, how let down I am—the equation will only come out to zero or infinity."

"Hey there, Ben," Paul ventures, peering into the apartment. "What a week and no kidding, am I right? I'm sorry I haven't had as much free time to follow up with you as you think you deserve. Am I interrupting anything?"

"Iiiiiiitty-bitty nervous breakdown. No big."

"And we have privacy?"

"I am as free as a quantum particle."

"Oh, good. May I come in?"

Paul carries a messenger bag. A sickly sheen coats his brow, as if a cue ball were suffering a fever, but then again Paul never looks well the day before the gala. And this is the first without Jackson.

"It's, uh, surreal that it's all going to go down tomorrow without him," Ben offers.

"What's that, Ben?" Paul looks up, almost startled.

"My dad. Jackson. I miss him, too."

"Oh." Paul chuckles. "Really, I can't imagine."

"Imagine what?"

"Missing him the way you must."

Paul returns to the middle distance as if he hadn't been interrupted.

What would Horatio do? Tea, yes. He'd make tea.

"So," Ben calls from the kitchen. "Tell me every single thing that's ever gone south between my dad and my uncle."

Paul brandishes a folder. "I always hate to disappoint you, even though, let's face it, that happens pretty much whenever we see each other, right? But no, I'm here for another reason."

A prickle of unease crawls over Ben's scalp. It's the exact opposite of the sensation Horatio left behind with his lips; if Horatio is a proton, Paul is an anti-proton. Ben drops two brown-flavored bags into the ubiquitous New World's Stage mugs. As he sets them down, Paul smiles crookedly.

"Boy, here's a trip down memory lane—what, twelve years ago? That was when we moved the gala from midtown to the Financial District, really got the thing moving. And what's yours there, five years back? You took Lia on that trip to the Finger Lakes, collecting foliage for her *Inferno* project. What a show that was, eh?"

Ben sets his tea down. He doesn't know what to do with his hands. They never talk about Lia—especially not anymore.

"Yeah," he agrees. "It, yeah."

Lia built a living room filled with secondhand furnishings. But on fire. She and Ben took a car, scoured sleepy hamlets for foliage in impossible bandwidths, colors so saturated they hurt the retinas. She cured them in water and glycerin and coated every surface with preserved leaves in hellish colors, unusually silent. Even for Lia immersed in work.

"What's that?" Ben nods at the folder, desperate for a topic shift.

"Oh, it's the board sign-off for the gala's insurance rider. One second, I must have a pen someplace, everything has been so topsy . . . ah! Goodness, it's not leaky, is it? Whew. Just signature here, and then initial here, please. Thank you! I always say, these events are—"

"Ninety-five percent preparation and five percent perspiration." Ben finishes with a flourish. "I hear you're worried about the theatre's money. Do tell."

Paul's lips tilt as he slides the folder back in his bag. Ben has seen a similar expression before: benign, ass-kissing, mostly directed at Jackson Dane.

Now it's a smiley face pasted onto a withered bag of skin.

"Sure, why not tell you?" Paul settles back into the cushion. "Jackson's more experimental forays have been driving New World's Stage into the concrete. Poor guy, always trying to outrun having been born in Texas. Desperate to escape the taint of the fortune he was *born with*. One more artsy show that gets on *Masterpiece Theatre* and is hari-kari for the box office and he'll be accepted by the Manhattan theatrical establishment? Despite the fact he's not an East Coaster or a Los Angeles import? Please. That was never going to happen."

Having never thought of his dad this way, Ben frowns. Having never heard Paul speak this way, he leans closer. It's like turning on his radio and finding it set to a random Christian rock station.

"Paul, are you all right?"

"Much better, thanks, Ben."

"Since . . . ?"

"Since you sent me your gala presentation. I'd have seen it anyhow, of course, the techs know not to incorporate content without my signing off on it. Your skipping the middleman was awfully gracious, though. Obviously, I can't let you go through with it."

Thoughts audition in Ben's brain, are rejected as unsuitable.

"It would deeply upset your mother," Paul continues. "It would wreak havoc with our theatre company, don't mistake me, but your mother has been through enough, don't you think?"

OUR theatre?

Are you in love with my mother?

"Holy shit, are you in love with my mother?" he blurts.

Paul's teeth show briefly. Neat, small rodent teeth, teeth for scavenging and for self-defense. "There's nothing I wouldn't do for your mother, but that takes the form of making her life easier. Nothing more, and god forbid ever anything less. She's a queen, Benny. You never understood that."

"Shit, shit, shit, you *are*."

"Young man, do not—"

"Oh god, Paul, that is just a, that is a *mess*. And I don't even have to go over your head to make this gala slideshow happen, I *am* over your head in, like, every way. It's happening."

"Not on my watch, Ben." The sweat on Paul's brow has evaporated. "I say the word, it all goes away. And I plan to."

"What the hell happened to you?" Ben demands. "I don't understand."

"No. No one understood. But you especially didn't, you pathetically self-obsessed asshole."

Ben stares, aware of nothing but

w h i t e n o i s e

white noise is not simply soothing sounds but is defined by the oscillation of the sound wave//if created in a studio an engineer would play every frequency audible at identical low volume// producing the same effect on the ear as white light has on the eye.

"I understand your confusion, I really do," Paul continues. "It wasn't ever easy acting this way. The boor who's triple-checking equipment, studying every ledger, but your father wasn't very easy to control, you understand. He was as headstrong as you are, maybe. Trying to get what he wanted. What Jackson didn't have was subterfuge."

Air slithers in and out of Ben's lungs. "And, uh, what you wanted? How'd you end up with that?"

Paul smiles a viper's smile. "Studying."

"Studying what?"

"Absolutely everything. Especially if it had to do with Jackson or Trudy or Claude Dane."

"You . . ." Ben tries. It doesn't work out.

"Or Ben Dane, for that matter. Anyhow. They need me back at the theatre. I really don't have long, I'm always telling you that, but you never listen."

Ben's chest feels tight. "My dad . . . What the hell, Paul, you stopped a robbery in an alleyway and my dad gave you a new career. You. I thought you were best friends. You fought for the company together, you, Jesus Christ, I think you love my mother, why would you try to *own* them?"

"Do you think you know what it feels like to be powerless?"

"Of course I do."

"You don't have the first clue, you spoiled modern aristocrat," Paul spits. "Lia and I were about to lose our home after Laura passed, about to be in a *shelter*. We'd suffered for years trying to save her, and all we had to show for it was misery. Do you know what any kind of hunger other than aesthetic suffering *looks like*?"

Ben has forgotten how sounds are formed.

It's something to do with waves.

If a tree falls in an empty forest,
   it doesn't make a sound,
      it makes waves,
         and it requires ears for the waves to become sounds,
            what no one thinks about is that
               the animal experience is the key difference
                  between sound and mere oscillation.

Ben is experiencing Paul Brahms, master manipulator, expound on his nefarious career, and he thinks a tree falling on him would probably feel similar.

"I recognized your father at the bar where I'd stopped to have one drink before heading home to my daughter with enough groceries for two more days." Paul's voice could save the polar ice caps. "Jackson liked dives, always did. The worse the neon flickered and the more cleavage the staff showed, the better, even in a five-thousand-dollar suit. You could practically smell it on him too—part of the reason none of the stage elites around here ever gave him the time of day. When he finished his beer, I followed him. I had management experience, did theatre in college—I thought I could beg for an usher job, anything. Jackson getting mugged in that alley was the turning point of my life."

"You were telling the truth all those times," Ben breathes. "That, that crap about not controlling your feet. You saved Dad because he was influential and you were desperate. If he'd just been some random—"

"I'd have called the cops." Paul checks his wristwatch. "From four or five blocks away, probably. But since the victim was your father, I couldn't leap into that crack between walls fast enough. It worked, too."

"What—but *how*?"

"Do you know what you can accomplish if you've read the entire biography of another human being?" Paul muses. "Well, I'll tell you, Benny, the answer is *anything*. Jackson liked cheap beer and cheaper women. He would have sold his soul to get Philip J. Smith or Thomas Schumacher or any of the real Broadway power brokers to invite him to golf. He was ashamed of the fortune I would have killed for to save my daughter, my *wife*. He was paranoid and suspicious, increasingly, and Trudy and I were forced to run things with Claude's help. He was disturbed. Where the hell do you think *you* inherited it?"

At least part of what Paul says is true. Ben remembers his dad getting snubbed by Disney, watched him crumple RSVPs declining the Danes' invites to donor weekends. Ben just worshipped him too ardently for it to register.

"He was a willing enough ally once you nudged him in the right direction. I never even had to tell him that his wife was sleeping with his baby brother practically since their wedding day. Something to do with Claude being charming, I'd wager, Claude being decent, Claude being *normal*."

"She wasn't," Ben husks. "You—"

Paul opens the satchel again, pulling out a sheaf of monochrome photographs. He spreads them on the coffee table in a careless smear.

trudy		hotel door	
sunlight claude			palm tree
hand	claude trudy	face	touch
gesture	concrete	hair	
skin			light
trudy claude trudy claude			

No matter how much Ben wants it not to be true, it was his first thought after they married, his first after Jackson accused his own brother in the videos. That this relationship between them was longstanding. And that certainties Ben had always trusted were lies.

"Why would you possibly have these?"

"Insurance," Paul replies. "Your entire family abhors the notion of a scandal—if they ever tried to oust me, well, I had leverage."

"So I guess you killed my father for them?" Ben's flesh crawls.

Paul's face lights, a sickly fluorescent-green satisfaction. "Don't be ridiculous. Of course not."

"Then Claude did murder him?"

"I'd say I hate to break this to you, but the pair of you always did deserve each other—both utter wastes of skin with delusions of grandeur. Your dad either overdosed by accident or design."

"You bastard. In those clips he said that eyes were always on him, he said it *directly fucking to you*."

Ben flashes back to his dad's videos and his gut boils.

And I probably won't need to make any more of these . . . confessions. It just feels like someone is always watching. I can't shake it. It's driving me up the wall.

Jackson was speaking straight to his own shadow governor, completely unaware that he was right.

So the paranoia wasn't paranoia. As for the death, though . . .

Ben understands not everything has a reason. Just because Spinoza argued that something could never come out of nothing doesn't mean that there's a *motive* behind every action. Determinate cause leading to a dramatic effect could be murder or suicide, sure. It could also be a pharmaceutical error or a coincidental overdose.

Meanwhile, numb fear inks across his heart at the look on Paul's face.

"Jackson was ruthless and so am I, in my own way," Paul says when he sees the penny drop. "Except in your father, you admired it, and I don't imagine you've ever admired me in your life. That's all right. I'm through giving a damn over being treated like some idiot lackey by my daughter's former fiancé."

The leather bag opens once more, and now there's a gun in Paul Brahms's hand, and Ben has no choice but to laugh hysterically.

"We're going upstairs."

"Wait, what? Why?"

"Benjamin, for once, you're going to do as *I* tell you."

The trip up to the rooftop passes in a blur. *This is another dream, it has to be.* Descartes worried himself raw over whether life might simply all be a dream. Ben once told Horatio about this and his friend replied that it could get a lot worse.

Chin up, in the Hindu Vedanta worldview, we're all just scraps of Brahma's dreams, which rather pisses on the notion of autonomy altogether.

The dream-roof is exactly as he and Horatio left it. Chairs, cinder blocks, the brick housing projects. Pigeons wheel above them, heedless and graceful. If he's dreaming, or even if it's Brahma dreaming, their dreams are incredibly detailed to include such individually painted birds.

"I don't suppose saying 'please don't do this' will help?" Ben attempts as adrenaline crawls up his throat.

Silence. Paul gestures him to the edge of the rooftop, where Ben can see the sidewalks stretching away in their great grey grid.

"If you're going to murder me, why and why *here*?"

"I'm not murdering you, I'm helping you fulfill a dream," Paul sneers. "You're trampling the system I've built, poking your nose in everywhere. As to why we're up here, because I can shut the door and no one will find you for a week. The gala will run as planned, and you finally get your eternal peace. Hereditary depression and insanity, they'll suppose. It isn't even a lie. Won't it be wonderful to cover what I did with the truth?"

"Lia wouldn't want you to do this!" Ben attempts. "Lia—"

"Lia isn't here." If Paul could slay him with a look, Ben would already be dead. "All you do is make people miserable. I want you to comprehend that, before the end. Your mother, your father, my *only child*, and you vowed to make her happy and she *disintegrated* right in front of your fucking eyes."

"That—I—no, that wasn't my fault, not entirely, do you remember the janitor from back—"

"Nothing is ever your fault," Paul says, disgusted. "You were given everything, and you tried to shove it all down the garbage disposal. So did Jackson, always preening about the theatre supporting itself. I've despised you for longer than I can even calculate, but I'm happy enough to do you this final favor. You don't want to exist anymore? I can arrange that."

Death, when contemplated, can look like temptation.

Death, when unasked-for, looks like being damned.

Paul raises the weapon. Ben's hand shoots out, and muscles

clench and grip and wrench and tighten

and then Ben registers a *bang* followed by a scream he suspects is his own voice.

Paul isn't moving. His eyes are open, though, clear as the morning sky reflected in them, as he reclines in a warm and ever-widening pool of blood.

LIA

In New York, when a tree dies,
    nobody mourns that
it was *cut down in its prime*. Nobody
    counts the rings,
notifies the loved ones. There are other
    trees.

—*Sarah Kay, "The Oak Tree Speaks"*

THE MORNING OF THE New World's Stage gala, Lia stands in a puddle of hose water on 28th Street between Sixth and Seventh Avenues, watching humanity flow around her.
I am a river rock, she thinks as pedestrians slip by.
I am smooth and cold and collected.
Following the meeting with Jessica, who dazedly accepted all proposals and even liked the ludicrous amount of lavender, they hastily quit the National Arts Club. Mam'zelle muttered something about *en taxi.* Moma glared at the iron fence defending Gramercy Park. Lia knew she only imagined it as sinister, but a flock of roosting pigeons burst forth from a neighbor's rooftop, soaring overhead like spies.

LAVENDER: *Mistrust or request for reassurance in the Victorian era, imports caution moving forward. Was given to soldiers going into imminent battle.*

"We'll send instructions, *chouchou*," Mam'zelle said, tapping away at her phone.

"Ready the flowers for us, yes?" Moma pressed her arm as a yellow cab rolled up. The driver stopped at the smallest flick of Mam'zelle's frosted pink manicure.

"Oh god, by myself?" Fresh alarm set in. "I can't!"

"You surely can."

"Please don't ditch me, I—"

"Don't fuss, baby girl. We ain't ditching you, we *need* you while we've business elsewhere, and you on our team, right?"

"I, well, of course, always," Lia stammered. "But what the hell just happened in—"

"The harvest is swollen," Moma whispered fiercely. "Ready to fall."

And then the sisters drove away.

Not knowing which was more frightening—Moma quoting Maw-maw, or the fact that Lia highly suspected they were off to deal with Robin in some fashion—Lia said nothing. Despite the humid funk of summer, she felt a cold thrill.

For all that events were unfolding so rapidly, they seemed planned somehow. Fated. So Lia did as she was told and returned home. She studied her sketch, pored over their design notes, readied all her ingredients in the basement workshop, and set to work.

PENNYROYAL: *While used primarily to foster peace and protection during a journey, combined with other ingredients useful for removal of curses.*

BUTTERFLY WEED: *Not as potent if employed alone, but indicates "go thy ways and leave me in peace," which when combined with more powerful flora will come to pass.*

CHESTNUT FLOWER: *I seek justice for a wrong to be righted.*

The air filled with scent until Lia could practically taste it, then vanished when her olfactory sense tired. A dusting of red pepper powder on the blooms was involved. Greedy stems drank essential oils. At first Lia's hands shook with the importance of the task—but that soon receded. She was sharply focused and mindless at once, the way she always felt weaving flowers into shapes. This act always soothed her, the way Maw-maw would spend hours muttering in the kitchen or Moma would twist herself into pretzels at the ballet barre.

When Jessica's bouquet was finished, Lia surveyed it in the lamp glow. It took her all night to complete and was a spectacularly odd wonder. Sprays in all directions, perfumed, a firework of texture and aroma.

Lia adored it in a way she'd never adored anything.

When she texted Mam'zelle, the sister, despite the early hour, immediately answered to wrap the bouquet and meet them at the flower market. One final ingredient remained to be added. Mam'zelle wasn't forthcoming about where they'd gone, but Lia didn't feel like pushing. They hadn't come home—but then, they often didn't. Her spine felt straighter after finishing, the thrill of completion making her movements deft and sure as she folded the gold paper. Tied the twine.

Tonight she'd be at the New World's Stage gala delivering this to Jessica. She was certain.

Which meant she'd see Benjamin again. Something complicated happened in her belly, a few organs readjusting. But nothing like panic—only anticipation, a clock ticking down to an alarm you'd set yourself.

Lia swept up her clippings and encased the bouquet in thin cardboard. Added a small rose quartz in a velvet pouch for lagniappe. She had no notion of what was going on. What the dreams meant, how Robin and the sisters were involved, where the hell her strawberry scarf was, or what would go down that night. But as she spared a last glance at the altar and the endless five-pointed symbol, she thought that time had wound to some sort of crux. And she was goddamn ready after two years to be back in the game of life again. Find out where she landed on Robin's and the sisters' opposing sides of the circle.

Now Lia stands, flowers in her arms, waiting on the corner. The market is in full swing, hoses spraying, corn palms being off-loaded from truck beds, lopped apple branches grasping at the clouds. The skies bleach their way toward a paler blue. Exhausted dog owners stagger past coffee shops.

Tap, tap, tap come jaunty fingers on her shoulder.

Lia gasps when her head turns, greeted by Robin's gleaming teeth. Lia doesn't like people who pry, or people who crowbar for that matter, and everything about this dapper, dashing older gentleman makes her stomach churn.

"What the hell do you think you're doing?" Lia clutches her bouquet tighter.

Robin Goodfellow makes a little bow. "Tip-top morning, wouldn't you say, my dear?"

Something odd happens to her eyesight. Lia blinks as hard as she can. For an instant, all the people on the street turned a horrible flickering monochrome.

But it's gone now. Everything is fine.

"Not anymore."

"There's the spark I like so much!" Robin clasps his hands. "Oh, just smell that! Bouquet construction completed without a hitch, I take it?"

Lia feels like she's baring her teeth, though she can't be sure.

"Masterfully accomplished—can tell without even a peep at it, if you know what to sniff for. And I do."

Lia glowers. "What was all that bullshit yesterday? My bag, *my* portfolio, my—"

"Illicit photographic proof of adultery?" Robin chuckles. "Clumsy of me, I know, my darling duckling. Apologies. Had my reasons, and I'll tell you all about them, too! Under *one* condition."

"You knew where to find me just now." Lia steps away.

"If you're of enough interest to me, I know where you are at any given moment. Just finished breakfasting with our sisters, in fact! They're a block and a half distant."

Lia's eyes slit at him.

"Oh, fine. Step under this awning, dear, we're frightfully underfoot. Over a lovely breakfast, I managed to steal a look at Mam'zelle's mobile phone by lucky chance, so knew just where to run into you."

"Why?"

"Business proposition." Robin nods his white head toward a diner. "Coffee?"

"Not on your life. Talk."

"Delighted. All is in readiness for the gala tonight. I take it you're quite . . . intimate with the family? What a remarkable circumstance! To think that you were once affianced to the son and heir."

"Tell me what you're up to or fuck off instantly."

"Can't be done, dear girl." Robin affects a look of sinister regret. "As I said, it's conditional."

"On what exactly?"

"On your defection, pet." Robin's lips make a pleased V. "To my side of the circle, as it were."

A dolly stuffed with hothouse tulips clatters past, *violet, yellow, pink*. Horns blare the instant the light changes. Lia thinks about being afraid and supposes she might have been before finishing the arrangement for Jessica. She isn't now. She doesn't even want a sip of something to take the edge off.

She's furious.

"Is this some kind of sick chess match between you four?" she growls. "Those women *saved me*, they care about me. They're like my family now."

"Canny choice of words." Robin is entirely unfazed. "Because there's a *very* great deal they aren't telling you. But isn't that what families do? Stay silent? Tell each other fibs?"

Flecked within the amber glow of Robin's eyes, Lia sees for the first time, are grey glints. They ought to be charming, but they're the color of something cold and ancient, like dessicated fog. They make her glad she's on a public street.

"Oh! Silly old bugger, me, nearly forgot." Robin whisks a piece of fabric from his inner jacket pocket. "Found something of yours. Wanted to return it in person."

It is Lia's mother's scarf, freshly pressed, its wild strawberry population altered. Where once were only berries dangling from their stalks, lush serrated leaves have been added in botanically accurate triplicates. A needle with poison-green thread still trailing from its eye pierces Robin's lapel.

"How dare you?" Lia snarls, snatching it away. "This was my *mom's*, you bastard!"

One hand flutters over where Robin's heart ought to be. "Had fallen on the ground, hadn't it? Might as well have rescued it, eh? Added a few of my own design improvements for you! My entire line of work, isn't it, improving designs?"

"Fell where? In my room, wasn't it? You searched my portfolio, you son of a bitch. My bag, my . . . that's where you saw the photo of Trudy and Claude, why you dumped it everywhere—"

"It may have crossed my mind to better acquaint myself with the new ally of my *very* old friends." Robin delivers a cheery grin. "Who really ought to be sharing more with you than they have done. Look, decide at the benefit this evening? I've a feeling it'll be a *smashing* success, and really, as an event planner, there's so much more opportunity for travel, exotic locales, pay's spectacular, and—"

"Outta her face or you will *learn* just what I'll do," Moma snaps.

All three of the sisters have appeared. Mam'zelle has her fists on her hips, Moma has a finger in Robin's nose, and Maw-maw holds a small garden spade like it's a lance. Lia twists her mother's kerchief. The strawberry leaves seem to glint at her, poisonous and alive.

"Ladies!" Robin throws his arms wide. "And so soon after our repast! Here for a touch of specialty shopping, I imagine?"

"Is this *sac à merde* bothering you, *chère*?" Mam'zelle growls.

"Yes," Lia replies.

"Can't deny it," Robin coos. "But she held her own."

"She's a lil' piece of leather and well put together," Moma says. "Best not to cross her, you want your balls to still keep you company."

"*Adieu, adieu*," Mam'zelle shoos him. "There's a bad smell lingering on this street."

"Begone." Maw-maw lifts the trowel, which has a tag dangling from it.

Rubbing his hands as if surveying a delicious feast, Robin laughs. "I'll pop off, then. Plenty to do before this evening! Pip pip! Enjoy having your scarf back, my dear, and do give a think to what we discussed?"

Robin swans off, a spring in his step.

"That Robin Goodfellow is on my last nerve," Moma announces.

"*Mange tes morts!*" Mam'zelle yells, which Lia knows is extremely foul language for her and means *go eat your dead ones*.

Maw-maw spits, hanging the spade back on its sale hook.

"OK," Lia says. "The three of you are taking me somewhere comfortable. With good coffee. And then you are going to tell me what the fuck is going on."

IT'S TOO EARLY IN the day for the Oscar Wilde restaurant to be open. But weird things happen around the sisters, so after Maw-maw pushes her tongue out and taps a text message, they are greeted at the door by a happily waving man wearing cleaning gloves. And ushered into Oscar Wilde immediately.

The trio lob sisterly smiles at each other. Their flower shop, the market, the National Arts Club: These are shabby house slippers compared to the glass slipper that is Oscar Wilde. Lia's friends swoon in satisfaction every time. From the green-patinaed statues lofting electric globes to the Carrara marble bar, Oscar Wilde restaurant looks like a nineteenth-century steamship crashed on it. Every square centimeter is swathed in damask, adorned with mustachioed gentlemen's portraits, or sheathed in velvet. The dim lighting likewise suits the sisters. If they were costumed, they'd look like they were about to take a foolish coal magnate for half a million dollars by rapping on tables.

Settling into a corner booth over coffees, the women fall silent. Moma and Mam'zelle angle eyebrows across the tabletop. Maw-maw glares holes in it.

"OK, I'll start," Lia proposes. "That jackass just tried to recruit me to *his* side of the circle."

The sisters emit discreet hoots. Lia imagines them in a lavish bayou parlor sipping spiked lemonade and drowning in petticoats.

Mam'zelle selects a sugar cube. "Oh, *petite chou*, of course he did, the reprobate."

"He also said there are aspects that you . . . haven't told me?"

They don't say yes, but they don't say no. Maw-maw tips the uncapped saltshaker over, starts drawing symbols in the grains.

"No, we're talking about this." Lia's rediscovered inner scaffolding grows stronger. She places the flowers on the table. "You three have *always* been here for me. When I needed you, before I knew I needed you. It's just as if you've always been *here*, the whole time . . . it must be more than your liking my art, and more than your being kind to walking disaster areas."

"*Nous amions*, Lia." Mam'zelle holds both hands out.

"Can't love be simple, baby girl?" Moma adds.

"Like calls to like." Maw-maw nods.

"Nah, nah. Let's try something else. Simple question: Are the three of you voodoo witches? With a secret cupboard of black cat bones and—"

Mam'zelle's hand flies to her imaginary pearls. Moma's cup slams in its saucer, and Maw-maw scrapes an angry fingernail through her salt creation.

"You think we practice that kinda dumbass cruelty?" Moma

demands. "My ears are burning, me. What do you think the
likes of them type do, baby girl? They take a black cat, a harmless little puss. Throw it into water that's supposed to be boiling
but ain't hardly is yet, these dumbshit sorcerers is so close bred
with their own pigs. Listen to the cat scream out its last wish,
which is to *die faster*. Black cat bones? Get you out—"

"You've seen this happen though, to a cat," Lia confirms.
"Thirty years ago, when you were nine? Two hundred years
ago, when you were fifty-three?"

The sisters clink spoons against porcelain.

"Never has it been polite to ask a lady her age, *chère*,"
Mam'zelle chides.

"How about the voodoo, then? Is all this window dressing to
run a hip boutique, or is it spellcasting?"

Moma scoffs. "Real voodoo ain't spellcasting. It's the science
of Them Who's Underneath. It's a rope back to the top of the
mountain. It's woman knowledge passed down and down and
down through the lines, and you'll learn it all. Because you are
apt, and I am practiced. Crossing, hexing, or blessing, I know
the ways of it, me."

"What does *apt* mean?"

Mam'zelle flirts through her eyelashes. "You've been studying
ancestor knowledge since you were a girl, Lia."

"Sure enough, we all the time telling you that you're gifted,
but *really*," Moma snorts. "Starting at that age? You're a prodigy, you."

"How . . . long have you known me, exactly?" Lia's lungs
don't feel large enough for air.

"From them gallery shows." Moma rolls her eyes. "That's
when we first *knew*. But we done seen all your pictures—school
projects, Polaroids. *Three-by-fives*. You spun funeral barges out
of twigs and snake grass and sailed them away praying to your
mamma. We got a hundred percent Mozart of root work right
here."

One midsummer day after Laura died, skies yawning wider

than Lia had ever seen them, she'd found a patch of buttercups along the riverbank. Lia had always loved buttercups. Shining like fresh yolks, heads bobbing. Her mother taught her the game of holding one under her neck to see if it glowed back yellow, which meant you liked butter, because her mother loved butter and buttercups, too. So Lia picked them all—every last one she could find—while they still shone like sun mirrors, wrapped them up in the strawberry scarf, and carried them home. She flattened their heads between two sheets of wax paper and ran Laura's hot iron over it. It's still resting in her portfolio.

BUTTERCUP: *In Latin, "little frog." Symbolically: humility and the freedom of childhood. They bloomed first when a miser refused to share his wealth with the pixies, and they slit his bag so that gold scattered wherever he went.*

"Are the buttercups watched over by pixies?" Lia asks.

A stunned silence falls.

"How in hell you know that, baby girl?" Moma asks incredulously.

"My mother always said so."

Maw-maw coughs, tapping the table.

"*Ça alors*," Mam'zelle says to Moma, impressed. "My sister, our Lia is surely ready as she'll ever be."

Maw-maw bangs the empty saltshaker.

"What I tell you just the other day now, my sister?" Moma agrees. "This one here—"

"*The time has come,*" Maw-maw growls. She thumps twice on the tabletop for attention and points to the scribbles she's drawn in the salt. "To teach her the way of things."

Moma tosses her hair till the tiny bells clack, and Mam'zelle makes a ladylike *pray continue* gesture.

This might not be witchcraft, Lia thinks, *but I am spellbound.*

"All is connected," Maw-maw says. "From the bright hot bang at the beginning, to the dark cold silence at the end, and back again. It is woven already. Alpha to Omega, from the first nothing to the final nothing, the nothings attached and the same nothing. The circle is closed. None walking the path of the circle can see forward—only behind. But those outside of the circle, those who do not walk it?"

"You can see both ways," Lia says softly.

"Not perfectly, not *altogether*. We puzzle. We scheme. But yes, we can."

Lia can't recall Maw-maw ever smiling this kindly, and she's now possibly doubled the amount of words Lia has heard from her during any given discussion. She ought to be terrified, because this sounds insane. But far more shocking to Lia is that she already knows this speech. Not in cryptic mythological language, but from sitting on a rock at Riverside Park with the nearest star to the planet kissing her hair, watching a mad-eyed Columbia grad student she loved to distraction expostulating.

No, no, forget all that time-is-a-flat-circle Nietzsche crap, Ben laughed. *It's close, sure, but there are better descriptors. Think of a loaf of bread, though. The whole loaf of bread exists, the slices are time, and each slice is marked differently. As you flip through them, of course you can remember the last one you saw, and you can't* remember *the next one you're going to look at. But if you were outside of the loaf, outside of time? Everything is there. Complete. The ones you already saw don't vanish, the one in your hand exists, and the ones you haven't looked at yet are already there. That's time. That's what the universe is like.*

"*Mon Dieu*," Mam'zelle chuckles as she studies Lia, beringed fingers intertwining. "She already understands it."

"Four-dimensional space-time? Yeah." Lia laughs. "I do. Somebody taught me. So who are you, then?"

Maw-maw flashes a devilish grin. "We see the foul and turn it fair, hover through fog and filthy air. Sometimes the other way around. We have many names. We are the apportioners, the destinies."

"Maw-maw, I love you, but can we do this in English please?"

Both Maw-maw and Lia are surprised to find this statement of affection perfectly true. Reaching across the table, they briefly grasp hands. Lia would be marveling at her own understanding, and still more shocked by her easy acceptance. But hardly anything can surprise you after it makes sense that a bouquet can twist the shape of Fate.

Moma finishes her coffee. "My sister speaks true, her. The circle is closed. But it begins again and again. Multitudes."

"Multiverses," Lia translates, marveling.

"As you say. We travel them with you, teasing out their rightful shape."

"And that Robin Goodfellow dickweed?"

Mam'zelle laughs. "He walks the opposite side of the circle, *chouchou*. Sometimes, we win the day. Other times, *il reussit*. We've known that rascal . . . well, time as such does not apply. We are locked in battle. Each circuit for us involves different wars, both small and great. Matters, they build, they build, *et voilà*, they conclude. When they are about to conclude, up pops Robin again."

"Reap the harvest?" Lia glances at Maw-maw, who nods.

"From the beginning to the end, this circle round, we's us, and he's him," Moma explains. "Done been three warriors and the poet, three saints and the leper, three kings and the prophet. Too damn many to name."

"Three florists and the event coordinator?"

"Sure enough, baby girl."

"And . . . not to oversimplify this, but are you the good guys?"

Maw-maw brushes the salt onto her saucer. "Yes. No. We create, he destroys. Or the other way around. He weaves disasters, we unmake them. Or we craft gardens, and he razes them. We are order, he is chaos. Or the other way around. We are the fucked, and he is the fucker. Or the other—"

"Maw-maw, *tais-toi*!" Mam'zelle yells.

"On my life, you will take your pills if I gotta push them down your gullet, me," Moma snaps.

"I'll count them every morning from the bottle, my sister, *tu vois?*"

Lia wonders if hiding behind her hands will disguise the fact she's helpless with laughter. Probably not. Her shoulders are shaking.

"Robin right now, he's the Needleman." Moma glares daggers at her sister. "Back in N'awlins, from our time, folk were much afeared of the needle men. They was studying to be doctors, but said to come by night to Black graves and steal their bones to cut apart and sew up again. *Anatomists*, you'd call them nowadays, but they was body thieves what stole and stitched under sickle moons. Some of that was gospel, some of it weren't, but best way to describe that sorry-ass scallywag is he's the Needleman. He sews crazy quilts. We put them back into whole cloth."

"It's our lot to stop his goings-on." Mam'zelle sighs. "Come to that, *chère*, do you know what answer you'll make to him?"

"About what?"

"Which side of the circle you wanna walk," Moma replies.

Lia considers the first gallery exhibits the sisters probably magicked into happening for her.

"That was never really a question," she says. "You're stuck with me. Like . . . floral tape."

The sisters smile as one creature. It's possible they are, it occurs to Lia.

Who could say?

"I don't like what's in my mind, me." Moma takes the long mass of her braids, wraps it around her skinny wrist, and ties it on her shoulder. "That Robin, we know him of old. And we might weave half the tapestry, Robin the other half. But ain't no weaver alive as knows *exactly* what it'll look like hanging on the wall. No matter how many times they've settled themselves down at a loom. Endings have a mind of their own."

Nodding, Lia thinks of every art installation she's ever created. A gust of wind or a change in mood will affect the outcome.

"This bouquet you done finished for Miss Jessica?" Moma nods at it. "You made real good on this."

Lia can't believe she's blushing. "You haven't even looked at it."

Moma winks. The gentleman who brought them coffee tasting oddly of chicory presents the bill, and Mam'zelle produces a pink calfskin wallet. Lia lolls her head, contemplating the chandelier. It wouldn't look out of place in Versailles except that it's blessed by a hearty layer of dust. It reminds her, in a dingier sense, of Trudy's clock collection. Trudy is nearly as preoccupied by time as her son—she just fetishizes it in another way entirely. Both mother and child are ferociously aware of the clock ticking. Ben deals with this by picking at the concept like a tiny wound, Trudy by deafening herself under its influence.

"I don't know why Dad had those pictures of Claude and Trudy," she says. "But it's safe to assume Robin was determined to out them as lovers. Why, do you think?"

Mam'zelle checks her lipstick in a silver compact. "*Je ne sais pas, chère.* But he was sitting next to your friend Horatio on the plane flight here from London town, we found out at our conference this morning."

"*That's* who he was talking about? The one he called bloodsick?" Lia exclaims. "Wait, how—no, no. Horatio is here, Horatio *left*? Why would Horatio ever leave, he loves . . ."

It's not quite possible for Lia to say *it here in New York* instead of *Ben*. Lia watched Horatio love Ben for years and could never pity him—partly because Horatio was the most self-made person she'd ever met. But also because he carried it as if he knew he was born to do so. Some men would have unfurled their battle flag hearts, demand that Ben choose. Some would have severed ties, cut losses. Not Horatio. He'd glance warmly at Lia as if they worshipped the same sports team or followed the same band. *Did you hear what that idiot just said?* his eyes would ask, and Lia would roll hers. They loved each other dearly. They were the first ones out of their chairs with Sharpies to write drunken quotations on the wall board. The more ridiculous, the better, his handwriting angular capitals and hers flowing script. Lia wished she understood Ben's mind the way he did, the labyrinths and the whims; Horatio wished he were the one gentling him out of consciousness, sweetly sore and satiated. None of it mattered. They were partners. Allies in a common war against tragedy.

"What were you up to last night, when you didn't come home?" Lia asks, shocked at this news.

Moma coughs lightly. "Scheming and dreaming, baby. Finishing the tapestry. Figuring what's best to do."

"Mam'zelle, you said that bloodsickness could get people killed," she recalls, pulse thumping. "When Robin was talking about it."

"I did at that, and so it does, too."

Not Ben or Horatio, though.

Please, for the love of God, let our side win.

"Why, you're shivering—somebody's just walked over our Lia's grave." Moma's fingertips brush Lia's cheek. "What's the matter, baby girl?"

"Oh, nothing, it's just . . . mortal terror."

"Of what, *chère*?" Mam'zelle asks.

"Mortality. I . . . have a deep fear of losing things. People. I've lost enough."

"You have at that," Moma concurs.

"Loss visits all," Maw-maw reminds them.

"May we live every day till we don't," Mam'zelle concludes, nodding.

I'll help you, Lia thinks in the vague direction of Ben and Horatio. *Not that I know how yet.*

But I'm learning.

Moma offers her hands on either side, as does Mam'zelle. Lia does the same. When Maw-maw completes the circle, something in Lia softly breaks.

Sometimes breaking, though, doesn't feel brittle or cracked. Sometimes breaking feels like new, green shoots sprouting up through old, dead detritus.

THE FLOWER SHOP GREETS Lia as if she's a sleek predator and this is her personal jungle. Bamboo leaves flicker hello at her from within their ceramic dwellings, and the orchids smile with purple lips. It's always been this way. A question has been growing in her along the entire journey home, and as the women walk up the stairs, Lia decides to ask.

It's the most important one, after all.

"So," Lia attempts as they set their purses down upstairs. "Uh, this is awkward. Thank you for telling me what—no, sorry! Thank you for telling me *who* you are. And who Robin is."

The sisters turn to her like flowers to the daylight.

"But . . . who does that make me, then?" Lia manages through a tight throat.

"Oh, *chouchou*," Mam'zelle says.

"Sweet baby girl," commiserates Moma.

Shuffling across the room, Maw-maw takes her face in both calloused hands. Her eyes are a strange but clear grey-brown and they extend back through her head for many long miles.

"Sufficient for tomorrow are the evils thereof."

Somehow, Lia makes it to the third floor. Rummaging in her small closet, she finds the nearest thing to black tie she still has, but the gown at least is a particular favorite. She'll wear it tonight. And every single threadbare sentiment about serenity she's ever learned will be put to the test.

Ben. You said, in the dream, you still loved me even though we can never be together.

Tonight we'll find out what that means.

But once she's steamed her dress and hung it with care against the shower curtain, Lia feels an irresistible urge to close her eyes. So she climbs onto the soft bed in her dragon's cave/princess tower, sets her phone alarm, and falls into a very deep—but hardly dreamless—sleep.

HORATIO

Now I've been crazy couldn't you tell
I threw stones at the stars but the
    whole sky fell . . .
            —*Gregory Alan Isakov, "The Stable Song"*

WHATEVER HORATIO RAMESH PATEL expects to happen upon returning to their flat several hours before the gala the morning after Benjamin presented him with a vegetarian buffet and his heart on a platter, he is dead wrong.

He's still furious. But the idea of failing Benjamin bleeds him dry as fumes. Horatio hangs up his keys in the empty sitting room. They've plentiful time for the fussing with cravats and cummerbunds, and his friend is home—the shower is running.

"Benjamin," Horatio calls toward the bathroom. "Hullo?"

Feet aching, he sinks onto the couch. He never really planned to scarper off again. But he needed time without being cajoled, wheedled, teased, or any of the other things at which Benjamin excels. At first, he walked—past a dozen shoe repair stalls and a hundred banks and a million drugstores. Thinking. Then he tried Central Park, with the grass sheep used to graze on tickling his back. Thinking. Then a scabby motel smelling faintly of stale cigarettes. Still thinking.

Love is clutter and you are a diagnosed hoarder, he recalls concluding as he drifted off at last.

Love is about as useful as a thirty-year-old atlas.

"What the hell are you doing, you daft thing?" he moans, forearms on his knees. "Shaving your bloody legs? And did you think earlier to put extra Bernardo's coffee in the fridge like we used to do?"

After three minutes, Horatio is stroppy, because Benjamin can hear him perfectly well in there, based upon years of experimentation. After five, he is hurt: Hadn't his friend wanted him back rather badly?

At the six-minute mark, a jolt of adrenaline shocks him.

He flies off the sofa, slamming against the door. "Benjamin, answer me!"

The patter of precipitation continues uninterrupted. But the door handle turns when he clutches it, so Horatio warns, "Oi, I'm coming in there," and shoulders through.

What he sees is so precisely identical to what he'd always imagined, the déjà vu stuns him. The shower runs without steam, and Benjamin is curled up in the far corner, *dead, so this is the way the world ends,* and his shed clothing is smeared with scarlet.

Horatio dives forward, clutching thin, cool arms.

"Benjamin! Benjamin, answer me for god's sake."

The water beats down on his shoulders. Horatio hunches forward, and Benjamin does nothing at all.

"Please no, please, you wanted—I thought you wanted . . ."

The sound ripped from his own throat stops his words. He tilts Benjamin's head back, checking for a pulse, and *it's not too late, call 999, no it's 911, they can still do things, Christ please, please,* when Benjamin gasps, splutters, and smacks Horatio straight in the face as he flails to life.

Horatio lands on his arse, gaping.

"What have you done?" he cries. "Yes, ambulance, right, where is my—"

"No!" A bleary Benjamin scrambles for the taps. "Ooooh, lord that's cold! No ambulance, I'm fine, I'm fine."

"Is this an overdose or, or an *attempt*, there is *blood*, Benjamin, on your—"

"Dammit, dammit, so cold." Benjamin twists the flow off and scrapes the water from his face. He's a white rat caught in a storm drain. "Drop the phone, Horatio, there was, sorry . . . it . . ."

"It *what*?"

"I fell asleep. Finally."

"Asleep, you thundering nob, what in hell—"

"Stop, stop, stop. See the bottle of scotch up there with the shampoo? Just got kinda tired. Shocked, shocked and tired. The shock part lasted pretty much all of last night from what I can remember. There was an, uh, a thing happened right after you left, a shocking one. But I feel better now."

Horatio breathes like he just finished the Tour de France. There Benjamin is in the tub with a flagging Lagavulin bottle displayed above his brainless head and a pile of gore-stained togs in the corner. Rolling to his own knees, Horatio sets his palms on the porcelain to see for himself, eyes darting everywhere, but yes, fantastic, no one has any stab wounds.

"What were you doing?" Horatio snaps.

Benjamin slowly comes to his senses. "Last night? Hyperventilating, mainly. Just now? Dreaming, actually."

"Oh. Well, then. Was it nice?"

"Parts of it. Not all, it had its moments. Yep."

Horatio is the first to realize that they're on their knees facing each other over a foot-high barrier and the Dane heir is spectacularly nude, collarbones dripping, but decides the less said the better.

Benjamin shakes his short hair like a fifties pinup model. The madman in the shower does smell of excellent scotch. And is breathing normally. Horatio can tell both because their faces are not so very far apart.

Inches, Horatio thinks. *Lifetimes.*

Benjamin settles back on his heels. "Shit. Are you OK, man?"

"Ah. Well. You gave me a bit of a scare."

"Yeah, I think there's a reason it's called having a shower beer and not a shower . . . bottle. I was in, uh, there's. A situation."

"What sort?"

"The bad sort."

A gallows laugh breaks free. "I should very much say so, yes."

Horatio would like to simply collapse. But he's distracted. Benjamin hasn't been eating, which means a droplet has settled in the curve of his clavicle. It's important that he catalogue this for some reason. Dragging seconds later, Benjamin's head tilts.

"I owe you another apology. You're like, *very* wet," he says, smiling.

"So are you."

"Touché."

"Right."

"That was really lame of me, but please don't assume I did it on purpose?"

"Perish the thought. What were you dreaming of?"

"Some . . . pretty important shit, actually. One of the, the vivid ones. But it'll all come out in the wash tonight, I think. Don't you worry."

"Me, worry?"

Horatio prepares to rise. It's a good job that Benjamin Dane is nothing if not clever. Because Horatio is a fossilized creature. But his friend is a very active one.

After another few slow blinks, Benjamin grabs his shirtfront, slotting their mouths together.

Horatio wonders how many people, medically speaking, have suffered two separate heart attacks in as many minutes, for completely different causes. He can't imagine heaps of such individuals exist. He is now one of their number. They ought to form a society. Benjamin keeps making breathy sounds, nipping and nuzzling for response against his lips like a lost puppy.

Something cracks, leaving a silt of hopes and dreams on the wet tile. It's too much and too suddenly. Horatio doesn't back away, but he does angle his face aside. Benjamin gives an *mmph* that's absolutely devastating.

"This is, um," Horatio attempts with his eyes resolutely shut, "a bad idea."

Benjamin huffs, against his temple now. "Come on, give me a break, you were always totally shit at chastity. What's that one called again?"

"Brahmacharya. No, not . . . oh god . . . not for religious reasons."

"Horatio," Benjamin intones against his eyelashes, "if we don't get this out of our systems *now*, before the gala, what's going to happen to me when you're back in that tuxedo?"

Horatio swallows.

Sod it.

Bloodsickness is meant to be fatal anyhow.

"*There* you are, yes yes," Benjamin gasps when Horatio parts his lips for him. Shaking, cold hands come up to circle his neck, the thumbs against his thorax, and Horatio doesn't know whether to laugh or sob. Both seem dodgy options, so he keeps kissing his friend, heart in his mouth, for long minutes, maybe it's hours, it's till Benjamin shudders softly. He pulls back but only to roll their foreheads together. He was exactly like this before, Horatio remembers—playful but grateful. As if the hated schoolkid was still in there and couldn't believe his luck.

"Beg pardon, whose blood is that on your kit, please?" Horatio recalls.

"Hey, shhhh, not right now. It's from yesterday. And I never liked the guy."

"But you said it's a problem?"

"For sure, absolutely."

"An immediate one?"

"Oh hell no, I can think of a much more immediate one."

Benjamin's fingers dart over shirt buttons. Horatio has him

by his birdlike rib cage, and Benjamin dives into his neck like he hasn't eaten in days, which is likely true. *This is a foregone conclusion*, Horatio supposes as he half-slips on the tile and the other man laughs. And Benjamin is quite right—there's nothing at all chaste about it save for where the flood of love is concerned, there's no holiness here, but nevertheless Horatio thanks every ancient prayer that ever taught him how important it was not to lose noble forgiveness.

How else but by forgiving Benjamin could he have earned something as precious as this?

AFTERWARD, BENJAMIN'S BED IS prohibitively wet. Horatio reclines against the couch arm, with pillows behind and with Benjamin Dane curled up on his chest like a cat. This particular cat prefers—they all have their little ways about them—Horatio's fingertips skating from behind his ear down to his nape and back up again.

Fuck you, Robin Goodfellow, and fuck bloodsickness, I get to have this.

"So you're, like, *officially* officially my date tonight now, right?"

Horatio shrugs. "If you say so. But I'm still incredibly cross with you."

Ben angles his head so his chin rests on Horatio's sternum. He's back to looking demonically cheeky, and Horatio reflects that he ought to be throwing him straight out the living room window. Repeatedly.

"Fine, you get to be mad at me as long as you like, but you gotta admit the makeup sex was leagues better than our first try."

"You—Christ. I admit to nothing whatsoever."

"No, for real, I can pat myself on the back now, because *those* were the kind of noises I used to have to crank up the stereo out here to cover—"

Horatio has no choice save putting his entire hand over Benjamin's mouth.

Benjamin's eyes shift from amused to pouting to impatient by degrees.

"Right, so first order of business," Horatio says as he removes his palm, "is whose blood that was."

Benjamin's lips twitch. If he weren't blissed out by a good shag, he'd already be heading for the Klonopin bottle, Horatio surmises.

"Just gotta say, your pillow talk is, like, subpar, which is surprising, considering how much prac—"

"Supposing I get to have you and supposing you're amenable, of course, I'd like to keep you. Um, for a bit. For—never mind. Whose blood?"

A smile flickers over Benjamin's mouth. Then he starts playing with the string of Horatio's hoodie. "You're not going to like it."

"No, but I already don't like it, so just bang right on."

"Like, head underwater in the ocean instead of wading in?"

"If you please."

"Paul Brahms is dead and his body is on our roof."

Benjamin is correct: Horatio does not like it. After the panic, and occasionally gripping Benjamin's hair to get him to stay on subject (the fact Horatio can do this sends him into mild ecstasies), he teases out that Paul arrived asking Benjamin to sign some paperwork, revealed that Claude and Trudy had a long-standing relationship (with photographic proof), that Jackson Dane was a paranoid narcissist, and that he, Paul Brahms, had been a master puppeteer working primarily for Trudy. None of this is shocking—it was Horatio who noted Paul couldn't possibly be a complete plonker, after all. But the part where bald, timorous Paul Brahms pulled out a gun and ordered Benjamin to climb up to a rooftop assassination horrifies him enough to wrap his arms around his friend, bricking him inside a human fortress.

Benjamin hums. "Not that I don't like this, I enthusiastically do, but I'll need intact ribs today."

"Er, I need a moment, pardon." Extricating himself, Horatio tries to regain some dignity by placing his feet on the floor.

"Get back—that was, like, absolutely not what I meant."

The grounded soles approach doesn't work, so Horatio tries pacing. It helps Benjamin. Sometimes.

"That is way *way* worse. Did I not mention the floor is lava? The floor is lava; the couch is safety."

"You were nearly killed, and . . . I was god knows where. Benjamin, I am so deeply sorry that you were alone when—"

"Nope, that's gonna be the road *not* traveled. You aren't my guardian angel," Benjamin scoffs. "They don't actually exist except in the Hallmark 'verse and the minds of women who have WWJD tramp stamps. You needed to untangle some shit. Probably still do, anyway you're not responsible for Lia's dad turning out to be a supervillain."

This doesn't loosen the knot in his belly. It only adds twists, tightens loops. And even through his gratitude that Benjamin escaped, a sick realization snaps Horatio's head up.

"You had to . . ."

He can't say it. Horatio, a modern city dweller, isn't traditional Jain enough to fret over rat poison or the pesticides spread for cockroaches. But it is one of the highest tenets that he murder no living creature, from eating a chicken wing to stepping on an ant, and even though he's reasonable about it, the thought of Benjamin—caustic, mercurial, but never willfully hurtful Benjamin—being forced to kill in self-defense is revolting.

"No, it wasn't, just *no*," Benjamin hastens to say. "It's hard to explain, but. He hated me. Said if I wanted to die so much, whoopee, he'd fulfill my wish. And that I didn't deserve anything I'd ever had, and that I ruined Lia's life."

Horatio's jaw drops. "That *you* ruined Lia's life?"

"Yeah," he says, eyes on the carpet.

"That's not—you *didn't*, Benjamin."

"I know that now."

"How are you this calm? How exactly do you suddenly know that?"

Benjamin makes a complicated gesture indicating *all of this*. "Paul had a gun and he said things I'd always suspected, things that made me hate myself, but when I heard the words out loud, from him . . . then they weren't true. I get the urge to destroy myself, but I don't *yearn* to die. Apparently. I might not deserve as much money as Oprah, but no one *deserves* that. Except for Oprah. Jesus, if you'd ever told me that Paul would force an epiphany on me, I'd have told you to check yourself into inpatient. Anyway, I never got my hands on his gun. We were . . . all tangled up, and it went off, it was in his hand and he pulled the trigger, and here I still am."

"I'm grateful," Horatio tries to say with a steady voice.

His friend shrugs his thanks. "So am I, weirdly. Then I just used Paul's plan—he was gonna leave me up there and close the door. That's going to work for a hot minute, until it doesn't anymore. And we won't have said anything to the police yesterday, or today, because I sure as *hell* am not saying anything till after tonight is over, so then hello, I'm a murder suspect, even though Paul was holding the weapon himself and tussling with me. Sure they can test for prints and powder residue and whatnot, but there was longstanding bad blood between us and I left the bastard to bake on a rooftop. Because of the whole, uh. Shock thing. Which I did *not* enjoy."

"*Why* wouldn't we call the police? We can ring Detective Norway this second and—"

"No can do."

"Tell me why not!" Horatio protests.

"Because I need tonight, or I'll never find out how my dad died. Paul had no reason to lie when he said he didn't kill him."

"But that's lunacy, what if no one at all—"

"Either way, I'll find out for certain."

Benjamin is eerily relaxed, as if a car with misfiring pistons was given the perfect kick in the tire. Chinese porcelain eyes, lotus position with an arm slung over the couch back. When he first woke up from that deathly shower, Horatio thought this serenity was drugs. In bed, looking up at him from priceless new angles, Horatio thought it was passion. None of that explains this new Benjamin. He remembers his friend trying to support Lia and putting serenity into his own words, just the three of them and a shared bowl of excellent weed.

We can only see this infinitesimally small slice of time, this instant, and now this instant. Maybe serenity is realizing that the only way to change your circumstances is to live right now. Otherwise you're either too early, or you're too late.

That's how he looks, he looks *serene*. The last thing Horatio wants to do is ruin it, but it's grotesque after Ben shot the man who could have been his father-in-law.

What does Benjamin need now? Questions? Quiet? He would give the man anything—his heart on a leash, his soul in a watch case—except for something that would hurt him. When Horatio kneels before the sofa with hands on his friend's thighs, Benjamin readily sits up, mussing with the Londoner's disastrous hair.

"You're *still* in shock," Horatio says clearly.

"Um, Horatio. Can you blame me?"

"No, but I—" Benjamin's fingernails on his scalp, those are distracting. "Stop that. We have to—"

"Horatio, I never *touched* the gun, I'll talk to them tomorrow, all right? We can't miss Mom's Cheater Extraordinaire–themed wedding reception."

"It isn't funny."

"Are you *kidding* me?" He mock shudders. "I *know*."

"When you . . ." Horatio attempts, measuring his words. "Um, when I came home and found you just now—"

Benjamin's laugh is explosive. "Oh my god, it was hardly *just now*."

"You said you were dreaming. And you're acting pretty barmy, even for you."

"Whoa now."

"Tell me please, what was it about?"

"It's hard to explain these dreams, they're some immersive shit. I mean. Lia was there."

"So you've said about the others. And?"

An eerie tale unfolds that turns Horatio's blood several degrees colder. In the dream, Benjamin and Lia were children again. Lia told him in much more detail about the janitor whose tricks both kids were so obsessed with—Jórvík Volkov, now cast as a nightmare figure.

"I didn't know it then," Benjamin explains, "but the theatre was geographically in the epicenter of these missing child cases. One missing kid's backpack was even found with a *Playbill* of ours, although we were running a production of *Peter Pan* right then so who cares, and another one's classmate said her friend gushed about going to see a play all week. Only problem was, the parents denied there, like, being any play tickets. But nobody could find anything. Any more than they could find out what started the fire or whose body that was. And in my dreams, Lia keeps telling me all this horrific shit about Jórvík, how he used to play a game with her about picking cards. Except the cards were school photos of the missing kids."

Horatio longs for a magic penlight to look straight through Benjamin's pupils into his brain.

"So on the one hand, here's Norway and Fortuna bringing up these cold cases to see if itty-bitty me knew anything. What do I recall? Could the missing kids be connected to Dad's death? They refused to say so, but I know they were thinking it. Different decades, different crimes, but you never can tell with that kind of thing. And then here's Lia in my subconscious—well, sometimes I'm in hers—telling me that the murderer was Jórvík, and that he made her pick the victims, and the guilt was killing her. Is that insane?"

Horatio struggles to keep his face blank. "I . . . let's hope not. No, of course not. But it's not calming, and you're calm as anything."

"Yeah, Lia said she's going to make it all clear when she comes to the gala tonight."

"Lia said in your dream she's coming this evening?"

"Don't look at me like that, it's not like I believed her," Benjamin grumbles. "It was only a dream."

"Right, um. Yes. Dreams can't be trusted on such subjects."

"Still. Like, what if she did—could you imagine the drama? I mean, glory hallelujah, that there's a showstopper. Not that I wouldn't love to see her, obviously. But just picture Lia Brahms walking into the middle of the New World's Stage gala."

Horatio does imagine. She'd be wearing some incredible designer dress she found in a bin for ten dollars, freckles dancing, flowers woven into that halo of hair as if she were a wood nymph. He's missed her and he'd tell her so. She'd burrow under his arm and he'd snug her closer, smelling rose water and cinnamon.

It would be wonderful. And Benjamin wouldn't so much as glance my direction for the rest of my life.

"Hold the motherfucking phone."

Benjamin drops a kiss to Horatio's eyebrow before springing away. It sparks a small catastrophe, like the fall of an icicle from a roofline. Horatio watched the same thoughtless gestures for years without pain. Now they open scars that were never there in the first place.

"What is it?"

"Behold these documents, brought from the mountaintop via the Prophet Brahms!" Benjamin plops on the rug to peruse. "Paul gave these to me, and—because I'm afflicted with the rare condition of cabbages for grey matter, suuuuper weird mutation, it causes total morons to sign whatever people put in front of them—I don't know what they say! C'mere, let's take a gander."

This is still manageable.

Manic Benjamin is funny and brilliant; Horatio knows how this Benjamin is wrangled. It's only been these few times that the new Benjamin slipped through the cracks, painting dreamscapes and scaring the daylights out of him.

"Ooooooh, Paul," Benjamin intones as Horatio sinks next to him. "You walking ejaculate hose, you said this was an insurance rider, but was this your idea or Mom's?"

"Benjamin," Horatio says incredulously, "these abdicate you from all your rights on the board of directors!"

"Cute, huh." Benjamin relinquishes the papers, starting one of his syncopated rhythms on the silent carpet. "Ariel told me that the theatre was in financial trouble. And Paul said yesterday morning that Dad would have shoveled it underground as a point of pride. They must have thought I'd want to, whatever you call it. Carry on his legacy. Pull up his bootstraps, as it were, posthumously. Continue to produce non-crap. Which is, by the way, correct: I would do that to a degree of certainty entirely outside of acatalepsy, categorically confirming that the Pyrrhonists were total crank yankers for insisting that only appearances could ever be truly known."

"Remain on topic, please?"

"So either way, Paul was getting rid of me—if I die, I'm dead. If I don't die, he has these papers for. Uh, Mom, presumably. Who is probably about to have me committed or something equally Victorian."

Benjamin plays a complex amalgam of piano and percussion, eyes focused on some part of the fourth dimension known only to him. Interrupting is a risk if he's following a train of real thought, but what good is this afternoon if it doesn't make Horatio more useful? They'd just closed over each other like two halves of a book with a story inside. He captures the nearest hand in both of his and starts gently pulling the tendons.

Ben doesn't so much startle as come up for air. He squeezes back gratefully.

"Soooo weird," he sighs.

But when Horatio tries to withdraw, Benjamin tugs him back in. "Nope nope, it's weird that you could have done that at, like, any point in our relationship and I don't think I'd have found it unusual. Neither would Lia, I'm guessing. So what have we learned today, kids? Mom wants me off the board of directors, possibly dead—"

"Benjamin, that was Paul being overzealous, you two have never got on and your own mum—"

"Has been doing the dirty with my donkey impersonator uncle Claude since I was a kid, and my dad, who I really genuinely thought ruled the world, was a wannabe New York power player ashamed of his big oil origins and under the thumb of a guy who pretended to be afraid of the bleach in toilet paper. Well, strike that, not *pretended* exactly. Anyway, a guy who had every dirty little finger and toe in New World's Stage's pie so it couldn't operate without him. And as a bonus prize, I'll be a part of a murder investigation tomorrow. Cool."

The skin of Benjamin's hands is softer than Horatio thought it would be, save for where music has scarred his fingers. Too much uncertainty and fear bombard them for Horatio to think about a single other thing. They sit on the floor of their flat, in Washington Heights, in Manhattan, in America, skin to skin.

How likely was this ever to happen again?

"That sounds like an impossibly shite day and I'm sorry."

Turning his hand over, Benjamin laces their fingers together and Horatio feels it flash through his entire spinal column.

"Nah, I dunno. I'm gonna go ahead and say the good parts might've outweighed the bad. Let's call it sixty–forty."

Horatio's heart does something incalculable, perhaps to do with fractals. He'll ask Benjamin. His friend's cashmere-pale eyes drift down to his Patek Philippe wristwatch, however (a gift from Trudy of doubtless obscene value), and Benjamin starts. Hopping to his feet, he pulls Horatio up with him.

"C'mon, let's get ready—you need time to throw six fits over the tux, which was delivered with mine just before the Great Regrettable Shower Incident."

Horatio retreats to his bedroom holding a garment bag, his mind off floating with the weather balloons and low-orbiting satellites. The chamber is as he left it down to the hastily made bed and the yawning suitcase. It's uncanny, considering the entire world started spinning in the opposite direction an hour or two ago. His teaching idol reposes on the shelf, the image of quietude, but Rishabhanatha's eyes could fly open in mingled awe and censure and Horatio wouldn't be surprised.

"I know." He releases his breath. "It's completely scatty, but I love him."

Approaching the figurine, Horatio lowers his voice.

"Didn't you ever love anyone like that? What else could I possibly do?"

Rishabhanatha says nothing, but he looks worried—which makes perfect sense. Because so is Horatio.

"You know, you might've at that." Horatio picks up the statue and rubs a thumb over the coiled snake on which he's seated so comfortably. "I mean, you had two wives and a hundred and one bloody kids before you renounced everything, after all. Maybe you loved to distraction, but you gave them up, and that's the idea. Maybe you were horridly in love and still left the palace to wander around without food for a year."

Rishabhanatha rests heavy in his hand.

"The food I could do without, I think. For a while. Possessions, fame, none of that matters. And I want nothing to do with this sodding tuxedo, you realize. Could I give Benjamin up, though? Willingly? For my soul?"

The teaching god looks doubtful.

"Right." Horatio returns Rishabhanatha to his perch. "I suppose that's why you're a statue and I'm not, mate."

Benjamin's velvet tuxedo turns out to be ethereal grey-blue like dawn on the coast, sleek along every angle, and Horatio instantly forgives Vincentio every discomfort ever inflicted. It's paired with a white shirt and pocket square, and a black bow tie, and Benjamin presently looks like a million dollars instead of merely being *worth* many many millions of dollars.

"Oh good, you like it." Benjamin does a shameless eye-rake, lips making a silent whistling shape. "You . . . ha ha. Look exactly like I thought you would. Planning ahead truly is so important. Yep, I was right, the sexing you straight into the mattress till you yelled was necessary."

"You need to desist, please."

"It'd be even better if you were walking funny, but thankfully you're a pro—"

"For god's—do you *want* me to wring you by the neck?" Horatio splutters.

"Wring me by pretty much anything else, but not that. Wanna hear what I think of yours?"

"Best not, I should say."

"Damn it!" Benjamin snaps his fingers, disappearing. When he returns, he looks even more pleased, which is to say as pleased as a tiny tyrant about to throw himself a military parade. He tosses a polished stick to Horatio. Turning it over, he frowns, puzzled. A silver tap and an embellished silver top complete the shining black cane.

When he does understand, Horatio laughs for all he's worth. He twists the handle. A blade emerges, edges looking extremely functional.

"You found me a sword cane. Everything about you is absurd."

Benjamin takes the weapon, studies it himself. "It's a good thing I know people, this cost more than the tux. Kidding! Cut it out, I'm kidding. Maaaaybe I'm kidding. Anyway, the gala wasn't going to go well unless swords entered into it somewhere, right?"

Horatio can't concentrate.

This situation is so complex, and my needs are so simple.

Benjamin's mouth pulls wide with happiness. His eyebrows tilt in concert with his question, and Horatio steps forward, wanting him very badly, and then Benjamin's hand is on his cheek with a low, "Thought you'd never ask."

Loud *whoop*s sound followed by a jolly banging at the door.

Benjamin's head falls onto Horatio's chest. "I forgot, shit, *shit*. Why did I forget they were coming? Oh, because I was drunk. That tracks."

"Benny!" crows Rory or Garrett Marlowe's voice. "Open up, dude, the Cristal speedy delivery service has arrived!"

Benjamin stalks to the door and the twins pour inside wearing immaculate matching black ensembles, a pair of ravens fresh off the runway. Likewise holding matching bottles of Cristal, they cheer and pop both corks with their thumbs, froth blessing the carpet. The overflow is stemmed by hearty swigs.

"Hi, guys," Benjamin deadpans.

"Let the games begin, right?" Rory offers his bottle to Benjamin at the same time Garrett shoves his at Horatio. "Drink deep, for the night is young."

"Do we think this is, like, safe?" Benjamin inquires, frank eyes on Horatio.

"Excuse me?"

"Considering yesterday and all. Well, I guess they did just uncork it. And drink it themselves. Should be fine. To a memorable evening!"

Horatio and Benjamin swallow champagne, returning the bottles to a set of confused Marlowes. They recover quickly, however.

"Guys, this is gonna be off the chain," Garrett announces. "Looking slick, Benny, slick as ever."

"Whoa, Horatio," Rory marvels. "We had no idea you cleaned up this nice. *Killer* tux, man, what is that, Armani?"

"It's Tom Ford, you peasant," Benjamin supplies smoothly. He pulls four mugs down from the cupboard, reaching for the nearest champagne bottle. "And of course he does."

The twins hover near Benjamin as Horatio leans on the other side of the counter, resigned to being commented on like a prize steer. Benjamin suspecting the champagne might be drugged or even poisoned mightily disconcerts him. Benjamin has always been a fairly even distribution of his parents' genetics, and apparently Jackson Dane was the prisoner of his own dark fantasies.

Paul tried to shoot him yesterday. It's not paranoia if you were nearly murdered.

"Shit!" The exclamation is from Rory, who glances at his twin.

"What's up?"

"Dude, Trudy just texted me. Odd, right?"

"Did she now?" Benjamin questions.

"Yeah, totally odd," Garrett agrees.

"Huh. Does my mom text you, like, a lot?"

"Of course not." Rory's eyes are blank with innocence. "Guess she's after a quick reply—you aren't really that great with answering, Benny, no offense."

"None whatsoever taken."

"Anyway, apparently Paul Brahms should be at the venue, but he isn't answering his phone."

Car horns bleat downstairs. A child is shouting in Spanish. A motorcycle backfires. Horatio doesn't dare to open his mouth for fear of what will emerge from Benjamin's. His friend just crosses his ankles, his lower back against the stove door.

"Not that I really know the guy," Garrett chimes in, "but isn't Paul super anal? And it's the big night and everything. Weird of him to go silent like that."

"Weird, right?" echoes Rory.

"Soooooo so weird," Benjamin agrees.

"You two haven't heard from him, have you?" Garrett asks.

Benjamin pushes off toward his bedroom.

When he returns, he carries the Teisco shark, which gleams an impossible mermaid color. He sets one foot on the lower rung of his barstool. Cocking his hip, he flutters his fingers over the shark's strings, and despite its not being plugged in, Horatio recognizes the famous Guns N' Roses solo from "Sweet Child O' Mine."

Finished, Benjamin brandishes the shark at Garrett. "Hey, man, why don't you have a go?"

The twins blink.

"Nah, but that sounded dope—you wanna plug in?"

"No, it's your turn now."

"Come on, Benny, you know I can't even pull off basic chords. Funny joke, though."

"I'm deadly serious," Benjamin replies silkily. "Play my guitar."

"Look, I don't know what's gotten into you, but I can't." Garrett extends his arm, and now there's a guitar and a champagne bottle in a bizarre duel. "This'll cheer you up, though!"

"Yeah, bro, have a drink," Rory urges. "And just answer me so I can text Trudy back—have either of you seen Paul Brahms?"

"What the hell, Ben," Garrett says when Benjamin proves unmoving. "Take a swig and chill out."

"Play me a guitar solo and I'd be happy to."

Garrett scowls before he can catch himself. "I can't; I don't know *how* to play the guitar, all right?"

"Then what the fuck do you take me for, Garrett?"

The twins' eyes widen in tandem.

"You're trying to play me, that much is stupidly clear." Benjamin spits chemical fire; Horatio can smell the exhaust. "Mom wants to know where Paul is and she texts *you*? I'm not supposed to, you know, realize you're in her pocket? So you can't play guitar, which doesn't surprise me, because you two are smart but you're also the least sophisticated pieces of shit I've ever seen, sorry, went kinda off track there, but you think I'm not more complicated than a guitar?"

When the twins remain as still as a razed building, Benjamin swings the shark back under his arm and plays an obscenely embellished version of "Wonderwall," pelvis swinging with abandon. His smile returns, the smile that means there's blood in the water and he's scented it, and Horatio is too stupidly turned on to question whether that's a sane response or not.

"Hear this? This is your exit music, chosen thematically and written by another pair of douchebag brothers. Get the fuck out of our apartment before I blacklist you from every bottle service club in the city and the only place you'll be getting blown together is behind Port Authority bus terminal." Benjamin sets the shark on the coffee table. "Leave the Cristal, Horatio and I like champagne."

"Benny," Rory protests, aghast.

"Ben, there's been some crazy misunder—"

"Hold on, are you working for Paul or for my mom directly? Hmm? That's all right, I guess it doesn't really matter either way. And if you talk to me at the gala tonight, you're going to be lucky to get a reservation at the Times Square Olive Garden. Go. Like, shoo, shoo. *Not* with the Cristal, idiots, that stays!"

The Marlowes depart. Benjamin locks the door, ricochets, rounds the countertop, steps between Horatio's legs, and kisses him. Bloodsickness must cause fevers, because Horatio's circulatory system instantly simmers, a hot spring flowing through too-narrow fissures. By the time his friend pulls away, Horatio's skeletal structure has melted and every synapse is firing *him, him, him, only him.*

"That was pretty satisfying." Benjamin glances at his phone screen.

"Doubtless I can do better," Horatio breathes.

"Jesus no, comprehensively owning the Marlowe brothers was pretty satisfying—the kiss just now was legendary, but you're right, we should keep practicing. The limo's downstairs." His friend pockets his mobile. "C'mon, and bring the bottles. We have a murderer to catch."

BENJAMIN

The soul is always beautiful,
The universe is duly in order, every
    thing is in its place,
What has arrived is in its place and
    what waits shall be in its place,
The twisted skull waits, the watery or
    rotten blood waits . . .

—*Walt Whitman, "The Sleepers"*

IT'S SIX O'CLOCK AND they only just left the apartment and already things aren't going to plan.

The cadaverous waiter is beginning his shift at City Diner. Outside, the limousine figure-eights under the spreading trees with two partial bottles of Cristal on ice. Ben supposes that the driver is confused. Horatio is beyond baffled, sitting across from him while Ben watches the waiter wrap an apron around his gaunt torso. Eyes full of the quiet sort of nothing, pad and pen in his front pocket. He doesn't seem to sense anything amiss.

But Ben does, ever since he threw the Marlowes out and kissed Horatio like he's the answer to the Poincaré conjecture. Because he is, sort of. Horatio can chart three-dimensional balls onto four-dimensional spheres.

HORATIO
CAN MAP THESE
SHAPES THAT LOOK
COMPLETELY ABSTRACT AND YET
STILL MAKE SENSE OF THEM
SOMEHOW

Something is changing too rapidly to stop or even to slow it down. They don't have much time. But what does that mean? And when did they run so low on it? The waiter opens the till behind the bar, deftly counts his starting cash.

"Benjamin, I can't honestly fathom what we're doing here."

"Have you heard of Muriel Rukeyser?" Ben asks.

Horatio's gaze narrows. His coffee-dark eyes have been doing that forever, but it's different now that Ben and Horatio combined themselves so messily and gorgeously, now that they're a *them*. Less Mozart. More Chopin.

"Um, should I have done?"

"Lia's favorite poet, a Jewish feminist and political dissident. She must've gotten wasted and talked about her at some point."

"Yeah, possibly. Are you going to order something?"

"Focus, Horatio—Muriel Rukeyser, born nineteen thirteen, Guggenheim Fellowship recipient."

"What about her?"

"She said that the universe is made of stories, not of atoms."

Horatio is trying fiercely to read him. But Ben is written in wingdings right now, and the comfort of the dream he shared with Lia has fast faded. He wants that sense of

DESTINY

back, where now he only feels

LAST CALL PLEASE IT'S TIME

"Stories-not-atoms is something I don't quite believe," Ben attempts. "Something I *want* to believe. I want to, like, try it out. It reminds me of you."

"Does it? Benjamin, what are we doing here?"

"Ending a narrative."

There's only ice water in front of them. This isn't padding the belly before a night getting shitfaced, this is a necessary stop on the road to completion. Ben needs to have this conversation before he and Horatio can possibly solidify whatever they are. Apart from *I don't think I can live without you anymore,* of course. The terribly thin old man leaves his computer station and Ben flags him down with a wave.

"How can I help you?" A lone strand or two pushes through his hairnet like seedlings.

"Hey, yeah, super-odd question." Ben tries a smile, finds it doesn't fit, trashes it. "I used to come in here with my girlfriend. Well, then fiancée, after, the beautiful one with the crazy hair, but anyway, we were here all the time during the wee small hours?"

His eyes narrow with recognition. "Yes, you had been out, I think, most of those times. Parties."

"Yep, right, yep, that was us, and my girlfriend, Lia, she always liked you. Seeing you."

The waiter purses his lips, listening.

"You were important to us—someone comforting when we needed you. A constant."

"Her I have not seen in a long time, I think?"

"No, she. She's not around anymore, but I just heard from her and she wanted me to thank you for being here and, like, for always being so patient. She's not . . . she was never an *empty* person. She appreciated you. Lia never drank to fill a hole," Ben insists. To the waiter. To the diner. To the world. "She drank to cover up a locked box."

The old man smooths gnarled hands over his shirt. "Better to stop trying, then."

"How do you know that?"

"The memories of my home, my family, my life before America—they cannot be buried, either."

"And how do you live with it?"

The glasses clink. The diners chew. Somewhere, the car drives around and around.

"I learned to put them at the edges of my sight," he says.

Horatio's voice breaks in, gentle and frightened. "Benjamin, this isn't . . . we should head downtown. Please."

"Just a quick sec."

"Let the poor bloke alone, for pity's sake."

Ignoring him, Ben asks with tears burning his eyes, "Where did you come from, if you don't mind me asking?"

Shaking his head, the waiter—he ought to have asked his name by now, Ben ought to have asked it years ago—returns his notepad to his pocket.

"It doesn't exist anymore," he says, and walks away.

Early bird patrons chat over tuna melts and spinach salad. They can't feel it, either. Horatio can't feel it, sitting there increasingly frantic, he doesn't understand why in order for something to officially begin, something else has to officially

FINISH

It's important.

There will be more changes, drastic and permanent ones, and Paul's death was the first of them. Making love to Horatio again was the second. Sending Rory and Garrett off was the third. This is the fourth. You can't feel motion no matter how fast it's going, supposing it's constant.

The rotational speed of the Earth is around a thousand miles per hour,
and the only reason we feel nothing is because
there's no discernible change.
We aren't slowing or speeding.   We're constant.
We're hurtling through space and can't even feel it.
Well, fuck constancy.
We've earned acceleration.

"In my dream," Ben says, "Lia reminded me that we always wanted to know this guy's origins. She said to pay attention to his answer."

"And?"

"It doesn't exist anymore. I guess that's the ending."

Standing, Ben takes a last look around. He doesn't need to return here.

"Are you disappointed?"

"Nah." Ben realizes it's true only as he says it. "We'll always have Bulvmania."

"You impossible nutter, what is it you're doing?" Horatio questions as they walk back into daylight, bells tinkling a farewell.

"Like I said, I always thought the universe was made up of atoms, but this time it needs to be a story, and that story needs to *end*."

"But why?"

"So that ours can start."

It's not the entire explanation, but it's the only one Horatio will stand for.

I don't actually know who's ending.

But someone is.

Lia said so.

And I would crack every unsolved equation left in the world to make sure that it isn't you.

They go back to the car. It's awkward pretending to laugh over champagne when they're both navigating the labyrinth of *what came before* and *what comes next*.

"Do you remember the day we met?" Ben asks.

"Ha, um, yes." Horatio tilts the neck of his champagne bottle. "But I don't suppose you do."

"What do you mean? Of course I do. *Rude*."

Ben was exploring the Columbia campus—trespassing recast as mapping. But he got bored with just linoleum and metal folding chairs. Columbia was meant to be exotic in the way only old things are; a penny is a mere penny unless it's an ancient penny, then it's an *artifact* or a *treasure*. So when he came to a door in the most castle-esque building yet, and it said **FACULTY ONLY**, he honored the spirit of Magellan and strode through corridors that emitted the inky-clean scent of midterms being graded. He reached a room, and Ben didn't know that he was about to meet him in person, this *person*, all he knew was that a handsome dark-skinned man chewing the end of a Bic pen was looking at a sheaf of papers like they needed stabbing.

> *"Need any help with that?" Ben asked, slouching against the carved doorframe.*
>
> *For some reason, the man's face lit up. "Oh, hullo. Why, are you much cop at papers on plagiarism and post-colonialism?"*
>
> *"Nope, I'm better with the conceptual foundations of quantum mechanics."*
>
> *The man offered his hand when Ben approached him. "Horatio Ramesh Patel."*
>
> *"Benjamin Jackson Dane. Soooooo, you're faculty, then?"*
>
> *"Oh, um, no. But you are?"*
>
> *"Absolutely not."*
>
> *"Ha! Well, I just started the graduate program, but Mum told me that if I was going to spend all our money going to America's Hogwarts, I had to find its hidden passageways and send her pictures. I'm not doing any harm, no one's booked in this room till a library staff meeting at seven. Cross my heart."*
>
> *Ben laughed. "America's Hogwarts is actually Harvard, I think. Any luck with the secret passageways?"*
>
> *"No, you?"*
>
> *No. But I found you, he thought.*

"It was when we were both invading the faculty wing looking for chambers of secrets."

Horatio laughs fondly. "It was not. It was outside of Pulitzer Hall, the first day, and you told me that we only marked time because it was passing. So we could orient ourselves. You weren't even showing off—the thought just sort of . . . delighted you. You could have been talking to your bedpost. I didn't mind."

Frowning in consternation, Ben answers, "Weeeeell, that does admittedly sound like me. So I believe you. Even though not remembering when we actually met makes me hate myself slightly more than the usual."

"Benjamin . . . for heaven's sake, I never. Please don't take it that way?"

Ben squints, trying to remember regaling a magnetic stranger about time. He can't for the life of him. The Cristal is getting warmer and flatter, but it's almost gone. South, south, south they go as the sun fades, toward the gala venue and the Dutch settlement of New Amsterdam.

In the alphabet of their personal time, of this story, where are they now? *C? Q? X?*

"Benjamin," Horatio's voice breaks in again.

"Yeah, sorry, right here."

"We've arrived."

Ben slides against Horatio, thigh to thigh. He sees red carpet through the tinted glass, thin people with thick wallets, strutting as if it's totally natural to stop, dislocate your hip, arch your neck like you're about to come, wait for the flash. *Repeat.*

"All right, let's get this over with. Just smile and know you look like a tasty, tasty snack. Or don't smile. You look fantastic like that, too."

Horatio's jaw drops. "We're . . . we don't have to . . . oh shit, you're *Benjamin Dane.* Of course we have to—"

"Gonna stop you right there." Ben plants a kiss on Horatio's shoulder, because he can. "Yep, we have to. Now, man up and get that Columbia-legendary ass on display."

Horatio splutters in annoyance, but it's better than the outright horror. They enter the line. Ben's entire neck feels like it's wrapped in a thunderstorm. He slides a Xanax out of his pocket, dry swallowing and covering it with a cough. When they reach the river of red and set sail, something still doesn't feel right. But Ben quickly susses out one of the things prickling like pure static charge.

"What . . . um . . ." Horatio squawks, staring down at their joined hands.

"Shoulda plied you with more Cristal." Ben beams. Everything is easier now. "This is cute too, though. Tallyho, as you would absolutely never say!"

the red carpet passes with dozens of
✳*flick*   ✳*flick*✳*flick snap* ✳*flick* ✳*flick* ✳*flick* *snap snap*

everyone absolutely rabid now they see Ben Dane is holding
   hands with
snap snap snap ✳*flick*✳*flick* ✳*flick snap*   ✳*flick*✳*flick*✳*flick*

a tall dark and handsome
✳*flick*   *snap snap snapsnapsnap*   ✳*flick snap*

and now they're yelling and doubling the rate of
✳*flick*✳*flick*   *snapsnapsnap flick*
  snapsnap ✳*flick*✳*flick*✳*flick*   *snap snap*✳*flick*✳*flicksnap*

But really it takes scant time for them to get through security (because he's goddamn Benjamin Dane and Horatio's sword cane looks like a Broadway-worthy accessory and that's all), and then they're past the bottleneck and the night is upon them. Which feels like nearing the end of a very painful line of dominoes.

"Killer job your first time getting papped. Mother of tap-dancing Christ," Ben remarks, craning his neck.

It's a South Street waterfront space hovering above the city like a helipad, the sheer bragging footprint spaced by pedestals sporting gargantuan floral arrangements. Shocking pink lilies, fruit tree branches, jungle leaves. Catering stations dole out champagne, mini-crepes with caviar, prime rib toasts. Spiral staircases lead to massive balconies where people survey the room like archers seeking a kill. It's grander than any of the galas his father ever lived to see. And even if Jackson Dane wasn't all he pretended, that makes Ben bleed under the leather cuff. A chandelier like a sun presides, metal rays shooting out with blazing illumination at the tips.

"T Tauri star," Ben says, nodding up at the light fixture. "Major X-ray flares, killer solar winds. One of my faves."

Horatio darts a smitten glance at him. "It's, um, really quite something."

"Hey, if you're gonna celebrate cheating, do it in style, am I right?"

"Benjamin, a word." His friend tugs him behind the closest floral monstrosity. "I detest prying, but, well . . . You've been acting quite oddly about this dream earlier, and I want to understand, so—are you willing to give me the SparkNotes version?"

Ben winces his eyes shut.

It just all happened so quickly. There isn't any *time*. Paul was alive **(then he wasn't)**, Ben was panting into his hands for hours **(then he wasn't)**, Ben's clothes were still hanging on his body **(then they weren't)**, the shower was hot and the scotch bottle half full **(then it wasn't)**, and before he knew it he was tumbling into

THE DREAM HE HAD TODAY THAT HE ALMOST
TOLD HORATIO ABOUT BUT DIDN'T
BECAUSE HORATIO WOULD HAVE LOST HIS SHIT:
A DRAMA IN ONE ACT

The fly system of the old World's Stage Theatre building was a relic of vaudeville. So the fly gallery offstage right was a charming eagle aerie, and he and Lia sat far above the proscenium, their legs skinny enough to poke through the gaps in the guardrail. Below, a stooped old man in a janitor's uniform pushed a wide broom, whistling something ancient and evil. A tune for luring wild horses or maybe enslaving a demon.

Ben reached for Lia's hand, tears threatening.

"I never knew."

"I never wanted you to. Anybody, really. But that's what the art was for. And the gin, you're probably thinking, but I'll say it first."

"What did he want?" Ben pleaded. "Shit, I just can't . . . why?"

Lia bit her lower lip. "What everybody wants, I think. What serial killers want when they taunt the police. Somebody to tell their story. That's what the universe is made up of, in the end. People's stories. If he got caught, then I carried his inside me."

Ben took a shaking breath. Jórvík looked like a Greek character from up here, but not Sisyphus of the eternal long-handled broom: King Sisyphus, before he was caught murdering hapless travelers.

"Is this your dream or my dream?"

"Does it matter anymore?" Lia chuckled suddenly. "Remember how we used to spy on that poor City Diner waiter? Because we needed to know his origin tale? Ask him straight out next time you see him, please."

"How can that still interest you?"

"Some weird shit has gone down where I live now. So . . . pay attention to whatever he says. It matters. To everyone. It might be the ending, I think."

Ben lifted their laced fingers, covering them with his other hand. He wanted to take Lia's prints and ink them and gently press them into very expensive paper like hide parchment or Egyptian papyrus or the gilt-adorned margins of an illuminated manuscript.

Jórvík's whistling grew fainter and fainter. A trapdoor staircase had opened in the stage floor. Down and down he went, broom and all, till his head disappeared, then the wooden handle. An easy stroll down to hell. Lia flicked her fingers and the trap slammed shut, locking. Wildflowers sprouted over its surface.

"My god, Lia," Ben marveled.

"Yeah, I did that once before." Lia squeezed his hand. "Minus the flowers. I was a young girl, and he was a monster, and the last time he made me pick and I'd put together what it meant, I thought, Someone else will die. *So I made sure all the exits down there*

were locked and shut him in, told him I thought I'd heard a rat or something, would he please check. I was going to go call the police."

Ben turned to her in shock. "What happened?"

"I got scared," Lia answered. "Like I said—I was a girl and he was a monster, and I thought no one would believe me. I waited too long, wondering about what I'd watched him doing before I shut him in there. He'd been planting what I now realize were tiny fuses, timed ones. Accelerants. Lord knows what arcane kind. I locked him in and went to stare at shit in the park, trying to muster the courage to go to the police. Wondering what my dad would think. What *your* family would think. If I'd go to jail for choosing pictures. Stupid kid stuff. Eventually I forgot about him touching all those walls, those curtains, planting things, and could only focus on the terror of what would happen to me if I tattled. World's Stage burned a few hours later."

Ben dropped Lia's hand. But only to throw his arm around her shoulders, and she nestled her head with a sigh.

"It's not that I . . . that I felt *bad* exactly. I knew I killed someone evil."

"How did you feel?"

"Corrupted," she whispered.

Flames licked along the stage, making patterns like glimmering snakes. Ben intended to tell her that Paul was . . . untimely deceased, if not exactly *how*. But after that confession, his own story was wiped from his mind.

"Remember how Jórvík was obsessed with fire tricks? I was sorta kinda starting to suspect his sick-ass brain burned down the theatre. Like a last hateful hurrah. But . . . that doesn't make sense anymore, for him to burn down his own refuge. Do you know why it happened?"

"No. I know what it did to me. I know it was him. But not why it happened."

The fire snakes darted up the walls, the curtains. Countless more now, a whole vipers' nest.

"I started a new art project." Lia nodded down at the burning *meadow flowers.* "It was going to be me trapped under him, pinned down by vines. But I've grown even since drawing the plans. Now I . . . I suppose I know I'm powerful. So I don't need to do that piece anymore."

Flower stems crackled, then vanished. Petals melted. The proscenium was covered in intricate swirling flame, whorls licking at the ceiling.

"Listen," Lia said. "A lot of pieces are going to fall into place at the gala tonight. And some of it will involve tragedy. Death. But you need to listen—no matter what happens, it's going to be OK. I promise. And I . . . I can do that now, I can promise."

Ben sank into the warm cloud of her hair. He believed her. More than that, he felt it ring true, somewhere at the back of his skull. Calm washed over him.

"We're gonna wake up in a second, and it's not going to be pretty for you." Lia laughed.

"Why?"

"Trust me."

"I do. But I don't want to leave you. I never did."

"That's not what your goodbye letter said."

"Oh. You got my goodbye letter?"

"Yeah, my friends made sure I did."

"Well. If I said that—then that part wasn't true."

Lia turned wide brown eyes up to Ben's. "It's almost over. The clock is ticking. Go get 'em, Benny. You can do this."

Sinking his fingers into her curls, Ben replied, "I am, like, way uncertain of that."

"But I am entirely certain." Lia smiled. "And I'll see you there."

FIN

Trudy floats into the room on Claude's arm, her honey-colored hair swept up, makeup so professional that you can't tell her face isn't exactly "procedure-free." Her poison-emerald gown plunges in a sweetheart V. Behind the complete assurance she radiates, something else simmers, at odds with her goddess half-smile. Ben swallows, thinking of holding her hand as they searched for antique clocks in the flea markets. Him adoring, her doting, licking it up, coaxing him to speak, and buying him treats. Trudy might just be the most voracious object science has ever encountered.

Oh Mom

I Love You

And You Look Very Pretty

But You Are Not A Size 6 Socialite

You Are A Supermassive Black Hole

Billions Of Times The Weight Of Our Sun

Uncle Claude, meanwhile, even outfitted by Vincentio, looks like a suburban real estate broker.

"Are you OK?" Horatio takes a half step to shield Ben from view. It is objectively adorable.

"Oh shit, listen, I have to talk to the techs, all right?" Ben watches Rory and Garrett Marlowe scuttle up to the happy couple, hissing reports under their breaths, and makes a face like he just chewed tinfoil. "Before you got back and I got plastered, I made a few changes to my speech for tonight. Minor ones. Go see if they have anything involving vegetables, and I'll, like, find you in a few."

Horatio struggles for calm. "But we don't know what the Marlowes just said, what if it's dangerous, what if you can't find—"

"Horatio Ramesh Patel." Ben slides his hands behind his friend's neck. "I will find you. They could stand a single atom from you in a huge police lineup of atoms, holding up little numbered signs, and I'd still see you. Yeah?"

His friend swallows. "Yeah. Be careful please?"

"When am I ever *not* careful?"

Air huffs from Horatio's nose, but Benjamin strikes off before he can lose nerve himself. A floating manager readily directs the Dane heir to a small tech booth hidden between a supply closet and a restroom on the second level. Away from skin contact with Horatio, Ben's stomach fires with nerves.

Lia thinks you can do this. Trust her.

He delivers the thumb drive. The staff press a remote into his hand to advance his slides. Thanking them, Ben takes the circular route back and finds himself passing the DJ booth, which has been producing party-guaranteed pop tunes, and is unsurprised to see Ariel Washington at the helm. One night a year, Ariel—repaid by Paul with a swag bag, free food, and a decent DJing fee—does what he's really best at, which is music. Since the swag bags are worth thousands, it's not such a terrible arrangement, and even though Ariel was a guitarist, he's worked practically every sort of gig known to man.

Keep it all in the family, Paul used to say. Ben shudders, knowing now that he meant *keep it all under my thumb.*

Currently Ariel is playing eighties music so white that Ben suspects sarcasm.

I GET FRIGHTENED IN ALL THIS DARKNESS
I GET NIGHTMARES I HATE TO SLEEP ALONE
I NEED SOME COMPANY, A GUARDIAN ANGEL

Ben approaches, waving warmly. All the wrinkles in Ariel's face sprout in an answering smile. He holds up a finger, enters some instructions, pulls off huge headphones, and comes down to wrap Ben in a hug.

"Eddie Money, Ariel, really?"

"Benny, my boy, you want a turn at this here gadget?"

"Dude, only you have the stones to play 'Take Me Home Tonight.' And no thank you."

"It's one of the nicest on the market, no kidding."

"Please. Like I've ever handled a DJ board in my life. Keep mocking us with your synth-riddled radio candy."

Ariel winks. "Listen, Benny, I'm glad you're here. Gonna fill you in on something real quick, all right? After our last talk, I did a little digging for you."

Ben crosses his arms protectively. "Yeah? Thanks, man, do tell."

Ariel, with his set of universally magic keys, had glanced at the theatre company's financial records himself. He'd been right—while Paul's nerves were understandable, New World's Stage wasn't nearly underwater yet, though water was sloshing steadily up the bow.

"But then I get to thinking, go back further, see what you can see, you feel me? And turns out, the old World's Stage *was* in some deep shit. And wouldn't you know it, that was right before we lost the place to the fire."

It's not that Ben is *surprised*. He's just feeling steadily sicker, like a light fever has exploded into chills. "It . . . you . . . is that why the insurance companies sniffed around for so long? I was too young and awkward to get any nuances of human interaction at that time."

Ariel lifts a shoulder. "Gotta be the reason, Benny. And no way I'm saying this is *proof*, but—"

"But someone probably torched it like a marshmallow."

Ben shoves his fingers into his eyes. Jórvík had the skill and was a psycho-clown child-serial-killer freakshow pyromaniac. It should be him. Lia said so, after all. But for what cause? The theatre was his sanctuary, as far as Jórvík was concerned, why would you torch a sanctuary, a killing ground, *what the hell is going on?*

Ben has only one suspect in mind: his late father, the revered Jackson Dane, whose gravestone read:

JACKSON JEFFERSON DANE
DEVOTED HUSBAND AND FATHER
RENOWNED ENTREPRENEUR
REQUIESCAT IN PACE

But should be changed to:

> JACKSON JEFFERSON DANE
> POOR MONEY MANAGER AND ARSONIST
> KIND OF A DOUCHE
> REQUIESCAT IN PACE

"So we're, like, saying that someone was definitely looking for a clean financial slate for the theatre."

Ariel presses Ben's shoulder in sympathy. "Can't say as I'm finding any likelier scenarios myself."

"Thing is, you can be super-duper certain about something and still be bass-ackwards wrong. Aristotle was super-duper certain that men have more teeth than women do, probably because he just thought it would be cooler to have more teeth than either of his two wives. Neither of whose teeth he bothered to count."

Ben answers the buzzing summons of his phone.

> **Not to imply you're dawdling**
> **but do have a little pity and get**
> **your arse back here?**

Smirking, Ben types:

> **so you want MY arse now**
> **is that it?**

To which he quickly receives:

> **I will absolutely walk out of**
> **this hellscape if you keep**
> **this up.**

Which can only merit:

as you must have noted I
can keep it up pretty well
don't get your knickers in
a twist I'm coming

"Hey, Benny?"

"Sorry, Horatio is making dirty jokes, it's completely uncalled for. Yeah?"

Ariel's eyes flick away. "You heard about Paul going missing, yeah?"

"Whoof, have I ever. Where the hell is that guy, this is his freaking Beatles live at the Washington Coliseum, nineteen sixty-four."

"Sure is, sure is. You got any theories, son?"

"Not a one!" Ben exclaims brightly. "Hey, Ariel, thank you for uncovering that, uh, petrified turd piece of evidence, yeah? I gotta go, and please by all means, keep insulting this crowd and deliver unto us a solid Rickroll. I'll give you my swag bag."

Not pausing over goodbyes, Ben darts off into the crowd of Broadway aristocrats. Jewel tones in taffeta and silk swirl around him. The centerpieces loom. They're in an enchanted forest, this is a fairy ball, and they'll be trapped here dancing till their shoes fill with blood. His pocket trembles.

Not just now, but you WILL be.

A few seconds are required for him to realize Horatio is answering his previous text—but when he gets it, he yaps a helpless laugh. Ben takes another pill, not bothering to check what it is, and while he's still looking down at his phone, almost slams straight into his mother.

"Hi, Mom," Ben attempts.

"Oh, Ben, *honey*, I was starting to worry when I couldn't find you." Trudy envelops him with lotioned arms. "You look so handsome, precious boy. Isn't it awful about Paul? We're all going frantic with worry about him."

Cornflower-blue eyes bore into his identical ones, and Ben can't help but stare back in wonderment. Trudy might not have tried to kill him. She might not know he killed Paul. She might not know he ever saw the papers eliminating him from the board of directors. But she obviously knows he's onto the Marlowe twins, and here she's smiling at him like a pediatric nurse.

"Benny, hey there, looking sharp," says Uncle Claude, sliding a hand around Trudy's torso.

"Uncle Claude, what a terrifically unpleasant non-surprise. Anybody confuse you with one of the catering staff yet?"

Claude just smiles indulgently. He is so *nice*, and that is *maddening*.

"Ben, don't be vile," Trudy sighs. "We're here to celebrate tonight, yes? To put all that ugliness behind us so we can be a family again."

Ben whistles, rubbing at his leathered wrist. "Ugliness? Wow, it's a good thing you asked *me* to do the eulogy-to-Dad part, because sounds like you mighta struck the wrong tone."

Trudy touches the emeralds at her neck oh-so-sadly. "We love you, Ben. And we loved your father. You are going to deliver such a fantastic tribute, I'm sure we'll both be crying all the way through it."

"That's the goal."

"And here we have him at last!" Robin Goodfellow croons, thrusting out his hand. He is impeccable in a tux that's so dark an eggplant it's nearly black, though oddly he has a number of needles thrust through the lapel. "Everything shipshape? Smashing look on you, I must say, you've outdone yourself."

"Benjamin," Trudy interjects, biting her lip. "This whole wretched Paul business—"

"There you all are, hullo."

Ben nearly startles as an arm snakes around *his* waist. Then he smiles brighter than

COMMON NAME	DISTANCE FROM EARTH	ABSOLUTE MAGNITUDE	SPECTRAL TYPE
Betelgeuse	700 light-years	-7.2	M2Iab

Horatio carries two champagne flutes in one hand, cane neatly tucked under his arm. Snaking further into Horatio's side, Ben accepts a drink, sipping with angelic innocence.

"Folks, you all know Horatio here."

Uncle Claude looks almost encouraging, Trudy shocked, and Robin Goodfellow absolutely over the moon.

"Honey!" Trudy gasps. "Oh, that's wonderful, that's just so . . . I can't even imagine a nicer surprise than this one."

"Me neither," Uncle Claude parrots.

"Absolutely *topping* development," Robin rejoices.

"There they are! Excuse us, Mr. and . . . well, Mrs. Dane?"

It's a fresh-cheeked pair of *BroadwayWorld* reporters. Trudy hesitates, but Horatio urges, "Oh, please don't mind us, do go on," and Robin shoos them toward the press chirping, "All part of our agenda, what?" and Uncle Claude says, "Time to face the music, pumpkin," and the new pair of Danes are gone.

Robin ducks toward Ben's ear, murmuring, "So jolly good to see you lovely young men together. And no doubt your eulogy will be positively *unforgettable*."

Then it's Ben who's being herded—which is just as well, since he feels as unwieldy as a baby deer—and they're back behind one of the fountains of artificial jungle. Horatio is saying something.

Horatio is saying something.

Horatio takes Ben's face in his hands and the volume comes back on. " . . . was admittedly distressing. Benjamin, speak to me, you're driving me spare."

"It doesn't make sense." Ben wants to cry, or possibly set something on fire.

"What specifically?"

"Ariel says the old World's Stage was in financial ruins, so someone must have torched it." Ben can't breathe. "Lia said Jórvík was the culprit but couldn't explain why. Mom, she—did she try to *kill* me or just disinherit me? *Fuck*. Vincentio says

Robin's poison, but Robin sounds like he's into my presentation, so I guess he's seen it, he's the event planner, and sure, he'd like it if he's pure chaos, but that doesn't bode well does it, and was Dad the real force behind the arsonist and if so did someone murder him for it and why did he think it was Uncle Claude or is it all coincidental?"

"Right, look at me."

"This is worse than knot theory," Ben moans.

"No, for the love of Christ, don't—"

"Are these descriptions of two different knots, or of the same knot? Is it actually more than one knot entangled together? Do I need to apply hyperbolic geometry? Did I, like, make all of this shit up and while it looks infinitely complex, it's only twists and layers, not a knot at all, it's an unknot, or what you'd call a three-dimensional circle? Like the geometric version of a run-on sentence fragment. Can I project it onto a plane and count the crossings? Which Reidemeister move—"

"Benjamin," Horatio says, calm as a frozen lake. "I know many things about you, and some fluctuate, but one is a constant. When you start talking knot theory, you are finished for the moment."

"But—"

"Hush. Let's find some coffee, or water, and—"

"Lia!" It all snaps back into place—the suggestion she gave him in the dream, *listen to the waiter.*

It doesn't exist anymore.

"What about Lia?" Horatio looks close to tears himself.

"She can help us. Look, I can try to ask her—"

"You cannot talk with Lia Brahms, Benjamin!"

There's a foot of space between them, but it doesn't feel like air, the gap feels as solid as a fortress.

"I've been talking to her for weeks, so why the hell not?"

"Because that's in your *sleep*, love," Horatio says, broken.

"And you're awake, you're here with me, and Lia has been dead for two years."

"But I can't—"

"This isn't about Lia anymore, Benjamin," Horatio whispers, pulling him closer. "You loved her so, and I loved her too, but please. She doesn't exist anymore."

LIA

I would rather dance
hoodwinked with the devil
than be alone.

—*Morgan Parker, "The History of Black People"*

AFTER LIA WOKE FROM the dream—even she couldn't tell whose—she put on her dress. Since Ben gifted it for one of her show openings, it was a ridiculous garment: a grey Marchesa gown with rivers of translucent fabric. Its bodice and sheer sleeves were covered with violet flora in crystal, glass, embroidery, beadwork. This dress screamed that a fairy godmother was about to free you from a wicked stepmother.

OK, Destiny. Lia finishes her mascara. *Bring it.*

She drops necessaries from keys to her mother's carefully folded scarf into a beaded purse, fetches Jessica Anne Kowalski's bouquet, eases into a cab. She frets over whether Benjamin visited City Diner and wonders what the old waiter had to say about his homeland.

It could be Moldova or the Moon, but it has significance. I know it does.

Lia seeks the gala's side security entrance when the cab pulls up. The one for sound engineers and head ushers, the people who don't get swag bags. Once inside, she squints in disbelief at the prows of heavenly balconies jutting outward, the frillions of dollars' worth of haute couture, and finally at the centerpieces.

What the hell, she thinks.

PİNK LİLY: *Riches, prosperity in abundance, excessive success.*

WİLLOW BRANCHES: *In Celtic, used to heighten psychic power; adaptability and survival; wands are powerful guides for underworld journeying.*

MONSTERA DELİCİOSA: *Used for honoring elders in Chinese culture, but bear in mind represents death in others due to its intense growth and dangling roots.*

These are some outwardly glam, deeply fucked-up arrangements.

Lia soon spots Jessica, who looks like it's her first dance at a new middle school. She wears a forgettable classic black princess gown, holding a martini nearing the end of its days.

They've prearranged for Lia to place the bouquet on a banquet table at precisely this time. For a tense two minutes, Jessica is preoccupied by her Louboutins. Then she looks up, startles, and makes a graceless dive for the flowers. Her expression is queasy, as if she's cradling a newborn who can't hold up its head yet.

That wheel is spinning, but the hamster may be dead.

Navigating the crowd is a nightmare—but there's a balcony that's still a good vantage point, and Lia climbs on simple silver heels. When she reaches the chrome rail, the perfect spot opens. The scent of the pink lilies drifts upward, rich as money, and willow branches truly do enhance powers, because this air tastes crammed full of promises.

"Utterly charming, just as expected, my dear."

Lia allows Robin Goodfellow to kiss her hand. He's immaculate, of course, a purple sheen to his black tuxedo, and the sinister tools of his trade pierce this lapel, too.

"If it isn't the Needleman."

"Oh ho!" Robin exclaims. "Topping! Given you a cursory briefing, have they? Much more forthcoming myself. One more chance to glory in the exotic world of event planning, what say you? Bali's next on my ticket."

"Save your breath."

Robin leans his forearms on the rail. "Can't blame a chap for trying, can you?"

"Actually, I kinda can."

"Well, did my best. Where are my beautiful sisters?"

"They said they'd appear when the time came."

"Typical. Good luck getting anyone to talk to you other than me. Robin to the rescue then, for I am nothing if not a hapless romantic!"

"I am persona non grata to a few of these attendees, but seems like I have my pick of two or three hundred other people. Why shouldn't any of them talk to me?"

"Why, because you're dead, of course." Robin chuckles. "But my stars! You didn't know, lambkins?"

Below Lia, figures flicker in and out as if they're in a horror film. Black, grey, muddy-grey, searing white, charcoal. She should be waiting for Benjamin's appearance, on guard against any violence from Jeremy. But with a few words, Robin switched the world to ghastly monochrome. He's had this effect every time she's seen him, she realizes. Lights in the shop, clouds in the street. When he approached tonight, for the first time, she wasn't frightened.

She's never been more terrified now.

"Oh, my dearie darling duck, what *fun*!" Robin's eyes are as yellow as a rabid tom's. "Didn't fuss over telling you, did they?"

Lia's lips tremble. "You're lying."

"Not much fun in that unless there's a smidge of truth present, though."

"And the sisters are on my side, they're a bit weird but—"

"Aaaah, yes, the *Weird Sisters*." Robin explores the railing. Up and down, *up and down*, leading her eyes up and down. "Rather callous even for them, if you ask me. Suspected as much, though. Reason I made my offer in the first place. They truly didn't tell you? You are passed on. You rest in . . . not exactly resting in peace, are you, love?"

Lia stumbles backward, nearly tripping on her beautiful dress. *No, this dress is precious. You cannot damage this dress.* She's going to faint right here, swan dive over the balcony rail. Robin turned the Technicolor back on, but she sickly suspects he's been doing the strobe effect every time he sees her for a reason.

The world doesn't look like this anymore. Not to you.

"It's not true." She hates how her voice shakes.

"Surely you aren't *surprised*. When's the last time anyone had a chin-wag with you, then?"

"I'm talking to you right now!"

"Ought to have seen that one coming, humblest et ceteras. A *human* person. And please don't come off a complete nitwit by suggesting the sisters are *Homo sapiens*."

"No, they're . . . much older. This is horseshit," Lia growls. "I . . . I can touch things, I just delivered Jessica's bouquet. I get supplies at the flower market."

Robin lifts a single finger. "How long was it after the sisters found you that you even tippy-toed out of the flower shop? A month? Two?"

"Longer," Lia whispers, ashamed.

"Oh, my heartstrings. Well, they made you their little errand girl, didn't they? Bound you to them somehow. Betting that outside the shop, you never manipulated anything but flowers, did you?" Robin inclines his head. "Naturally you can handle flowers—they wanted you to, and it's your oeuvre. Disgraceful how speedily they trained you into their lackey. Never were early risers, those three."

"The picture!" Lia gasps.

"Always appreciated the word 'lickspittle,' it's gone out of fashion but—"

"The picture of Trudy and Claude, I took it from my dad's coffee table."

"Didn't you just!" Robin trills. "That's all to do with who *you* are, I'm afraid. Or what you are. You're coming into your own, and I'm positively awash with feeling. Should you prefer I plan a celebratory bat mitzvah, or go rogue with a quinceañera?"

"Who am I?" Lia steps close enough to smell cedar cologne and something darker, like an alley without any end. "Tell me."

"Ah-ah-ah." Robin pouts. "Made you an offer, didn't I? Twice. Don't be fussed, I'm sure they'll tell you themselves in another few thousand years."

Tears crowd behind Lia's eyes.

"Christ, *here's* a dismal sight." Robin slinks around her, mocking and admiring and cruel. "No home, no friends or family, never going to eat a peach or share a kiss or take a shit or feel the rain again, and you thought what, some divine wise women arrived to nurse you? My sisters *collected you*, Miss Brahms. Running a Red Cross, are they? Do you even know what happened that night?"

Grief tears at her seams because no: Lia can't remember. So many of her stories must be narrated by others. Autobiography aped by biography. Forensics pieced together.

I can't remember.

She'd eaten the last Greek yogurt in their fridge. She'd packed that threadbare Talking Heads T-shirt Ben said was sexier on her than any lingerie. Lights in their apartment were off, the dozen plants watered and misted. She'd been sober while getting ready to leave so they didn't end up in London needing to visit a Tesco for socks with Ben wearing *that face* and Lia drowning in shame. Downstairs the snow fell like cherry petals, and she checked their flight wasn't delayed, and headed for her studio to ensure the seaweed was drying correctly. Once she'd arrived, there was only a quarter left of that bottle of gin, and a quarter bottle would be the perfect amount, and not a drop more.

After that, nothing. Not even static. Spliced tape.

Robin leans forward as if she's a stupid child. "Here's one gratis, duckie dearest, even though you fucked me over by not joining my side. Luggage? 'Fraid not. Wallet, keys? Nix. Empty pint of corner-store gin in one hand, MetroCard in the other. God knows how many bars before that. Various unexplained bruises. Took a nap *under* the park bench, like a moron, so no one saw till far too late. My sisters whisked off this Lia, the one I'm speaking with. The one frozen in the snow of many colors didn't have an ID, lads in blue had to do some digging, but a few days later . . ."

Robin's lips nearly touch her ear. "Paul Brahms arrived at the morgue."

"You bastard!" Lia cries as she slaps him.

And she runs.

Down, down, down to the ballroom. She's dodging at first, then stops avoiding the patrons and . . . nothing happens. No one collides with her, no one glares.

"Excuse me," Lia says to a man in an all-white tuxedo.

"Hi, I beg your pardon," she tries on a woman in a lace gown.

"Can you hear me?" she shouts at a trio of chorus girls in pixie cuts.

"Will somebody *help me please*!" Lia screams in the middle of the ballroom.

No one helps her. She isn't there.

THE INSTINCT TO USE the ladies' room to cry is strong, it turns out. Even postmortem. Lia sobs in a stall for half an hour before emerging. She stands before the mirror. On this ephemeral plane or whatever the hell it is, her hair is mussed enough to look runway-worthy, so she embraces entropy and drags her nails through it. She redoes her makeup, stares herself down, remembers who she is.

Who she has become.

Her curls are insane, her lips blood-red, she's basically wearing grey gauze covered in sparkling blossoms, and the light Robin keeps referring to burns in her dark eyes like a bonfire.

Lia looks, in short, like a witch.

"Nice knowing you," she says to herself as she exits.

She goes to the other side of the event space and finds a new lookout. It's so unnerving to think that she's not physically present. If she even has nerves. She can smell the Wagyu sliders coming out of the kitchen, feel the bounce of the carpet beneath her heels. But she realizes that in the last two years, she only ever eats the food the sisters make, and traverses their rugs. Before having made Jessica's bouquet, Lia would have fallen apart over this. She'd known her last chance with Ben was gone, but not that *she* herself was. Alive, Lia was in a tortuous limbo of longing and regret. Dead?

Fucking roll dice.

A series of technical cues cascade. The chandelier dims, the DJ shifts to a theme from *The Light in the Piazza*, a huge projector screen descends. Lenses tighten and blaze, and where nothing existed, there's a platform with a podium and a microphone, and Ariel Washington's buttery voice makes an offstage introduction, and then the space is occupied by Benjamin Jackson Dane.

Lia's heart stops.

You don't have one.

Ben smiles sideways, and the crowd erupts in applause. Apparently he ordered Vincentio to find a tux made from grey thistledown, and it looks spectacular. His softly punk blond hair is identical, his weight is a mess, there's a cuff on his wrist although he never wears jewelry, his eyes are fifty years older, he's exactly the same.

And a new ink-black pain spills in Lia, because now she remembers the goodbye letter from him that the sisters gave her.

Lia thought he'd finally left her. Her friends never contradicted the idea. But it wasn't a *Dear Jane* missive at all.

She was reading the eulogy he gave at her services. She knows it the way she'd know his voice in the dark.

I loved you then. I love you now. I love you everywhere, and everywhen, and after what you did this time, I can never be with you again.
    How am I ever going to recover from something like that?

Ben squints at the followspot in his eyes, but it's for charm. "Hey, everyone, hi. My name is Benjamin Jackson Dane. Thank you for supporting the annual New World's Stage Benefit Gala, which this year is significant to us for so many reasons. Your ticket sales tonight will enable us to keep providing the highest quality art for our community—that's you, you're the community, you guys are dropping your cues already. Let's hear it for our donors!"

Lia's cheeks ache with pride. He was so different when she met him. Funny and fascinating, tongue-tied and abused. This Benjamin has taken scores of remedial speech courses, taught thousands of philosophy students, studied hundreds of hours of live theatre. Lia wants to strip him down and crown him entirely in laurel, and they aren't even in the same corner of the universe.

Ben has been speaking. " . . . they have dedicated their lives to this theatre, and now, ladies and gentlemen, be it known that they've dedicated their lives to each other as well. May I present Claude and Trudy Dane . . . man and wife."

Outright gasps from the crowd. A solid effort at applause. Shock, mainly. Lia can't believe that Ben just delivered that introduction with so little venom. Unless he's changed—and he hasn't, she's been dreaming him all this time—Benjamin has more private vengeances planned.

"And now," Ben states, "it's my sad duty to deliver a short presentation memorializing the life of my late father, Mr. Jackson Jefferson Dane. He was the founder of the old World's Stage, he pulled up his bootstraps and dragged it from the ashes to unveil the incredible space you all enjoy now, and he was larger than life in every possible sense. But speaking for myself, he was Dad."

Ben stops. Clears his throat, shuffles notecards. The audience waits, still reeling from the marriage announcement. Lia spies Horatio's imposing form, with his hair in a low knot and his arms crossed. He looks sick with worry, he looks like the brother she never had, and she badly misses him, and Lia only wishes one of them could go to Ben.

"Right, sorry," Benjamin gasps, coming out of it. "This, um, this is not easy. I'm going to conduct this tribute to my late father in the form of compare and contrast, which is a pretty venerable rhetorical mode, gotta be one of my faves, and so allow me to present the first slide."

Jackson Dane, midtwenties. Sweat streams down his bared muscles. Wasteland and derricks in the background, a dry sky above. Jackson looks as careless as a man in a cigarette ad. But she knows he hated that life, was even ashamed of it.

When Ben wolf whistles, the crowd relaxes a little. "Right? Let me tell you guys, I have *never* looked like that. Anyway, here's my dad back in Texas where our holdings come from, the ones that have helped bring so many unforgettable performances to the public by founding the original World's Stage. We're looking at unforgettable abs now, but . . ." Everyone chuckles. "My dad was the hardest worker I knew, and here he is out in the fields. Jackson hated what he called 'nuts and bolts.' Fixing things, dealing with hoses and drills. What he wanted to do was make people feel powerful emotions, and . . . well, if you straight ladies feel nothing about this picture, I know a lot of the chorus boys here, and they feel very deeply."

His audience grins. Broadway Twitter has probably gone off like a nuke, Lia thinks. Hashtags like "Claudy" and "Trude" being explored. But here, it's a son who loved his dad showing the world his heart, and it's a room full of kindness.

Until the next slide shows up. Gasps, cackles, an audible *what the hell*.

"You really can't understand how much I agree with you." Ben beams at the heckler.

Present-day Claude is poolside at the Danes' summer Hamptons residence. Flabby absolutely everywhere, he sports swim trunks with dolphins printed on them, streaks of white sunscreen under his eyes and down his nose, and a floppy hat reading **CARP EAT 'EM: SEIZE THE FISH.** Hapless and genuine.

"What you just saw was my mom's first husband, my dad, Jackson. This here is the new guy, Claude Dane, his half-brother. I gotta say, Mom: Mad points for mixing it up. Let's not leave the buffet till we've tried *everything* on offer, you feel me?"

Cell phone cameras feast voraciously. Somewhere in a Hell's Kitchen walk-up, Lia thinks, a Page Six freelance reporter just had an orgasm.

"I'm kidding, Mom, I'm kidding, we need to lighten this up or I wouldn't live through it otherwise." Ben crosses and uncrosses his ankles. "Sorry, folks. The evolutionary root of laughter is actually survival, not pleasure, did you know that? Well, I did. Back to Jackson Jefferson Dane."

Jackson in a full three-piece suit, going over documents with men who look comparatively shrunken. One hand is cocked on his side; the cowboy hasn't left him entirely. The confidence he exudes must be seeping into the paper fibers.

"This is Dad going over plans for New World's Stage." Ben's voice softens. "As I said, he didn't want to tinker with physical objects. But he did like to dream them up and *make* them exist. Which I think is objectively nine hundred times cooler, not to cast any aspersions whatsoever on elevator maintenance employees. I chose this slide because in it, Dad has been doing some dreaming, sure, but he's willing it into creation. He was a great one for winning allies over, because he loathed even thinking about using family money for an artistic venture. We fought all the time and he didn't approve of me, but. It didn't matter. He had me won over from the start."

Ben swipes at tears. The assembly careens between sympathy, shock, and bizarre glee at witnessing a masterful performance. He didn't study acting, and he certainly wasn't talented—but Ben Dane has been beaten to a pulp, taunted, and literally pissed on. Which means that Ben is very *very* engaging.

"OK, bit too much of this, apologies again." Ben pockets his handkerchief. "Let's see who replaced this guy."

The audience, thoroughly warmed up by now, points, howls, says outright *girl he did not* and *snap that is low* and *they can't be in on this joke, can they?*

Lia recognizes the ornately carved stones of the Lopburi temple and recalls a rare Dane family outing to Thailand years previous. In the foreground, Claude Dane in a Pepto-Bismol pink polo shirt is being mauled by a monkey. Because of course he is, Lia thinks, groaning. The monkey is either about to munch on Claude's face or initiate the most passionate kiss since *Pretty Woman*. Claude's obscured expression is probably a scream, or maybe his face is just being yanked by a hungry (or horny) monkey.

"So here again we have a subtle contrast to my dad," Ben continues.

Lia knows this tone.

It has said to her, *Lia honey, vomit isn't so much for inside my backpack, are we on the same page here?*

"Credit to my uncle Claude—I took this picture, and he totally had a sense of humor about it. So I knew he wouldn't mind my showing it tonight! Cool guy. So yeah, what's next after Uncle Claude, Mom? Because this monkey sure looks ready to go."

Flashes from the press illuminate every expression of delighted horror imaginable.

What are you doing, Benny? Lia thinks frantically. *What have you already done?*

"Please, ladies and gentlemen!" he calls. "My word of honor, not one more embarrassing picture of my uncle. I didn't really think I could get through this sorta surreal experience without some jokes, but it's a memorial, not a roast. Back to my dad, Jackson Dane."

Lia's eyes fill. Trudy, lithe and gorgeous, sits on the white carpet in the townhouse. She is laughing, reaching her hand toward the couch. Jackson holds small Ben easily in his quarterback hands. He's whooshing his son like an airplane, and Benjamin doesn't know that things are going to get so much worse after this, for so long, before they get better again. But right now? He's blissfully happy with two loving parents, and Lia faintly, like an echo, remembers what that felt like, too.

"I was a year and three months, I think, in this picture," Ben says hoarsely. "Which, like, obviously means I don't remember it. But I do remember my dad always trying to lift me, even when he was ham-fisted at it. Look at my mom too—you look gorgeous, Mom. You look just as gorgeous tonight. And yeah, it took me a hell of a lot longer to achieve liftoff than is reasonable." Ben takes a shaking breath. "But my dad, even when he was knocking me, even when it hurt, he did it because he wanted me strong. That's a legit retro parenting style. But this image—this is what he wanted for me."

Ben glances out at the crowd. "No more jokes at my uncle Claude's expense. Just one more family portrait."

It's a balcony walkway outside a row of hotel rooms. Trudy, sun-kissed and soft-lipped, gazes at an infatuated Claude. It can't possibly be less than twenty years ago.

"Congratulations, Trudy and Claude Dane," Ben declaims, lifting a champagne flute. "Or is it more like Happy Anniversary? Whatever, same-same. Fuck if I care! To the happy couple!"

"Lights! *Lights!*" Claude Dane's voice bellows. "For god's sake, will somebody shut that screen down and turn up the lights!"

The star chandelier blazes to life, the projector disappears, the patrons make no effort to disguise their dark delight or total revulsion or both. Ben vanishes, thank Christ. Lia is mystified that no one shuts down the proceedings. The only return to normalcy is Ariel playing "Everybody Wants to Rule the World."

Then she recalls that this fundraiser is a giant percentage of New World's Stage's budget. Trudy's relentless quest for swag pays off yearly in the form of very real stage furnishings and costumes, fixing the hand dryers, vacuuming the carpets. They cannot permit hundreds of important donors to walk away without their rose crystal–infused water bottles. The horse has already fled the barn, after all—admitting guilt by throwing everyone out is the worst thing they could possibly do.

Meanwhile where the hell is my dad? Lia wonders.

"Hello, our *petite chouchou*," says Mam'zelle, approaching the rail. She wears four cakelike tiers of palest pink tulle. "We don't want to see your Ben like this—my spirit, it was so torn apart."

Moma passes an arm around her, clad in a black strapless sheath topped by waves of 3D printed lace. "How I'm supposed to look nice tonight when you all dolled up like some kinda fairy queen?"

Maw-maw shuffles over in a couture sack made from crushed metallic copper fabric. "The harvest is upon us. Ready the scythes and the sickles."

"That is seriously just sinister, Maw-maw," Lia says, and Maw-maw winks.

"There's our Miss Jessica." Moma nods, leaning on the rail. "Any time now."

"I was talking to Robin earlier," Lia begins.

All three sisters roll their eyes.

"Yeah, for real. Anyway . . . so I'm dead? That would have been good to know."

Moma's neck arches. "Ha! It would not, baby girl. The kinda state you was in, that would have sizzled your soul to a crisp.

You weren't nohow ready. This Lia right here with us is your *mind*, and it had its work cut out for it."

"Rest," Mam'zelle agrees soothingly. "You needed affection. A change of scene."

"Hell, when you first woke up, body or no, you coulda still drank the river Jordan and then licked the rock. I had to coax it back to other cravings, me."

"Us, *ma chère* sister."

"All of us and never say otherwise, my sister," Moma agrees.

Despite the extremity of the situation, Lia is already battling to look severe. "Cards on the table, I've been dead well over a year?"

Moma's braids are piled vertically in a huge headdress and she pats them to check the sturdiness. "Give or take. Year and a half, I'd say."

"The goodbye letter from Ben." This time her voice husks. "That was his funeral speech."

Mam'zelle presses her hand. "We couldn't tell you, *chère*. You had to find it out yourself. But we understand why you loved him so. *Il est un homme juste, un homme bon.*"

Lia nods. She wishes she knew quite where this good, just man is, but at least he's coming back this way soon. She can feel it.

"So, give it to me plain: Am I your bitch, then?"

"*Pardonnez-moi?*"

"Robin seems to think that you put me under some sort of binding and have been using me for your servant."

Maw-maw stomps a foot, Moma guffaws, and Mam'zelle clicks her tongue in disbelief.

"That man can't picture nothing saving as a conquest, him," Moma scoffs. "What an ape. Me stronger than you, you serve me. Him stronger than me, I serve him. Caveman bullshit."

"He's unevolved," Mam'zelle agrees.

"Robin wants a binding spell, I'll give him one next time he wants to wipe his ass."

Lia has never struggled so hard not to laugh, and it's the least appropriate time and place possible.

"But I'm somehow important to the . . . grand scheme of things? I was never your pet charity project?"

"*Mon Dieu*, Lia, you are one of the most key players," Mam'zelle gushes.

"What kinda time I got for a charity project?" Moma glares down her nose. "The *idea*. We watch you, we guard, we guide, and you don't figure there's something in it for us, too? What kinda magical negress home for the stupid you think you landed yourself in?"

"That would have been ridiculous, *chouchou*," Mam'zelle agrees. "Winning your trust was a triumph. Robin said all those things because he's hot under the collar."

"Oh, we dilled his pickle all right." Moma smirks. "He dangled this in front of our Lia, dangled that."

"The main thing he dangled was who I am." Lia pauses, then presses on. "He even implied it would take you thousands of years to tell me, seeing as I'm your magical indentured . . . thrall . . . thingy."

Maw-maw tugs her shiny dress collar impatiently. "What is freely given must still be freely received."

"I had a choice, working for you," Lia translates.

"It woulda stopped the second you said no thank you," Moma agrees.

"What am I then? A spirit? A ghost?"

"Our *friend*," Mam'zelle chides gently.

"And a goddess," Moma adds, shrugging.

"An *excuse me*?" Lia cries.

"You wanna go back to the Greeks, you're Heimarmene." Moma's brow lifts, amused. "Doing that kinda root work at your age, strong as you are now, couldn't be nobody else. The goddess of cause and effect. This action produces this result. *A* leads to *B*. Not a lotta forces in this existence more powerful than cause and effect and, well . . . that's your jurisdiction right there."

"Not individual lives, that would grow so tiring," Mam'zelle coos. "More . . . how to say it?"

"Fate of the universe," Maw-maw assists.

"Oh," Lia says, dizzy. "OK. Well. Guess I better read the handbook soon, then."

"There are my divine sisters!" Robin exclaims. "All looking ravishing, I might add. What's a poor tailor to do?"

Moma mutters a suggestion that Lia doesn't think anatomically possible.

The silver tray Robin carries is laden with five glinting champagne flutes. He raises his eyebrows when he sees Lia looking significantly more demonic than previously. But his cheer returns, and he tosses the empty tray over the ledge like a Frisbee.

"A toast!" Robin proposes. "To the circle of life. Long may it grind!"

"To the next beginning," adds Mam'zelle.

"Unto death," Moma continues.

"Into dust," says Maw-maw.

Everyone stares at Lia.

"Mazel tov?" she hazards.

You fucking bitch, I'll kill you! comes from the ballroom below them.

Over the course of the next minute or so, a series of events unfolds below them, the instigating factor being Jessica Anne Kowalski's bouquet. While matters progress quickly, the climax of the scene features Horatio Patel holding one Jeremy Bradford, hedge fund manager, at bay with the point of a sword cane.

"Lord have mercy," Robin comments during these proceedings, sipping his champagne. "What fools these mortals are."

HORATIO

DON'T CARE!" BENJAMIN YELLS, waving his arms. "We needed a fundamental shift, Horatio, a quantum jump if you will, and here's this nifty secret cheating bit that they didn't want anybody to know. Hokey-dokey, what if *everybody* knew? This is a filthy long-term affair, now how are you guys gonna behave? They could never have anticipated Paul ordering those pictures taken, and *definitely* not his smearing them in my face for pure uncut spite right before I accidentally shot him dead."

"It's not, ah, the likeliest of scenarios."

"Damn straight it's not. Talk about a quantum jump, I just took their electron and kicked the shit out of it."

"There's a world of difference between the atomic electron

transition and asking your mum if she'd care to shag a monkey'"
Horatio groans from behind his fingers.

The part of him that can feel Benjamin's anguish, as if jumper
cables connected them, burns. The part repulsed by Claude and
Trudy applauds. But every British instinct sparked while watching that spectacle made Horatio want to relocate to a moon, and
preferably not Earth's.

They sit—rather, Horatio leans while Benjamin paces—in a
cul-de-sac bordered by an electrical room, a service elevator,
and the unmarked staircase they used to flee. If the Danes
wanted them, they'd be caught by now; a security camera stares
down unblinking. And if Paul Brahms were alive, they'd have
been whisked to the nearest cement-shoe-fitting salon. But neither scenario is occurring, so Benjamin schemes while Horatio
rests against a stack of boxed tile cleaner.

"Fine, there are hardly ever monkeys mentioned in conjunc-
tion with the creation of a photon, what did you see?" Benjamin
demands.

"Um. See?"

"See, while I was giving the most memorable eulogy known
to civilization, what did you *see*? That's the whole reason we put
you so close to my mom and that broken breast pump Uncle
Claude."

"Right, I need one thing clear first. You surveyed this cata-
strophic situation in which multiple people are dead, you were
nearly murdered, and you were disinherited before you burned
those documents, and you thought, you know what this calls
for? *More* chaos."

"Exactly!" Benjamin snaps his fingers as if Horatio just did a
cool trick, and Horatio might genuinely push him down the
service elevator shaft. "Chaos theory."

"Chaos theory?"

"The tiniest alteration in the initial conditions of a highly
complex situation can produce a wildly different outcome. Your
dad makes one joke his boss appreciates, he gets the better job

posting, you marry a different person, and you die in a different freak traffic accident than if he never pulled that crack about bad golfers. This is a deterministically chaotic system, which means that even if we knew atom by atom what happened just before my dad died, it would be, like, beyond arduous to figure out where this is headed. But we *don't* know what those initial conditions were, so I reset the clock. The initial conditions are now the present."

Horatio attempts to think of a meditation prayer.

All that comes through is *buggerfucking hell.*

"By doing that slideshow, I intend to restart all my thought processes under the assumption this is the beginning. Horatio, what did you see?"

Horatio isn't the shirking sort, so he says, "Whatever happened to your father, it wasn't Claude."

Benjamin worries at the cuff. "Good, now we're getting somewhere, why do you say so?"

"Because he was narked off but mainly worried over Trudy. Not once did he look frightened. And even when the final slide showed up, he was shocked, granted, but not defensive. More protective."

Horatio does not want to tell Benjamin what else he saw.

"OK, so my dad was wrong. That leaves accident, suicide, or someone else was the killer. This is sooooo good, finally, this is progress."

Horatio pictures Trudy Dane, Claude's hand finding soothing places to alight. He's never observed a woman less in need of being comforted. Trudy's eyes were arctic blue, love and loathing congealing into a noxious expression. If she'd been born a few hundred years ago, Horatio thought, Trudy would have been a remorseless queen, and her subjects would have trembled and worshipped at her golden slippers. She would have made for a stirring biography.

But this was Benjamin's mother. And when he'd shown the final slide, she'd flinched before baring her teeth like a predator.

"Horatio?"

"Present, yes."

"There's more, isn't there?"

Benjamin's entire body is a question—the half-frown, the madly tugged hair. Horatio holds both his hands out. The smaller man readily approaches, and with Horatio propped against boxes, for once they're the same height.

"Hey," Horatio begins.

Benjamin slides into his arms. "Hi. We're investigating, don't try to distract me. The tux is distracting enough."

"I'm not, love."

"That's weird."

"Oh, I didn't even notice that I . . . My apolo—"

"Nope." Benjamin smooths a palm over his hair and Horatio doesn't need a skeletal system, this is fine. "Your inner monologue being . . . outer, it's strange. Just because I couldn't hear it before doesn't mean I couldn't *hear* it. I'm sorry."

"That's all right." Horatio doesn't need whatever throat impediment this is. "I was happy enough."

"In fact, this doesn't feel like happiness."

"What does it feel like?"

A sad smile emerges. "What you said before."

Love.

Do what you need to do before he renders you sodding incapable of human speech.

"Benjamin, about the investigating. Claude wasn't overtly fussed when you showed the final slide."

"You said so. And?"

"Trudy was."

Horatio misses nothing of Benjamin's full-body tremor. His friend closes his eyes. They're glassy when they open and have been red at the edges for days now, painfully blue within.

"So, right. Right. Maybe Mom really was trying to off me. That's disturbing."

Horatio can't imagine any possible response.

"I, we, I need to get back inside," Benjamin stammers. "Where's the bunch of dudes in black-tie security-detail uniform? I know they hired extra muscle for this so where are they, why aren't they here, because they should be so what's the holdup?"

Horatio gathers him closer. "We can just—"

"No, we're going back in, and then. Then we can leave. But I need to gauge the aftermath."

Horatio studies him, all the brackets around his eyes that weren't there before Horatio left for London, the way the corner of his mouth tucks down miserably.

"Then let's get it over with, shall we?"

"Let's shall."

They link fingers and return the way they came. The gala is a firestorm of gossip and speculation. There's more programming to come—a medley from their current rock opera production of *Paradise Lost*, Ben thinks—but it hasn't begun. It's as if a lion-mauled Christian is still bleeding out, and the Romans are salivating for the next course.

They circle the room slowly, readying to leave it. But everyone is so preoccupied by exactly the same thing that a single dissimilarity stands out. Horatio finds himself tuning in to an unrelated conversation, out of context and none of his business. A thin, processed-looking young woman holds out a bouquet to the man before her. She's so frightened her arms shake.

"Please just take it." The young lady's mouth wobbles. "It's, it's an apology bouquet."

The man's hands are wedged in his pockets. He is superficially good-looking, with a cleft chin, though his hazel eyes have the depth of a goblin shark's. This chap would just drift toward his prey on a deep-sea current and then lazily snap teeth. He's also three or four sheets to the wind.

He's a discount Marlowe twin, and Horatio prickles with loathing.

"What is wrong with you, Jessica?" he demands. "Look, I

said I was sorry about punching your date. You wanna get back together with me and you think a bouquet is gonna cut it?"

"No, I don't want to get back together, I just, this is an apology." Jessica takes a deep breath. "At least let me read you the card. 'May you have all the happiness that you deserve.'"

Jeremy shakes his head. "This is the saddest shit. You're bringing me flowers and wishing me happiness but you *don't* want me back?"

"This is, uh, to smooth things over at work."

"Pathetic. Things are totally smooth there, it's outside of work you're a total nightmare."

Jessica starts to cry. Horatio's aunt in Norwood had a terrier that sounded like that when it was hungry.

"We should—" Benjamin starts.

"Just a tick, love." Horatio squeezes his hand and goes to Jessica. "Are you all right?"

Jessica thrusts the bouquet out with both hands. She shakes her head. The canine crying intensifies.

"Hey, who the hell are you?" Jeremy sneers.

Horatio doesn't understand anything about this situation. Jessica is terrified of Jeremy; she's handing him a unique, large, and frankly costly looking bouquet. People don't behave so, and if Horatio is an expert at anything whatsoever, it's how people behave. Jeremy snatches the bouquet out of her fingers, to her obvious relief.

"My name is Horatio," he answers. To Jessica, "If you need anything, say the word."

"Look man, she doesn't need some Arab guy hitting on her."

Jeremy puffs himself bigger. Or attempts to. Horatio fights the urge to wince in distaste. The incorrect racial slur he ignores, as he's been doing periodically since he was a child.

"He's not hitting on her, he's with me." Benjamin peers intently at the bouquet, as if trying to place it. "Dude, I dunno what your deal is, but it's shadier than a back alley."

"My *deal*? I'm a fucking Two Sigma hedge fund manager!"

"Oh my god, you say that as if you *want* people to hear you. Do you need us to stay with you, miss?"

Jessica shakes her head so hard that Horatio worries about whiplash. Benjamin slips his hand through Horatio's arm, and they step away. Obviously too legless to recognize the Dane heir, Jeremy turns back to his ex and almost staggers at the change of direction alone.

"Something super weird is going on," Benjamin decides.

"Agreed." Horatio does a perimeter check, but the Danes are nowhere in sight. "I've no idea—"

Jeremy attempts to swell like some none-too-bright species of poultry. Horatio is about to bodily whisk Jessica away when a newcomer arrives. Her hair is Coke label red, she's dipped from décolletage to ankle in silver sequins, and she's several shades beyond angry.

"*Jeremy!*" she brays. He startles. "What the fuck is this?"

"Brittany, calm down, it's nothing."

"Hi, Jessica," Brittany says coldly. "What, you're back with this ugly bitch now? You got a nice romantic bouquet and everything? That's sweet, Jeremy, that's the sweetest thing I ever seen."

"This isn't what it looks like, calm down."

Brittany swings ample hips at Jessica. "Did you just tell me to calm down, you cheating piece of shit? Jessica, did you give Jeremy these weird-ass flowers?"

"Uh," Jessica sniffles.

"And he *took* them?"

"Yeah. But they're not—"

"Have a nice life, then." Brittany, with a conviction Horatio can only admire, turns on a gravity-defying platform heel and sashays toward the nearest champagne station.

"That's not—no," Jeremy snarls. "Brittany!"

"I should be going, too," Jessica says in a tiny voice.

"Jessica, how exactly do you manage to ruin *everything*?"

"It, it was just meant, I have to—"

"*You fucking bitch, I'll kill you!*"

Benjamin and Horatio are both in motion, but it's too late. Horatio doesn't know the number of drugs in Jeremy's system, nor drinks. But he recognizes the nasty power play of an impotent man, and they're both too late to prevent Jeremy from throwing his ex into the nearest floral display. The centerpiece shudders but is heavy enough to remain standing.

Jessica hits the ground, stunned. Horatio dives to her side while Benjamin, bless him on occasion for the fearless bastard he is, grips Jeremy by the tux lapels and shoves him several feet backward.

"Night watch! Palace guards? Sorry, *security*? Right now would be a good time!" Benjamin shouts.

Horatio helps Jessica to stand.

The patrons notice the show isn't over yet and scuttle back for a better view.

Jeremy sizes up Benjamin and decides he likes his odds. A knife appears in his hand, the sort of concealed switchblade that idiots bring with them to drug deals—which likely happened a few hours back—and are easily overlooked when screening at large events.

"I'll teach you to touch me, you little faggot," he snaps.

Benjamin rolls his eyes.

Jeremy lurches forward, finding himself at the business end of Horatio's sword cane.

Horatio cannot believe that any of this is happening.

"Yes, I do actually know how to use this," Horatio warns him. "Oddly enough, I was ranked third in the Eton College Fencing Club my final year. Drop the knife if you please, mine is longer."

"Holy unmarried teen mother of god, what are you doing?" Benjamin marvels.

"Not now, Benjamin."

"I think I just came in my pants."

"Security is en route and I'm holding an illicit sword, so if you don't mind taking matters just the slightest bit seriously?"

"I'm taking them seriously, I'm taking them so seriously that . . ."

When Benjamin trails off, Horatio follows his line of sight. His friend stares in bafflement at an empty balcony. Security shoves their way through the crowd, the Danes still ominously absent, and Benjamin studies a railing as if he's being visited by an angel.

With an audible frizzle, all the lights go out.

Screams clang against each other, glasses break from every direction, a chorus of wild suggestions vents forth. Horatio has enough wit to put the sword on the ground before someone is impaled. He was close enough to Benjamin that when his friend reaches blindly backward, they're connected, sure of each other by touch alone.

Horatio has never been afraid of the dark—but he doesn't know where Trudy Dane is. And there's already been one assassination attempt too many.

"Right, we're off." He tugs Benjamin toward the gleaming red emergency exit signs, which aren't being stampeded yet because Trudy's swag bags are reason enough to remain on the *Titanic* while the orchestra plays "Nearer, My God, to Thee."

"Wait, I thought I saw—"

"No. Come with me."

"She said she'd make everything clear tonight, she said she'd help—"

Horatio will not collapse over this. He simply will not.

"We're going."

"But Lia—"

"I'm not disputing this with you. *Move.*"

Benjamin complies, overpowered by bulk and determination.

And if Horatio thinks he saw a flicker like an afterimage of someone on that balcony—someone with wild hair and a familiar gauzy gown covered in glittering flowers—then he's mistaken, and there's nothing more to be said about it.

It's only a few more yards to the door. *Nearly there, nearly safe*. They can see one another painted in hellish scarlet by the light of the exit sign when an almighty crash occurs, a miniature explosion, and Horatio has never been more certain of anything: It was the centerpiece Jessica was thrown against like a worthless doll. Either off balance from her collision or deliberately tipped.

And he can't help but surmise that it landed square on top of Jeremy.

BENJAMIN'S HAND IS THE only anchor keeping Horatio from flying out the cracked window of the taxi into the breath-warm night air. Streetlights stretch into eerie taffy. Every car's crimson brakes glow with a sinister aura. Horatio replays peering up at the balcony dozens of times, and after each, the Lia figure is left more brittle, like a piece of potting clay that's been worked for too long.

"Music," Benjamin announces.

He's much calmer following the altercation with Jeremy. Or he's much calmer after staring up at the spectre of his late fiancée. Horatio doesn't want to know right now.

"Is the only reason we recognize the name Willie Nelson," Horatio supplies.

"Nah," Benjamin dismisses, though he smiles. "He'd have been a famous marijuana advocate. The Harvey Milk of wake-and-bakers."

"Occasionally I can't fathom why I speak with you."

"Me neither, seriously. It's mind-blowing. No, *music*, I need to look at this case like music, considering what we understand now. There's a rubric, a system. There has to be."

Horatio hums. Is this what lightning rods feel like after they've conveyed elemental energy from the sky to the ground? They turn off the West Side Highway, losing sight of the glimmering New Jersey shore.

It cannot have been Lia.

It looked exactly like Lia.

An enervating cocktail of fear and desire and bafflement are pulling Horatio under. He's nearly fully submerged when Ben snaps at the cabbie, "Whoa, stop right here." Then quieter, "Yeeeeah, that's what I should have predicted from this system. That looks right. Son of a bitch."

Horatio jolts upright. Their building is surrounded by flashing squad cars. Cops mill about on the sidewalk. Tape cordons off the steps to their front door. One of the policemen is on a radio, one writing in a notebook, another directing a pedestrian to the other side of the street. It looks like a crime scene from the telly.

Because it is a bloody crime scene.

"Drive!" he orders. "Benjamin, Fortuna and Norway will be here."

"Yes, and?"

"And Norway will notice a taxi idling across the street from her investigation."

Horatio twists around fully just before they turn a corner. A stretcher is being carried out the front entrance, one with a not very bulky figure under a sheet. He can barely make out Fortuna's bulk following Norway's trim figure, and every follicle on his arms bristles in dismay.

"Did you see the third car illegally parked?" Benjamin asks dully.

"Not as such."

"One of our town cars. Mom was fast, though I guess it was an easy conclusion . . . Paul shows up to eliminate me, Paul vanishes, where else could he be? Point to you, Mom, I didn't expect you to leave your own gala to throw me under the bus."

"Hello, where am I taking you people?" the driver demands.

"The Four Seasons," Ben calls. "Central Park South, east side of the park. And step on it, or whatever they say in the movies. Speedily, please."

"The Four Seasons?" Horatio studies him. "Why on earth would we go there?"

"Because we wouldn't go there." Benjamin's eyes lose their glow as he slumps against the opposite window, a light-year away from Horatio. "Never on earth would we go there. But seeing as we're in hell, it's just the spot."

TWO YEARS AGO, WHEN Lia Brahms was found frozen to death in a public park, Horatio's life went from low-grade excruciating to unbearably simple.

Benjamin was in a bad way. After the screaming, which was finally ironed out chemically, and after he read a gutting letter at Lia's funeral, he refused to leave their old flat.

Horatio put sheets on what had been Benjamin's bed and settled in for the long haul. His friend would sit under their wall of Sharpie quotations, eyes tracing things Lia said. Adding ones when he recalled them. Novels and curriculum were abandoned in favor of poring over the lovers' gargantuan text thread. The Sunburst strummed out bizarre chords warping classic love ballads.

Horatio was the sole person he'd tolerate other than Ariel or occasionally Jackson. So Horatio went with Jackson to the sleek West End Avenue residence Benjamin and Lia rented when they moved in together, the two men packed his belongings, and they brought them back to the Washington Heights flat Horatio thought he would never abandon. And since Jackson neither needed to impress nor intimidate Horatio, he remembers that grief-washed day of mournful work was punctuated by honest conversation.

We appreciate the care you're taking of Benny, Jackson said as they collected clothing, vinyl, electronics. *He's closed to us in some ways. I'm grateful you're up to the challenge.*

Horatio swallowed, thanked him, fought not to think of Lia falling into an endless sleep in a bed of snow and cigarette butts. He brought Benjamin the daily allotments of Bernardo Brothers. He got Trudy to find a psychiatrist who made house calls. In increments, Benjamin came back. One day he showered without being marched to the loo, one day he vanished for a nerve-wracking six hours that turned out to have been a walk in Central Park. After a month he was functioning, after two he could laugh.

Horatio was single-mindedly devoted through every second of it. It was simple. His own schedule fell into place like grains of sand, the hourglass containing them his loyalty to Benjamin.

The six-month mark passed. The year anniversary.

Then Horatio gave the most ill-advised blow job of his life, Benjamin dismissed the event as a check on Horatio's scorecard, and one month of grotesque normalcy later, Horatio was shaking with tears on a transatlantic flight home.

Therefore, he forgives himself for being somewhat at a loss over sharing a Four Seasons hotel room with Benjamin Dane.

They haven't any luggage, but when the desk clerk saw Benjamin's credit card, that apparently became an opportunity instead of a detriment. His friend rattled off items Horatio cannot recall. He stands in the middle of the living room—there's a living room—not knowing what to do. The décor is all pleasant neutrals, like a beach with the saturation turned down. Beyond the sitting area with its couch, desk, mini-bar, etc., is a queen-sized bed he's not going to consider yet.

They're on the thirty-seventh floor. The lights of Manhattan shine like a pretty toy world.

Horatio goes to the floor-to-ceiling glass. All those biographies swarming about, the incessant flow of cabs ferrying strangers. The vast blank rectangle of Central Park, and that's not even empty, it's crawling with crosstown pedestrians and joggers and people without roofs seeking them among the spreading trees. It's dizzying. Ordinarily New York fits Horatio—his size, his curiosity, his efficiency. He feels outside of himself. As if he went too far being a chronicler and is trapped observing.

Benjamin investigates the fridge. "Come on, Four Seasons,

you can do better than this. Oh well, the concierge will solve it soon. Horatio, I get that you're, you know, out of your element, but could you maaaaybe please stop looking like someone's about to jump out from behind a curtain and catch you in a luxury hotel?"

"Apologies." Horatio loosens his tie. "It's been a rather eventful evening and I'm knackered."

"Oh god, too true, I've never seen you hold someone at sword point before. And you gotta admit the gala would not have been complete without it. That was, like, the ultimate aesthetic check mark."

"If you say so."

"Excuse me." Benjamin holds a pair of neat brown drinks. "I've had a crap day, too. Here's to it ending in a couple hours?"

They clink glasses and they stand, gazing down at the city, two men who know one another like they know their own flesh. Many minutes pass watching the traffic and imagining where people have been. Where they might be going to.

"Weird to think about how empty all that is," Benjamin comments.

"How so? It seems outrageously full to me."

Benjamin gestures with his tumbler. "Scientifically, there's almost nothing there, and I'm not even talking about the spaces that *look* empty. Even inside the solid objects. This right here?" He raps on the glass. "Tiny particles bound and repelled by powerful forces with massive gaps in between. And this?" He waves at the building they stand inside. "Primarily the, like, blanks between protons and electrons and such."

"By that token, we're made of mostly nothing as well. That's almost Eastern of you, philosophically speaking."

Benjamin looks pained. "No. You . . . no, you aren't. You're here. You're solid matter. You might be the only solid thing in the multiverse, Horatio."

Horatio doesn't know what to say.

"And despite the fact that all this is mostly nothing," Benjamin adds lowly, "I'm touching you right now. From a foot away, invisible particles buzzing around as if we were both swarming with comets. Me in your skin, you in mine."

Horatio doesn't even have an early draft of a response to this before brisk footsteps approach in the hall. A discreet knock announces the concierge service, and a gentleman passes Benjamin several shopping bags. He trades them for a twenty-dollar bill and tosses them on the carpet, kneeling to rummage.

"Two sets of sweats in distinctly different sizes—oh nifty, I did not ask for cashmere joggers, but fine, try to impress me. Two bottles of pretty decent cab, one Tullamore D.E.W., toothbrushes, socks, boxers, snacks, this is a good job he did. You, sir, are getting an early Christmas bonus."

Horatio doesn't realize tears are pooling until he scrapes them away. Of all the times to feel so utterly lost.

He needs you.

Horatio clears his throat. "So the plan is to hole up in a couple-thousand-quid-a-night hotel room?"

Benjamin's head lifts. "Yeah, I guess it is."

"For how long?"

"I dunno. Forever?"

"Those police officers will be watching our flat, we can't go back there, it's the first place they'll try to trap you. They'll trace your credit card here as well."

"Kinda aware of that, but the warning is appreciated."

"What are we going to *do*?" Horatio folds his arms around his torso, feeling sick. "They found Paul Brahms bled out from an unreported bullet wound, they could charge you with manslaughter or god forbid—no, never that, but you just gave this, this public speech to reset the beginning, except it proved the worst possible person was the one who definitely had something to do with it, and I can't sodding think straight and I can't let anyone hurt you and you're going to be taken into custody because of your own mum and I—"

Benjamin deposits Horatio in the nearest chair. Then he slides his knees in against the seat arms and Horatio has a lapful of his friend, which is shamefully wasted if he's also having a panic attack.

"Er, sorry." Horatio tries to breathe. "That was appalling, please erase the last thirty seconds or so."

"Nah." Benjamin tugs Horatio's hair, shaking it loose. "If you're going to defend me with a sword, I'm going to make sure you don't lose it from the strain. Anyway, every sensation we've ever experienced is still knocking around in there someplace if the residue theory of memory holds true. I can't erase it. It's the pathways we lose track of."

"Benjamin, what did you see on that balcony?" Horatio asks hoarsely.

His friend flicks his eyes to the gleaming electric metropolis beyond the window. All the shapes and shadows and what flits between them unseen. He stays that way for a long time, contemplating the universe outside their fishbowl.

"What I wanted to see," Benjamin says at last. "You know, as prisons go, this one isn't too shabby. I could do this for maybe the next five or ten years without suffering much."

"You'd not consider it undue torment to stay at a five-star hotel with a bloke who fancies himself a genie ready to pop up with cashmere and good scotch?"

"Nope, it would be just this side of bearable, I figure."

"You really are horridly out of touch, do you realize this?"

"What? Oh god no, that's not what I meant," Benjamin protests, embarrassed. "I've never been picky that way. How fast did I move out of that townhouse and in with you? You could stick me inside a marble and I'd consider myself a king of infinite space, as long as I had good dreams."

Horatio imagines Benjamin's recent dreams and sees the translucent figure on the balcony. His stomach twists.

"What sort of dreams?" he rasps, not certain he can cope with the answer.

Benjamin's head lists fondly. "Ones about you."

Horatio makes a hurt sound but then they're kissing, Benjamin's lips pliable and urgent and Horatio's hand sliding up his chest to his face. Horatio's mouth gives way. His friend is right. Any place can be a prison; but if all his dreams were of Benjamin, he would have something that meant more than his freedom. When he pulls back, Benjamin targets his neck instead and Horatio gasps.

"Let me," Benjamin hums. "You always take care of me, and how often am I going to get to take care of you in an iconic hotel? Don't answer that. You want me, you did from the beginning, and I can give that to you. Let me—"

"Jesus Christ." Horatio pushes his friend's shoulders back. "Is . . . is that what this is? You aren't even interested, you just think well, he's earned it?"

"No!" Benjamin denies, aghast.

"Because if so—"

"Stop it, Horatio."

"You don't have to, to *indulge* me, you don't have to dress me in a designer tux and make yourself want me, I don't—"

"Shut up," Benjamin snaps. "I've been shit at this. No, that's not quite right, I've just been shit, absolute shit, period."

"You aren't shit, you're possibly the kindest—"

"For over a year now. Whatever happens tomorrow, I need you to understand something tonight."

"Never mind me, we need to focus on—"

"Listen," Benjamin commands.

Horatio stops talking.

"Most people's feelings override their logic and thus their decision-making. Christ knows mine do, right? But you're different. It would never occur to you to manipulate others, broadcast your emotions to get something you wanted or to change theirs. And your feelings don't affect the things you know to be true, or change what you believe is right. Those stay constant. Do you have any idea how insane that is?"

Blood migrates to Horatio's cheeks. "Good lord. I'm in no way out of the ordinary."

"That's a load of garbage," Benjamin growls. "There's no one else like you."

Nothing emerges when Horatio's lips part. He's got it backward. *There isn't anyone like Benjamin, he should be saying that about himself.* Surely Horatio is a dime a dozen, just an average scholar with an even temper, a solid brain, a love for good storytelling, and too much educational debt.

"Are you still listening?"

"I, yes," Horatio manages.

"Are you *sure* you are?"

"I think so?"

His friend leans forward until their brows are touching. "While you were gone, I . . ." Benjamin takes a steadying breath. "I wore you in my heart. Every day."

"Benjamin," Horatio says, shocked.

"No, I did. I *do*. More things in earth and space exist than you ever dreamed, you know."

"Do they?"

"Yeah. I wore you then, I wear you now. I wear you in my heart of hearts." Benjamin's voice catches. He brushes Horatio's lower lip with his thumb. "Do you understand?"

All Horatio can do is go back to devouring him. It escalates to *come to bed* and *please don't stop* and tearing at tuxedos and not bothering to close the curtains on the diamond-strewn satellite orbit they inhabit up here. And when their pulses are slowing and the world begins to reappear, Horatio curls up with his head on Benjamin's shoulder and regulates his lungs and his friend places the gentlest kiss in his hair he could possibly imagine enduring.

HORATIO CAN BARELY SEE by the light from the surrounding high-rises when his eyes crack open again. It can't have been very long—he wasn't sleeping, he'd just been blissfully warm and shagged out and dozed off for a few minutes.

The side of the bed next to him is empty.

When he flicks the lights on, he sees that Benjamin's tuxedo is missing. Tripping, Horatio casts about for scattered togs, muttering a mad series of incoherent chants.

Shit, shit, shit.

We are helpless in the face of death but the inner invisible force always lives.

You bastard.

I am light and only light can come to me.

How fucking could you?

When he's half-dressed in trousers and an untucked dress shirt, Horatio dives out the door. He flings himself bodily in front of a cab. But his directions, when he gives them, are clear and distinct despite his voice shaking.

He knows where Benjamin went, after all.

BENJAMIN

You're going to die
in your best friend's arms.
And you play along because it's funny,
because it's written down . . .

—*Richard Siken, "Planet of Love"*

B ENJAMIN DOESN'T FEEL LIKE hurrying. The thought repels him, and Horatio sleeps unawares. Exerting an unconscious gravitational pull, lining Ben's dress shoes with lead weights.

So he walks to the subway instead of hailing a cab, thinking about how Manhattan looked from the sky while he made a home inside his friend. They couldn't see the city's more than 250,000 streetlights, of course, and they were preoccupied anyhow. Entirely. But the NYC Department of Transportation is worth cogitating over, because it employs possibly the coolest unit of measurement ever to categorize its lamps:

	AVERAGE ILLUMINANCE	ILLUMINANCE UNIFORMITY
Roadways		
Collector	8–12 lux (.74–1.1 footcandles)	4:1
Local	6–9 lux (.56—.84 footcandles)	6:1

Horatio, you're measured in footcandles, not inches or pounds or even years, did you know about that?

Ben hopes he can explain it someday.

He crosses a green signal, a red one, zigging and zagging. It's probably not worth puzzling over when he fell entirely madly for Horatio, but sometime between the seven thousandth *oh, hullo* and the Four Seasons hotel, it happened, and Ben walks faster, face to the night wind. His thoughts aren't smooth, they chatter along like a sunlit brook, and if he weren't heading to visit his mother, he'd feel about as happy as he ever has.

it isn't that I love you I mean I do love you
but this is something else; I have to keep you
may I please keep you
and if you understood what looking at you feels like . . .
I mean it's all about perspective isn't it,
everything is relative except for light, it's the only constant,
the speed of light, which means that you can't ever
catch light at the end of a fishing line
hold light in the palm of your hand
make a soft bed for light and tuck it in and kiss its
forehead lips nose
and I never really understood that before, the sicksweet urge to
catch starshine in a butterfly net
own it
keep it in a box lined with blankets
punched with air holes but with you
you're constant just like light is constant and I only want to
keep you
to us a photon takes light-years to arrive, but to a photon
it's   traveling   at   the   speed   of   light
which means time literally stops for a photon
do you understand how light you are, and how much I want to
travel with you? because

I do
I do
I do

When he reaches Grand Central Terminal to take the cross-town train, he goes into the rotunda. It's an indulgence. He deserves those just now.

The night sky spreads above him in rich aqua and gold, a pantheon of Greek heroes and astrological signs. When he was a boy, he told Trudy he wanted to be an astronaut. He would live in space without the eerie lag between people's questions and his answers. She didn't take him to the Hayden Planetarium; Trudy took him to Grand Central and showed him the sky as reimagined in myths, pointed out that Orion was flipped backward, that east was really west and west was east. Ben remembered this when he studied philosophy and Einstein, that

perspective

w

a

s

everything.

The scientist they consulted for this ceiling was named Dr. Harold Jacoby, Trudy told seven-year-old Ben. *He went to Columbia University and then chaired the astronomy department. He even went on an adventure to West Africa to study a solar eclipse! And now sixty-seven million people a year see the constellations he helped create. You could do the same if you tried, honey.*

Ben decided he would go to Columbia too and never changed his mind. He would always have met Lia, that was inevitable.

But Trudy was responsible for his meeting Horatio.

"Fuck," Benjamin says as he heads underground.

When he arrives at Port Authority and emerges with the rest of the moles, he walks north. Their townhouse is only half an hour away. The air is heavily warm, like a weighted blanket, the trees sluggish and still. A thunderstorm approaches. Presently the city will smell like damp asphalt and petrichor.

> **Petrichor** (/ˈpɛtrɪkɔːr/): the odor the earth emits when raindrops strike dry ground and it releases scent-carrying aerosols.
>
> **Ichor** (/ˈaɪkər/): the ethereal blood of gods and goddesses.

Benjamin knows it was Lia on that balcony. Wearing the fog-grey dress covered in purple wildflowers he gave her for the *Elegy for a Life Lost* installation closing, her curls snaking Medusa-like, looking more herself than Ben had ever imagined. Everything in him screamed to run to her. But in the millisecond before the lights shorted out, he thinks he saw four others flanking her, and that they were the ones who plunged everyone into midnight. Three crone-shaped hooded figures draped in black, as faceless as holes, and a tiny creature with pointed ears and cloven feet.

Not so much the sort of thing to tell Horatio.

The townhouse appears empty, but a light glows in the front room, another upstairs.

You already did me proud today, son. But it's high time this was resolved.

Yeah, pulling up bootstraps. Ben rubs the cuff. *I put that in the speech for you.*

I heard you, Benny. It was right on the money. You really showed those two whose kid you are. Now go talk to your mom and settle this.

The entryway looms silent and unlit. Heading toward the back of the townhouse, Ben brushes his fingers against the walls, the doors, the fridge, the furniture.

I was here. I probably won't be, ever again. But I was here, now, before my family disintegrated.

Several antique lamps illuminate Trudy's study in amber pockets. The clocks envelop him as he enters. He feels warring comfort and abhorrence at the

clickclick tick click click clock ticktock click clock clickclick
    click clock ticktick
tock clickclickclick clock click click click clickclick click
    clickclick click tockclick
click click click click clock clickclick tock click click click
    tick click tock tick tock click

that Trudy wraps around herself like a protective cloak or maybe an unyielding straitjacket.

"Benny! Oh, I looked everywhere for you." Trudy appears from the shadows, likewise still in her gala attire, the green silk gown trailing after her bare feet.

"We're not still doing this, are we?"

Trudy steps farther into the light. Despite the memorial debacle and subsequent discovery of Paul Brahms's body, her face is cool and calm and her mascara could have been applied lash by lash.

"Still doing what, honey?"

Ben's hands twitch in his pockets, but he refuses to muddy this with more pills. There have been enough pills, there was enough champagne, more than enough ghostly visitations, nearly enough heartbreak.

"It's amazing to me." He shakes his head. "It's not exactly that I think you don't love me. I think you do love me, in your way. But it's like you were born with one face, and you paint yourself a totally different one. Depending on who you're with and what you want. I have no idea who you are."

Trudy's lips twitch. A flash of hurt, a calculated deflection—who can tell? She goes to the buffet housing a hidden fridge drawer and retrieves a bottle of white wine. The bones of her spine snake upward in a gentle S.

"I'm your mother, Ben. That's all I ever wanted to be. Before you abandoned me, I got to play that role, and it was the most cherished I ever felt in my life. You were so fragile, but you trusted me. We understood each other. I would have kept on protecting you for the rest of my life if you'd let me. You have no clue what that feels like, to have been everything to someone, to be their *lifeline*, and then turn into some kind of joke."

When he was nine years old, at a private school on 82nd Street, Ben was introduced to a new torment. Bloodied noses were too noticeable—the perpetrators knew the consequences for visible cruelty. So they started breaking into his locker during his honors math class, and while he studied number theory and probability, they copied his answers for US History and Biological Sciences. Changing their responses individually, of course (these thugs weren't stupid), but when they started tearing his work into little pieces after plundering it, Ben felt like nothing in his life could ever be safe again. Physical abuse he could withstand, but now his teachers would think he himself was

s l o w

and they didn't

b e l i e v e   h i m

and it was so much worse than his body being abused, this deliberate sabotage of his already wretched reputation and his mind, and Trudy held him as he gagged on his anger and she whisked him into another school where the students saved doggy waste bags to drop into his lunch, but hey, at least his homework survived.

Trudy is right; they understand each other. But Ben has spent enough time with Horatio to recognize what selfless love sounds like, ditto what it sounds like when someone wants to appear a combination Mother Teresa and Angelina Jolie.

I'm your mother, Ben. That's all I ever wanted to be. Before

*you abandoned me, I got to play that role, and it was the most
cherished I ever felt in my life.*

"You liked me helpless," he realizes, awed.

"What a horrible thing to say to your own mother—but it's
what I expect these days."

"Is this, like, make-believe time at the Dane manse? You
hired the Marlowe twins to spy on me because you're never ever
squeezing anything out of Horatio. I'm assuming they reported
to Paul, who showed up at my apartment with paperwork to
boot me from the board of directors and a gun to kick me out
of this whole 'being alive' business. He was shot—totally by
accident—after he outed your affair with that bag of rancid hot
dog water Uncle Claude. Where is he, by the way?"

"Upstairs making some calls." Trudy eases the cork off the
screw. "We can't reverse what you did, Benny, but we can put
our own stamp on it. A few New York morning shows, the *Post*.
I describe being married to a paranoid egomaniac with a star-
fucker kink and suddenly an affair with a normal, loving human
makes sense."

"Cool. Does that mean we can stop playing nineties sitcom
family now?"

"Only you would consider our being a family an exercise in
make-believe."

"Only you would consider your being a diabolical wannabe
murderess forgivable. It isn't."

"Why are you here at all, Benny, if that's true?"

Ben's emotions lap against the levee. He has about ten more
minutes of preternatural calm in him before the vision of Lia at
the gala will fade like the dream did. Then the river is going to
crest the embankment and drown god knows who.

"Because people are dead, and since you wanted me dead too,
you owe me an explanation."

"*Owe* you," Trudy muses. "How exactly, entirely like you.
All right. Since you asked so nicely."

She sets their wineglasses on the coffee table, going to the bookshelf. It holds far more clocks than it does books, and she selects one resting on a small marble base, decorated with silver pieces including a bird.

"This is the first gift your father ever gave me." She brushes her fingertips over it. "A William Comyns miniature carriage clock from nineteen-oh-five. He didn't know how appropriate a present it was. These blue dial numbers are hand-painted on the porcelain, and the tortoiseshell encasing isn't really something you can find in this quality today."

"If I live to inherit it, I'll buy it a pedestal."

"Don't sound so dismissive. You always understood clocks the way I do."

"I'm not so sure about that, and why do you say Dad didn't know how appropriate it was?"

Her forefinger comes to rest on the bird. "This is the Eagle of Preparedness. When Jackson drove through that pitiful town where I was born, I didn't know a thing about sophistication, but I knew I needed money and a husband to escape being ground into the dirt like my own mother, so I was *ready*. Every day going to work in that filthy junk shop I wore the best secondhand clothes I could find. I kept my face clean and when we couldn't afford lotion, I used Crisco. When my parents threw bourbon bottles at each other, I swept up the glass. Jackson walked inside the pawn shop and I *made* him love me. Whatever comes my way, Ben, I am prepared for it, and somehow Jackson foretold that with a clock."

Ben hesitates. "What else were you prepared for?"

Trudy smiles, catlike. "What do you mean by that?"

Ben's chest feels too small for his heart. "The original World's Stage Theatre was dying before somebody set it on fire. Was that you?"

"Of course not." Trudy begins a tour of her timepieces, glass in hand, stopping to wind mechanisms. "That was Jórvík Volkov, the theatre's custodian. I might have suggested it to him, of course, and offered a hefty fee. I'd have paid him too, if he hadn't vanished—though I won't deny I was glad. I always suspected his was the body that was so badly incinerated. But I didn't mention it, and no one asked after him. Life can be much easier when risk factors are eliminated."

"Yeah, I can, um. See that. And after Dad died, you'd planned far enough in advance to have Uncle Claude. Did you plan for Paul to fall for you too, or was that just a side casualty?"

Trudy touches a 1940s round Masonite clock that looks designed by the Jetson family. "Jackson wanted an angel who worshipped him instead of the Almighty, so that's what I was. I never had to see my stepfather again, or rummage through restaurant trash for food. Paul wanted a queen to give his life meaning after Laura died, and I gave him that. In return, I controlled everything, though I admit the photos came as an unwelcome surprise. I thought he trusted me. But it must have been pure self-defense, I realize now. He always was so lost after poor Lia passed, always looking to lay blame. The slideshow stunt doesn't matter though, because I'm prepared, and Claude will help me deliver the message the world will forgive."

"What's Uncle Claude getting out of it, then?"

"Claude wants proof that he's as good as his brother. I'm his proof and have been for decades. He also wants someone to watch over. It's a match made in heaven, when you think about it."

He was never as good as me, you know that, son. He sells property, but he doesn't *create* anything, not the way I did.

Jackson's voice is getting alarming enough that Ben touches the pills in his pocket, finding a shape that'll make him feel that crucial bit more sane, and popping it down.

"And what do you get out of Uncle Claude?"

"Devotion. You'd be surprised at how useful he is, especially when it comes to tedious business formalities."

"Is that why you killed Dad? He wasn't useful anymore?" Ben forces the words out before they can rob all the air from his lungs.

Trudy pauses over a Lux clock with a black and gold face and four tabs meant to be screwed into a car dashboard. She smiles again, and again the smile is

B   L   A   N   K

"Spiritually, your father was a small man," she answers. "His obsession with leaving a legacy crippled him. He'd have ruined us, the way I let him operate before the first theatre burned. To be honest, I don't know exactly how he died. He was on any number of medications by then. Afraid of Claude, cloying and overprotective with me, completely useless at running a business. I hate watching miserable creatures suffer. If he took some of his pills and forgot to keep track, and I reminded him to take them again, whose fault was it?"

Even though she did kill him, it can never be prosecuted, Ben thinks. *Horatio already said it to you: What happens, once you find out?*

"How did you know where to send Rory and Garrett? My place is one thing, City Diner is something else."

"There have been cameras in your apartment hallway since you've had an apartment. And I know you, Benny. I know what you do when you're having an episode. Crashing out of this townhouse the way you did, I had no doubt whatsoever where you would go."

"Mom, it's not unnatural for me to have left here," Ben pleads. "Isn't independence the goal of good parenting?"

"Maybe so." Trudy's hem flares as she spins on him. "But you didn't leave here, you left *me*, entirely. Just the way your father did. Do you have any idea how toxic this self-obsession of yours is? The universe doesn't have enough time for your *shit*. While you still needed me, and I could still do something for you, it was bearable. Only just. You have everything you could ever want, honey—a mother who loves you, an endless fortune, people who are devoted to you, and you still tried to die. It's shameful. When I think of my life at your age, still smiling over the fact there was more than one kind of fork, I can't bear to look at you."

"That's . . . not unfair, really. But you're the person who tried to murder this ludicrous human being. For more easily manipulating the board? What in even your malignant brain could possibly justify what you've done?"

"You're right, Benny. We don't understand time the same way." Trudy raises her glass to him as she takes a deeper drink. "You understand it as something that's always there. Forever, flies trapped in amber. I understand time the way it actually works."

"And how is that, then?"

"Never current," she snarls. "We are forever and always already a step behind—and meanwhile, you have *never* had to face what would happen when you were no longer young."

Benjamin blinks—she isn't wrong, there's a gap between:

1. SIGHT
2. THEN SOUND
3. THEN BRAIN INTEGRATION TO MAKE THEM
   SIMULTANEOUS
4. THEN THE MEMORY OF WHAT HAPPENED

Time is like watching a commentator on a live talk program. The flat-ironed woman or the gelled man receive the signal and process it; but there's always a lag as their answer returns via lazily orbiting satellite.

"You said that I was born with a face and painted myself a different one." Trudy shakes her head. "I was born with nothing whatsoever and made my own paints out of mud. Then, after you were born, I painted *you* a different one. Who you survived to be is my greatest achievement."

"You're putting a lot of effort into killing that achievement!"

"And you're relentlessly ruining everything," she volleys. "It was obvious you'd have kept the theatre going exactly the way Jackson did, and I was *finished*. That cuff you're wearing out of Jackson's belt . . . so morbid. So obviously refusing to move on."

"When am I meant to move on?" Ben cries out. "Right, OK, I'll play this shit game with you, let's set me a clear timeline. When the *fuck* is the right day for me to forget about Dad? Is it one day, two, a hundred? You hated him, and now you clearly hate me too, but this is just a cruel version of the heap of sand paradox. Is a single grain of sand a heap of sand?"

"Well, no. Of course not."

"How about four?" Ben growls, advancing.

"Benjamin." She steps back.

"Twenty?"

"Probably not, honey, and you're being—"

"How many does it take, for fuck's sake?" he shouts. "How *many*? How many days does it take until I begin to forget my father, and how many until I struggle to remember? What about Lia? How many minutes need to trickle by? How many infinitely divisible increments can exist between two human hearts? How many is a fucking heap, Trudy?"

He's cornering her beside a display case of monstrously ticking clocks, her chest heaving in alarm under emerald silk. Ben doesn't know when the rage and hurt turned from messily smeared coal to diamond hardness. It feels like a stranger who's noting a strand of her golden hair unpinned, that there's a sheen on her healthy skin now, that her mouth is flushed with biting. He doesn't think he's nearly as strong as this strange Other-Benjamin. He doesn't believe he can control him. When Trudy reaches for his arm, Ben wraps his fingers around her wrist and pins her left hand hard against the wallpaper.

Her wine trembles in her other fingers but doesn't fall.

All right, that's enough, be more careful with your mother there, son—I love her, we both do. Don't frighten her like this.

"Shut up," Ben snaps to his invisible father.

Your mom is a delicate lady who deserves your protection.

"No, she is not, that's seriously the most ridiculous bullshit I've ever heard."

"Benny, please," Trudy whispers, "who are you talking to?"

"You. And you're going to listen."

"All right, honey, I'll hear whatever you have to say—just let go of me?"

Ben laughs blackly. Dropping her forearm, he rests his palms on either side of the still-beautiful mask she wears, pressing intimately into the wall although no longer touching her.

"Right, to conclude the heap of sand paradox," Ben hisses. "In ancient Greece, they didn't mathematically have 'to the power of,' and so they came up with the term 'sand hundred' to mean these . . . these unimaginably big numbers. Understand something: Sand hundred days is how many I will need to forget Dad, and forget Lia. And ever forgive you."

When Ben launches himself away from the wall, his fist strikes it, and Trudy gasps. Stumbling, she reaches her gilt-edged desk and presses the silent alarm Ben knows is there. It doesn't matter. They're coming for him anyhow, thanks to Paul. Shoving his fingers into his eyes, Ben fights the growing chaos in his head.

Meanwhile, he watches Trudy straighten. Her chin raises.

"You called the cops just now," Ben rasps. "Probably Norway and Fortuna on a direct line."

"I had to. You're frightening me."

"You're frightening *me*."

"All right, I'm through with this." Downing the last mouthful of wine neatly, Trudy goes to the small sink and rinses the glass out. A superfluous gesture that belies having both multiple live-in housekeepers and a robot dishwasher. "Sit down until they get here, please. We won't have long to wait."

Fuck it, Ben concludes grimly.

Picking his own wine up as if it's the heaviest thing he ever lifted, Ben downs it in two swallows. Trudy lets out a tiny hiss of air.

Aha, Ben thinks, as his universe shatters.

Once upon a time there was a soft little tabby in a box with a hammer poised to strike. If a radioactive atom decayed, the hammer would crush the kitty's skull; if the radioactive atom did not, the hammer would not fall, and the tabby would live. Before actually observing the decay of the atom and thereby selecting a definite thread of the multiverse as our own path, the cat would remain both alive and dead in separate potential worlds.

Giggling like a child, Ben sinks to the couch. His cheeks are wet. Why are his cheeks wet? At the same time, he hears his mother whimper.

Trudy stares at her own empty wineglass in horror. "What did you do?"

"Nothing that ought to matter."

"No," she chokes. "You did something. Benny, what did you do?"

"I didn't want to believe that you actually were trying to kill me. I switched them," Ben says, barely loud enough to hear.

Trudy Dane falls to the carpet.

The police are already coming. He goes to his mother without any idea of what she just consumed, and he cradles her head. The tears come in a soundless waterfall now. Trudy is still warm, still solid, as he pulls her to him.

"Mom, why?" he gasps.

"I didn't want to," she answers in a cracked voice. "But you made it impossible."

Look what you've done now. My god, son, what a failure you always were, all along.

"*Go away!*" Ben closes his eyes, burying his nose in her hair.

"All right, I'll just. I'll tell you the story of what you did. If that makes it easier."

Trudy nods. Her body begins to curl in on itself.

"I was suicidal, I was insane at the gala, I more or less murdered a family friend, and I was caught. What simpler thing than to make it look like I killed myself here?"

Trudy is turning whiter by the second. She clutches at her belly.

"Mom, you didn't even poison me and you're killing me, please tell me if that was a true story?"

Her lips lock together as she nods. A shudder wracks her small bones, then another, then another.

"Do you want me to tell you a different story, Benny?" Her eyes wince shut. "For old times' sake?"

"Yeah," Ben whispers. "Please, Mom. Tell me anything you want. They're on their way. They're coming."

"The Greeks created the most incredible clock," Trudy gasps. "I want you to know about this. A jewel-encrusted gate, hung . . . hung with twelve golden orbs. One for each hour of the day. It was hydro-powered, and called the Clepsydra. Do you know what that means, honey?"

Benjamin shakes his head.

"*Water thief.*" By now she is haggard even beyond her years. "It reminds me of you."

"To measure one thing, you always have to steal from something else. Distance or velocity, never both. Space or time." The panic rises, clutching at his throat. "Mom, stay with me. I know Norway and Fortuna are coming, but I'm calling an ambulance."

"It won't do any good." Her voice is barely audible as he lays his mother reverently on the floor.

Ben's hands are palsied as he pulls out his phone.

take the device
type three numbers

　　　using non-ionizing radiation
　　　from the electromagnetic cell fields
　　　　　　　　　　　　　　to save the mother
　　　　　　　　　　　　　　you just murdered

Ben remembers nothing of the phone call. They tell him to stay on the line, but he can't possibly, he needs to do something, he needs to *save her.*

Trudy has already gone still, mouth slack. Eyes unblinking.

Ben can only stand there looking down.

The sound of the door opening snaps his head up. But it isn't the paramedics yet, not even Norway and Fortuna, it's Claude Dane, wearing reading glasses and a ravaged expression, dropping a legal pad and a pen on the carpet.

What did you do? he mouths.

"Technically, I switched wineglasses," Ben forces out. "Please help me."

"Dear God in heaven." Claude's face turns scarlet, then ash white.

"I didn't put anything harmful into anything, I just survived my own mother trying to kill me, please for god's sake help me. I know you would, you're. You're a decent man."

But whatever poison Trudy Dane put in the wine, it was swift. Claude rushes to her, but it is already too late. Her eyes are soft white pearls.

"No," Ben moans. "No, please. I didn't want this."

It takes Claude several seconds to gather himself. But when he does, his eyes turn dark. Claude goes deliberately to the desk, opens a drawer, and pulls a gun out of it.

"I loved her. She was all I had," he says.

"Yeah, she was all I had once, too. I know how it feels. You don't—"

"You are not going to dismiss me ever again."

"No, no, the ambulance is coming, they're almost here, I called them, I didn't—"

Claude fires the gun.

A BRIEF INDEX OF WHAT BEN DOESN'T
NOTICE AFTER HE'S BEEN SHOT:

—the metallic aromas of hot metal and spilled blood
—the continued ticking of the clocks
—the sound of Claude's shoes pounding away in panic
—fresh air seeping in through the townhouse's open front door

He does notice a tiny crack in the ceiling when he blinks, and the sudden sharp agony of being lifted up, and a new voice begging for something indistinct. Ben struggles to open his eyes more fully.

When he does, he smiles.

Ben never appreciated how beautiful Horatio is. His body still isn't fully processing being shot. The hole where his heart still beats and hemorrhages is just another emptiness in space. But he does note how much he simply loves the sight of Horatio, how everything becomes better when Horatio is there to share it.

Except that Horatio is probably about to watch me die.

Horatio is still talking. His tears spill like the blood from Ben's body. If only they were somewhere else, maybe they wouldn't be ruined. Maybe somewhere else, they would have had more time. A gentler country, a kinder one. As imaginary as the one conjured in City Diner. A faraway place that doesn't smash people to pieces and discard them like so much ceramics.

It depends on geography because here in America

if I so happen to fall and I

<break>

then I'm buried in the ground, but in

THE ANCIENT EMPIRE OF JAPAN

cracks are marks of resilience and are repaired with gold and no matter

what happens here, *my heart, o my heart,*

every shattering of you patched with precious ore

every loss every hurt

shone so brilliantly you all but blinded me

"Don't look like that," Ben manages. "I've hurt you too many times, and you never deserved any of it."

"This isn't happening," Horatio pleads. "No, no. You—I've already watched you die once. You cannot do this to me again."

"I was always going to die. It was the one certain thing in my life."

Horatio's hand is warm on his cheek. "Please don't."

"I can't do that. It's a candle flame, and candles go out."

"That's just poetry."

"No, it isn't." His eyelids flutter. "Life isn't a noun, it's a verb."

"Life isn't a biological process."

"No?"

"No."

"Then—"

"It's a story, just the way you told me." Horatio's voice as he gentles his fingers through Ben's hair seems to come from a dark void. *Across an event horizon.* "It's my autobiography, and yours, and Lia's, all bloody crashing together like the entropy you love to go on about, you utter *utter* prick."

"Horatio?"

"Yes, love?"

"If life is a story, then it's written by a real idiot."

Benjamin cannot believe that this makes Horatio smile. He hears sirens wailing in the distance. They speed as fast as they can. They will be too late. He slides his hand up to Horatio's open collar and clutches, not wanting to let go.

"I don't want a life without you in it," Horatio whispers. "I won't stay here without you. I can't."

"You have to."

"For god's sake, *why?*"

"No one's written the stories down yet." When Horatio makes a sacrificed noise, Ben stares up. "Hey, I have to tell you . . . Sorry, this is. It's all getting . . ."

"Shh, it's all right. I've got you, I'm here. Tell me."

The gap in his body is just a gap, does it have to feel like wolves' teeth tearing into him? "I have friends in high places, I think. Other places, other, are they planes or mirror universes or . . . I'll find you. I can't explain. I'll talk to them and I'll get you back, Horatio. You can't die, promise me you won't? I'll do this part. Live first. You deserve it. No one deserves it like you. And then when you're ancient, then if you still want me to, I swear on every thread of the multiverse that I will bring you back to me."

"You mad bastard," Horatio answers brokenly against his cheekbone. "I love you, too."

The sirens are louder, and louder. Ben wants to spare Horatio's feelings. But the blood is everywhere, and the light is dimming. Nothing can save either of them. It was always going to end this way. And since the initial shock has passed, everything hurts more than he thinks he can stand.

"Please don't go," Horatio begs.

Ben cannot register anything very well after this. Shouting, weeping, running, lips against his skin. He falls into a memory of Horatio when he first knew his friend was in love with him, but didn't allow himself to recognize it.

LIA

And when wind and winter harden
All the loveless land
It will whisper of the garden
You will understand.

—*Oscar Wilde, "To My Wife"*

LIA HAS BEEN MAKING too many bouquets, pouring her mourning into them the way she fills their vases with oil-blessed water.

The first funeral she attends is the least connected to her own life. It turns out that Jeremy Bradford, hedge fund manager, had no parents and few friends. It is an ash-scattering ceremony in the Battery, tinsel scraps of light glinting off the waves at the southernmost tip of the island. Five of his coworkers show up for it, an aunt, two cousins who also live in the city, and Jessica Anne Kowalski.

Jessica isn't crying any longer. She looks hollow, but she stands straight. Her dress is a simple charcoal sheath with a large gold necklace. She looks more capable, more adult, than Lia has ever seen her. Brittany is not in attendance.

This wasn't a funeral at which Lia had lost anyone. When she selected a single white lily to bring, the sisters smiled at her, and she knew she'd made the right choice. It meant nothing to her; it was simply corporate America's choice of mourning bloom.

Lia, Robin, and the sisters stand a discreet distance away. No one notices them. Lia is beginning to realize that if they don't want to be noticed, they won't be. It's as easy as that.

"Did we *make* all of this happen?" Lia asks.

"*Mais non, chouchou,*" Mam'zelle replies. Her black dress has a pink silk ribbon at the collar. "We nudged these things. We placed people where they should be."

"They done decided what to do once they got there," Moma adds.

"The seeds were in the ground," Maw-maw agrees.

Lia nods. Robin vanished after the lights went out at the gala, and apparently witnessed shocking events. He bragged about them as if they were his needlework, but Lia isn't so certain. He said he helped Trudy Dane come to power and then be killed by her own son. That he forever tarnished the name of New World's Stage, ruined Horatio Ramesh Patel's life. That he had a hand in Paul Brahms's killing. That he cut down Benjamin Dane.

But Lia is beginning to understand cause and effect. Definitely better than Robin, though probably not as well as the sisters do. Not yet. But she knows the story isn't quite finished.

The second funeral is the simplest. Lia leaves a trio of pink carnations at Trudy Dane's elaborate ceremony—a yacht voyage down the Hudson, all the corporate tributes and offerings from carefully cultivated friends piled near the bow of the boat as the attendees sample caviar and drink moderately good champagne. Her carnations are ridiculous next to all the ostentatious offerings.

Lia smiles, looking at them. When Trudy's ashes are given to the river, a few tears are shed, but none of them are genuine.

PINK CARNATION: *Remembrance.*

Don't think I'll ever forget what you did. Or who you really were.

For an instant, Lia is saddened that such a vibrant woman has so few people at her glib socialite funeral who actually cared about her in the daylight, in restaurants and crosswalks and bedrooms. She may have been dark and grasping to the core, but she *lived* her life. She took her chances.

Then Lia recalls that Claude Dane would be here, but he's awaiting trial for the murder of Benjamin Dane.

She doesn't feel quite so sorry for either of them anymore.

The third funeral is eviscerating.

Paul Brahms is laid to rest at the largely Jewish Mount Carmel Cemetery in Ridgewood, Queens. There are around eighty people in attendance this time. No matter what she knows about him now, how ruthless he was and how desperate, how ready to wield a gun, her father was decent to his employees, and he worked so many hours and put his fingers in so many pies that practically everyone at New World's Stage was at least his acquaintance.

Lia learns, and it touches her deeply, that some were even his friends.

"Paul saw me leaving the building around one in the morning this time I had a late shift, stopped me and asked if I had a ride. I didn't," one of the cleaning staff says. "He called me a car right there. Said I'd never been late a single day in four years, and it was on the theatre. What he didn't know was that my son was home sick, and I got back to him that much faster. How do you ever forget something like that?"

Walking up the simple paved walkway with a huge armful of white gladioli almost taller than she is, Lia kneels beside the hole in the earth.

GLADIOLUS: *Shaped like a sword, which is the meaning behind their Latin name. They take traits associated with gladiators—agility, courage, power—but have also long been a symbol of infatuation.*

"Hello," Lia says softly, through her tears.

Paul's grave doesn't answer her. She didn't expect it to. He's somewhere else now.

"You did a lot of terrible things I didn't know about," Lia tells him. "I was surprised when Robin told me. He seems to know just about everything. But then I remembered the way you loved Mom, and the way you loved me, with everything in your soul, and . . . then I knew I was stupid for your choices to have shocked me. You put the two of us first. And when you didn't have either of us to put first anymore, you changed."

She lays down the enormous bundle of white gladioli on the half-green, half-amber grass. She could always carry flowers, even when she didn't exist any longer. The sisters would have had no use for her otherwise. There are clumps of dirt visible in the landscaping, whole streaks of fried ground cover. The cemetery is meticulously kept, but no matter how well-maintained, Mount Carmel is visibly imperfect. It's the perfect resting place for her father.

"These are the right flowers for you, Dad," she whispers. "You were maybe preoccupied by the wrong things. But you fought like hell for them. I'd have brought you violets, you know, which stand for faithfulness and humility. That's how everyone saw you. But it felt like they all withered when you died."

Lia doesn't attend Benjamin Dane's funeral, because she has a plan.

"All right," she says, walking into the sitting room above the flower shop. "Ladies, I have questions. Actually, for you too, Robin."

Moma, who was approaching the barre with a water bottle, pauses. Maw-maw enters from the kitchen, drying her hands on a rag. Mam'zelle looks up from her book on the sofa. Robin wriggles in his chair, where he's finishing a stitch on the dress sock he's darning. He announced he's leaving for Bali in the morning, and Moma muttered *good riddance to bad rubbish*, but Lia is grateful he's still here.

"Is it . . ." Lia pauses over her wording. "*I* can communicate with Ben, there's this in-between place we go to talk. I can find him. But for other people, when they die, where do they go?"

"Everywhere, *chérie*," says Mam'zelle.

"Far away," says Moma.

"In the ground," says Maw-maw.

"OK, I gotta be real here, that was spectacularly unhelpful," Lia remarks.

Robin laughs, loud and long. "Oh, precious duckling, you really ought to have defected."

"I think we're pretty well past that."

"Checked the weather in Bali, it's—"

"It's going to be hurricane season in a minute if you don't answer my question."

"You wouldn't," Robin says with a comical look of shock. "Don't even know how, do you?"

"Sure, I do. I convince a butterfly to flap its wings. Cause and effect. Can I influence where the dead go? *Where* do they go?"

Robin, after a satisfyingly stunned moment, rouses himself. "That . . . is exactly how you would go about making a hurricane, tip-top. Ah, let me see. Most of the dead are relatively settled in their lives. Had a smashing life! Had a rotten one. Had an ordinary one. Any which way, they're returned to . . . what to call this, there aren't really words as such . . ."

"They're returned to the everywhere and everywhen," Lia supplies.

All three of the sisters sit down, and Robin drops his sewing.

"Really rather good, isn't she?" he coughs after a few seconds. "With whom do you want a chin-wag, you magnificent entity? Martin Luther King Junior? Hammurabi? Alexander McQueen?"

"Oh," Lia realizes. "Sorry, I wasn't expressing myself very well. See, I myself can find Benjamin whenever I want to if I decide to dream him. I don't think that'll change a bit now that he's dead, we're so connected. What I'm curious about is whether there's a way for a person who *isn't* dead yet to find Ben after *they* die."

The silence that follows this suggestion seems exaggerated to Lia. But then again, all four of these beings are entirely melodramatic and completely out of proportion, so it does make sense.

"Now, that there's just too much generosity," Moma says, looking equally adoring and skeptical.

"Heart like an artichoke," Mam'zelle breathes. "A leaf for everyone. Oh, Lia, *Lia*."

"The harvest is sweet." Maw-maw wipes a tear from her eye. "The harvest is bountiful."

"Merciful heavens," Robin exclaims. "*That's* what you want to do?"

"Look, you all can like it or leave it, but here's what I'm trying." Lia tightens the knot on the scarf in her hair. "Obviously Benjamin has unfinished business and hasn't just dissolved, or I'd sense that he was gone for good. I feel like the five of us are generally really . . . occupied. With the entire universe, and all. We're too busy to fret over one ghostly consciousness. Can I make it so that *two* people who have unfinished business can . . . finish it? Find each other?"

The sisters smile their slow, one-minded smile. Robin laughs hard enough to lift the ceiling.

Then he jumps up, snatches Lia's hands in his, executes a twirl, and when she's spun around, finishes by kneeling at her feet with their fingertips barely in contact.

"My fairy queen," he says, all his teeth showing. "You absolutely *can*."

"How?"

"You need a talisman. An object imbued with love and power by a magical creature, enough strength to make this mortal being findable if they keep it with them. Like a beacon, or a distress signal."

"That's all it takes?"

"From you? That's all it takes." Robin's eyes gleam like molten ore. "What a pity. Can't imagine you have any such item lying about. Do you?"

WHEN LIA WALKS DOWN the aisle of the old World's Stage Theatre this time, she arrives here on purpose. Which makes the experience altogether individual.

Ash still floats in the air, but it reminds her of snow. The smoky atmosphere is a fireplace on a cold winter's night with the promise of an ugly blanket and a mug of something steaming arriving soon. As rickety and ruined as the structure seems, it's a relief to see that it's crumbling. There's no debate now. No *is this worth saving* or *is it still beautiful*. She knows that in New York City, it was rebuilt through grit and force, and continues to showcase art. But here, in the place where she meets Benjamin, the finality of its demise soothes her.

A loud crack sounds, and a chunk of ceiling falls. Lia smiles at it.

"What the ever-loving fuck is happening to me?"

Lia climbs to the stage. Benjamin isn't so much sitting as huddling, arms wrapped around his knees, staring at his surroundings. A crack in the wall sends a puff of plaster dust into the air.

"Oh god," he breathes as she walks up to him. "It's . . . you're here, you're *really* here."

When Lia laughs, he springs to his feet. They close the distance between them at a run, falling into each other's arms. Both are adults, the age they were when they died. Both are cracked and completed. Neither is a terrified kid in this space anymore, confused about how they got here. Ben spins them in a circle with Lia's feet off the ground, and she hasn't felt anything as wonderful as this in a very long time.

"You're different." Ben is panting when he finally sets her down, slotting his fingers into her hair in the exact way she remembers. "It took you so much effort. Like, attempting to be different, and then staying the same no matter how hard you tried. You've changed, what is this?"

"I'm actually not sure yet." Lia smiles. "I guess that we know what we are, but we don't know what we might become."

A slow smile trickles from Ben's mouth toward his eyes, against all gravitational sense. "Where is this? Another dream? It feels a lot more, uh, very? Extra? Cranked to eleven?"

"I wish I could say it was that, but." Lia links her fingers behind his neck just the way she used to do. He half-laughs, half-sobs, his brow coming to rest on her shoulder. "God, Benny, I missed you, too. I missed you so much."

"This is the cool part then, where we can stop missing each other?"

"Not—"

"I'm dead, aren't I?"

"We shouldn't—"

"Ooooh no no no, it's coming back, my *mom* killed me, Jesus of Nazareth on a rickshaw, this is—"

"Ben, please stop till you remember the rest of it."

Lia waits as his face changes.

She watches Ben remember her own death more vividly. She watches him see his demise, too. His mother's treachery flickers in his retinas. She waits while he recalls Horatio and tears flood his eyes, and she waits while he tries to stop them and can't.

"You want him back, don't you?" she says in his ear. "I need to know."

"Yes, but I . . ." He shudders. "You, you're my—"

"I'm sorry, but I'm not your anything anymore," Lia says softly. "I haven't been for a while. What do you want your future to look like?"

"It reeeeally sounds like I don't have one."

"Oh, you do. I never got the chance to tell you at the gala what was going to make things more clear. I should've said in the first place that it would be the same message from the Bulvmania waiter, reinterpreted. That's why I needed you to get it."

Ben kisses her temple, leaving salt water on her cheek. "It doesn't exist anymore."

"Yeah." Lia hugs him tighter. "I didn't know either, at the time. But, I do now. I don't exist anymore. At the same time, I'm pretty hardcore, as you'd put it."

Ben's head falls back as he laughs. Lia hasn't seen it in far too long. He's just as absurd and as beautiful as she remembers, and their time together was never wasted, no matter what the ending looked like. They survived in one another's company. That was always going to happen, and it always will have happened.

Nothing can take what they were together away from them.

"I really get to decide my future?" Ben marvels.

"Yeah, I'm fond of you, so you get extra perks."

"I, um." Ben shakes his head. "There's someone I did not treat well I would like the chance to treat better. If possible."

A massive chunk of ceiling collapses. Soot and wood and plaster fly everywhere. Standing on the stage, however, Lia and Ben don't flinch at it. This place is supposed to come down. It burned a very long time ago, and maybe it was always the pair of them who allowed it to keep existing.

They'll find someplace better to dream one another.

"I was hoping you'd say that." Lia lays her head on Ben's shoulder. "Consider it done."

A FULL MONTH AFTER the deaths of Jeremy Bradford, Paul Brahms, Trudy Dane, and Benjamin Dane, Horatio packs his bags for London.

He isn't really present. There is also less of him physically than previous. He's tried sobbing and tried not sobbing. Being busy and being curled in a quaking ball under Benjamin's blankets. Everything hurts so much that he can't remember what it was like before. When muscles didn't scream and his skull wasn't fissured. He doesn't remember life before bloodsickness, and he can no longer imagine the warm weight in his palm of an unshattered heart. It was never in his chest, not really. It lived in his hand. It might have been cracked, but he was always offering it to his friend. Every day, in countless fashions.

Here. It's yours for the taking.

Do you want it?

I don't know whether you do, but your wanting it would be the greatest gift of my life.

Now he puts clothes from the dresser in his bag. His mum flew out for two weeks during the worst of it, held him while he disintegrated. They did video calls with his dad, all wept together.

But he really only had time for one parent, because Horatio has been on every news and talk show in the greater New York area, and two in Los Angeles. Telling Ben's story. Over and over, mostly through tears, but coherently. Concise and eloquent.

No, he had no intention whatsoever of killing Paul Brahms. Benjamin was no angel, far from it, but he only hurt people by accident or in self-defense, and never violently. I don't suppose I even saw him punch someone's arm as a joke. He suffered terrible violence as a boy.

You'd think that we would have, but it never occurred to us to imagine Benjamin's own mother was such a ruthless woman. I mean, I found her wonderful company for a decade. Then she went and . . . it's difficult for me to grasp. And it hasn't got any easier.

Yes, he was always different, but in that special way where everyone else suddenly seemed the same. As if he was the only original person present and the rest were copies of each other. Yes, I suppose that does sound extreme, but . . . Well, he had that effect on everyone, it wasn't just me, despite . . . yes, I did love him, of course I did. Do.

I do love him.

There's nothing left to attempt within Horatio's purview. Everyone has been buried. Claude is in prison awaiting trial, and Horatio dreads flying back for that wretched business, but he will be ready when the time comes. He's spent more hours than he ever expected with Ariel Washington, who keeps popping up at the flat with Bernardo Brothers coffee, talking about Benjamin.

Do you remember when he set up a booth at the Union Square subway stop offering Free Time Lessons?

Do you remember when he first started working at the youth centers, the way he'd talk about those hurting kids?

Do you remember when he said everyone worth their salt should know how to escape a supervillain and decided to learn horseback riding, scuba diving, and get his pilot's license?

Horatio is stacking boxer-briefs when he finds something unexpected. To say he's stunned would be far too extreme for what he's capable of feeling. But he's surprised, and these days that takes a great deal.

Tucked between a black pair and a navy pair is a scarf. It's embroidered beautifully with wild strawberries, all lush red fruit and writhing green vines. He knows at once it was Lia's but can't fathom how it came to be here.

Of Benjamin's, Horatio is taking only a few keepsakes. The pocket square from his tuxedo, that night. His favorite New World's Stage coffee mug. And the black leather cuff.

Brow furrowed, Horatio continues packing.

Of course he will keep this, too. He loved Lia.

He will keep it when he returns to London and finally to work. When his first biography is published, it will be tucked in a teak box with Benjamin's things. It won't have moved when he publishes his twelfth. All the objects will be safe in their dark home when Horatio wins the Costa Book Award, the Specsavers National Book Award, and finally the Pulitzer. He will keep it when he moves to the Sussex Downs at age seventy with his Staffordshire bull terrier, keep it close along with his memories of a philosopher who loved the stars.

Horatio will keep the strawberry scarf for the rest of his life.

ACKNOWLEDGMENTS

There were aspects of this book for which I needed to do no research whatsoever, neuroatypical brains and addiction struggles in particular. But I've always been riveted by the mysteries of the cosmos—quantum mechanics, paradoxes, cosmology, and the like—and for that, I had the best of assistance. My deepest gratitude to Charles Seife (*Zero: Biography of a Dangerous Idea*), Daniel J. Levitin (*This Is Your Brain on Music*), Simon Singh (*Fermat's Last Theorem*), John Gribbin (*In Search of Schrödinger's Cat*), and Brian Greene (everything the chappie's ever written, but in particular *The Fabric of the Cosmos*). It's likewise with humble gratitude that I thank Columbia University for allowing me to audit some of the classes Benjamin would have been taking for his very real master's program. I might not have understood half of it, but it deeply enriched my experience of the program, familiarity with the intersection between physics and philosophy, and the actual halls Ben and Horatio would have haunted as grad students.

The culture of New Orleans is one of the richest in a rich nation, and I'm delighted to say I've been there multiple times, as I'm not comfortable landing readers in geographies I know nothing about—even if the book physically takes place in New York. However, when writing the Weird Sisters, I relied heavily on a single text: *Jambalaya: The Natural Woman's Book* by Luisah Teish, which is a fascinating combination of autobiography, history, feminism, self-help, and spell work. As for the language of flowers employed by Lia and the sisters, that was my own amalgamation of Teish's recipes, Victorian lore, and herbal cures borrowed from other cultures. Hey, just because the sisters are from the American South doesn't mean they can't dabble in the wisdom of Chinese apothecaries. It made sense not to bind them to a single way of manipulating flora, and my research for that spanned many a tome and encyclopedia.

As ever, I can't sufficiently express my gratitude to my agent, Erin Malone, foreign rights agent Tracy Fisher, and all the other heroes of William Morris Endeavor. Erin, you've been a champion for the entire time I was writing this—don't think I haven't noticed. I have. Boundless thanks to my editor, Sara Minnich, who took a manuscript that occasionally went off the rails (all of mine do, let's be real here) and applied a fine-toothed comb to it during 2020, The Year During Which We Largely Abandoned Combs and Just Said Screw It No One Cares About My Hair. Sara, this is a vastly better book because you've been such a dedicated, intelligent, caring, and thoughtful part of it. The entire team I work with at Putnam is very dear to me (I'm looking at you, Katie McKee and Alexis Welby), and in short, I couldn't have a better support system if I magicked one up myself.

My dedication at the front of this novel is to the Groundlings. During Shakespeare's time, *groundlings* were the riffraff who couldn't afford seats in the mezzanines and were instead packed shoulder to shoulder standing in the yard below the stage for the price of a penny. It was actually in *Hamlet* that Shakespeare invented the slang—he quite liked inventing slang—during the speech when Hamlet is begging the Players to speak the speech trippingly and not chew the wallpaper. "O, it offends me to the soul to hear a robustious periwig-pated fellow tear a passion to tatters, to very rags, to split the ears of the groundlings," he laments. (I adore Hamlet, but he is one meticulous little snot.) Previously, *groundling* had meant a wide-mouthed fish, so it was a clear dig at the impoverished denizens of the theater's pit staring up at the stage, who were notorious for creative misbehavior like chucking un-fresh fruit during the duller stretches.

My own Groundlings, however, are very real and alive today. There are about a dozen of us, give or take, and every year without fail, we get up before sunrise to wait in line for tickets to Shakespeare in the Park at the Delacorte Theater. We snooze in sleeping bags, order breakfast from Andy's Deli (they deliver to the line—one indicates "by the water fountain," "near the big rock," "close to the Pinetum"), talk, laugh, collect tickets, and then reconvene for a picnic at Turtle Pond before the show. You aren't allowed glass in the Delacorte; but you are allowed box wine, or on one memorable occasion Ziplock bags of premade margaritas, and we howl with laughter at all the jokes and are very much the groundlings minus the fruit. They're some of the dearest memories of my life. I've seen Ann Hathaway in *Twelfth Night*, John Lithgow in *King Lear*, Al Pacino in *The Merchant of Venice*. And I've loved Shakespeare with all my heart since I was a little girl, when my parents took me every summer to the Oregon Shakespeare Festival. But it was my Groundlings who made those dozens of shows so precious to me. This book is for each and every one of them.

Finally, as always, it's for my readers. Thank you from the bottom of my heart, readers. Shakespeare and I have one thing in common: we are (or were) commercial authors, people who live and breathe and buy groceries by sharing stories. I wouldn't exist without you.

DISCUSSION GUIDE

1. Though *The King of Infinite Space* is primarily a contemporary retelling of *Hamlet*, author Lyndsay Faye also infuses other elements of Shakespeare's canon. Did you pick up on any other references or parallels? How has Faye altered the characters, and what do you think of these changes?

2. Benjamin Dane's mind "operates as part philosopher, part scientist, and part torture device." As readers, we are privy to the complex inner workings of Ben's mind. What did you make of his perspective and the ways that Faye experiments with style and form to depict his interiority?

3. Discuss the dynamics among Horatio, Ben, and Lia. What is their history as a group, and how have their relationships changed over time? What did you make of the budding romance between Horatio and Ben?

4. How do botany, the language of flowers, and the magical shop play a role in the story? Discuss Lia's perspective, particularly her relationship with the Weird Sisters and how her distanced narrative arc ends up converging with the larger plot as we near the conclusion of the novel. What is the relevance of the scarf that is referenced throughout?

5. *The King of Infinite Space* is set in and around the theater world in New York City. How does this setting impact the tenor of the book? Discuss the history of the Old World and New World's Stage, and how its mysterious burning is tied up in the central conflict of the story.

6. At the beginning of the novel, it is apparent that Ben's father is dead, presumably by overdose. What do we eventually learn about the circumstances around his passing? Discuss how Faye inserts a murder mystery into this story, and why it becomes pivotal to learn the truth of Jackson Dane's death.

7. At one point, Ben says, "Time . . . You can't hide from it. There's no hiding from anything, and especially not endings." To what extent does this sentiment prove true for the characters? How does Ben think of time and space in a metaphysical sense?

8. What is Robin's role in this story? What did you make of his character, and how is his entropic nature revealed throughout?

9. Much of the narrative leads up to the New World's Stage gala. Why is it an important event, and what are each char-

acter's motivations ahead of that night? Discuss what ends up happening, and how Faye brings all the various plot threads together.

10. How did you react to the novel's ending? What surprised you?

Photograph of the author © Anna Ty Bergman

Lyndsay Faye is the author of six critically acclaimed books: *Jane Steele*, which was nominated for an Edgar for Best Novel; *Dust and Shadow*; *The Gods of Gotham*, also Edgar-nominated; *Seven for a Secret*; *The Fatal Flame*; and *The Paragon Hotel*. Faye, a true New Yorker in the sense she was born elsewhere, lives in New York City.